Destined Hearts Dangerous Secrets

Anthea Laurelton

Book 2 of the Hearts of Sparta trilogy

Independently Published

First Published – 2026
This edition published 2026 by Anthea Laurelton
Sydney, New South Wales, Australia

Title: Destined Hearts Dangerous Secrets / Anthea Laurelton

ISBN: 9780987640772 (paperback)

Creator: Laurelton, Anthea, author

Edited by: Stephen Black of Black Thoughts Editorial Services

Cover art by: Sheridan Kent

Printed and bound in Australia by Ingram Spark

AUTHOR NOTE

Dear Reader,

Like its predecessor, ***Fearless Hearts Forbidden Love***, this fictional love story contains mentions of historical persons, sites and events, as well as exploring the norms of Spartan cultural customs.

Xanthia's name came to me while watering my flower garden way before the first words of the story were written. The Greek name, *Xanthe*, means yellow or yellow hair. Xanthia has dark hair and by the time I checked name meanings, her name had stuck and I couldn't bring myself to change it!

Melos Island, or Milos as it is more commonly known, was the site where the famous ***Venus de Milo*** sculpture was discovered in 1820. Believed to represent the goddess, Aphrodite, it is on display in the Louvre, Paris.

The word ***laconic*** derives from Laconia (also spelt with a 'k'). The Spartan dialect had limited words, hence one of the reasons why, particularly the men, spoke in such abbreviated sentences.

A glossary is included at the end of the book.

Thank you for taking a chance on this story. I hope you enjoy the read.

Anthea Laurelton

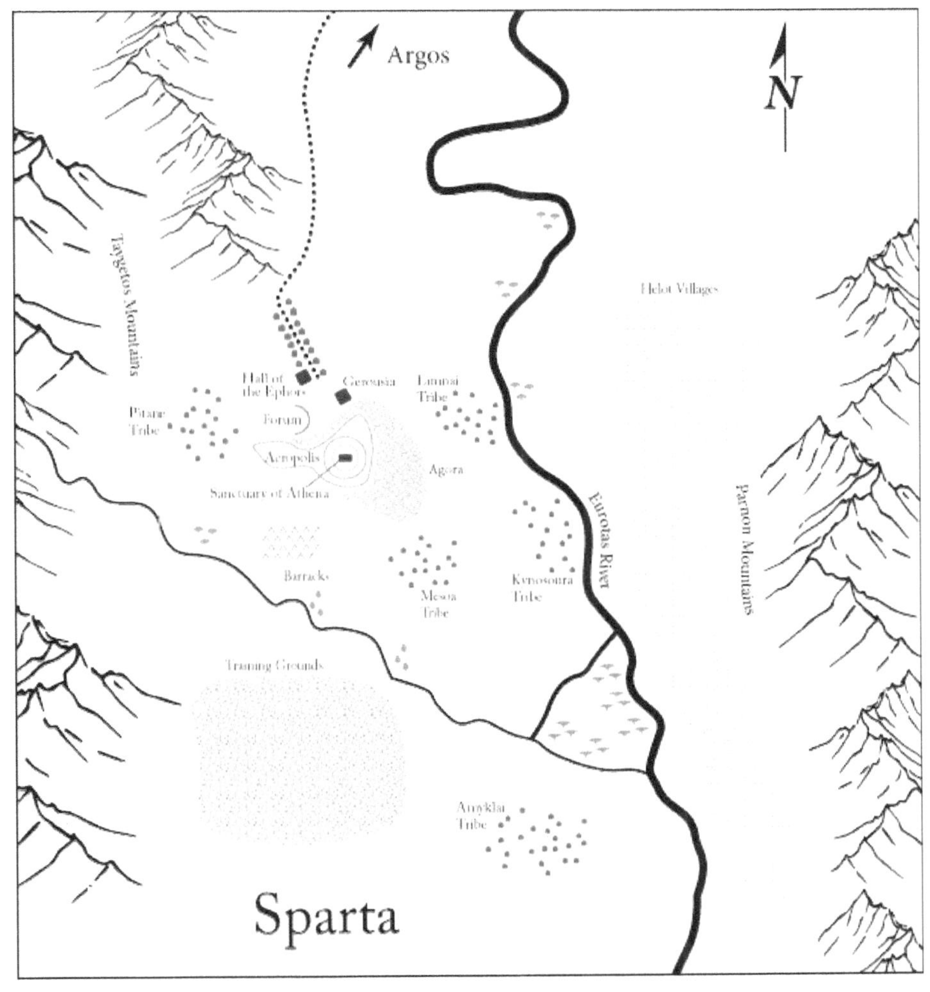

Map credit – Jeremy Brown author of ***Akon's Mission***
Reproduced with permission.

CHAPTER ONE

Island of Melos, circa 450 B.C.

"Must you go, Xanthia?" Kallios shaded his eyes from the morning sun streaming in through a small window of the neat, compact dwelling. "For once, I want you here with me to enjoy the days before the festival."

Xanthia clenched her hands over the light woollen chiton she held. Releasing a long sigh, she laid the tunic-like garment to one side and turned to face her lover. "You know I always visit my parents before the fertility festival. My time is my own, Kallios."

At the thought of Philodemos and Euphrasia, a small smile lifted the corners of her mouth. They were the ones who had fostered her, nurtured her; the couple she embraced in her heart and mind as her *real* parents.

"I don't need a reminder of your refusal to open your heart to me," Kallios said accusingly, sitting up and reaching for his clothes. "You've made that clear every year since you came to us."

Xanthia wrapped her arms around her waist, a defensive gesture she had adopted to make clear to anyone who endeavoured to command her affections, her intent of keeping them at bay. She contemplated the man who had shared her bed through the night, as he had through all the agonising nights she had battled with her demons. She began to worry her lip with her teeth, reminding herself of the blessing bestowed by Aphrodite in helping her find this group of the goddess's acolytes, a group she joined after her world came crashing down around her.

Gratitude for Kallios's attentions came easily. She had taken lovers before him, casting them aside when she discovered the power her face and form wielded over men. Something about Kallios earned her respect, however, and not just because he was the acknowledged leader of their group, but for four years she had waited for real desire to stir. Waited to feel the leap of excitement in her belly.

Love remained elusive, as it should, she mused, to keep her heart safe. He was, after all, a man. A man who could abandon her at a whim. Just like the others had a long, long time ago.

"I don't know if I can ever love any man." She hesitated, then chose words intended to remove the sting of the avowal she had just made. "Don't be concerned, Kallios, you know I always return, and this time is no different. There is no reason to leave Melos and my parents."

She tensed as Kallios approached, desire and possessiveness clearly written across his features. He stood close enough for her to feel the rise and fall of his chest as he ran a gentle finger over her cheek. Xanthia managed to control her flinch, but he must have felt her withdrawal because twin lines of disapproval formed between his drawn eyebrows.

"No reason to leave me either," he argued, attempting once more to change her mind. "The fertility rites hold no meaning unless you are there. We have given so much to each other."

Xanthia flattened a hand to her churning stomach. Once, he had given her a gift she had rejoiced over, only to have that gift reject her. Just like another man had rejected her not long after she had taken her first breaths. She called on all the years of practice in cloaking her emotions to not shout at Kallios to leave her alone so she could deal with a grief that still bubbled like lava beneath the surface of her emotions.

"I know we have," she murmured, sweeping her lashes and tilting her head to one side in a practiced move that never failed to bend a man to her will. As a lover, Kallios was generous even if he had failed to touch her heart. She gave a mental shrug. No man would penetrate that stronghold. A raging fire of torment and loss ringed it, refusing to relinquish its protective hold.

That fire kept her alive. Kept her sane. From the moment she had taken her first lover, she had vowed not to pour water onto it for any man.

"Then why deny us both the time together before the festival?" he complained, pulling the chiton over his head.

Pushing her long, sleep-tousled hair over one shoulder, Xanthia overlooked his petulant tone. "Are you still afraid I may choose another to enjoy the fertility rites with? I haven't done so since we became lovers."

"I know that, but what if you change your mind?"

"I won't." She studied him almost dispassionately. Attractive enough, he possessed a reasonable build any other woman would find desirable. Despite his standing in their group, and the freedom he had to choose someone more amenable than herself, he had respected the limits she placed on their liaison.

Now, for the first time in the four years since her initiation, remorse entered her soul. Pressing fingers to her temples, she massaged the tightness there and speculated whether the tension sprung from using Kallios for her own ends, or for the pain she had caused, and indeed still did, to her parents during a time when bitterness had infected her soul.

The struggle with this dilemma remained constant. Her fellow worshippers were her extended family. They had taken her in, accepted, and saved the girl ready to throw herself off the highest cliff, all because of a revelation not meant for her ears. Their wholehearted welcome continually fed the empty part of her that needed a reason to keep living.

It was futile to wish she could scrub away all memory of that fateful day, seven summers ago, when she had walked by an open window and overheard her parents talking about her past.

"What troubles you?"

She kept her eyes downcast, reaching for the chiton to resume folding it with meticulous care. "Nothing. I'm just tired." The lie came easily. She had mastered the art of lies. "The time away will do me good. It's so peaceful where my mother and father live, I always sleep well there."

The tiny muscles around her eyes tightened. It had taken years to regain any semblance of peaceful sleep. In her mind she was back on Kythera, her first home, clapping her hands over her ears to forget what she had heard, knowing forgetfulness to be impossible. The carefree, innocent girl vanished, replaced by a woman who had pledged to make every man's life a misery.

The pledge brought a timely recollection when Kallios leaned in to embrace her, pressing his lips to the smooth skin where neck met shoulder. She resisted the urge to pull away and wipe off all traces of his caress.

He lifted his head to murmur near her ear. "You will need the rest. This year I plan to keep you all to myself. I have prayed to Aphrodite to bless our coupling. I want to see our passion bear fruit again."

Xanthia yanked herself out of his arms. Heat, wholly unrelated to desire, stoked a raging furnace within her. "Never! Never, I tell you! If a child is your greatest wish, then take Zenais to your bed. She'll gladly give you what you want."

"Are you doing something to stop conceiving?" His scowl carried the weight of his displeasure. "Going against the will of the goddess? You have become a little too sure of yourself these last two years."

Xanthia stabbed a finger into his chest. "And *you* have grown arrogantly possessive. You've the gall to speak of the will of the goddess, then remember the goddess doesn't force anyone to bed with another. I choose who I take to my bed and whether I want a child."

She would never bear a child even though she longed for one with every fibre of her being. The ongoing war in her heart threatened to rip it apart.

Kallios drew back to look haughtily down his nose at her. "Why are you pushing me to bed Zenais? This isn't the first time you have suggested this."

Xanthia angled her chin in answer to his hard stare. She did not care if he refused to look at her again. He was easily replaced. There were many men in their group who desired her. Time and again, she had witnessed their eyes light up with undisguised passion whenever she deigned to notice them.

"Zenais is lovely and gracious. From among you all, she welcomed me first, offered guidance. I know she desires, even loves you." Xanthia had sworn to never forget the woman's kindness to her in those first turbulent days, when she had struggled to find her place.

"What if I don't feel the same?"

She pressed a hand to her forehead and shook her head. "I don't feel the same way you do about a child. How are your feelings any less of an affront to the goddess's will than mine?"

"I wager you may feel differently after your visit." He backed toward the door, staring with displeasure at her. "If you persist on this path, you may find yourself barred from our rites."

Kallios's cold dismissal of her accusation carried an empty threat. He could glare all he liked. She knew he was aware of how much competition he faced for her attentions. A smug smile tugged at her mouth as she purposely arched her back, generous breasts thrust forward to taunt the elemental hunger in his eyes. "Don't threaten me with banishment. Your decision would be very unwelcome."

Mouth twisting, he tore his gaze away from temptation. "Go then. Visit your parents. I may see you on your return."

Muscles tense, she watched him fling the door open and storm out into the crisp morning air. As soon as he was gone her shoulders slumped on a outrush of breath. If he truly meant to reconsider their liaison, she would be spared his following her like a lost lamb trying to win back her attentions. Not that she would entertain any qualms about ending it herself if he continued to pressure her to conceive. The customary stab of pain this evoked remained as intense as ever.

In walking away first from the men she had taken to her bed, she believed her spirit reclaimed a measure of power over those who had turned their backs on her.

She stretched her arms up, reaching through her fingertips to release the stiffness in her upper back. Conflict with anyone left her feeling wound up like a coiled snake ready to strike. Up till now she had been satisfied with her lot. Her one regret was the heartache her decision had brought to Philodemos and Euphrasia.

Xanthia inspected the organised chaos waiting for her to pack into a large bag. The clothes she had selected lay over a stool in a jumble of blues, whites and violets. Tapping her bottom lip, her gaze fell on a small leather pouch. Yes, she would take some of her herbs, too. Her parents, or perhaps their animals, might require her healing skills.

A genuine smile curved her lips as the sweet notes of cooing filled the room in answer to the morning calls of birds beyond the still-open door. Two steps brought her to the wicker cage she had woven with her own hands. Xanthia lovingly stroked the dove perched on top. The beautiful white bird, sacred to Aphrodite as all doves were, was the only being in the world she truly loved other than her parents. The dove went wherever she did. This visit would prove no exception.

"I won't ever leave you, Calliope, or Melos," she vowed, picking up the dove, who she had named after the Muse of singing, laying a light kiss on its back. Despite the dove's injuries when she had found her, Xanthia's pain had been lessened when its heartfelt song of gratitude for being healed, had poured balm into her heart. She returned Calliope to the cage with a heavy sigh. Securing the door shut she vowed, "And, no man will ever claim my heart."

CHAPTER TWO

Sparta, one month earlier.

Acastus drew his shoulders back and stood uncowed before his peers, his unwavering stare meeting the sceptical gazes of the dour faced gerontes, the members of the Gerousia who made up the senate of Sparta. "The general has approved my quest," he informed them in a strong voice.

A storm of whispering broke out in the wake of his announcement. He ground his teeth. Did they not comprehend the importance of this undertaking? Urgency to begin his hunt for Xanthia warred with the discipline instilled in him over the years.

The discipline won.

No use wishing he could bang heads together to obtain a favourable outcome. The two kings who presided over the Gerousia might be absent, the senators might be past their fighting days, but the latter, like himself, were all trained warriors who had earned their position. His sense of duty compelled him to listen when one of the senators raised his voice above the muted hum of conversation.

"Confirm for us your mission is to seek out this woman, and bring her to Sparta, so that a former citizen may also come home."

Acastus clenched his left hand around the hilt of the xiphos sheathed by his side. The short, dual-edged sword bumped against his hip. "Not just any woman, a woman born on Spartan soil, the child of two citizens." He pressed his lips together. It was wiser to not say anything about her unjust removal from her homeland because of her parent's identity. To convince them to allow a former, in their eyes a disgraced peer, to return would prove enough of a challenge.

"A Spartan who flees his native land is hardly to be considered noble or heroic enough to welcome home."

He glowered at the man who had voiced the insulting remark. A recent appointee, Acastus noted he deliberately withheld attention to the details of his proposed objective, preferring to recline in his seat and stare at Diokles, who stood behind and a little to Acastus's left. Even though the slight to himself grated, Acastus raised a cautionary hand to his friend, whose face wore a black frown.

"I will answer," he muttered out of the side of his mouth, the assertion a reminder to Diokles of his insistence that he alone would present the case.

At the edge of his vision, Acastus caught Diokles's subtle nod, followed by a half-step closer to where he stood. This show of solidarity caused another eruption of whispers among the senators, who sat arranged in semi-circles facing the area where he and Diokles stood. He allowed a brief surge of triumph to wash through him. Yes, he still needed to convince them, but their denying him would prove difficult. Not just because of Diokles's support, but the fact that both had returned from a more than successful mission to Apollysis.

He raised his voice over the continuing whispers. "That may be so, though he isn't the first to flee, or be outcast, on the advice of an oracle." Acastus's lips twitched at the sight of his audience gaping at his temerity in referring to Demaratus, a former king who had been dethroned and banished after his co-king had bribed the oracle of Delphi to find in another's favour.

"You claim an oracle warned this Spartiate to leave?"

Acastus turned his attention to the senator who had first questioned him. "Yes. Aeschylus sought counsel in the temple of Athena here in the city. He followed the advice of the goddess to save his daughter, Callisto's, life. After the recent threat from Apollysis was defeated, they were told by the high priestess of Olympian Zeus that Aeschylus could only come back to Sparta if his missing daughter, Xanthia, is discovered and brought home first."

More uneasy rustling filled the chamber. Acastus worked hard to not reveal his satisfaction until the outcome went his way. All Spartans were pious to a fault; such a trait would give him the needed impetus to gain his way. He pressed home this advantage. "If Zeus has ordained this course through his priestess, are we mortals prepared to argue with the king of the gods?" Even though the gerontes had begun to shift uncomfortably after he posed this challenge, he could not resist adding, "By honouring Zeus's will, we regain two citizens, one of them a trained warrior."

The assignment he had requested fired his blood. Its purpose filled his mind. It was, perhaps, his one chance to restore his honour. A chance gifted from Olympus itself to atone for the wrong he had done to the friend standing in silent support beside him.

To atone for his part in the banishment of Diokles's half-sister, Xanthia.

He had to win this vital battle.

The wait tore at his control. He listened and observed, the tension leaving him by slow degrees. The urgent hum of the gerontes debating among themselves sounded favourable, more heads nodding in agreement than shaking in denial. His confidence grew with every heartbeat and he half-turned to raise a brow at Diokles, receiving the barest of nods in acknowledgement, indicating his friend had reached the same conclusion.

The whispering suddenly stopped, and a spasm twisted in his gut. The absolution of his guilt, perhaps his very future, hinged on their answer. He held the gazes of the senators, trying to imbue a favourable outcome into their collective consciousness. As the spokesman rose to his feet, Acastus felt his pulse trip in an erratic beat he had never experienced, even in the heat of battle.

"Our decision is agreed. If you succeed in restoring this woman, Aeschylus may return to put his case forward to be readmitted as a Spartiate."

~*~

Acastus strode past the imposing Doric columns that supported the roof of the senate building, Diokles at his side. In unison they stepped out into the agora, the great marketplace where a couple of vendors immediately besieged them. He tossed a coin to one in exchange for two apples, handing the larger one to Diokles.

"We ought to celebrate with a kylix of wine but I find myself hungry. That exchange proved as testing as any battle."

Diokles nodded. "You argued well. The Gerousia members sometimes forget the fire that fuelled their bellies in their younger days."

Biting into the crisp apple, savouring its tart sweetness, Acastus clasped Diokles's upper arm. Swallowing the mouthful, he grinned. "You can now go and tell Callisto she'll welcome her father home." He let loose a full-throated laugh. "I'd rather take my chances amongst the Argives than be anywhere near your wife if you had to tell her otherwise."

With a smile of agreement, Diokles clapped him on the shoulder. "One day you will learn what it means to have a Spartan wife." The smile grew wider. "Perhaps the day will come when I call you brother-in-law as well as friend."

If you only knew, my friend, you would understand why that day will never come.

Acastus pushed the dark thought away and shrugged. "Perhaps," he lied. "We part here. I'll sail to Kythera first, it's the closest island to the Peloponnese. My father's old servant confirmed the legend of the horses Callisto saw in her meditation." He ignored the baffled look Diokles sent him, knowing the time might never come when he could explain his lack of enthusiasm for the hint.

"What provisions and servants will you take?"

"One helot servant will be enough. Any more might risk my merchant disguise." Acastus waited and was rewarded with the anticipated frown.

"A merchant's disguise is beneath a Spartiate," Diokles objected.

"Agreed but recall our discussion at Amyklai a few weeks back. I'll do whatever needs to be done to succeed, and that position is not beneath a Spartan warrior."

He met his friend's probing stare calmly until Diokles spoke.

"Will you now tell me why you are so eager to take this mission?"

"No." Not until he had discovered Xanthia, Aeschylus had returned, and he had come to terms with his role in her disappearance.

Diokles shot him an incredulous look but asked no further questions. "Then, may the gods grant your plan success. I'm surprised the Gerousia came to a decision so quickly. On occasions they debate for days."

Acastus released a derisory cough. "Had they refused it would have been an insult to you, given your resounding victory in Apollysis without losing one hoplite."

"Just as much an insult to you," Diokles countered. "You held the city until I returned from the shrine, where the threat to Sparta was discovered and removed."

Acastus kept his tone neutral. "True, however the senators are now aware how much is at stake for you as Aeschylus's son-in-law."

No-one, not even his closest friend, had any idea how much was at stake for him.

The sudden animosity wreathing Diokles's face tightened his gut. Surely no-one remained who knew of the fateful event that had led to Xanthia's expulsion. Acastus relaxed a little on seeing Diokles's focus was on someone, or something, behind him. A glance over his right shoulder revealed the hostile senator speaking in close confederacy with another man a short distance away. Acastus trained his gaze on the newcomer, who boldly returned their stares, his narrow face wearing an expression akin to sizing up an opponent before a wrestling match.

The skin at the base of Acastus's neck prickled. Glaring at the two conspirators, he sensed a secretive, sinister energy ringing them, his suspicions strengthened by their furtive discussion. Without taking his attention away from their every nuance, he addressed Diokles. "What do you know about Theron?"

"He's Callisto's uncle. I've never trusted him. He's cunning, avoids his duty in the mess. I hear things about his conduct in battle."

Acastus's fingers tightened over the apple in his hand, appetite suddenly gone. "I hear the same. It wouldn't hurt to uncover what plans those two are hatching." He looked back at Diokles. "I'll take leave of you to begin preparations."

Diokles raised a hand in salute. "And I must return to the barracks. I call on Athena to grant you swift passage."

Disturbed by an inner prompting, he called out just loud enough for Diokles to hear. "I sense treachery so watch your back."

Face set, he began to walk towards the two men, only to have his intent to confront them thwarted when both hurried away separately as he drew closer. Heeding his gut, he chose to pursue Theron who had sought to escape via the stoa. Acastus angled across the square, cutting his quarry off before the latter lost himself in the crowd. "What brings you to the senate building, Theron?"

"Nothing you need to know about," Theron replied in an affronted tone. "Merely some business in the city. I met Laomedes as he came out."

Acastus weighed up the beady-eyed look directed his way. Theron stood a head shorter than himself, and his limbs, though hardened by physical exercise, were gangly, almost like a rodents. He had no trouble envisioning Callisto's uncle in the middle of a phalanx, pressed forward into battle by those braver than himself. "A convenient meeting then." He crossed his arms over his chest. "Perhaps he disclosed some senate business."

Theron moved a step back. "Perhaps. I hear you have a mission. I wish you good fortune."

"Do you?" Something in Theron's voice hinted otherwise. Spartans weren't above scheming; even their own kings had done so in the past, but he sensed darker undercurrents threatening his mission before it even began.

"Yes. No doubt it will prove a difficult task. If you succeed, well…" Theron gave a light shrug. "I'm needed at home."

Reflexively, Acastus grasped the hilt of his xiphos. Watching Theron scurrying away towards the east of the city, instinct whispered he might need to watch his own back, too. Turning his gaze in the direction of Athena's temple, high on the hill overlooking the city, he vowed, "With your aid, goddess, nothing will stop me returning Xanthia."

CHAPTER THREE

Theron hurried across the small courtyard of his house to seek out the woman who had come to live with him since his wife's death. Sidling into the room where she usually sat, his lips pursed on finding a servant clearing the remains of a half-eaten meal. Ignoring the woman's deferential bow, he demanded, "Where is my sister?"

"She has gone to speak with the wine maker, master."

Not bothering to thank her, he hurried away to the single domed building a short walk from the house. *There should be more than one outbuilding.* His jaw clenched in a tight, painful line. A citizen of his standing *deserved* more than one.

Before the stream of envious thoughts became a raging torrent, he spotted the blonde woman emerging from where the wine press was housed and beckoned her to him.

"There is a risk Aeschylus will return." He huffed out a disparaging breath as her eyes widened, their light brown depths taking on the look of a hunted rabbit. Quickly, he filled her in on the information given to him by his ally in the Gerousia.

Akantha knotted her fingers. "He mustn't be allowed to. He won't take me back. Even if he does, you will lose everything you've schemed for, regardless."

Seeing her knuckles turn white, his mouth twisted in frustration.

"I told you to go live in his house rather than here." Heart racing, he paced, considering the consequences should his brother-in-law reappear. Not just the failure of his plan but possible expulsion from his mess group. He punched a fist against the palm of his other hand, vowing to avoid such a humiliation no matter the cost.

Akantha rolled her eyes. "The land might be cleared, but who would have sown and harvested crops? Continued to keep the house liveable? Certainly not you."

The constant reminder of his lack of any real wealth rankled. "Which is exactly why I need you to claim your husband's kleroi."

"Of course I will claim it. By law, I'm still Aeschylus's wife. Our only child, Callisto, is married, so she is out of the way."

"Yes, yes, his wife," Theron scoffed with a wave of his hand. "And while you're his wife, you cannot help me. As his abandoned wife…or his widow…you can."

"Are you suggesting Aeschylus be killed? No. I can't, I *won't*, condone murder."

He gave his sister a pitying look. "If you want to help me, your own flesh-and-blood brother, then you will. Either he dies, or his and Ianthe's daughter must. If the first, you inherit your husband's lands outright. If the second, your husband remains an outcast leaving you free to claim them." Theron cocked his head at the myriad emotions crossing his sister's face. "I'll wager you'd prefer the second course of action."

She shot him a baleful glare. "Do not utter that woman's name. Even dead, she continues to blight my life."

Theron clasped his sister's arms as an idea took root in his mind. "I will do everything I can to ensure Acastus doesn't succeed."

Akantha eyed him warily. "How?"

"Better you don't know. Leave it to me."

He circled back to the house to search out his most trusted servant. Theron dropped coins into the man's hands and murmured precise instructions before the servant nodded curtly and ran off to do his master's bidding.

Theron rubbed his hands together. He had waited long enough to lay claim to Aeschylus's valuable land even by way of proxy through his sister. Now, nothing remained to stop his acquisition.

Except for a girl who would soon be dead.

CHAPTER FOUR

Coarse sand covered the beach for the entire stretch he was able to see. Inhaling a lungful of salty air, Acastus angled his way to the cliff face where Philodemos had indicated he wait for Xanthia. Recalling the former servant's shock at his appearance, a wry smile lifted one corner of his mouth. Beyond a cursory greeting, he had lingered only long enough to learn of Xanthia's whereabouts.

Beneath the light cloak he wore, the comforting weight of his xiphos bumped against his hip. It did not matter that he had adopted the guise of a merchant, a warrior always carried his weapons. His leather sandals sank into the sand with each heavy tread, abrading the soles of his feet. The stinging sensation raised memories of running barefoot over stony ground as a boy in training to become a man, a warrior of Sparta. A warm breeze swept his long hair across his face. Hardened to all discomfort, he nevertheless rued not having braided it for this confrontation.

He needed to see clearly in more ways than one.

A natural indentation in the smooth rock caught his eye. Hollow and high enough for him to stand in, the recess provided concealment from anyone who might pass in the vicinity, including the woman he sought. He welcomed the advantage to assess his quarry before she noticed his presence.

Ever alert, his probing gaze raked over the stretch of shoreline as he studied the vista before him. Close to the shore a pod of dolphins frolicked, their calls to each other wild, melodic, and full of freedom. He sank deeper inside the rocky recess, gratified to note the light-coloured cloak blended seamlessly into the chalk-like cliffs.

Then he saw her.

The lissom woman who materialised on the beach, almost in a direct line to his hiding place, matched the description Philodemos had given him. Fire kindled in his belly, a fire which stoked unwanted passion the longer he stared at her while she danced in the glistening shallows.

He swore he could feel every blood vessel dilate as his heart began to pump blood at a speed he feared would tear veins open. Aware that his hands were shaking, Acastus flexed his long fingers, concentrating on the task to reimpose control over his riotous senses.

It was her.

Xanthia.

Worshipper of Aphrodite. Half-sister to both Diokles and Callisto.

The woman whose forgiveness he might one day earn. Even if he met his end at the hands of her brother when the truth came to light.

Another swift scan of the beach satisfied him that no threats, either human or animal, lurked nearby. They were alone. His eyes were drawn back to her, enthralled by the joyful bliss on her face. Her dancing mimicked the dance of the dolphins – wild and free. Arms outstretched, face lifted skyward, he could almost feel her drinking in the very essence of the sun and wind.

Satisfied she had not seen him, he allowed himself to further savour the sight she presented. The diaphanous white material of her chiton swirled around long, shapely legs. Hair, the colour of a raven's wing, flowed down her back in a thick glossy wave, contrasting sharply with her smooth skin, which gleamed golden in the sunlight. The next breath he took shuddered to a halt in his chest.

Her chiton hung around her waist, the half-twirl she made gifting him a vision of her breasts, bared to his hungry gaze. Acastus briefly closed his eyes, battling a powerful urge to go to her, cup those golden globes in his hands, and fasten his mouth over the erect buds crowning their fullness. He shifted his feet in a vain attempt to relieve the vice clutching his groin.

In the blink of an eye, he saw her freeze mid-step. A silent curse flew from between his dry lips. Had even that small movement given him away?

Across the expanse of sand separating them, his keen sight caught the widening of her eyes and the small 'o' rounding her mouth. To brand those parted lips with his suddenly became as necessary as breathing. She tossed her head, hauteur settling over her strong, proud features. Excitement filled him to bursting at this display of fearlessness, and for the briefest of moments, he forgot the reason why he had travelled to this island to find her. She was a woman worth fighting for and winning. A woman to challenge and fire his blood.

Instead of running away, she faced him head-on, giving him an even better view of her delectable form. The languid way she swept back the unruly hair blowing across her face summoned a momentary fantasy of its rich blackness adorning his naked chest. Lust punched a heated fist through his vitals.

The sensual pain jolted Acastus out of his trance. In the early days of his training, his mentor had sometimes called him out for not focusing on the task given to him. Now, he castigated himself for allowing physical desire to override his purpose.

Holding her insolent gaze, he pushed away from the rock face and walked towards her, bound by an inexplicable yearning to tether her to him. Why did she not cover herself now that she was in his presence? He pressed his lips together. Perhaps as a worshipper of the goddess of love she possessed no qualms about appearing half-naked in front of a man.

His steps faltered as a stab of unfamiliar emotion pierced his gut. "Xanthia."

Her large, almond-shaped eyes, irises dark and glossy as the olives gathered on his lands, grew wider.

"Who are you, stranger?"

Like liquid nectar, her voice flowed over him. Would it have the same honeyed tones in the throes of shared passion? Acastus clenched his jaw, furious with himself, and furious with her for the effortless way she had summoned his ardour. He would not allow an inconvenient desire to sway him from his goal.

He drew himself up to his full height to deliver an ultimatum she undoubtedly would be loath to hear. "My name is Acastus. I am here to escort you home to Sparta."

Her response confirmed his expectation.

"You are mad."

The frigid tone those three words were stated in rivalled the freezing snow which crowned Taygetos, the great mountain of Sparta, in the middle of winter. The expressions crossing her lovely face stirred an emotion he hesitated to label as possessiveness inside him. By Zeus, he would bring her home with him.

His eyes strayed to her breasts, their pale brown crowns tempting him to reach out and claim them. Acastus swallowed and fisted his hands. They were not his to claim.

"I am far from mad." He summoned his anger, the only defence against her allure. "You would be wise to cover yourself. I could overpower you, take what I want. Your lack of modesty invites it."

Her derisive laughter fanned the flames of irritation. She could laugh all she wanted, but no derision would sway his mind from a task he needed to accomplish as much as he needed to breathe.

"You hypocrite! I happen to know in Sparta the women parade themselves such as I am now." She looked him up and down, her gaze lingering a fraction longer on the betraying bulge of his chiton. A knowing smile curled her lips. "Are you afraid you like what you see?"

He bit the inside of his cheek. The goad had struck too close to home. "Only during exercise, Xanthia. They don't flaunt themselves otherwise."

The glint in her eyes mocked him. "But I am exercising. I swam with the dolphins and rolled down my chiton to dry myself faster. I was quite alone until you intruded."

She truly possessed no understanding of his capabilities, of the promises he made to himself to redeem her out of an exile a few careless words had caused. His mind remained clear enough to recognise the difficult task ahead of him, and not just because every cell in his body clamoured to know her better.

Far more dangerous was her indomitable spirit.

Like a hunter stalking his quarry, his deceptively leisured steps closed in on her, until little more than a hand span of space remained between them. Except for the disdainful tilt of her head, she remained motionless, watching his approach with a confident half-smile.

Passion flowed in a tidal wave he feared would leave him at her mercy. Acastus pushed it back with the same unyielding power he used to push back an enemy shield in the thick of battle.

Droplets of sweat tracked down his forehead. Ignoring them, he held her gaze and reached one hand out to encircle her wrist, his forefinger sliding over the point where her blood pulsed. Its frantic beat resonated against the pad of his finger. Calling on the discipline instilled in his mind, body, and heart since boyhood, he conquered the sensual message conveyed there.

She tried to tug her hand away, but he tightened his grip; strong enough to hold, gentle enough to not bruise. Acastus grasped the shoulder sculp of her chiton and tucked her hand through the sleeveless opening, pulling the fabric up slowly. He repeated the task on the other side, even as everything primal in him objected to covering the bounty that provided such a feast to his eyes.

It was a power play.

His gaze lifted to her face. The displeasure blazing from her eyes told him she understood the game he played.

"Now you resemble a woman of Sparta." The slight tremble of his voice unnerved him. His composure wavered further when he drew his hand away, a finger lightly brushing the peak of one breast. The sudden hiss of indrawn breath betrayed her awareness of him.

He stiffened and looked into her eyes. Eyes which glittered almost black above a clenched jaw.

"I am *not* a woman of that accursed land," she spat.

CHAPTER FIVE

Fear and defiance clashed and swirled in her stomach, its potent mix creating a nauseating maelstrom. Xanthia breathed in through her nose, taking the air as deep into her lungs as her tight chest allowed. Slowly, the urge to throw up lessened. By all the gods she would not betray panic in front of this man, whose deep brown eyes examined her as though he fathomed the depths of her soul.

Nor betray how much his demand, and his presence, affected her.

He was magnificent. The simple clothing he wore failed to hide his warrior's physique. The short beard and the scar running down one cheek served to add character to the strong planes of his face. Her fingers itched to bury themselves in the thick, long hair crowning his scalp. She had known men, conquered their desires, then used them for her purposes. Instinct warned her Acastus could never be conquered, no matter how much she believed she could best him in a tussle of wills.

Xanthia snatched a furtive breath to steady her wildly beating heart. If he had been from anywhere else, she would have dragged him to the sand and revelled in the pleasure her body clamoured she take.

A great pity he was Spartan. Her enemy. The epitome of everything she loathed.

And if she allowed him to take her away from her island home, she would lose the foundations of her life for a second time.

Her gaze darted up the looming cliff face, mind rejecting one escape plan after another. No use trying to outrun or fight him. A subtle shake of her head confirmed her choice to heed the inner voice that argued the best course of action was to outwit him using any wiles at her disposal.

She raised her chin. Staring down her nose, she willed him to fall to his knees and beg her forgiveness for his outrageous pronouncement. "You say you are here to take me to Sparta. After all these years, why now? Who has sent you?"

Chest heaving, she stared suspiciously as he crossed his arms across his own broad chest and planted his feet apart as though he was a wall preventing her escape.

"Your family in Sparta sent me."

His deep voice gave off an unmistakeable tone of command. It shivered through her, igniting a wildfire of defiance in her chest, serving only to increase her urgency to escape his presence.

"And, what if I refuse to go? My family are here. Will you force me to leave my home? Leave my parents who love me? The friends I consider my family." She glared at him. "Are you Spartans always so ruthless and single-minded?"

The flaring of his nostrils sent a thrill of disquiet racing down her spine. The twitch near the corner of his eye roused a reluctant admiration for his self-control. It was ridiculous to imagine she possessed the strength to stop this superb specimen of manhood tossing her over his shoulder and striding off to wherever he chose.

To her chagrin, her imagination taunted her with that very image. Her blood heated, leaving her legs weak and forcing her to lock her knees to stay upright. The last thing she wanted to do was collapse against him.

"Have a care, Xanthia. Whenever Spartans are fixed on a purpose, we always achieve it. You'll learn soon enough this is the way of our people."

There was no denying the subliminal threat behind the words delivered in his deep, deceptively quiet voice. "You presume too much. Do you think I'll fall on my knees and beg you to take me to Sparta? I hate Sparta!" She spat near his feet. "You are brutes—"

"And you are the child of a Spartiate and a Spartan mother. You'll return to your rightful home as your half-sister did."

Ice coated his pronouncement, but his tone failed to hold back the disdainful explosion of her breath. "What is a Spartiate?"

"A full citizen of Sparta. Descended from the ancient Dorians who first came to the region of Lakonia."

Grief clogged her throat. Was she *someone* after all? A half-sister? She fought the unwelcome curiosity over the family lost to her because of an unknown man's decree. Still clear in her memory was the day her rage had subsided after learning she had been banished from the land of her birth. An intense longing to belong to someone, somewhere, had swamped her soul.

To confess her longing to Acastus, though, would be to confess weakness. Thanks to the goddess, she had found a sense of belonging among her fellow acolytes.

"You mean two Spartans who abandoned me to die. I don't know them, and they don't know me. They didn't want me then, so what reason do they have to insist on my return now? Tell me how I can leave the two people who nurtured and raised me with all the love they possessed?"

Her chest heaved, anger ripping open old wounds. Who was he to expect her to drop everything and accompany him? He knew who he was, confident in his standing amongst his own people. She had lived a lie and still had not fully recovered from the knowledge.

The baleful stare she gave him gradually morphed into a frown. Guilt, inflexible will, and something else indefinable, flitted through his eyes before a veil fell across them. Xanthia looked away to stare at a group of noisy gulls fighting over a dead fish. Why did her tirade affect him so much?

A thrill lanced through her gut. The answer might prove an invaluable weapon in resisting his attempts to kidnap her. And, to resist him.

The drawn out silence, a profound silence full of hidden hurts, plucked at her composure. A silence where all she heard was the lapping of waves on the shore and the cry of gulls taking to the air. Her lips parted but no sound emerged from her dry mouth.

Xanthia started at the clipped voice breaking the uneasy standoff.

"Philodemos understands you must go. He and Euphrasia don't regret their sacrifice taking you to safety."

"I don't believe you." She turned her face away to stare out over the sea. The sea she would fight with every weapon she could to not cross to a land foreign to her.

"Come with me. Let him tell you for himself."

She shot him a narrow-eyed glare. "Even if what you say is true, I won't go anywhere until after the festival. Philodemos must have told you."

"He mentioned a festival. He didn't say you would be attending."

She rubbed her face with both hands. "I won't leave until the festival to our goddess is finished. Must I beat that through your thick Spartan skull?"

"No, since you will leave on my say so."

The half-smirk curving his full, masculine lips contained sufficient provocation for her temper to flare. Xanthia closed her eyes. Taking a moment to tell herself losing it would not achieve the result she desired, she opened them again to find him studying her with what appeared to be a haughty tolerance. Her hand itched to slap the expression off his ruggedly handsome face.

Then an idea struck her like a thunderbolt.

"What if I promise to go willingly to Sparta if you agree I attend the festival first?" She had no intention of keeping it, and the distrustful gleam in his eyes clearly showed he considered it a delaying tactic.

"Tell me why I should believe you?"

Think! If she managed to convince Acastus to attend the festival, Kallios and the other men could overpower him. No-one would know any better if he never reached Sparta again. She trusted with unshakeable faith to her parents keeping their silence.

Perhaps she could use the sensual skills she had cultivated to convince him. Eyes half-closed, Xanthia ran a fingernail down the hard planes of his pectoral muscles in a provocative message meant to tease and arouse.

"The festivals honouring Aphrodite are vibrant and erotic." She kept her voice low and seductive, reining in a triumphant smile when his eyes turned opaque. "Dances petition for fertility. They are followed by a feast and other rites lasting all night. Everyone is welcome to attend."

There was no time to escape the hand that shot out to fist around her thick hair. Unable to look away from the irresistible power in his face, Xanthia bent her head back in response to the gentle tug he exerted, sucking air into her lungs and failing to release it. The sun's warmth seeped through the soft skin of her neck, melting resistance away. She waited, spellbound, unable to utter a protest, watching his head come closer.

For one short, sweet instant, she felt his warm breath hover over her skin, inhaled his heady masculine aroma…curled her fingers into talons, ready to scratch his face if he dared to kiss her.

Then his warm fingertips traced the pulse beating in her neck in a caress as gentle as it was commanding. A soft moan escaped to mock her control over a predicament of her own making. What mystical power did he possess to make her heart race like the immortal horses that drew the chariot of the sun?

In a daze she reached up to clutch his head, a silent plea to keep stoking the passionate fire now making her heart sing. The warm breath he exhaled close to her ear floated through every trembling limb.

"I'll discuss this with Philodemos."

The spell broke.

Xanthia tore herself away. "Speak with him, then. I suppose it's because I'm only a woman." She was far too angry to care that displeasure twisted his mouth into a hard line.

"You'll find out how wrong you are once you are in Sparta. Our women are valued more than anywhere else in Hellas."

"I don't believe you." Whirling away, she stalked towards the path leading to her home, not caring whether he followed her or not.

CHAPTER SIX

Xanthia broke into a run when she spied Philodemos walking around from the back of the low, white-washed dwelling she called home. "Father, this…this man is threatening to kidnap me! I won't go back to that place with him or with anyone!"

The sorrowful frown creasing her foster father's face froze her heart. Surely, he would not take the side of Acastus over her. He was the only father she knew, his arms the only arms she remembered holding her, keeping her safe. She needed his support now more than ever.

Philodemos heaved a long, pain-filled sigh. "My child, four years ago you already left us to join Aphrodite's worshippers, but I always expected the day to arrive when you might be called upon to leave us and return to your rightful home. I never spoke of this to you because you wouldn't have listened."

Pacing in circles gave her time to think, find reasons to enlist her father's support. "This is different. I'd be forced to leave you, our home, everyone I know, for an uncertain life in a land I hate!"

"How can you hate something you haven't seen?"

She gritted her teeth. Acastus's voice should not possess the power to pluck at her nerves as easily as a musician strummed the strings of a lyre. She spun to face him, ready to argue him away from Melos and out of her life. Finding him almost by her side, her pulse tripped over itself – she had not even noticed or heard him approaching. "Everything I've learned is enough to warrant me refusing to set foot there. Why are you doing this to me? To us? Is it because my parents were helot slaves, useful to be hunted down by the likes of you?" Seeing his face darken at the accusation, an irrational satisfaction summoned a smirk despite the gravity of the moment.

"I'll overlook your rash words. You're not of their blood. Your father is alive. You owe him your return."

Philodemos's exclamation stopped the insult she was preparing to hurl at Acastus.

"Praise the gods, Aeschylus is alive!"

"It doesn't matter," Xanthia insisted, worried by the joy spreading over Philodemos's features as he absorbed the news. This Aeschylus, whoever he was, may have fathered her, but she knew him about as well as she knew a wave rolling onto the beach. There for a fleeting moment then gone forever.

"It matters more than you think," Acastus countered. "We'll go inside. Philodemos will agree with me once he hears what I have to say."

She shot him a mutinous look and pointed to the door. "You go inside. I'm going to find my mother. Euphrasia will take my side. You don't know her. We're a formidable force together."

"Maybe you are, but she'll agree you need to return home."

Xanthia planted her hands on her hips. "I am home," she snarled. His implacable stance hardened her resolve. No matter what Acastus claimed, she knew Euphrasia could convince Philodemos to change his mind. Xanthia moved to clasp her father's hands. "Please don't betray me. I've been betrayed enough."

Gritting her teeth to avoid giving in to the bright moisture filling his eyes, she turned on her heel and stormed off to find her mother, who had been pasturing their flock during the cool morning hours. She ignored Acastus's command to stay, heart leaping into her throat in case he tried to stop her.

Hearing no footsteps following in her wake, Xanthia squared her shoulders and kept walking.

~*~

Philodemos wiped his rheumy eyes, then tilted his head to listen. "I hear sheep, which means my wife will be home soon." He gestured towards the doorway of the small house. "Come in and refresh yourself."

Acastus entered first, stooping to fit through the door. He straightened to his full height to take in the large, single room, looking around with keen interest. Bright and clean, a welcoming fire burned in the hearth. Light woollen curtains were drawn back, two beds arranged side by side behind them.

The smaller one was covered by a jumble of bright chitons. Xanthia's? His gut tightened. A flash of white caught his eye. Why would she have a dove next to where she slept? Remembering doves were sacred to the goddess she worshipped, he wondered idly whether she was taking the bird to be sacrificed at the upcoming festival. He shrugged. The reason mattered little.

The scent of wood smoke blended invitingly with the aromas wafting from the pot hanging over the flames. His stomach growled, demanding food it had not received for some days. He ignored it, having perfected the skill of controlling hunger. He had gone without eating often enough during forced marches on a campaign.

The sound of liquid being poured brought his attention back to Philodemos, who handed him a kylix. Acastus sipped thoughtfully. One concern ate into his unshakeable confidence. If his disguise was so transparent, then it would serve him well to understand the reason. "When I first came to your door, you recognised me being from Sparta. How?"

Philodemos spread his hands out. "You may wear the garb of a merchant, but even though only a helot, I lived in Sparta and recognise a warrior when I see one. Your features, too, show your heritage, but I doubt anyone else would notice."

Acastus grunted in disbelief. "You sound very certain."

"I am. No-one would believe, or expect, a Spartiate to travel disguised as a merchant."

"There is truth in what you say." Nerves poised on a knife-edge, he prepared to ask the question that had haunted him since his encounter with a woman who had stirred him more than he imagined any woman could. "Why does Xanthia hate Sparta?"

He caught the flash of pain in Philodemos's eyes before the old servant gestured to a seat. Acastus stifled the impatience to know everything immediately and sat heavily on a three-legged stool by the table. It spoke of its workmanship that it did not collapse beneath his weight. Philodemos sank wearily onto the stool across from him. The muscles in his neck grew tight while he waited for the older man to speak.

"There is much I need to explain, Acastus, and much you will need to contend with."

"I've contended with challenges enough. I don't baulk at what is thrown in my path."

The older man clasped his work-roughened hands on the wooden table. "You'll face a battle convincing Xanthia to leave Melos. I've tried my best to lessen her aversion, but I must warn you she carries a loathing, even hatred, of everything Spartan."

Acastus raised his eyebrows. "Why?"

"My master learned of Xanthia's abandonment on Taygetos," Philodemos said in a tight voice as he stared at the opposite wall. "It saddened me to witness his despair, so I begged him to let me save the infant. He agreed readily, paying a trusted perioikoi to escort us out of Sparta. I feared for Xanthia and Euphrasia's lives, terrified how we would explain ourselves to any kryptos if one or more found us."

The former helot had been right to fear. Acastus recalled his own time as a kryptos, the punishment he had dealt out in similar encounters. "No-one must know Aeschylus let you go. I've never heard of a helot being set free." He was taken aback at the hard look the man gave him.

"After all of my master's kindness to myself and Euphrasia, the gods would surely punish any betrayal. Aeschylus's secret is locked in our hearts."

So was his own. Locked away, although the time for revelation, however slowly, grew closer. Acastus pressed hard on the bridge of his nose. "How did you escape?"

"The perioikoi paid our passage from Gytheion and gave us the remaining coins as our master had instructed. We fled to Kythera first." Philodemos clenched his hands together. "We found a new home and life with help from the people there. Xanthia's childhood was spent on Kythera, and in her ninth year she came across a small herd of horses. She loved those horses, ran with them on the beach. They seemed to accept her."

"I heard of that legend," Acastus said, thinking of the island in the Ionian Sea where some held Aphrodite first came to shore, borne on an open shell. Perhaps this had drawn Xanthia to worship the goddess of love. "Callisto received a vision of horses near a sea when she entreated Apollo's help to find her half-sister."

A smile lit up the older man's eyes. "Is Callisto married? She'd be a woman now."

"Yes." Acastus harboured no scruples over his terse reply. A warrior did not indulge in idle talk. "Why did you leave Kythera? I sailed there first believing it the likeliest place you fled to. It didn't take long to discover you had left for Melos."

Philodemos's shoulders drooped. "Thirteen summers passed, happy and peaceful. Until the day Euphrasia and I were recalling our flight from Sparta and wondering whether anyone would search for Xanthia after so much time had passed. Neither of us realised she'd returned from visiting a friend and was listening near the door. She burst in, her face paler than the white rocks of Melos itself, demanding answers, covering her ears while we tried in vain to calm her and explain what happened. I will never forget her anger, the wildness in her eyes, even though only a young girl. The wound festers to this day."

Acastus drew back to stare at the shepherd's bent head. The fault lay with him, not the loyal servant who continued to twist his hands together. Now, he understood how far the ripples of one careless, however innocent, remark had extended. An innate ability to control his emotions did not gift him the defence against the self-loathing that clawed at his insides like the talons of an eagle, ripping his heart to shreds. The grief on Philodemos's face, when he looked back up at him, served to deepen his guilt.

"What did she do?" His voice sounded rough even to his own ears.

"She grew almost wild, unable to deal with the truth, uncertain of where she belonged. It took a long time for her to accept what she'd learned. Murmurings reached my ears that people had begun to speculate about us. With each passing year her Dorian heritage became more apparent. Anyone who saw her questioned our claim to be her parents." Philodemos passed a gnarled hand over his face. "I thought it best if we moved further away. We left our home, our life on Kythera, and came here to Melos. Xanthia was a lost soul until she stumbled across the acolytes of Aphrodite living on the other side of the island. Against my advice, she joined them, saying she had found people, other than myself and Euphrasia, who accepted who she was without question or judgement."

Acastus rested his arms on the table and considered everything he had been told. His first impression about her had been proven correct; no innocent like her half-sister who had been a virginal priestess of Apollo when reunited with Diokles. Would this make the task of returning her more difficult, especially given his body's inconvenient response to her allure?

He harboured no illusions he might need to throw her over his shoulder if she refused to go with him. There would be no asking, just taking. Exhilaration bubbled in his gut at the prospect of such a challenge.

"She mentioned a fertility festival." He drew back when Philodemos looked down to study the beaten earth floor.

"I dislike to admit it, but I know she has taken men to her bed. Two summers ago, something happened to her. She refuses to speak of that time, though I pleaded with her to ease the pain by unburdening herself to Euphrasia. She was like one dead, the light gone from her eyes. Xanthia lives mostly with the acolytes. She always visits us before the festival begins and arrived two days before you did. You won't convince her to go with you now. She is strong-willed and won't give up the time she spends with us. Once she leaves for the festival, she returns only briefly to collect her dove and make healing potions if we need any."

"She is unwavering like her half-brother. Why does she value the dove so much?"

"All I can tell you is that she first brought the dove here the same summer she withdrew into herself."

There would be plenty of time to discover the importance of the bird to Xanthia and perhaps find a way to use that bond to convince her to return with him. Acastus digested the thought of a fertility festival. An insistent tug had him gritting his teeth. His body could clamour to know her intimately all it wanted. Honour demanded he first atone for her almost losing her life before it had barely begun.

The trials of a journey home with a reluctant companion loomed large in his mind, but a self-assured shrug dismissed such concerns. Never in his life had he experienced female rejection. They were desirous and more than willing to follow his lead.

"When I'm ready to leave, she will come with me."

"Only if you call on every god in Olympus to drag me away."

Acastus swivelled on the stool, blinking to dispel the bright light hitting his eyes. Xanthia stood in the doorway, sunlight streaming around her like an aura. Behind her hovered an older woman, her work-roughened hand clasping Xanthia's shoulder. As both women entered, he was able to see the sadness in Euphrasia's eyes and the blazing anger in Xanthia's. Both emotions pulled at his control, but he turned his hard gaze onto Xanthia.

"The choice is yours," he stated with quiet menace. "You'll choose to return to Sparta. Choose wisely or I won't hesitate to force your return." He pressed down hard on the desire to laugh aloud at the angry dismay suffusing her face.

"What sort of choice is that!?" She turned to the silent couple. "I won't leave you no matter what this Spartan bully says."

Acastus felt the knife of his betrayal sink deeper into his soul. He had broken up one family, now he was going to break up another. "You'll return to take your rightful place as a citizen of Sparta."

"And my parents," she demanded. "Will they return to their rightful place? Or are they safer here? As I am."

Time to explain the situation to her in a way that invited no argument. Before he could, however, Philodemos spoke.

"Xanthia, recall what I said earlier about expecting this day. Euphrasia and I love you as though you are our child. We gladly gave up our privileged position in your father's household to save you. But your real family, who you are bound to by blood, is in Sparta." He cast a questioning look at Acastus. "I leave it to the will of the gods whether or not we return."

Witnessing Xanthia's lower lip tremble, Acastus clenched his hand. Giving reassurance, especially to a helot servant, was foreign to him as a Spartiate, yet the compulsion to do so in this case proved stronger. "Also the will of Aeschylus. Once he is settled in his old house, I have no doubt he'll send for you."

"Since you insist on dragging me away, why can't they come with us now?"

"Because our life is here, child. We're still considered slaves, so we must take care not to be punished for our escape."

"I was right about you Spartans. No—" Xanthia shouted when Philodemos tried to interrupt her. "Are such people what you expect I'd gladly return to?"

Acastus pressed his lips together to prevent a torrent of rash words. Once he reimposed control, he spoke with conviction. "Your safe passage is guaranteed. Only three people know of what transpired, one being Aeschylus. His gratitude for saving Xanthia cannot be underestimated." One corner of his mouth tilted upward as Xanthia pushed her bottom lip out, every line of her face mutinous. "See, I'm not a brute as you've already called me."

"Let me be the judge of that. Mother?"

"You have to return," Euphrasia insisted in a soft, pain-filled voice. "Your father risked punishment to save you. Don't let his efforts be in vain. He'll be over-joyed to finally welcome you home."

Acastus met Xanthia's scowl with a composure he did not really feel. The tight muscles around her face were evidence she was not yet convinced despite the assurances she had been given.

"I'll think about it," she demurred. "In three days I leave for the festival. You can come with me or not. I'll return briefly for my dove and…other things. Only then might I consent to leave."

His forehead crinkled. *Why not take the dove now?* Skilled at uncovering a person's motives, it would only be a matter of time before he understood her odd decisions. He leaned to one side, resting a forearm on the table.

"Depend upon it, Xanthia, I'll accompany you."

A mysterious smile pulled the corners of her mouth up. Acastus set his jaw while a finger of distrust worked its way down his spine.

CHAPTER SEVEN

A cool breeze softened the sting of the warm afternoon air. This was the late spring day Xanthia anticipated each year, the day she thanked Aphrodite, through her festival, for guiding her to this place. Anticipation danced through her nerves until she trembled from the excitement.

"You celebrate the Aphrodisia early on Melos."

She took a careful step away from Acastus, who walked beside her, close enough for their arms to brush. Xanthia rubbed at the tingling beneath her skin. "It's sometimes too hot here to celebrate when the other cities do. We're a small company of acolytes, not a populous city."

His mysterious smile set her heart thumping to a slow, heavy beat. Looking away, she struggled to compose herself. Why did he have to be so tall? Her neck ached from having to look up at him during their long walk to the small community where she lived for most of the year.

Some of her fellow acolytes had already spotted their approach and were now hurrying to meet them. Seeing Kallios among their number, Xanthia blew out a nervous breath. The closer they came, the more she could discern that his features were livid. The women on the other hand...

"Tell them I'm from Kythera."

His low demand startled her. "Why?"

"I prefer no heroics of anyone challenging me."

She tossed her head and looked down her nose. "Afraid of being beaten? How would that Spartan pride recover."

"Keep your voice down," he growled.

After a short, internal debate, she decided to play along. There was plenty of time to betray him if she needed to. "If you insist. Although anyone with healthy eyes can see you're more than just a shepherd."

"You like what you see?" he smirked.

"No, I don't," she lied hotly, leaving his side to hurry towards the group closing in on them.

Xanthia hugged each of them in greeting, except Kallios, who leaned down to claim her lips. For the first time she hesitated, unsure of her feelings. He lifted his head to send a cold look in Acastus's direction, whose features, she was apprehensive to see, wore a dark, thunderous scowl.

She gestured towards him, needing to remove the tension in the air. "This is…Acastus," she hesitated over his name. Apart from Kallios, everyone else swarmed the newcomer to their festival in welcome. Watching the women drape themselves over him, Xanthia was stunned by a burning sensation in her stomach. No! Their attentions meant nothing to her.

"Why did you bring him?"

"He's a guest of my parents." Not strictly true she admitted to herself with a tiny shrug. "Others bring guests and he'll be gone tomorrow. Come, the festival begins soon."

Kallios snorted, then took her hand, leading her away. "I'll make sure he does. I've prepared offerings for you, and the fire is lit upon the altar."

The offering of myrtle leaves was not what concerned her. A dove had to be sacrificed at the start to call on Aphrodite's favour. Xanthia's stomach clenched as she followed Kallios to the large grove fringed by myrtle trees, where the festival was always held. Where her dove was concerned, she trusted no-one, choosing to leave Calliope safely behind.

She looked over her shoulder to find Acastus, eyes boring into her back, being followed by a trail of women in his wake. She bit her lip. Maybe it would have been better to leave him behind. He dwarfed the other men, both in height and build, and as much as she hated to admit it, the raw masculinity that exuded from his mere presence. Her belly flipped. If there was any trouble, it would be her fault.

Or, she could use any trouble to her advantage.

CHAPTER EIGHT

Arms folded across his chest, Acastus acknowledged the anger coiling like a snake in his belly. Prayers and offerings to Aphrodite had been made, a dove sacrificed, sheep roasted over open fires. Wine had flowed freely. Once the meal ended, a sultry atmosphere descended swiftly over the those present.

Flames flickered in the twilight, the air scented by the blooms of the myrtle tree he leaned against, from where he had watched the proceedings unfold. Fragrant wood smoke drifted over to tease his nostrils, imbued with traces of scented oils rubbed into bodies to heighten anticipated pleasure. In the firelight, the women's skin glistened, inviting the touch of a lover's hands this night.

Earlier, a few revellers had approached, trying to entice him to join them. A menacing look had sufficed to send them scuttling away. His aloofness guaranteed him solitude to watch the proceedings in relative peace. He stifled self-deprecating laughter. Peace was the last thing to be found among the carnal dancing on display.

The women conjured passion with liquid, flowing movements of hands, their bodies undulating in time with the deep, slow, throb of drumbeats, calculated to burn through the strongest defences any red-blooded man could muster. Two of the dancers had draped their tunics over the knotted cord under their breasts, leaving a simple garland of Adonis flowers to cover their bare skin. While such temptations might glaze the eyes of the men present, they failed to sway his fixation away from a certain dark-haired woman who commanded his attention.

If Xanthia had deliberately set out to rouse his anger, she was succeeding beyond her wildest dreams.

Her lithe body swayed in time to the evocative sound of flutes, movements made all the more seductive by graceful hand gestures meant to entrance and entice a lover into their silken hold. His mouth tightened when she glided over to dance before Kallios, whose face wore an expression of naked desire.

Acastus resisted the urge to spit on the ground. The coil of anger rose to settle in his chest as disbelief questioned how a woman of Xanthia's mettle could consider such a man worthy of her attentions. Suddenly, he tensed as she twirled with a suggestive rocking of her hips to face him.

Their eyes locked, and the world around him ceased to exist.

His burning gaze bored into her. Like him, she held herself slightly aloof from the others, although her eyes dared him to join the group by the fire. Her tongue traced her lips, a half-smile curving their fullness. Her blatant mockery of his self-control pushed his tension levels higher.

But he saw her intent stare drop to, and linger, below his waist. A feral grin teased his mouth and eased some of the strain keeping his nerves tight. If she sought to play games, he would demonstrate his adeptness in those passionate games, too. Acastus tilted his hips just enough to allow his chiton to shape his burgeoning vitals. Despite the sudden dryness of his mouth, his grin widened in satisfaction at the sight of her parted lips.

Until she ran a languid hand over one breast, tracing slow, seductive circles around its fullness in time with the whispering sighs of flutes. Blood rushed to his head.

He clenched his hands to control the impulse urging him to snatch her up and carry her away, denying anyone else the right to claim her tonight. Acastus read defiance in the way she tossed her head, the flickering firelight providing the perfect backdrop to the glistening strands of her hair and strong, yet beautiful, features. She rejoined the other dancers, who were now moving among the seated men. The tiny muscles circling his eyes tightened, his vision tunnelling the same way it narrowed prior to a battle.

He drew back slightly as one of the dancers came to him, seemingly unperturbed by his forbidding stance. The delicate material of the chiton she wore presented a scant obstacle to his imagination. He ran an impassive gaze over her alluring figure. Dark eyes thrown into prominence by soft, golden-brown hair, she was attractive but could not match the women of his homeland.

"Come, join us," she whispered, pressing herself suggestively against his unyielding bulk.

Whatever flower she had infused in the oil slicking her skin, its heady fragrance was intoxicating. He rocked back on his heels, reluctantly enjoying the sensation of her hands sliding over his chest and arms. A quick glance showed him Xanthia, now nestled in Kallios's lap, glaring his way, and with a sudden indrawn breath he realised her glare emanated jealous disapproval. He licked his lips, tasting victory.

"I'm here only to observe," he managed in a guttural voice as the woman tempting him ran her fingers lightly over the swollen evidence of his arousal. In another time, another place, he would have accepted the inducement to carry her off and give her the pleasure she so willingly sought.

Withdrawing from him, she looked him up and down almost pityingly. "Then observe," she scoffed, flouncing off to seek someone more amenable.

His mouth twitched at her pique. No matter how alluring the offer, no matter how much his lower body protested this mad denial, his training ordered him to keep focused on Xanthia. He received her smug smile with a yawn to show his indifference, until she began to slowly pull grapes off the bunch she held and feed them to Kallios, letting his lips slide over her fingers, while he caressed her back and hips with long, indulgent strokes.

Acastus flexed his fingers. His own stimulation heightened, fighting to reclaim control was proving a challenge. The pain in his tense jaw was nothing compared to the pain he was ready to inflict if she continued her obvious efforts to provoke him.

He caught the sultry glance she cast in his direction, caught the delicate arching of her eyebrows, as she covered Kallios's mouth in a hard kiss. A conflagration of furious desire raged through his veins, ripping his self-control to shreds. She was about to receive her first lesson in the true nature of her heritage.

Acastus pushed away from the tree. Reaching the would-be lovers in a minimum of strides, he snatched Xanthia off Kallios's lap, smirking when the latter overbalanced and fell off the log he had chosen to sit on. Tossing his quarry over one shoulder with no more effort than he flung on a travelling cloak, his focus closed out the cries of the crowd. Satisfied he held her legs firmly, Acastus marched away without a backward glance.

"Are you mad?" she cried, beating his back with her fists. "Release me and let me return to my friends. Now!"

"The only place you are returning to is Sparta," he growled, suppressed desire deepening the threat in his voice.

Anger he had no right to feel consumed him. Battle-honed senses caught the sound of running feet rapidly closing on them. Heard Xanthia exhort them to hurry. Acastus risked a look over his free shoulder to see Kallios approaching, along with a few men following in his wake.

"If you value your lives, keep away," he warned.

"Fight him, Kallios," Xanthia shouted, her command echoing painfully in his ears.

Acastus made a sound of contempt. Turning, he confronted his would-be opponent, who had been swaggering towards him, fists raised. His cold stare stopped Kallios in his tracks, and he saw a sliver of doubt crossing the man's face.

"Is this how you treat guests during your festivals?" Acastus taunted, "even during wars, fighting is stopped if either side hold a festival to honour one of the Immortals."

"You abuse our hospitality," Kallios snarled, "let Xanthia go or I'll kill you to ensure you do."

Without releasing his quarry, Acastus balanced himself and waited for the first blow. Holding a squirming Xanthia limited his offensive moves but gave him an unexpected advantage. The tactical part of his mind deduced that much of Kallios's hesitation came from not wanting to endanger Xanthia as much as it did from doubting his chances of winning against him.

A mere flicker of motion was all Acastus needed to swing his free arm and block the first punch. Quickly reversing direction, his fist connected with Kallios's chin, the force of the blow snapping the man's head to one side and sending him sprawling to the ground.

Tightening his grip on Xanthia's legs, Acastus eyed Kallios while the latter rolled on the ground, groaning and clutching his bloodied nose. He glared at the hesitant onlookers, who now shuffled out of his reach. "Anyone else brave enough to fight me?"

He heard Xanthia call out to her would-be rescuers. "Rush him! He's one man even if he is—"

"Quiet," he thundered. "I'm not letting you go now that I've found you." It was imperative he keep his identity secret and restrain Xanthia from announcing his intentions to the world in general. He flexed his bare arm, solid and muscular from years of brutal training. The men who had followed Kallios fell back to mutter amongst themselves.

"You chose wisely. Go and enjoy your lovers with your faces intact." Confident they would not pursue him, after witnessing how easily he defeated their leader, Acastus left them with one last warning look to keep their distance. Having pursuers on his tail simply added another obstacle to leaving the island quietly. He had enough problems with the woman still beating his back with her fists.

"Put me down!"

Xanthia's voice was muffled, where her mouth buried itself against the material of his chiton. He could no more ignore the way her warm breath heated his back than ignore a spear tip thrust towards his face. "I don't trust you. We go straight to the port. My servant waits for us there."

A horrified gasp greeted his announcement.

"We can't go yet," she pleaded. "I need to say goodbye to my parents, collect my dove, and…and…there are other things I need to take."

Acastus rolled his eyes. "There are plenty of doves in Sparta. You can leave this one here to be sacrificed to your goddess for our safe return."

"No!"

The hysterical half-scream rent the air. It ripped through him with an energy that almost convinced him he had emitted the crazed sound himself. Gripping her waist, Acastus lowered her to the ground, forced to grit his teeth to counter the effects evoked by her body sliding over his. He grasped her arms and gave her a gentle shake. "It's only a dove."

"Please, you don't understand."

In the moonlight her face glowed with entreaty. Once again, he was overpowered by the urge to kiss her until she thought of nothing but him. He wanted to pry the reason from her right there, but the fading sounds of the festival tempered his impatience. At any moment, those men might work up the courage to arm themselves and attempt to retake her.

"You're right, I don't understand. One day you'll tell me." He grasped her upper arm, not letting go until they were amongst the acolyte's homes and he had received reluctant directions to the one she inhabited. "Pack what you need and don't try to escape."

He spied her bared teeth before she tossed her head defiantly and entered the domed house. He could admire her powers of recovery without being ready to trust her, so he followed her inside. His enquiring gaze saw her snatch up a small bag fashioned out of animal hide. This she hurriedly filled with a number of items including a small pouch that inexplicably brought a frown to his face.

Suppressing his curiosity about the pouch's contents, he waited until she securely tied the bag closed. "Ready? We go see Philodemos and Euphrasia, then we leave."

Nose in the air, she stalked past him, the scent of roses rising from her skin drawing him into the web her mere presence wove around him. Acastus motioned her to lead the way along the rocky path, so he could bar her way back to the settlement while keeping a sharp lookout behind him. No more sounds of music or laughter followed them into the night.

Wary of the silence, he stretched his awareness out, readying himself in case of a surprise attack.

CHAPTER NINE

Releasing an indignant *huff* at Acastus's high-handedness, Xanthia started the climb up the steep cliff, which rose to one of the highest points on the island. A fresh breeze stirred the mild night air, the crash of waves surging against the jagged rocks at the base of the cliff invigorating her soul, the tang of seawater flavouring every breath she drew.

Arousal continued to feather in her belly, made impossibly more potent by its light touch. There was no hope of relief unless she suddenly lost her wits and seduced the arrogant man who followed close behind, the sound of his heavy, confident footsteps stretching already strained nerves to breaking point.

She told herself not to be impressed his breathing remained light despite the steep incline. In comparison, her own gasps grew heavier and more frequent. She scowled, promising herself a brief rest when they reached the summit.

A grin, prompted by a spontaneous image of pushing Acastus over the cliff, relaxed the tight muscles of her face. The thought brought her to an abrupt halt, Acastus crashing into her back, almost sending her toppling to the ground.

"What is the matter?"

"Nothing," she croaked, heat flaming her cheeks at the hoarseness of her voice.

Xanthia clenched her jaw and shut her eyes, fighting the sensation of his broad chest cushioning her back, the heavy arm around her waist that had stopped her from falling face-first onto the gravel beneath their feet. His breath whispered over the crown of her head. His voice, deep as the deepest black of night, vibrated within the depths of every cell.

What would it be like to tame a man like him? Be the one to command his desires.

She gave an imperceptible shake of her head. Under no circumstances could she afford to consider him a potential lover, so why did her treacherous body find him so captivating? He was her enemy. He meant nothing to her except a threat to her peaceful existence. Someone to be forever avoided and banished from her life.

She concentrated on placing her feet carefully on the slippery ground. A plan, born out of her earlier thoughts, took root in her mind. Xanthia chewed her lip. It might not work, but she had to try.

The wind picked up once they reached the exposed pinnacle, sudden gusts whipping the chiton's length around her legs. Dark sky met black sea on the horizon. Stars glittered. Air moved in the limitless expanse. Any other time she would have gloried in this natural beauty. Right now, she needed to plan the demise of her kidnapper.

She dropped the bag and doubled over to clutch her chest.

"Are you ill?"

It could not possibly be concern she heard in his voice. No, he had a mission to accomplish. That was the beginning and end of his concern. "I'm trying to breathe after that climb."

She wheezed audibly and braced her feet, readying herself in anticipation of the right moment. She must take care to not follow him off the edge.

"Rest awhile. I'll carry your bag."

Out of the corner of her eye she noticed him moving to her left to pass her on the seaward side. Ah, there it was – his mistake. Thanking the goddess for confounding him, Xanthia threw all her weight against his unsuspecting bulk. The air left her lungs on impact. She may as well have attempted to tackle a mountain. She sensed his footsteps falter, his body swaying as he overbalanced.

Push!

Teeth clenched from the effort, she obeyed the silent command of her mind, pouring anger, fear, loathing – all her darkest emotions – to summon the power to free herself from being taken against her will to a place she never wanted to see.

Her feet began to slip, the heavy thump of her heartbeat resounding painfully in her ears. As her desperate efforts nudged them closer to the edge, where rock met air above the tempestuous sea far below, Xanthia pushed harder, the effort pulling guttural moans of frustration from her throat.

Then the world upended and she found herself flat on her back, propelled there by a powerful shove she could not remember giving. Acastus's bulk dropped on top of her, emptying her lungs of air with a forceful *whoosh*. The sharp stones stabbing her flesh drew no painful cries. Rather, she yearned to scream, to pound her fists into the man whose weight pressed against every part of her body.

"Don't ever try to kill me again."

She did not care his eyes blazed with a fury impossible to disguise. Did not care his voice sounded like the roar of Ares on the battlefield. She had failed to make this Spartan pay. "If I have to try again and again, I will," she yelled, thumping her clenched hands on the ground, ignoring the scratches tearing her skin. "Whatever it takes, I won't go back to Sparta. Do you hear me!?"

He rose to tower above her, his face set in hard, disapproving lines. "Then I'll bind and carry you all the way to Sparta's agora so all citizens witness I keep my oath."

"Your oath means nothing to me...*oomph*!" Pulled to her feet, Xanthia spluttered into silence. For one brief, wild moment she considered another attempt to push him toward oblivion, but the just discernible censure in his expression gave her pause. There would be other opportunities to make good her escape.

"Here." He thrust the bag into her hands.

Xanthia glared daggers at his broad back as he walked off, assurance in every line of his magnificent physique that she would obediently follow. Why not turn and run? Grimacing, she looked behind her and instantly dismissed the idea. She did not doubt he could outpace her easily, and she was not ready to end her life by running down a steep incline in the dark. One misstep could mean the risk of a broken neck.

It galled her to admit she had handed him the sword he held over her head. Acastus would wait at Philodemos's, knowing she would never abandon Calliope after witnessing her reaction to his preposterous suggestion to sacrifice her dove. Growling low in her throat, she prayed to Aphrodite to smite him. When the prayer failed to be answered, she reluctantly conceded she required shrewdness to win their battle of wills. A moment ago she had received overwhelming evidence that mere physical strength, no matter how expeditiously timed, would end in failure.

Her eyes narrowed. The best weapon she possessed was to make the journey miserable for him. Starting now, she determined to be the thorn in his side he could not remove.

"Is this how all Spartan men treat women," she jeered, walking quickly to catch up to him, meeting the contemptuous look he sent her with a sneering one of her own. Aware she played with fire, she told herself the need to rattle his self-control would give her satisfaction like none other.

"I'm surprised there are any Spartans left. Do you even know how to pleasure a woman? You barely talk I'm told, you abandon children to—"

This time it was her turn to slam into him as he whirled to face her. The impact left her breathless. Glancing up, she beheld eyes blazing in a face tight with rage. She swallowed past a throat tight with nerves, her innate courage abandoning her in the tense moment.

He gripped her arms. "You know nothing about our ways, but you'll learn."

The heat of his body kindled an answering warmth in hers, dissolving any remnant of fear. Xanthia attempted to pull free, instinct warning her to keep a safe distance from Acastus. "You have to get me there first. I don't want to go to some foreign land where all the men know is how to fight. Aren't you interested in anything else?"

The taut lines of his face suddenly relaxed. An enigmatic light gleamed in his eyes, their obsidian depths made more potent in the silvery light cast by the moon. She laboured to breathe, prompting the terse command, "Let go of me."

"Once your lesson is finished," he said cryptically, removing the bag from her unresisting fingers to place it beside his feet.

"What do you mean?"

"This."

The starlit sky vanished before her eyes as he covered her mouth in a kiss that surely only a god could bestow. His lips were firm and warm, commanding a response against which she struggled to raise resistance. Her mind spun, dazed into compliance by the passion erupting in every erogenous point she possessed.

Resist!, the logical part of her brain insisted, but the feeble protest faded away like mist evaporating in the warmth of a summer sunrise. The hands she lifted to push him away instead curled around solid biceps, her heart skittering at the strength her fingers found there. Willing her trembling legs to keep her upright, Xanthia clung more fiercely, her fingers digging into his upper arms for support.

The kiss turned gentle, persuasive. Her lips parted like the petals of the first spring flowers, impulsively inviting him to deepen it. Head lolling back against the forearm curled around her shoulders, she kissed him back, her tongue tangling with his in a mutual dance of need. She whimpered when he abandoned her mouth to plant fleeting kisses along her cheeks. Drowsy eyelids half-opened, the glitter of stars coming into focus. Awareness crawled in like a ship-wrecked sailor crawled onto the shore as she became conscious of his hard length pressed between them.

"Let me go." She winced at the huskiness of her voice.

To her surprise, Acastus released her immediately. A forbidding frown settled over his features, yet he too, breathed heavily as though he had just battled a score of enemy soldiers.

"You see, Spartan men are interested in things other than fighting. Your lesson is finished."

"Thank you, O wise teacher." She injected as much frosty sarcasm into her voice as her galloping heart would allow. "It still doesn't mean I want to go there."

"You will." His voice rang with certainty. "Walk in front of me. You waste time arguing if you mean to see your foster parents before we leave."

Intense sadness gripped her even as she admitted he was right. Keeping her mouth tightly shut to stop the flow of imprudent words, she snatched up her bag and walked ahead of him. Her heart ached at the thought of saying goodbye to her family, just as it ached with the remembrance of the kiss. It had made her feel alive, desired, safe. She wondered whether Acastus felt the same or had kissed her simply to prove his dominance over her.

What a fool you are, Xanthia.

Of course he did not feel the same. The kiss served as a cruel reminder that the two most important men in her world had rejected her. Even the man she called father had stepped aside, abandoning her to an uncertain fate in Sparta. Men could not be trusted, she reminded herself. Her strategy to be the first to walk away from a lover went some way to pour balm over the anguish still present in her soul.

Acastus threatened to haul all the bleakness of her past into the light. The fine hairs on the nape of her neck rose as she glanced into the night sky, swearing she would do whatever was in her power to stop him.

CHAPTER TEN

Acastus looked down at the subdued woman standing beside him. "Once I find my servant we can board ship." When she remained silent, he scanned her features closely – the tight-pressed lips, the shoulders slumped as she withdrew into herself, the revealing moisture which had turned her eyes into luminous orbs with every step that had brought them closer to the port. Hardening his heart, he rested his hand firmly on her back, guiding her to where he had left his servant, Drakon, when he and the latter had first landed on Melos. Once she accepted, and adapted to, her Spartan heritage, she would learn to face any situation with resolute courage.

The parting between Xanthia and her foster parents had been drawn out and tearful. Acastus had managed to hold onto restraint long enough to remind them that if they chose to rejoin Xanthia and Aeschylus, an escort would be sent for them. He could understand their hesitation. They had built a life for themselves on this island, free from the fear that one day they would be on the wrong end of a helot hunt, regardless of their standing in Aeschylus's household. He had also welcomed Philodemos's timely reminder to Xanthia that one day she would marry and, whether on Melos or Sparta, she would leave them to live with her husband.

"Should I feel gratitude you allowed me to spend an extra day with Philodemos and Euphrasia before we left."

The cold, biting sarcasm in her tone pulled him out of his introspection. He went to pass a hand over his face and stopped.

Xanthia wielded words like weapons and, by Zeus, he would not allow them to find his vulnerable spots.

"Yes, since we lost a day because I allowed you more time together," he announced in equally cool tones.

The tacit agreement on his part to linger an extra day, even though his hosts protested his sleeping outside in the elements, was attributed to his assessment of the risks involved, rather than yielding to any weakness. He would feel disappointed to know Xanthia's friends had not followed them to the port yesterday. Let them think he had slipped away with her during the night.

"I'm certain you're capable of rowing the boat by yourself to Sparta if the tide proves unfavourable."

She might have been baiting him but the realisation did not stop him grinning from ear to ear. "I would be. It is good to see your spirit is unbroken. It's a ship, a merchant vessel. Stay close while I look for Drakon."

He took her elbow and steered her towards a cluster of low buildings that ringed the port, confident that his servant had carried out his orders to purchase the supplies they would need, along with two donkeys to carry them. A quiet bustle filled the small port, but people moved out of his way, his strides proclaiming an arrogant certainty that his path would remain clear. Seeing the curious looks directed Xanthia's way, he could have sworn there was recognition in one or two of them.

The muscles at the back of his neck became rigid. Perhaps they past lovers of hers?

A glance showed her face remained impassive. She did not even attempt to look over her shoulder as the crowd of people passed by them. The painful tightness in his neck lessened just as he spied Drakon weaving his way through the throng. As the servant drew nearer, Acastus caught the furtive look he gave Xanthia, a fleeting shadow of something not quite right crossing his features, before the servant lowered his gaze to address him.

"Master, I've purchased everything you told me to. I talked to the captains of ships that are docked and the one yonder is sailing to Gytheion early tomorrow."

He looked over to where Drakon was pointing and nodded, "Good," he replied, then addressed Xanthia, "Drakon will take care of anything you need."

Xanthia sidling closer alerted him to the strained air between the two people who would be under his protection. Between half-closed eyes he studied both her and his servant. Nothing about Drakon's curtailed bow suggested anything amiss, but he sensed an undercurrent in the servant's demeanour, in the studious avoidance of Xanthia. Clearly, she had sensed the same, her perception surprising him into looking at her with a fresh appreciation.

Making a mental note to keep a close eye on his servant, Acastus issued further orders. "I'll speak with this captain. You wait here with Xanthia until I return." Turning to her, he said, "We stay here tonight."

"I hope I don't have to sleep in your presence," she exclaimed.

"Not tonight but sleeping on a ship will be a different matter."

He shrugged and walked away from her spluttering objections. Would she be foolish, and brave, enough to attempt to escape? Would Drakon betray more hostility towards her without his presence? He had purposely left them together to find the answer.

Reaching the vessel Drakon had pointed out, Acastus found the captain and haggled over the payment. He then informed the man of something important, which made the latter smile, and give assurances he would tell his crew.

Although inside he shook with laughter, Acastus kept his features impassive as he started towards Xanthia, using the opportunity to watch the interaction between her and Drakon. They kept well apart, avoiding each other's gaze, the space between them emanating a palpable coldness even from this distance. He jammed his fingers into his braided hair, their obvious dislike of each other squashing his amusement.

It was as if the gods were determined to test him with as many difficulties as they could devise for him. He hoped it was not blasphemous to liken them to the twelve labours of his ancestor, Herakles – the demigod all Spartans claimed descent from – and wondered how many more would be thrown at him. Still, he accepted these challenges, seeing in them a way of atoning for the wrong he had done.

What he did not expect was a loud, angry voice he thought he would never hear again.

"Where is Xanthia?"

Acastus plunged his hand under his cloak, fingers tightening over the grip of his xiphos. In the same fluid movement, he spun to face the man whose shout had echoed along the waterfront. He retained the presence of mind to keep his weapon concealed. He might still be dressed in merchant garb, but as soon as anyone spied his weapon's length, they would know he hailed from Sparta.

"No concern of yours, Kallios. Do you harbour some foolish hope to spring a trap?" His initial surprise had worn off and questions battered at his mind. Who had told Kallios they would be here today? He could discount Philodemos and his wife, which left Xanthia and Drakon. But how could either have found the opportunity to betray him?

"Kallios!"

Xanthia's desperate shout spurred him into reflexive action. Side-stepping to meet her headlong rush, he swung an arm out, grabbing her by the waist and holding on tightly.

"Let me go!"

"Stop kicking," he grunted, absorbing the pain from a particularly well-placed kick to his vulnerable shins. Worse than the pain, her struggles were attracting a ring of onlookers. Acastus glowered and all, except one or two, fell back.

"She belongs with us," Kallios snarled. "Give her back and we leave peacefully, otherwise we fight. The festival is over, Spartan, no truces to observe."

Acastus stilled, feeling as though an icy spear had been plunged through his core. Cold, merciless anger swelled his heart. It must have shown in his expression because Xanthia, her face turning pale, ceased squirming as soon as he looked at her. "You betrayed me," he bit out between bared teeth.

"I didn't," she shrank back, "I swear by the goddess I didn't."

"Then how does Kallios know who I am."

"I swear by Aphrodite that I don't know," she whispered.

Acastus ground his teeth. This was the last thing he needed: a fight to delay him further. His suspicions now turned to Drakon, but how could his servant have known who Kallios was, or even when

Kallios had arrived? The servant's loyalty, proven over many years, cleared away the niggle of doubt.

Kallios was staring at him with lethal intent, so it would prove pointless to pray that the man possessed enough sense of self-preservation to leave. "Then we fight," he agreed, stifling a smirk at the way Kallios's eyes bulged, revealing that Xanthia's lover had not wagered on his acceptance. Acastus called out to the silent crowd, "Is there a pit or arena nearby?"

Over the excited muttering, someone answered there was none. He looked around and saw a sandy expanse not far away. Stabbing an index finger towards it, he commanded tersely, "Clear that patch of ground." His mouth twisted at the way locals and sailors alike fell over themselves to avoid him and clear the area he had chosen of any obstructions to a fair fight.

He carefully loosened his hold and pulled Xanthia over to where Drakon stood guard over her dove and the bags they had brought with them. "Stay here," he commanded her, "if you run, Drakon will throw the cage with your dove inside it, into the sea." Ignoring her gasp of outrage, he removed his himation and xiphos and handed them both to the silent servant, then strode over to the makeshift arena.

"Well?" His hard voice shattered the stillness that had descended over the onlookers.

Kallios glared at him. "Pankration. Strato here, is undefeated on Melos. He'll fight you first, then I will. If both of us lose, you can leave."

"No!"

"Accepted." Acastus shouted over Xanthia's denial, struggling not to laugh out loud in their faces. They had unwittingly chosen the one combat he was a champion in, winning every match in Sparta and the neighbouring towns. Even once at Olympia as a boy. Certain they would not honour their word, he ran a few well-rehearsed moves through his mind, which would allow him to finish the fight by immobilising both opponents.

Moving to the centre of the cleared area, Acastus crouched to remove his sandals. Springing up once finished, he peeled the tunic over his head and tossed it to one side. Murmurs rose around them like a horde of angry bees disturbed from their hive. A corner of his mouth quirked as he stood, naked and waiting. He never gave his physique a thought beyond ensuring he kept himself fit and ready for battle.

He looked over his shoulder and grinned at Xanthia, who averted her eyes, cheeks overspread with an alluring blush. "You may want to leave. It'll be brutal."

"I'll stay," she called back, still refusing to look at him. "I want to see you on your knees and begging for mercy before I return home."

No point crushing her fantasy. He sent a quick prayer to Zeus, stretched a few vital muscles, and waited for Strato to disrobe. The watching faces blurred into the back of his perceptions, all his focus on sizing up his opponent.

They began to trade kicks and punches, each attack becoming more vicious as the fight wore on. Acastus gave credit to a worthy opponent, all the time searching for a weak point. Surprised by powerful kick to the stomach, he rolled with the blow, then heard a triumphant yell as Strato followed him down to place him in a choke hold.

Dots swam in from of his eyes as air struggled to get into his lungs. He dug his fingers into the arm squeezing life-giving breath from his body and heard a voice growl in his ear.

"Do you yield?"

He answered by snaring the fingers of the arm choking him, bending them backwards forcefully enough to hear the satisfying snap of bones. A scream of pain almost deafened him. The pressure on his trachea lessened, allowing him to gulp life-giving air. Bracing himself on one hand, Acastus slammed an elbow into Strato, aiming high to reach the chest. A loud grunt was his signal to roll out from under the injured man and drag him upright by the hair to place him in a deadly hold. "Yield!"

He did not have to demand twice. Strato retched, then held up the index finger of his uninjured hand in submission. Acastus released him and watched his defeated opponent stumble out of reach, clutching his broken fingers. Wiping the sweat off his forehead with his arm, he swept a hard gaze around the circle of watchers. "My win. Kallios."

He waited, intrigued by the expressions on Kallio's face as the latter divested himself of his clothes. There was murder in the man's eyes, although he read fear in them as well. Acastus entertained no doubt of his own victory while acknowledging it would prove to be a lengthier and more punishing one.

He was proven right as he resumed the fight. He traded stronger blows with Kallios, neither gaining an advantage. Kick after kick, punch after punch, and he knew he would feel the blows the next day and possibly beyond.

"Tired? Yield and I take Xanthia and not beat you into submission."

Acastus absorbed the taunt with the contempt it invited. Wasting breath to speak during a match proved his opponent was no true warrior. He was good, but his weakness lay in his smug assurance that he could win simply because he believed his opponent had already been weakened.

His sense of danger niggled as he continued to circle Kallios. In the next instant he understood why. Focussed on his opponent, the clouds parting in the heavens had escaped his notice. The sun came out, its blazing light hitting him squarely in the face.

He squinted, felt air ripple around him, then heard an exultant roar, followed by a blow to the jaw that snapped his head back. Feinting, Acastus allowed his knees to buckle, then grabbed Kallios's arm as the man swung another punch to his face, the force of the intended blow sending both of them sprawling.

Acastus drove a fist into the nose he had injured two nights ago, the crunch of shattered cartilage still failing to stop Kallios who continued to fight like a man possessed. Driven by the icy rage which had filled him before the fight, Acastus slowly wore down his opponent, waiting for an opening to place the unsuspecting man in the Wolf's Embrace, a hold from which there was no escape.

Feeling his opponent's blows weakening, Acastus locked his arms around Kallios's chest and squeezed with all his strength until the man struggled to breathe and raised his finger to signal submission.

His own body was already feeling the pummelling it had taken. Despite the clear rules, he kept a close eye on his challenger. Once a loser yielded, any attempt to ambush the victor would be heavily punished.

"As agreed, Xanthia leaves with me." He eyed Kallios warily as the defeated man glowered at him with hate-filled eyes.

"You may have won today, but this isn't over."

All his muscles tightened as a cold trickle of dread shot through his core at the threat. "Follow me only if you are tired of living."

Retrieving his chiton from the ground, he quickly dressed and made his way back to where Xanthia waited. The mixed emotions playing across her face as she glanced between himself and Kallios made him wish he could read minds. "So, having won the right to take you, it would be wise if you don't make things difficult."

A corner of his mouth lifted as she tossed her head. The disdain in her loud sniff could not have better conveyed her reception of his demands.

"Like declare to all who didn't already hear that you are from Sparta," she flung at him in an undertone. "You couldn't possibly defeat everyone."

"If you're interested in reaching Sparta alive, then hold your tongue." He paid no concern to her paling at his hostile tone.

"I don't want to reach Sparta at all, but it seems I have no choice."

"You are learning."

Acastus grabbed her hand, gave Drakon a sharp order to follow, and dragged her towards the lodging the servant had held until his return. He was brought up short when she dug her heels in. A rebuke on his tongue, he turned in time to see her prise her dove's cage out of Drakon's fingers.

"Now we can go," she said haughtily.

There was a gleam in her eyes and the hint of smugness playing around her mouth. "What have you done?"

"Nothing," she replied with a wide-eyed look. "I'm treasuring the memory of you on your knees in front of Kallios."

He laughed. "Don't bother. I allowed myself to fall. Tactics. He had none."

He admired her spirit, even when she pointedly turned her face away. A quick, backward glance revealed Drakon following with their bags and a calculating look fixed on Xanthia. The warning bells in his mind grew louder and refused to be silenced as Acastus reconsidered who had betrayed his identity. The thought was galling, but he conceded that time might prove his family's up-till-now faithful servant, might not be so faithful after all.

CHAPTER ELEVEN

A blustery breeze teased her hair out behind her like a pennant. Xanthia breathed the tangy air slowly, imagining each breath cleansing and preparing her for the challenges ahead. Face turned to the sun, its warmth caressing her closed eyelids like a lover's kiss, she reflected on Aphrodite's birth from the sea.

The meditation acted like a soothing balm to her nerves.

She held tightly onto the rigging of the pitching merchant ship, which had taken her away from Melos a few days ago. Glancing down with a smile, she checked on Calliope, perched on the cage near her feet – her beloved dove was with her, safe. Every day she brought her onto the deck for light and air. The faces of the crew were easy to read – they thought her a fool for caring for a creature they probably saw only as food.

Xanthia scowled. It did not matter what they thought, and if any of them dared to touch Calliope…

A grim smile lifted the corners of her mouth as she ran a hand over the pouch secured around her waist. Most of the crew continued to treat her respectfully since she had first come on board. Having mastered the art of managing men's desires early in her life, the scant few brave enough to cast avid looks her way found their overtures smothered by a contemptuous tilt of her chin.

She gusted out a breath. Her natural honesty forced her to acknowledge there existed a much more powerful reason keeping the crew's baser instincts in check. That reason stood talking with the ship's captain.

She cast an assessing glance over Acastus. At first she'd been blisteringly angry with the way he'd overruled her every objection. Only to her innermost self did she acknowledge the misgivings she – refused to label them fear – of returning to the land of her birth. Her foster parents and Acastus could heap reassurances on her all they liked, but what if she was judged unworthy to remain in Sparta? Banished once again by perhaps the same men who had commanded her exposure to death in her infancy.

Hugging an arm around her waist, she stared blindly out to sea. No matter the outcome, she was older and wiser now; a grown woman, blessed with inflexible resolve to save herself if exiled a second time.

Stretching her arms to ease the ache between her shoulders, she mulled over the memories intruding into her mind, reliving those last moments on Melos. No matter how hard she tried to avoid speculating, she continued to wonder who had betrayed Acastus's identity. Thinking of Drakon, coldness washed through her, his mere presence casting an oppressive cloud over her that she could not shake off. She blew out another heavy sigh – she must be imagining Drakon's hostility because of her own fears.

She shaded her eyes and swept her gaze over the limitless expanse of water around them, her scrutiny coming to rest on Acastus again. These few days crossing the Myrtoan Sea had given her an insight into the man, not just the warrior in merchant disguise, who had torn her away off the bedrock on which she had rebuilt her life. She used his distraction with the captain to study him minutely. Why had no-one challenged him after his two fights? He was only one man, perhaps tiring or, she frowned, did Spartans carry some mystique with them wherever they went?

His broad shoulders proclaimed a strength to heft two grown men. There could be little doubt some of the crew had witnessed him fight before they had sailed from the port. Her own mouth had dropped open at his sheer determination to win and the endurance he had displayed. He might have been breathing audibly when he had returned to her side, but she would have wagered the armband

Kallios had gifted her some years ago that Acastus could have fought at least two more men before even thinking about defeat.

Of course, there was the way he had looked naked. That memory was seared in her mind for eternity. Tiny bumps rose all over the skin of her arms. Did he have to be built in a way that made her question whether one of the Olympian gods had had a hand in his shaping? All she saw now were long, tanned legs, every muscle delineated, emerging from the short tunic he chose to wear on the ship, braided black hair reaching almost to his waist.

Faint tremors gripped her as she tried to subdue the onslaught of a sensation akin to every nerve ending being set on fire. In the name of all the gods, why did he, the man she planned to escape from, summon such intense, yearning desire that she had never felt in the past for anyone else.

Just then, he turned to pin her with a dark-eyed gaze. The gulp of air she sucked in lodged high in her chest. Unnerved by the way he always appeared to know when she watched him, she consciously fought to relax muscles, which had tensed as soon as he had looked at her. Pressing her free hand over one hot cheek, Xanthia prayed he remained oblivious to her thoughts.

She held her breath, as with a final word to the captain he sauntered over to join her, swaying with superb balance in time with the ship's pitching as it cut through a moderate swell. Much like the pitching of nervous energy in her belly. Moistening lips dry from salty air and nerves, Xanthia broke their eye-lock, kneeling down to feed the dove scraps of moistened bread. Bare feet materialised in her peripheral vision.

"Have you kept your food down this morning?"

She growled deep in her throat. "I have, no thanks to you. I'm sure your concern is simply because your honour is at stake. How much longer before we reach land?"

Seeing him close his eyes and rub his forehead, knowing she had caused him more annoyance, filled her with a kind of morbid glee. That same annoyance etched across his face, however, was nothing compared to the relentless nausea plaguing her since they had sailed.

He released an exasperated sigh. "You're succeeding in your mission to irritate me. It depends on the wind. Once we reach the gulf of Lakonia, it's only a few days sailing to Gytheion. You need to be rested and fed for the trek to Sparta itself."

"Then what?" she prompted insolently, "a trek across mountains until we reach Sparta? How many days will that take? How safe will I be? No, don't bother answering. Throw me overboard now. I'll probably die either way."

Her eyes grew wide when he stooped to clasp her shoulders, giving them a gentle shake.

"I promise to guard you with my life. There are no mountains to cross. We walk along the Eurotas Valley between two ranges. A few days, no longer."

His hands were large and warm, and Xanthia fancied she felt the power radiating out of them. Beside the pankration fight, she had managed to glimpse the moment when he had knocked Kallios down at the festival, swatting him away like a fly. "I don't doubt your commitment," she conceded, "but what if that isn't enough?"

He released her and straightened. "It is enough."

"You are still bruised." She cast an eye over some of the livider ones on his legs where kicks had connected. "What if you are challenged to more fights because of who you are?"

"They won't be as foolish or ignorant as your Kallios was," he mocked lightly. "Apart from our reputation as fighters, many know that without our king's sacrifice at Thermopylae they would be groaning under the yoke of invaders."

Rolling her eyes at his over-confidence, she turned her back to him, making a show of feeding the last few scraps of bread to Calliope. "I don't understand, what sacrifice?"

"You don't know? You'll start to learn of your heritage after we make landfall."

She did not want to learn anything about Sparta, but he was right, now was not the time to start voicing her objections with nowhere to escape. Preparing to rise and take Calliope below deck, his next words stopped the breath she was about to exhale.

"Will you tell me now why this dove is so important to you?"

~*~

Acastus stepped in front of Xanthia when she hunched her back as though defending herself from a blow. The tiny jerk of her head enabled him to spy momentary grief tighten her features before she looked up at him with a face devoid of all expression. Such an odd reaction raised further questions rather than giving him answers. The more she withheld, the stronger his motivation grew to probe deeper.

From his earliest days of training, he had displayed uncanny skill in reading another person's emotions. This ability provided one of many weapons at his disposal, which made him such a dangerous opponent. That skill insisted she hid a disturbing secret.

"Xanthia?"

He met the glare she speared him and schooled his expression to be equally blank as hers. Rather than aggravating him, the look burned hot enough to draw beads of sweat from his pores. His grip tightened over the rigging to stop himself dragging her to her feet to brand those soft lips. The kiss they had inadvertently shared on Melos tormented him each night before he fell into a restless sleep.

"Calliope is my friend, my familiar, my solace," Xanthia intoned. "The one being on this earth, apart from my parents, who never abandoned me."

Dark foreboding filled his chest. Within those words so much remained unsaid. Winning her trust to release the unspoken hurt presented one of the hardest battles he had faced, a battle promising victory only through careful strategy.

"Your foster parents," he corrected. "How long has she been your companion?" He did not miss the colour ebb from her face, leaving the skin almost as white as the dove's feathers.

She twisted her hands. "Almost three summers. I found her injured, her wing bent, a toe missing. Doves are sacred to Aphrodite, so I took her home, healed her wing as best I could. Although she can fly, she never leaves me. She sensed my suffering at the time…"

Acastus stilled. She had clamped her mouth shut tighter than the monster, Typhon, had tightened its coils around Zeus during their battle. His instincts could not quite put a finger on the reason for the suspicion niggling at him. Whatever it was, the emotions crossing her face betrayed its profound effect on her. "What happened?"

"Nothing," she mumbled. "Why were you sent to kidnap me? Surely a warrior such as yourself is needed in that land of warriors."

"Keep your voice down," he warned. The ship's crew did not need constant reminders of who he was. Having left the relative safety of Melos, concealing his identity from now on became paramount. His sole aim was to return her safely and swiftly, not fight every man he met along the way who thought he could best a Spartan. "Your brother is my best friend. I owed him your rescue. That's all you need to know."

"Really!?" She jumped to her feet, the abrupt movement sending Calliope flying into the safety of her cage, wings flapping madly. "You insist on knowing everything about me but won't reveal anything in return."

Acastus jammed fingers through his hair, pressing them down hard on his scalp. From the time they had departed Philodemos's house, her constant jibes had slowly ground what little patience he possessed into dust. "I didn't kidnap you," he seethed, ignoring the fact he had hoisted her over his shoulder and marched away from the festival while her yells pierced his eardrums. "You were able to see your foster parents before you left. You would've already arrived in Sparta had I kidnapped you."

A smile tugged his mouth when she lifted her nose in the air. Summoning control through supreme effort, he managed to keep his expression from betraying amusement.

"How noble of you," she scoffed. "I'd wager any of these men on board would have shown me more courtesy than you. They at least are polite to me."

He half-smirked. "Some witnessed the match, but the greater reason they are polite is because I told the captain, who warned his crew that you are my wife."

"You…you…!"

This time he was powerless to stop a grin. Given all her verbal barbs directed his way, it gratified him to witness her spluttering, lost for words. "Would you prefer they know the truth?"

"Do you even know how to be truthful?"

He knew far too well the potential truth possessed to ruin lives. Maybe that explained his success in disguise and deception. These skills somehow salved the open wound in his soul, providing lessons in avoiding past mistakes.

For now, there remained some truth he was able to share. "The captain informed me we'll sight Kythera by the morning. If the gods grant a good wind, we reach the Peloponnese shortly after rounding the island."

"Kythera!"

The knife of guilt dug deep into his vitals. Longing, joy, despair, mingled in her breathy exclamation. "The ship won't stop there," he warned.

"I can still come out to see the island which was my first home."

About to argue, his attention was suddenly caught by a sight beyond the boat's stern. He was no sailor, but the buildup of clouds on the far horizon had him straining his eyes to assess the threat. "Only if the weather holds."

He watched her back away and briefly glance in the same direction.

"Even if I have to stand in a raging storm, I want to see my childhood home one more time. I'm going to stretch my legs. I don't need company."

The ship pitched sharply, and Acastus reached out to steady Xanthia when she over-balanced. The wariness which sprang into her eyes stopped his hand short. Turning to seek the reason for her discomposure, he saw Drakon hastily cross to the hatch leading to the lower decks.

"Drakon's presence troubles you?" His misgivings rose when she rubbed her arms as though warding off a malignant spirit.

"He…" She hesitated, worrying her lip and staring out over the expanse of blue water. "I've caught him staring at me strangely ever since we sailed. He's done nothing, but I feel uncomfortable around him."

"You're worried because you're uncertain of the future." She was imagining things. Drakon had entered his father's household a scant three years after Acastus had commenced his agoge tenure at the age of seven. "Drakon has been a trustworthy servant to my family."

Xanthia sent him an odd look as she left to walk the deck. He found it difficult to drag his eyes away while she paced the length of the ship, captivated by the sway of hips, the hem of her ankle-length chiton sashaying invitingly. Clearing his throat loudly to break the spell, Acastus removed himself from the temptation to stay and watch her, choosing to escape below deck and check on their supplies, also to ensure the two donkeys purchased on Melos were fed and watered. Their very survival depended on the animals carrying all the provisions once they made landfall.

There was no reason to not check on Drakon at the same time.

CHAPTER TWELVE

A rough jolt woke Acastus from a light sleep. Rolling onto his side, he instinctively searched out Xanthia. The sudden, sharp roll of the ship sent him sprawling towards the hard deck. He braced one hand to prevent himself from hitting it face-first as the creaking timbers were drowned out by a deafening thunderclap.

His heart slammed against his ribs. He had been tossed right across the empty space where she usually slept.

A burst of energy sent him leaping upright at the same moment the vessel pitched more heavily than before. He flung an arm out to grab hold of an overhead beam, knuckles white from the force of his grip. Another thunderclap resounded in his ears.

Over the thunder's fading rumble came a woman's scream.

He launched himself from the hold, gaining the deck powered by a burst of speed that would have secured him victory in any sprint race in Olympia. Frantic activity greeted him, the crew securing anything not washed overboard; sails taken down, hatches being shut.

A flurry of motion at the edge of his vision spun him to face the bow. Rain battered his face, blurring his sight, but not enough for him to miss Drakon, kneeling, both hands attempting to peel fingers off the gunwale.

Blood rushed to his head. He knew to whom those desperately clinging fingers belonged.

The wind howled and jostled him, threatening to send him toppling over the starboard side of the ship. He leaned into it, resisting its force, aided by the muscular strength of his legs. Another gust whipped his hair off his face, enabling him to make out a crewman crawling along the deck to assist Drakon. He started to run, slipped on the rain-lashed deck, and crashed onto his knees.

Not stopping to check whether any bones had broken, he threw himself into the wind, running and swaying in time with the ship's wild movements, one purpose fixed in his mind – to save Xanthia.

Almost there. He saw the crewman reach Drakon. Anger blazed, hotter even than fires lit by Hephaestus, when he saw Drakon shove away the helping hand extended to him. The moment of inattention gave Acastus the time to spring forward, grab the crewman's shoulder, and push the man out of danger.

In the next breath he dug vice-like fingers into the servant's arm. He met Drakon's dismayed look with bared teeth and saw the rain-soaked face turn white as he instinctively let out a great battle cry and threw Drakon across the deck.

Driving rain battered his face; thunder resounded its displeasure; on the horizon lightning speared into the sea. His senses acknowledged, then disregarded, the storm's fury. Nothing mattered except saving the woman he had exposed to danger yet again.

He anchored one foot to the hull and leaned over to wrap his hands around her left arm. He roared over the booming of another thunderclap, "Xanthia, trust me. Do exactly what I tell you."

Her frozen features stared back at him, lips clamped together, terror slowly receding from her eyes.

"I won't let you go." He imbued every last drop of power and confidence into his voice.

Rewarded with a barely perceptible nod, he forced himself to breathe slowly in order to steady his racing pulse, then tightened his fingers over her wet skin and pulled with all his might. His toes gripped the deck, cramping the longer he stood there. He fixated on the hand still gripping the gunwale, knuckles white from the effort to push herself up and over the side. It gave him impetus to keep going, mouth contorting into a rictus grin as he battled the elements and took her weight.

Then her head cleared the side of the ship. Relief expanded his chest.

It was short-lived.

A large wave crashed over the deck. Her hand slipped out of sight. Acastus cursed over the sound of more thunder, spitting out rain and sea water that had engulfed his mouth. He tightened his grip on the arm he held and prayed her shoulder would not be wrenched out of its joint.

"Lift your arm."

His roared command lifted her stricken gaze to him. Fear, frustration, and fury edged her dark eyes. Hope filled his heart that together they would succeed in saving her life.

Her movements were sluggish, but she managed to lift her free arm towards him. When the ship climbed the next wave, Acastus grabbed her right arm while she was clear of the storm-tossed water. He could just make out, through the rain driving in to his face that she was trying to help by bracing her feet on the hull as best she could, refusing to give up even when one of them slipped and swung out into the waves. Witnessing her strength, her fight, her determination, he managed a quick grin of encouragement despite the dire situation they found themselves in.

Certain an eternity had passed while they battled together, he roared in triumph when her head cleared the side a second time. Acastus gritted his teeth, braced himself for one more supreme effort, and pulled, Xanthia's cry reaching him as she slid over the gunwale.

He allowed himself to fall, barely wincing when his back impacted the hard wood. Her startled cry spurred a final effort to pull her on top of him. Allowing her to tumble onto the deck and be injured further, after everything she had been through, was unthinkable.

For a long moment he lay there, chest heaving, relief rather than effort making him breathe heavily. His mind taunted him with images of the moment Xanthia's arm had slipped from his grasp. He saw again the terror that had flared in her eyes, felt the clenching of his stomach over the renewed dread when he thought he had lost her to the wild sea.

Acastus shifted uneasily, the movement bringing awareness of the shudders wracking Xanthia's body. With a savage oath directed at himself, he tightened his arms around her shoulders and waist, sitting up to begin a torturously slow slide across the sodden deck. He dare not risk standing with her, although the storm had eased somewhat, the ship not pitching violently like before. Gusts of wind plastered his wet clothes to his skin, his teeth chattered, but he first needed to get Xanthia dry and warm before tending to himself.

Once he had gained the relative dryness below, he set her carefully on her feet, not relinquishing his hold until satisfied she had the strength to stand without his assistance.

Someone pressed a kylix of wine into his hands. He grimaced at the first mouthful. A Spartan never imbibed undiluted wine, but in this instance, he had no choice. He drank deeply, the cold bands compressing his chest eventually giving way to the warmth infused by the strong wine. Wrapping a supportive arm around Xanthia's shoulders, he pressed the two-handled drinking vessel to her bluish-tinged lips.

Her dark eyes half-opened to stab him with a look that clearly blamed him for her close brush with death. Pushing aside remorse he insisted, "Drink. It'll warm you," and watched in satisfaction as the tentative sips she took restored colour to her cheeks.

She spluttered a protest when he tipped the kylix at a sharper angle. Acastus took the hint and returned the two-handled cup to Drakon, who had reappeared by his side. Propping her against himself, he rubbed her arms vigorously. Even though she winced repeatedly, he kept up the steady massage until her shivering stopped.

The agitation racing through his limbs at nearly losing her would take longer to control. "You need to change into dry clothes."

"I need no reminder. I'm freezing."

Her hoarse voice sent a fresh wave of compunction crashing through him. Rummaging in the supplies, he found a homespun woollen blanket and wrapped it around her. He bent to pick up her bag, staring incredulously when she snatched it out of his hands.

The furtive lines of her face set him on guard. "I only intended to find you a chiton." He enunciated each word slowly, watching for any flicker of emotion which might reveal a clue to her caginess.

"You have no right to touch my clothes. You can turn away while I change."

Her order brought back the memory of the first time he had seen her on the beach. The way she had appeared – wild, abandoned, free. The way she had felt – soft, womanly, but also strong. The battle to control his body's unwanted reaction had tested him more strongly than expected.

He turned his back to her and spread the blanket out between his arms. Jaw clenched, Acastus doggedly gazed at the opposite end of the ship, although the sight of her wet clothes dropping to the floor as she flung them to one side, severely tested his restraint. The wine he had drunk moments ago failed to heat his blood to the same degree that it boiled in his veins now.

A tug on the blanket, the way the material almost slipped out of his fingers, told him she used the trailing edges to dry herself. He inhaled a rough breath, silently praying to Ares for the discipline to resist the temptation to sneak a glance behind him.

"I'm dressed." Her voice carried all the warmth of a mountain stream at the start of the spring melt.

Acastus ran an eye over the blue chiton she had donned, noting in satisfaction it was less transparent than the one which lay in a damp pile. "Tell me everything." His chin jutted when she bit her lip. "Xanthia? The truth."

She shot a venom-filled look in his direction. Amazing how those flashing eyes had failed to send him to Hades for judgement in that very instant.

"I wanted to see Kythera again. To remind myself why I was banished there, since I'm being returned, grudgingly, to the place which banished me."

Her pain-filled words burned through him as though the arrows of Herakles, dipped in the Hydra's blood, were sinking their deadly tips into his flesh. He rubbed both hands over his face, not wanting to countenance how close he had come to losing her. "Didn't you realise the danger you were in? What possessed you to not return below deck when the storm hit?"

"I did try, but the ship tilted when it crested a wave. Someone, I don't know who, pushed me. Only the protection of Aphrodite saved me from falling into the sea." She hesitated, crossing her arms around her middle. "Your servant…I'm not sure…"

There was no need for her to say anymore. Distrust reared its ugly head. Reliving the – he hesitated to call it a rescue – in vivid detail, Acastus battled to keep his burgeoning rage at bay. He caught sight of a still dripping wet Drakon skulking in the shadows.

"Come here," he thundered, watching his servant shuffle toward them. "How did Xanthia end up over the side."

"Master, I lost my footing and fell, hitting my lady's legs. Before I could stop her, she went over the side."

Acastus stared hard at him, unable to comprehend any reason for Drakon to deliberately harm Xanthia. Yet, the image of his servant attempting to loosen her fingers remained imprinted on his mind. "You were forcing her to let go," he accused in a rough voice, "why didn't you call for help? And, why," he roared, "did you refuse help when it came?"

The recriminations were delivered with the same rapid force he delivered blows to an enemy in battle. His servant appeared to shrink into himself, wringing his hands, looking stricken.

"I'm sorry, Master. I panicked because I didn't want the man to be hurt, too. All the other sailors were busy saving the ship." He added a sullen aside, "I tried to hold onto her hands to stop her coming to harm."

"Did you?" Acastus challenged, the clamour of misgiving inside his head growing more insistent. He swung round to interrogate Xanthia, who he noticed had listened without attempting to correct Drakon. "Does he speak the truth?"

She turned her head aside, bringing a frown to his face.

"Yes," she mumbled.

"You don't sound certain." Was she unwilling, or afraid, to admit Drakon had possibly tried to drown her? That made no sense.

"Drakon seized my wrists while I held onto the side." Her voice rose. "I'm alive and unharmed. Nothing else matters."

A donkey braying from the deck below them broke the troubled silence holding them in its tight thrall. His imagination mocked him with images of Xanthia falling below the waves, dragged deep into the halls of Poseidon, never again to rise to the surface. He longed to embrace her, to give reassurance he would protect her, even if it cost him his life.

Acastus took a half-step towards her only to see her step back out of his reach. Ignoring the twinge of his conscience, he studied the hands she held together in a white-knuckled grip.

"Leave us." He impaled Drakon with a look and waited until the servant made himself scarce, then laid a gentle hand on Xanthia's shoulder, unprepared for her sudden intake of breath and sidling away. "The truth. How did you fall?"

She sent him another of those looks that would have frozen the river of fire in the Underworld. "The truth is I want to go home. The truth is my life seems more in danger now than when I was abandoned to die. You want truth, Acastus, well, sometimes, the truth is uncomfortable to hear."

He made no move to stop her when she walked away. Rubbing the back of his neck, he decided to question the crew once the storm subsided. Despite the pandemonium on the deck, he hoped one of them may have witnessed how she came to fall overboard.

It was a sign of his deep unease that he retrieved Xanthia's wet chiton instead of ordering Drakon to perform the menial task. Acastus wrung the remaining moisture out and hung it over a beam to dry while he reluctantly considered some unsettling possibilities.

Servants were sometimes bought. He did not want to believe he was dealing with such a situation, but what if he was? Nothing could be done until they reached dry land and he prised the reason out of her why she seemed to be protecting Drakon.

Until then, he would need to keep a watchful eye on the man he had always believed to be a faithful, trustworthy servant.

CHAPTER THIRTEEN

A bleary sun fought its way through scattered storm clouds. One hand shading the glare from his eyes, Acastus scanned the heavens and judged it close to midday. Glancing portside, he resigned himself to the sight of the mainland to his left and the mountain range he could just make out in the distance.

While the ship, some sails ripped and rigging swinging uselessly, limped its way to the nearest port, his mind raced through the adjustments he would need to make to get Xanthia home. A wry smile lifted his mouth, imagining her reaction to the news that their trek to Sparta promised a longer, more difficult walk. More strenuous for the others, certainly not for himself. Because Aeolus, keeper of the winds, had unleashed the combined power of the west and south winds to push the battered ship close to the gulf of Argolis.

A feral grin curved his mouth as he wondered whether they would meet any Argive pirates. He cracked his knuckles in anticipation.

"I suppose we'll have to climb mountains after all. Is that why you're smiling?"

Acastus allowed himself a moment to relax his shoulders, which had tensed at the sound of Xanthia's voice. He turned slowly to meet her unsparing gaze, his own running an assessing sweep over her. "I'm glad to see your trial earlier this morning hasn't weakened you."

He watched her pull her shawl around her slim form, fighting back a sudden desire to grab the garment, pull her into his arms, and kiss away the tension pressing her lips together in a thin line.

"I suppose I must thank you for saving me," Xanthia replied in a strained voice. "Though I sometimes wonder whether I'd be better off dead."

Her words stunned him. Not just what she said, but the obvious effort it cost her to thank him.

"Don't say that." His voice was sharper than he intended. "Many would mourn your death, your father, brother, and sister among them."

She sent him a sideways look. "You keep saying my brother and sister. How can they be married to each other."

Acastus drew closer to where she stood holding onto the rigging as the ship ploughed heavily through choppy waters. He reached out, clasping a reassuring hand over her arm, and blinked, fingers tingling at the contact, the warmth of her skin seeping through the thin material of the shawl. He looked into her eyes and spied confusion in the dark pools of her irises. Very slowly he drew his hand away.

"Callisto and Diokles are not blood kin. You, however, are kin to both, sharing a father with Callisto and a mother with Diokles." He clenched his hand and considered how much to tell her. No. The tragic details needed to wait until she reunited with her family and saw for herself that they rejoiced at her return. "It was Callisto, through Apollo's guidance, who advised where to begin my search. She's desperate to find you."

"And my brother?"

How could he answer her? Spartan men did not share their feelings, and Diokles had naturally mentioned nothing of his thoughts about his sister's return. "He agrees you need to be restored to your family and homeland. Why do you ask?"

Xanthia gave a cynical laugh. "Since my birth, men have made life-changing decisions for me. I was cast out, left to die, rescued, taken to one place, then another, when too many questions were asked. Only recently, the father I knew all my life betrayed me. To side with you!"

Running stiff fingers along his scalp, he released an exasperated sigh. "Philodemos explained his reasons to you. Nothing about his actions bordered on betrayal."

Acastus heard the captain call out to him, relieved to have the discussion cut short. She skirted too close to the scars which riddled his soul, threatening to rip them open. He strode over, frowned at the information the captain related, then gave a resigned shrug. He looked back at Xanthia, standing where he had left her, arms folded across her middle. Scratching at an annoying itch on his chin, he would have wagered her jaded expression meant she anticipated the tidings she was about to hear.

He cleared his throat and went to rejoin her. "The storm blew us off course, " he began, fully prepared to have another one break over his head, "the captain must dock at Zarax to repair a crack in the mast. We can't wait, meaning a walk around the lower slopes of the Parnon range to reach the Eurotas Valley."

Xanthia let out a sound akin to a hissing cat. "Why can't we wait? Wouldn't it be quicker to sail to wherever you said we were going?"

"Gytheion. Perhaps, but it will take more time than we have to repair the mast. There is every chance we might encounter Argive pirates even this far south. Sparta and Argos are mortal enemies. I need to consider your safety so prefer not to wait for them to show up in Zarax."

"Is there anyone Sparta doesn't consider an enemy," she huffed, rolling her eyes for good measure.

A gust of wind blew her hair across her face. Impulsively, Acastus pushed the unruly mass behind her shoulder. His fingertips burned with a heat as though he, not Prometheus, had lit the torch from the chariot wheel of the sun. Her gaze singed him; anger or desire, it was hard to tell. He released the last silky rope of hair still contained in his hand, taking pleasure in the way the length slid through his fingers.

"I'll make time to explain about our homeland," he promised. "You won't be so quick to disparage it when you arrive there."

~*~

Xanthia leaned away and clasped her hands. A seed of victory, if she could call it that, had been planted this morning despite the terror she had experienced in almost losing her life. For the first time since she had met Acastus, she had caught a hint of fear in his eyes when he came to her rescue. The goddess had granted a glimpse of the human who lived behind the over-bearing Spartan male, confident his every order would be obeyed without question.

As much as she hated to admit the galling truth, her curiosity about the land of her birth had been aroused. She still wanted some form of revenge on those who had cast her out. She still wanted to see their faces when they witnessed her survival. But, for whatever reason, she wanted to know how being in Sparta would affect her. What might she learn of herself?

"That remains to be seen," she demurred, finally responding to his assertion. "Since I'm in this crisis thanks to Spartan men, I have no choice but to go with you and decide for myself."

The sheer frustration wreathing Acastus's face made her lips twitch.

"You will drive me to madness." The words exploded out of his mouth, turning heads their way. "The people who banished you are…"

Her eyebrows shot up close to her hairline. "Are what? What do you know?" The way his mouth clamped shut and the closed expression piqued her curiosity more than ever. "Acastus. I want an answer."

"You'll receive your answers after you are safely back with your kin."

Xanthia lifted her chin, staring hard at him as though her gaze could rip out the secrets and lies relating to her birth. "I want to know now. I have a right to know."

"You do have that right and the right people will tell you."

She drew in an indignant breath when he left her, without apology, to retreat below deck. Restraining the urge to go after him with more demands, she stared blindly out over the expanse of shore line the ship clung to as it sailed further up the gulf. Deep in her heart, questions bubbled upward, demanding answers. What did he know? If he knew anything about her exile, was that why he was utterly determined to deliver her to Sparta?

She sighed and shifted her feet to a more secure stance. This morning, she had stared into his face and seen her saviour. This morning, discomforting realisations had hit her. She did not want to die. She wanted to find the truth, and afterwards, she could leave for Melos, once she satisfied herself that living in Sparta with the family she had never seen was not for her.

Of course, if there was a way to return to Melos immediately, she would take the risk and prise the real truth of her exile from Philodemos, even if her foster father never spoke to her again after she compelled him to the revelation.

CHAPTER FOURTEEN

Xanthia stared at the rocky coastline for so long, that her eyes started to water. Far too quickly, the vessel closed in on the port. Tight bands circled her chest, the pressure forcing her to fight for every breath. Soon, she would walk down a plank onto the soil of Lakonia. Not even the glimpses of verdant fields, or the fact she would finally be on dry land again, could ease the shakiness of her hands and legs.

Nerves already stretched to breaking point, she started at the loud shouts which sounded surprisingly close. Blinking, she was startled to see the ship had docked while she was lost in her uneasy thoughts. There was frantic activity wherever she looked – men loading, while others unloaded, the few merchant ships already moored. Dogs yipped near their master's feet and curses flew freely. Compared to the tranquillity she had left behind, the mayhem below felt like a physical assault. The noise was too loud, the smells too many, the sights too numerous. Xanthia swayed from the sensory overload and clutched the side of the ship to steady herself.

She picked up her bag, holding it to her middle like a shield. Earlier, she had declined to secure it onto one of the donkeys. It might prove burdensome to carry all the way but distrust of Drakon had influenced her decision.

A burst of raucous laughter on the dock sent her sidling closer to Acastus. Enemy or not, he represented safety here in this sea of humanity now crowding around the ship. A furtive sideways glance revealed his face set in inscrutable lines. Her stomach rolled at the sight of the gangplank being lowered. If only she possessed Hermes winged sandals to speed her over the sea back to the serenity she had been taken from.

She risked another glance at the silent man next to her. "How soon can we leave?"

"Once our supplies and animals are unloaded."

With no further information forthcoming, she studied him with a puzzled scowl. Rather, he continued to stare intently at the flurry of activity below. The tight jawline, the squared shoulders, gave her a glimpse of the highly trained warrior. She waited, biting her lip, then shivered on hearing the thud of the heavy wooden plank hitting the ground.

"Come."

Hurrying down the plank after Acastus, Xanthia staggered as she stepped onto dry land. She looked down, fully expecting to see the ground rolling like waves beneath her feet. Swaying, she concentrated her efforts on remaining upright.

Once she had steadied herself, the murmur of nearby conversation brought her head up to observe the flurry of activity swirling around her. She sized up a circle of rough-looking men, the majority of whom ogled her with ill-disguised interest. Unease prickled between her shoulder blades. Her life, she understood now, had been sheltered, leaving her no real experience of the world beyond her home.

But she had survived. She would survive this rabble, too.

Although she loathed being reliant on any man, the present circumstances gave her no choice. Walking swiftly to catch up with Acastus, she reached his side and muttered, "Everyone is staring. Can't you rebuke them for ogling your wife."

He stopped abruptly to turn an incredulous look on her. "You scolded me for telling the crew, now you want me to announce you're my wife?"

"Yes," she hissed, gritting her teeth against the flare of heat where the bare skin of their arms collided. "Any lie will do to convince these scruffy men that I'm yours."

Something moved across his face and disappeared before she could fully understand it. Perhaps she had overstepped some unknown cultural line. Well, if she had, the fault lay with the culture, not her.

"Stay close to me. You're a beautiful woman, it's natural you'll attract attention."

A fire erupted in her pelvis when Acastus draped an arm around her waist. *Don't let him captivate you, Xanthia, no matter how impressive his physique or looks.* They might captivate other women, except she was not like other women, as she bristled on seeing the smug smile pulling at his mouth.

"Don't think you've won," she warned testily. "Once we're away from here, I could go back to making your life miserable."

His deep-throated laugh served to garner even more attention. The looks were curious, some interested. She wrinkled her nose. Men were so…

Possibilities shivered right to her fingertips.

What were her chances of persuading someone to give her passage back to Melos? The gold armband, Kallios's gift to her two years ago, would secure payment. She had brought it with her for just such a purpose. In the past, she only wore it to festivals to placate him, otherwise keeping it out of her sight. She had fastened it on this morning to ensure she did not lose it. In her heart of hearts, she admitted it would be a relief to rid herself of this reminder of a time she tried every day to forget.

With a roll of her eyes, Xanthia silently scolded herself back to reality. Asking some stranger for assistance posed a huge risk. If only she possessed the power of second sight to help her choose, because curiosity pushed her towards Sparta, but her heart drew her back to Melos.

Mouth flattening at the dilemma, she unobtrusively studied the men in the vicinity. An older man, almost fatherly, caught her eye, even though he appeared oblivious to their presence. He would be safe to approach. The rest were younger. They might demand a much higher payment.

She sniffed. So what if she bent one more man to her will. Casting her gaze around the port with renewed interest, she tried to frame her question with an air of indifference. "There's so many people. How do you know who the captain of a ship is?"

Acastus angled her a narrow-eyed stare. "Why ask?"

She looked away. "No reason, I just wondered."

"Don't bother thinking of escaping."

His voice rang with a hard menace, forcing her to press her lips together to restrain the intemperate words forming on her tongue. While her mind raged, she settled her features into what she hoped were bland lines. Catching Acastus's piercing gaze, she tamped down on her guilty thoughts and lied without qualm. "Of course I'm not thinking of running away. After everything that's happened to me, I'm in no hurry to set foot on another ship."

"You won't be boarding another ship." The emphatic statement was followed by his turning to call out to Drakon who led the now-laden donkeys in their direction.

She fumed at being denied a disparaging retort by his leading her further away from the wharf. Forced to quicken her pace to keep up with his longer strides, concentrating on not losing her footing, she grunted at the lack of opportunity to think through any options she might have which would determine what she would do next.

A sudden queasiness settled in her stomach. The reason became clear when she noticed a burly, unkempt man taking a keen interest in their small group. Covertly studying his movements, she became convinced he kept pace with them while pretending interest elsewhere. Xanthia casually swung her left arm until her shawl slipped to her elbow, allowing the sun to flash on the gold band secured around her upper arm. A significant sideways look, a half-smile, brought an imperceptible nod of the stranger's head.

"Smile at him again, and I'll carry you all the way to Sparta over my shoulder."

Her loud gasp could have been heard on Melos. "Have you suddenly turned into Argus!?" He surprised, no, astounded her yet again. Lingering thoughts of slipping away unseen died right there. Foolish to think she possessed the skill to evade someone like him whose senses were constantly attuned to whatever environment he found himself in.

"Do I look like a hundred-eyed giant?" He drew her closer and dropped his voice. "That man is possibly a robber, a pirate, or a kidnapper. Are you so keen to discover which of those is true?"

Her heart quailed at the potential danger she had placed all of them in, even though she ground her teeth at this reluctant admission.

"Not really," she averred in an intentionally ungracious tone while squirming under his assessing stare. "I'm also not keen on climbing mountains. How is what you're making me do any different?"

"I'm taking you home, there is your difference. Did you pack a himation?"

"Only my shawl," she grumbled, thinking of the heavier travelling cloak she rarely packed when visiting her parents. "Thanks to you hurrying me off, I didn't remember to take it."

"I'll buy one from the vendor ahead. The nights in the mountains are cold unless you want to sleep next to me to keep warm."

The indignant breath she had intended to release stalled in her lungs. She relaxed her chest, releasing the trapped air, but her heart kept galloping like the wild horses she remembered from her childhood on Kythera. There was a gleam in his dark eyes she had never seen until now. Well acquainted with lustful looks, the light-headedness gripping her insisted this was different.

Her physical vision faded as an image filled her mind's eye – her naked body pressed against Acastus's in the heat of passion. Mouth dry, Xanthia blinked to dispel the sensual scene. There were only two things to keep uppermost in her mind – her retribution and eventual escape.

Taking Acastus as a lover was impossible. Yet no answer presented itself when she questioned why she mourned that simple reality.

"I don't want to sleep next to you. Buy me a cloak, quickly, so we can leave. This place is making me nervous."

"Sleeping next to me is repellent to you?"

The smile playing around his mouth irritated to the extreme – he was mocking her, she was sure of it. "I'd rather sleep next to a snake if I knew it wouldn't eat...my dove! Where is Calliope?"

A line of cold sweat broke out on her forehead. Even lingering terror of possibly going to an early death in the storm, amounted to no excuse in forgetting the dove. Heart in her mouth, she pivoted swiftly, slumping in relief when she saw the cage secured on one of the donkeys, Calliope balancing on her perch, swaying in time with the animal's gait. For the briefest of moments her eyes met Drakon's. He averted his head, but not before she spotted a shifty look flitter briefly across his face.

Xanthia worried her lip as she recalled those panicked, storm-tossed moments when she thought her life was about to end. Alarmed at losing her footing when she had tried to retreat below deck, the impact of someone slamming into her back had terrified her. But, what if the push had been unintentional, and Drakon had indeed lost his footing? What if his attempt to lift her fingers had simply been so he could grab her hand? Despite her dislike of the man, he was a helot servant, the same as her foster parents had been. If she had stated he had tried to kill her, she knew Acastus would not have hesitated to kill his servant.

"There's a vendor there," Acastus said, pointing straight ahead.

She surrendered her arm to his gentle, but firm grip. Must her pulse jump every time he touched her? Venting her exasperation with a heavy sigh, she followed in his wake.

They reached the vendor, who she noticed had immediately sized up Acastus and inflated his prices in the belief he was a wealthy merchant. Acastus had begun to negotiate a lower price, but it was obvious he was more warrior than negotiator. One skill she had learned from Euphrasia, who had regularly bartered her sheep's milk and cheese, was how to haggle.

She stepped forward, ignoring the vendor's dismissive look as she did. A hard lesson was coming his way. "How can you dare ask so much for this inferior cloth?" she chided, laughing silently as the vendor's face reddened in affront. "There are better cloaks to be bought for less money on the islands."

"Do you allow this woman to speak for you?" the vendor demanded angrily. "What kind of a man—"

It had been a long time since she had reason to laugh, but she shook with it now, as the man hastily swallowed his words when Acastus glowered at him and removed his cloak. The sight of his arms would be enough to make any antagonist think twice about engaging him.

"No need to fear," she broke the tension, "your cloaks are well-made, but the price you ask is too high." She named an amount well below his. Seeing him glance at Acastus, realising he had no choice but to deal with her, she grinned and with gusto began bargaining.

Pleased to secure her new cloak for well below what the vendor had tried to extort, she turned to Acastus. "Thank you. I don't have room in this bag and don't wish to carry the cloak. Where is your servant so I can place it in the packs?"

The words had barely left her mouth when a shout whirled them both around in unison. One of their waterskins lay open on the ground, contents spilling over the sandy path. Losing a waterskin was a blow. Unsurprised by Acastus's order to wait while he marched off to remonstrate with Drakon, she wondered whether he would risk the loss and continue their trek.

As she watched the exchange, noting Drakon's shamefaced, yet defiant, expression, the tiny hairs on her arms rose. Once again, she spied the unkempt man whose attention she had foolishly attempted to capture earlier. He motioned to the waterfront and smiled to reveal a broken tooth, greed shining out of his beady eyes.

She flinched and questioned whether she had done the right thing?

Xanthia managed a tiny shake of her head, then Acastus appeared by her side to clasp her elbow. Her trembling must have given her away. His fingers tightened a fraction, then she saw him plunge his free hand under his cloak to where she knew his xiphos was secured. The raw power blazing from his face, the aura radiating a menacing readiness, widened her eyes.

She glanced back at her potential conspirator and had to tamp down hysterical laughter at the fear so clearly written on his face. She watched him take a cautionary step backwards, narrowed eyes obviously sizing up his situation, eventually deeming it wiser to scurry back toward the dock.

Acastus bent close to whisper in her ear, increasing her trembling ten-fold for an entirely different reason.

"Don't court danger our way."

"I—"

Fuming, she opened her mouth but the sharp words she intended to utter died away unsaid. Alertness radiated palpably off him, every muscle in his tall body bunched and ready to pounce. She longed for some water to relieve the dryness of her mouth.

"Keep walking. Next time you attract attention I *will* throw a sack over your head."

Nose in the air, she hastily packed the cloak away without looking toward the silent servant standing between the donkeys. Annoyance rose like flames from a newly lit fire when Acastus clamped her firmly by his side. Grumbling under her breath about high-handed Spartans, she marched beside him. However, she did not have to stay silent.

"Had you listened to my wishes, I wouldn't need to find some means of escaping from you," she accused in a low voice.

"Sometimes it's best not to say anything. No-one hears what they shouldn't."

A sideways glance showed her his rigid jawline. After a prolonged, tense silence, she half-shrugged and told herself worrying about his tangle of words served no purpose.

She had more to worry about than Acastus. She did not need to look behind her to confirm Drakon's eyes were boring into her. Twin spots on her back throbbed the warning. He warranted keeping an eye on once they left behind any semblance of civilised life. Her free hand drifted to the satchel of herbs hanging over her hip. If she were wrong about what had happened and Drakon was intent on harming her, she had the means at her disposal to stop him.

The sun was beginning its slide to the horizon by the time they came across a small valley hidden between low hills. Xanthia's heart pounded, its heavy beat setting off whorls of trepidation. She studied the warrior striding slightly ahead of her. Out here, only he stood between her and whatever danger lurked along the way.

If she reached Sparta alive, the first thing she would do was take his xiphos and run the sharp weapon through him for putting her through this ordeal.

CHAPTER FIFTEEN

Acastus tossed a piece of wood onto the fire with enough force to send embers flying. They landed on him, scorching his skin. He brushed them away, mere pinpricks of pain compared to the battle wounds he had received in the past. He had called a halt when he had noticed Xanthia's steps growing more sluggish the longer they walked.

The idea of throwing a sack over her head grew more appealing, if only to save his sanity. In attempting to lure the stranger who had raised every one of his hackles, she had imperilled them all, never mind placing his mission in danger. Not long after leaving the port, his danger sense had started to tingle sporadically. Now it clamoured an insistent alert in his gut. Had the ruffian followed them? Did he have cohorts? Acastus kept both xiphos and kopis sheathed by his side.

He glanced towards the silent woman seated to his right, chewing slowly on the remains of her meal. So far, she had tried to push him off a cliff and then fallen – or been pushed – over the side of a ship to where certain death awaited in the storm.

His conscience smote him. She would not be in mortal danger if not for an unthinking remark which continued to cast a pall across the intervening years.

As though aware of his scrutiny, she stopped eating and eyed him cautiously. Desire slammed a fist into his solar plexus. Impossible, and dangerous, to succumb to whatever inconvenient attraction drew them inexorably into its silken net. He was a Spartan warrior on a mission of honour, not some green boy just coming into manhood, unable to resist the allure of a woman.

"Have you eaten enough?" Earlier he had scouted the valley, more a dip between hills, and decided to stop for the night because of the shelter it afforded, especially the small cave he had discovered. Decision made, he had trapped and skinned a rabbit which Drakon roasted over the fire. Acastus then dispatched him to refill the remaining waterskin from a stream they had crossed along the way.

"Yes. I'm surprised I have any appetite for food given my kidnapping and how close I came to drowning."

Hauteur dripped from her voice, the reminder of her ordeal cutting him to the quick. "I didn't kidnap you; you came willingly."

"You practically coerced me," she shouted, "and, even worse, convinced the man I consider my father to agree with you!"

"Once again you conveniently forget that he said he always expected the day might arrive when you could rejoin your blood kin as a citizen of Sparta."

He caught the disdainful smirk as she turned her face away. In profile, she was just as beautiful, the otherworldly air surely gifted by the goddess of love herself. The urge to kiss her, until he rendered her pliant to his caress, gathered strength the longer they spent together. Acastus stood and stepped back from the fire to escape the web she had begun to weave around him since he had first set eyes on her.

"Tell me about your life on Melos." The very subject was sufficient to cool his ardour. Her dark beauty must have easily ensnared the male acolytes.

She eyed him suspiciously. "Why do you want to know?"

"It interests me." Although honesty prompted him to admit he did not want to hear about her many lovers, Acastus waited while she stared off into the distance. In those drawn-out moments, the muscles in his neck grew stiffer from the waiting tension. He bent his head side-to-side to relieve the ache.

"There's not much to tell. We left Kythera because my parents grew worried about some things being said about me. They wouldn't tell me what, and I was too young and naïve to argue with them. I cried when we left. I missed the horses and running with them."

"Philodemos told me questions started being asked about your parentage. He, himself, saw your Dorian heritage emerge as you grew."

She gazed into the fire, then continued in a cooler voice. "We made our home on Melos. One day, I overheard my parents talking about how I had been left to die on that accursed mountain and how I was rescued. Something died inside me that day. I was lost, though a wildness gripped my soul. In our third year of living on Melos, I encountered the acolytes of Aphrodite and joined them a short time later."

There remained much she held back. His gaze narrowed on her slender hands, clenched together, noting the tension in the smooth jawline. "And took lovers?"

He met her mocking look with a narrow-eyed stare.

"Of course. It is expected during fertility festivals. That is the point after all."

Disapproval tightened his face and he refused to consider the source of it. Even Spartan society encouraged the use of progenitors if a husband proved infertile. He ploughed on, driven by a need to know everything about her. "I'm surprised a woman of your beauty and spirit doesn't have a child."

Intense pain clouded her eyes. Acastus sucked in a breath, mesmerised at the obvious effort she made to wipe her face clear of emotion. His suspicions that she hid some important part of her life intensified.

"There are ways to stop conceiving, Spartan," she chided him in a bored voice. "While the rites are meant to produce children, sometimes pregnancy doesn't happen. Other times it might not be desirable."

Trained to read nuances, the nonchalant tone failed to convince. Hurt resonated deeply beneath her careless words. Had she borne, then lost a child? The possibility hit him like a debilitating blow to the chest. If true, it mirrored her own mother's tragedy.

Although, if she were already a Spartan mother, she would have been obliged to give up any sons when they reached the age of seven to be raised amidst the rigorous agoge education. Would she have fought the warriors who came to take her son like other mothers who had been known to reach for knives? The determined set of her chin alone made it easy to assume she would fight like a lioness to protect her own.

"So, pleasure is more important?" He decided to be wise and refrain mentioning his own pleasurable encounters at the behests of older husbands.

She gave him a pitying look. "I don't understand why people think pleasure in lovemaking is wrong. It enhances the chances of conceiving a child."

It was an odd sentiment to express from someone who obviously enjoyed the experiences of the fertility rites yet had birthed no children. Acastus hid a rueful grin despite the seriousness of their discussion. If she was a mother, he harboured no doubts she would strike him with his own weapons before she left any child of hers behind on Melos. "By your own words you are admitting you have never known such pleasure."

She jumped to her feet, the look in her eyes impaling him as efficiently as any spear. "It's none of your concern."

The ice in her voice stoked his temper. "It is my concern when you attempt to lure every strange man you meet. If you'd managed to escape and pay your passage back with that armband you flashed, do you believe payment would have stopped there?"

Annoyance pressed her lips into a tight line. The smile tugging his mouth, when she realised the corner he had backed her into, died when she jutted her hip and swept an assessing look over him.

"You men are easy to control." The husky voice dripped with a sensual promise, guaranteed to inflame ardour in anyone.

If he did not believe it blasphemous, he would have sworn it was Aphrodite in human form come down to tempt him. "Take care, Xanthia. Not every man will fall for your wiles."

The tip of her tongue delicately swept the upper lip. "I wager I could make you."

His manhood instantly begged him to take the wager. Taking his time, he rose to his feet, moving closer until her scent teased him, capturing her chin between his thumb and forefinger to stop any retreat. Acastus bent his head until his lips hovered a hairsbreadth away from hers. The sudden hiss, the glitter in her eyes, stoked the embers of passion to full arousal. "I wager you can't. Ever."

Lifting his head, he drew back to study her flushed, angry face. When she flounced off, he kept an eye on her movements, certain she would not go far. She was intelligent enough to understand the utter madness of escaping with dusk falling.

Once Xanthia left, the servant's continued absence stoked his uneasiness up another notch. Had Drakon returned to Zarax to refill water or fallen foul of some wild animal? Or human? Expanding his senses outwards, he leaned against a tree trunk to wait, while the clamour of his concern grew louder with each moment that passed.

CHAPTER SIXTEEN

The dense bushes he sheltered within parted above his head with the violence of a summer storm. Drakon squeezed his eyes shut, a reflexive move, and prayed to the gods his painfully thudding heart remained inside his chest.

"Well, by the goddess, see what I've found."

Drakon cowered away from the rough, drawling voice, which set every one of his limbs trembling. Opening one eye so only a slit of white showed, he tilted his head. Both eyes gaped open to stare at the apparition standing over him. It was the man he had seen at the port. The same ruffian the little whore had lured into their path.

Uncaring that his hands visibly shook, he stretched them out in supplication. "I beg of you, don't kill me. I'm a helot servant lately escaped from my brutal Spartan master." The lie came easily to his tongue despite the clammy sweat covering every last inch of his skin. The brigand who towered above him spat on the ground.

"Spartan, you say."

Drakon swept a swift, furtive glance over the five men surrounding him, careful not to make full eye contact. They resembled pirates, but he allowed himself to breathe just a little easier. If they hated Spartans, it seemed fate finally smiled on him.

What can I say to convince them to let me go?

The answer required more bravery than he had ever needed to show. Choosing the right words meant life or death. He must survive to fulfil the task of stopping Xanthia returning to her homeland. He had been paid handsomely to accomplish that by whatever means available to him.

All I need do is not let fear addle my wits.

"Yes. A Spartiate travelling in disguise as a merchant." If betraying his master to these pirates, and he was fairly certain now they were pirates by their dress and speech, resulted in Acastus's death, leading to his freedom, then he considered it a gift from the gods.

The pirate peered, then grinned, revealing a chipped tooth that somehow enhanced the menace of his appearance. "And where do we find your master? Why does a Spartan hoplite lower himself to that sort of trickery?"

Drakon looked from one brutish face to the next. Their reactions, at best, would be unpredictable, leaving his very existence in question. Feverish shivers wracked him.

"He's on a mission, which is the reason he wears merchant's garb. There's a woman with him and he's armed." Until he gained surety they would not kill him on a whim, he was not going to disclose his own covert plans.

The pirate leader sneered. "Armed, is he? One man versus five Argives won't last long even if he is Spartan." He turned to grin at his fellows. "We can thank the storm for this chance at some entertainment. Let's go greet this Spartan warrior." He spat the words out like an epithet. "Once we've finished him, we'll have some fun with the woman."

Drakon blocked out the noise of their laughter and ribald remarks. This might prove the opportunity to extricate himself, unharmed, out of a deadly situation. What could he do? What plan of action would aid him the most? He entertained the idea of hiding on the outskirts of the camp to make certain of Xanthia's demise at their hands, then steal back, somehow, to Sparta to report on his success. "If I show you where to find him, will you swear by Aphrodite to release me to return home?"

"You say you're a helot," a second hulking brute challenged him. "Why would you want to return to Sparta? Us killing you now, or the Spartans hunting you down, makes little difference."

Muttering a quiet prayer to Hermes to endow him with the right words, Drakon turned to the leader. "If you kill me, I'm dead. By going back, I might have a chance to escape the helot hunts ensuring I can feed my family. If not for them, I would never return but seek sanctuary elsewhere." That much was at least true.

The pirate captain crossed his arms, hard eyes boring into him, a sneer contorting his features into an evil mask. Drakon shivered and stared nervously at the group enclosing him on three sides. The threat relayed in their positioning was intentional. Desperation plucked at him; he wanted to run, but the panicked impulse died the moment it arose. They would hunt him down and kill him if he did.

Yet, despite their number and bulk, they were over-confident in thinking it would be an easy task to take on and beat a trained warrior, unless all five attacked him together. Unlike the pankration match participants, pirates respected no rules. He had no personal quarrel with Acastus, although the way the Spartans treated his people meant he was more than happy to betray him.

The pirate leader speared Drakon with a pitiless look. "I swear by Aphrodite I'll free you after you lead us to your master."

Drakon gulped air into his starved lungs. He picked up the full water skin and rose to his feet, managing to stay upright despite his legs feeling unsteady like a child taking his first steps. "We camped not far from here. Follow that path."

He nodded in the direction he had come from, except the pirate's imperious hand signal left him no choice but to walk in front. His neck tightened. Drakon rubbed the muscles there, feeling as though the area had turned to stone. Not only did they have no rules, but pirates possessed no honour. There was nothing to stop them stabbing him in the back once he led them to Acastus and Xanthia.

Inhaling a jittery breath, he counted on their historical hatred of Sparta to allow him to make good his escape.

CHAPTER SEVENTEEN

"Tell me, my resourceful warrior, are we sleeping under the stars or have you found shelter?"

"Keep your voice down."

Acastus swept an uneasy glance over the nearby rocks and bushes, which provided a natural barrier to anyone stumbling upon them during the night. Even as he acknowledged no better place to be ship-wrecked than the Peloponnese, they were still many days away from real safety. Wild beasts and the odd bandit always lurked where least expected.

Pushing aside the disquiet still holding him captive, he had risked lighting the fire for their meal which had long finished, though embers still smouldered. He placed another branch on them despite his better judgement. Without Xanthia, he would have easily borne cold and hunger. It would not have been the first time he had starved in order to conquer the natural demands of his body.

Too bad he failed to conquer certain of those demands whenever his gaze fell on the woman who now rejoined him after feeding her dove. Acastus ground his teeth together with a frustration mostly directed at himself. It went beyond reason that she possessed the ability to ensnare him in such a way when danger weighed heavily in the air. He would breathe easier once they reached the valley where the Eurotas River would guide them home. His tension levels had soared after one brief glance at the man Xanthia had enticed at the port. Something about the ruffian had set his nerves on edge.

Whether the man was a pirate or some other threat, both of them remained vulnerable. Only his training, his merchant guise, and his weapons stood in her defence against whatever they might encounter.

He drank in the sight of her as she lowered herself to sit opposite him, tucking long, shapely legs to one side. "There's a cave at the top of that hill." He pointed in the direction of a stand of trees providing camouflage to his chosen spot. "It's sheltered and well-hidden."

"Is it large enough to fit all of us?"

He nodded approvingly. "Your forethought is commendable. We'll rest here tonight and move at first light. Make sure you eat enough and don't try slipping away if you think I'm asleep."

She turned an incredulous look on him.

"Why would I run away? I don't know where I am. I don't know how to live off the land. You do, which means I stay alive."

"Once you are home, you'll learn to survive in the forest." Acastus studied her, marvelling once again how much she resembled Diokles. Ianthe's genes had been strong. The train of thought produced a stab of guilt so strong he could be forgiven for thinking he had driven his own xiphos into his heart. "And you'll be educated in ways no other city-state educates its women."

She snorted. "Education is somehow meant to make amends for me losing twenty years of my life? Help me forget my banishment during which my real father disappeared and my real mother died? I don't know if I can ever come to terms with what happened and live in Sparta in spite of it."

Every word cut like a knife slashing his skin. Acastus threw another log on the fire, the small task masking his silence because he knew there was nothing he could say to alleviate her pain. He could only give her this assurance. "I know a way through the lower slopes of the mountain range. Once we clear that, the going is much easier."

He stared into the flames, their hypnotic flickering turning his sight inward. How indeed could he atone for the mistake which had caused her banishment?

A voice whispered that he offer to marry her.

His body jumped as though he had sat on a thorn bush. While his heart shouted its agreement, the logical part of his brain resisted. Once his role in her exile became known, and it would if they wed, there was no predicting Diokles's reaction. He would not risk the friendship forged from their earliest days and strengthened through countless battles.

Nor would he tear apart a family a third time.

He made to reach out, give comfort, then slowly withdrew his hand to his side. If he touched her now, one of two things would happen – either he would find his face slapped or he would lose himself in her warmth. He closed his eyes, searching for control…

When suddenly his gut churned, his hearing intensified, his fingers tingled.

How many battles had these same involuntary reactions warned him of danger? Of an enemy about to strike a death blow? A blow avoided, enabling him to deliver one to his opponent instead.

In the quiet of the twilight not a breath of wind stirred the leaves, yet he just knew danger lurked.

Meeting Xanthia's frown with one of his own, he pressed a finger to his lips. She gave him the faintest of nods, her throat working as she swallowed an emotion at which he could only guess. Once more her life was in danger because of him.

He stretched his arms above his head, casually, to make it seem he was relieving an ache, then drew them down, crossing them beneath the cloak he still wore to grip both his swords, grateful for the hours his mentor had trained him to wield any weapon with both hands. His mind raced through tactics while knowing the crucial one was to convince whatever foe lurked that he remained unaware of their presence.

"Tell me about the customs of the people on Kythera." He made an imperceptible movement of his head, indicating for her to answer. In a more relaxed setting, he would have laughed at her comical expression, which plainly showed she thought he had taken leave of his senses.

She shrugged. "There is not much to tell. Aphrodite is worshipped as the patron goddess because it's believed she first came to Kythera after her birth from the ocean. My parents herded sheep there as they do now on Melos. We live as anyone else in Hellas does. How did you become a warrior?"

Only he could have heard the tremor in her voice but carrying on this charade might save their lives.

His pulse began to drum a battle tattoo.

"All Spartan boys become warriors, although girls too, are trained to fight so they can defend themselves…"

The threat closed in stealthily.

Almost within striking distance.

"…Like this…"

In a whirl of motion, he sprang to his feet, brought both weapons to bear, and thrust viciously through the tangle of laurel bushes behind him.

He heard Xanthia scream, the sound drowned out by two agonised yells inside the bushes. No time to confirm they were dead. There would be more than just these two.

Acastus yanked his weapons out of their victims, warm blood splattering his hands. A blur of movement to his right sent him spinning to deliver another death blow.

Something hard hit the back of his head. He fought to remain conscious, to save Xanthia from the remaining threat, but was quickly consumed by a fiery pain radiating out from where he had been struck.

Another blow buckled his knees, and he knew no more.

CHAPTER EIGHTEEN

Guttural laughter penetrated the relentless pounding in his head.

Acastus carefully opened his swollen eyelids and struggled to focus his vision as the dim light of evening slowly filled his watery gaze. He swept his parched tongue over cracked lips, tasting blood oozing from a deep split in his lower lip.

He made to step forward – but a pain like stabbing knives arced through his hands and brought him to an abrupt stop. Resting his chin on his chest to convince anyone watching he remained comatose, he blinked to clear his vision, suddenly understanding why it felt as if he had been crushed between the clashing rocks of the Bosphorus.

Blood spattered his shredded tunic. He tried to breathe deeply into the pain, but shards of agony sliced through his chest. Bruised or broken ribs, then. To a Spartan warrior, fashioned in the fire of the agoge, pain was his friend, the momentum needed to keep going and take down an enemy.

Even if he descended into the Underworld alongside them.

Ignoring the spasms threatening to tear apart his aching muscles, Acastus lifted his head just enough to observe a chunk of meat roasting over the fire *he* had built, stoked higher than before. Three brutes sat warming themselves, laughing, calling to someone he could not see. He went cold all over, then an inferno of bloodlust followed in its wake, blinding him to everything.

Argives.

Their speech betrayed them. They would have had no qualms beating him to a pulp while he hung unconscious. Why they had not killed him outright remained a mystery. The tree they had tied him to stood enough of a distance from the fire to set him shivering, but more importantly, enabled him to watch his attackers without being noticed. Pressing against the rough bark helped ease the chafing of his bound wrists.

He assessed the situation through hooded eyes. None of the ruffians paid him any attention, so he risked tugging at his bonds which confirmed his wrists were securely tied, though not tight enough to numb his hands. He began to saw the rope over the rough bark of the tree, disregarding the protest of his shoulder joints.

Then his mind blanked, followed by a torrent of fury scalding his heart and soul because, at that moment, Xanthia stepped out from behind a tree trunk, laughing, and serving wine to the greatest enemies of her own people. Had she lain with them while the cold night air bit his wounds?

Diokles's sister or not, he would wring her neck if she had.

Urgency infected his mind. He leaned forward to place greater pressure on the rope, sawing faster than wisdom dictated. It increased the risk his enemies would notice, but if he managed to cut his bonds in time, well, he would be free to wring the Argives necks, too.

Low in his throat, a feathery tickle grew in intensity. He sawed faster, trying to swallow any moisture he could summon into his parched mouth to suppress the irritation. Sweat broke out on his face and neck. Despite his best efforts a hacking cough escaped. Instantly, every eye turned his way. He prepared himself for more punishment as the largest of the three stood and sauntered over to where he was bound.

"Ah, the Spartan awakes. Well, my fine specimen, tonight you die." The Argive rubbed his chin, grinned at his cohorts, then turned back to Acastus. "Better yet, we take you with us and kill you in Argolis. Your blood will enrich the soil like the blood of our forebears whom your king slaughtered."

Acastus impaled his assailant with a look he knew conveyed all the hatred and contempt he could muster. Knew that he had succeeded, because for a heartbeat, fear suffused the hateful face.

The face he recognised as the man whose notice Xanthia had tried to engage in Zarax. It all made sense now. They were Argive pirates, ready to plunder any ship damaged in the storm.

A fist planted to his middle doubled him over, the pain in his ribs intensifying. Acastus swayed, pretending the blow affected him more than it did. In truth, the swaying helped disguise the fact the rope was starting to fray, the hanging fringes tickling his thumbs confirming it.

"What a gift the gods have given me," jeered the pirate captain. "To see a Spartan swinging from a tree. Nothing to say my fine Acastus? Yes, I know your name. Before I kill you, I will tell you mine." He called out to his companions. "What say you, shall I tell him so he remembers my name for eternity in the Underworld?"

The other two pirates guffawed. Acastus's lip curled – only Xanthia could have told them his name. He directed a hard, accusing gaze towards her, refusing to see the angry plea in hers. She had threatened him, warned him she would try and escape. Now it appeared she had chosen to take her chance by throwing herself on the mercy of Argives.

He squashed an insane impulse to laugh at her foolishness and forced his aching body upright. "I say, untie me, return my xiphos, then we'll see whose blood nourishes the soil first."

He braced for the expected blow. When none came his eyes narrowed, suspicious of the lecherous smile curving the pirate's mouth. The unholy glee in the soulless eyes warned him that the Argive might be entertaining a more sordid plan. He looked down his nose, disgusted, as the man leaned in closer, breath smelling of soured wine.

"How much does the woman mean to you?"

"Nothing."

The lie was necessary to his mission and to keeping them alive. Out of the corner of his eye he caught a glimpse of Xanthia's face blazing with loathing. She could hate him as much as she liked – she had made her choices clear. Though his gut churned at the thought of her defilement at the pirates' hands, her obvious betrayal seared his mind. The one stain on his honour would be in failing his mission.

If this was his last day, he would face death like a warrior and not think about a woman who had chosen to embrace their mortal enemies, rather than see him live. The Argive leered, his chipped, yellowing teeth disgusting Acastus even more.

"Then you won't mind watching us pleasure her."

A knife in my guts would be preferrable.

Acastus shook his head much like a dog shook off water. Where had that thought come from? He argued with himself that his concern only lay in the knowledge she was Diokles's sister, leaving him unable to cleanse his guilt. She meant nothing to him.

He leaned forward. Eyes burning, voice hoarse, he mocked the pirate. "Pleasure her? May the gods grant you luck."

~*~

Xanthia stood open-mouthed, hearing every word because neither man bothered to lower their voice. All her preconceived beliefs were proven true by the short exchange.

Spartans were mad!

She knew men could be ruthless, but the knowledge did not stop her longing to vent her fury and, for good measure, hit Acastus over the head like the Argives had done.

She needed to think, fast, if she was to save them both from the precarious crisis they found themselves in. Acastus's punishment would suffer a delay. Her stomach rolled and twisted at the thought of being forced to pleasure this group of unkempt brutes. They would be the first men to feel the wrath of the revenge she planned, or she would die in the attempt before she gave herself to them.

Xanthia waited, heart racing, as ideas came and were discarded on how best to stall them until she could execute the plan she settled on. The pirate leader strolled over, stopping barely a pace away from where she stood. Rank sweat and unwashed body odour wrinkled her nose.

"Which one of us first, my beauty? Should be me, of course, but capturing a Spartan has me in a good enough mood to let you choose." A lascivious gleam appeared in his eyes. "Later, we can take our pleasure all together."

Her fingers tightened painfully around the handles of the wine jug she carried. The madman was fortunate she restrained the urge to throw up all over his brutish face. *Breathe, Xanthia. Pray to the goddess for guidance. He is just another man to bend to your will.*

She feared the breakneck speed of her thudding heart might suffocate her. Surprised her chiton remained still, instead of moving in time with each powerful beat, Xanthia swept her eyelashes downwards to hide her disgust.

"I will consider this," she murmured in a sickeningly fulsome voice. "The night is young. There is time to offer sacrifice to Aphrodite and for another drink. I have herbs to enhance our pleasure and your stamina."

The bag of herbs she had had the foresight to take. Her secret weapon.

"Whatever you say." The pirate captain licked his lips, beady eyes transfixed by her curves. "We do the sacrifice now. I don't want to wait."

"Alright." She inclined her head. She must remember to keep her eyes downcast to hide the revulsion they would surely see. Xanthia stifled a nervous laugh. All three ogled her in a way, which betrayed their interest in what lay under her chiton rather than what her expression might reveal.

Deep breathing helped release some of the anxiety stiffening her muscles. She grimaced over an unexpected pang of guilt, which forced her to acknowledge her part in having to play this perilous game. Acastus had abducted her; her naivete had placed them in their current danger. The power to save him from death, and herself from gruesome violation, rested in her hands.

What could she suggest using for a sacrifice? If the night provided a wild pig stumbling upon their encampment, the Argives were allowed to offer that. Anemones! The idea flew out of her mind like Hope had flown from Pandora's box. Praying she could find at least one bloom in the dark, Xanthia took a few hesitant steps to go search when one of the seated men called out.

"There's a dove with the donkeys. They're the goddess's sacred bird. You can use it."

Her blood ran cold.

"No!" She bit off the moan that welled up from the depths of her frozen heart. "I will gather—"

The pirate leader captured her arm and pulled her roughly back. "Why not? I said I'm not waiting. Who knows how long it'll take you to find something else."

Xanthia struggled against the rough hands restraining her. Still in her cage, her precious Calliope was brought to the fire. "Please, not the dove. I can show you pleasure like nothing you've experienced, but don't sacrifice her."

He leaned in to bite her neck. "You'll give us pleasure, whatever we do."

A bitter lump of despair fomented in her stomach, rising to burn her throat. Xanthia controlled the violent urge to sink her teeth into the hands restraining her and bite through to the bone. She pressed her lips together with such force she lost feeling in them. A tidal wave of grief overwhelmed her, watching Calliope flap her wings to avoid the grasping hand, instinct sensing the end.

Just in time, she stifled the keening wail which started in her throat when the knife was driven into the pure white breast. Red blood crimsoned the feathers and the hand of the murderer. Her beloved solace was thrown onto the burning logs like a piece of trash. Flames hissed and spat, turning a once living being to ash.

"Sacrifice to the goddess done, now we celebrate. Pour more wine."

The man she had foolishly imagined paying to return her to Melos rubbed his filthy hands in anticipation. She angled her head invitingly, although the effort to feign excitement while her heart was breaking cost her dearly.

It was not excitement that roared in her veins. Summoned from somewhere in her heritage, a wildness built, thrumming through every cell, a frenzy of violence worthy of Ares himself. She would entertain these pirates in a way they never imagined.

Reaching past her grief, embracing the formidable spirit inherited from her ancestors, Xanthia gave a wide, perfidious smile. "I'll get my herbs and more wine."

She risked a glance at Acastus as her heart gave a little flip of fear.

The fixed stare conveyed his utter determination to kill her and take satisfaction in doing so. She had underestimated his fierceness yet again, but there was no time to explain her plan. She looked away, a strange feeling of loss consuming her, no less intense than when she had witnessed Calliope butchered.

A hard ball of anger constricted her chest. Why should she care what he wanted to do to her? If circumstances rendered it necessary, she could finish him off anytime she chose. Whirling around, she went to retrieve the herbs and wineskin, purposely keeping her gaze averted from Acastus when she returned. Xanthia laughed at the lewd comments meant to arouse her, boasts about their prowess, how they intended to take her.

Steady hands poured wine into three kylikes, while inside she was a seething mass of rage and revenge.

"These herbs enhance the flavour of the wine, not just your stamina." The husky voice she affected masked their real purpose. She knelt to measure out the dose, mixing the fine powder into the wine, leaning well forward to let the front of her chiton gape open and give each of the ogling monsters an eyeful of her breasts. Watching their eyes turned glassy, it took all her self-control to not snatch up one of the burning logs and run it across their hateful faces.

She then stood, sinuously flexing her body as she rose, intent on keeping them focussed on their desires without frustrating them, mindful that at any moment, the pirates might lose their patience, leaving her at their mercy. Keeping her voice low and sensual, she murmured, "Here, drink the wine of passion."

Once she had given each pirate his wine, she stretched her arms to the sky and swayed her hips in a parody of a dance. All three lifted their kylikes with obscene haste. The two underlings drank so fast that one almost choked. She smiled, taunting their haste, then glanced at the captain. His own drink remained untouched as he continued to point and guffaw at his men's desperation.

Her smile died. "Drink," she urged him.

"In a moment," he laughed roughly.

The first flutters of panic began to beat inside her chest. "You'll be last," Xanthia lied, "the herbs take time to work."

There was murder in the glare he turned on her. Her legs shook like leaves in the wind. To diffuse his anger at being told what to do, she ran fingers through her long hair, fanning the strands out in a halo as she pouted. Risking everything, she dipped her shoulder to let the sculp slide down her arm. The pirate's mouth fell open, his eyes staring at the partially exposed cleavage. *Pitiful.* Elated to see him at least raise the kylix to his mouth, she fought to keep calm and work out what she could do if he refused to drink.

Her frantic gaze darted around the campsite and she inhaled a sharp breath. *There!* Acastus's xiphos, the short blade half-hidden under an abandoned cloak, glinted in the firelight. The overconfidence of the Argives was about to be paid back in full, very soon.

Except, disaster struck first.

The two pirates who had already guzzled their wine, dropped their kylikes to clutch their throats, sputtering and gagging before toppling to the ground. The leader's mouth gaped and fury darkened his face. He swore so obscenely she flinched and gulped past the knot of fear in her chest, her stomach pitching and rolling over itself.

"You whore! You've killed them. I'll take you now. Then you'll wish you'd never been born." He threw the tainted contents of the kylix at her.

She dodged the foaming, contaminated wine, the sideways jump bringing her within reach of the weapon. Acastus was yelling something, but her senses tuned him out, all her focus on the remaining pirate, teeth bared, hands clenched, striding menacingly closer.

Xanthia spun on the spot, intending to flee but tripped on the torn hem of her chiton, and fell on all fours. She had no time to pound her fist on the ground at this injustice – the mishap might prove to her advantage.

Breathe. Be ready.

She had never handled a weapon in her entire life. Her assailant's feet loomed closer, and her tunnelling vision warned her she had only one chance. She relived Calliope being torn open with the knife. Rage lent her raw strength which consumed the fear.

As the bellowing brute reached down to grab her hair, her hand closed around the hilt of the xiphos. *Now*, her mind screamed. Teeth bared, the blade shot out, slashing the pirate across the stomach, more by luck than skill. A bestial roar of pain deafened her as she dived out of his reach, coming to a stop beside the fire. Her eyes bulged as the pirate, blood staining his ripped garment, staggered after her, face twisted in demented hatred, a fist raised and ready to smash her to a pulp.

In the split second she stared certain death in the face, a myriad of thoughts flapped like trapped birds in her mind. One remained to torture her – she had failed. Sucking in short breaths that brought no air into her lungs, Xanthia shut her eyes and resigned herself to the final moments of her life. Far from home. Far from the family she would never meet.

An enraged howl filled the small valley.

Her eyes snapped open in time to see a sandalled foot driven into the Argive's knee from the rear. He collapsed into the fire, a xiphos protruding from his back, driven in to the hilt. Slapping a hand over her mouth to stifle a scream, morbid fascination kept her gaze trained on the doomed man, whose attempts to crawl out came to a gradual halt as he collapsed into the remains of the fire.

Silence.

The smell of scorched flesh sickened her. She pressed a hand to her stomach and gagged. Xanthia tried to push herself up, but every limb trembled as shock began to subside.

Turning to seek out her rescuer, she fell on her bottom, mouth agape. Acastus, face gleaming with sweat and pain, swayed above her. Her gaze dropped to his hands, dotted with blood, where it seeped out under the rope still attached to his wrists, the middle of it sawn in two.

"How," she croaked, "did you cut the rope?"

Despite his split lips and swollen face he smiled. "I did what I had to do. I was right about you."

Head shaking in disbelief, she wondered whether Spartans were indeed mere mortals. "Right about what?"

"Your bravery proved your heritage as truly a woman of Sparta."

She yelped as he collapsed in a heap beside her. Still dazed they had managed to avoid a brutal death, she shook his shoulder. No response. Fingers trembling, she lifted one eyelid, then noticed his torso moving in time with his breathing. He had passed out.

Xanthia dropped her head to her knees, her entire body shaking now, and allowed the tears to come and wash away the appalling anguish she had faced this night.

CHAPTER NINETEEN

"I can heal your wounds, but you must stay still!"

Xanthia's voice penetrated the haze of pain holding him in a vice-like grip. The mere act of focussing his vision hurt, and each time he squinted, the muscles around his eyes ached. From his prone position, Acastus stared at the muted blur of the rocky ceiling. He blinked a few times to clear the watery film covering his eyes. Lifting his head a fraction enabled him to glimpse beyond the cave mouth, where night reigned, limned by the glow of a full moon.

How had he ended up on the ground here in the cave? Straining his memory, he managed to recall the laborious climb up the hill, trying not to lean on Xanthia's supportive shoulder, every step feeling as though the point of a xiphos pierced holes all over his legs, grateful when he finally collapsed on the sandy ground, where he now lay.

He studied the outline of the woman kneeling beside him. Every breath jarred, but his sore ribs failed to dampen his appreciation of the feminine silhouette she presented. He caught the hand trying to restrain him, heard her gasp, felt her attempt to pull free. A grunt of remorse prompted him to ease the pressure of his grip.

"I don't want you to save me. Nothing is more worthy than to die in a battle. Anything else dishonours me."

He swore he heard a growl rumbling in her throat before her rage broke over him, her voice reverberating inside the cave and in his ears, intensifying the pounding in his head.

"How can you be so foolish to talk of dishonour at a time like this!?" she shouted. "Where is the honour in leaving me alone and defenceless in a strange land at the mercy of unknown dangers I may face?"

Even believing he hovered on the threshold of the Underworld, even as outrage shimmered in every cell at her implication he was a fool, he still managed a weak laugh that further inflamed his bruised, possibly cracked, ribs.

"You, defenceless?" A hacking cough abraded his throat. Turning his head to one side he spat out phlegm, wishing he could see if it was stained red, which would show whether he bled internally. "The way of our people is to face death with courage."

"The Spartans are not my people," she hissed with a venom to rival the Hydra. "They abandoned me, left me to die. I've learnt better. I won't allow you to die."

"You are one of us," he grunted, licking to soothe his cracked lips. "Your blood is Spartan. That cannot change."

"Every word you speak saps your strength. Be quiet or I'll hit you over the head and gag you."

Acastus started to laugh and stopped immediately. He lifted a hand to his ribs, pressing down, absorbing the pain until he pushed it to a deep corner of his awareness. He could consider himself fortunate the bones only felt heavily bruised rather than broken. The latter problem meant delays in conveying Xanthia, now ministering to his numerous wounds, home.

And therein lay his blinding dilemma. He had sworn on his honour to her family to return her to them. To fall in battle against a worthy opponent was the honourable way to die. The men who had ambushed them, though mere pirates, were nevertheless Argives, sworn enemies of Sparta. To have bested them all, to have fallen worthily, taking down as many of the enemy as he could, would have earned him glory in the eyes of his people and in the afterlife.

Forcing his shoulders to relax, he ran the events of the attack through his mind. The threat of danger he had been unable to shake, the ambush, the…

"Where is Drakon?" Xanthia's swift indrawn breath, the way she abruptly stopped tending him, told him much before she even spoke.

"I remember now! While you were unconscious, the pirates drank a toast to your servant for leading them to us. Do you think he is still alive?"

"If he is alive, he won't be after I find him." On his return home, no reason existed to stop him extracting that price from Drakon for his betrayal. Under his breath, Acastus called down curses on the treacherous helot who had betrayed them.

Did she plan to extract a similar price for his abduction of her. He studied her bent head while she carefully dabbed a cold salve into the many lacerations covering his arms and face. In the hushed darkness of the cave, the touch of her soft fingers on his skin tripped his pulse. He frowned, intrigued, annoyed and questioned whether it was the heat weaving tendrils through his body because of her, or worse, the first stirrings of fever?

If Xanthia, she had no business affecting him in this way. *Focus on your mission.* He clenched his jaw, clamped down on his rebellious thoughts, and went on the attack.

"What is in the salve," he demanded. "You say it heals, but how can I believe you?"

"I told you to save your strength. Are all Spartan men this pig-headed?" She dabbed the salve less gently this time. "I blended a paste containing herbs which clean wounds and speed their healing. Fortunately, you found a place to spend the night with fresh running water."

"Learning to live off the land and seek shelter is a skill all young Spartan boys learn." He certainly would never forget the first time he had been cast out of the barracks and forced to survive using only his wits. As her words sank in, he stiffened. "Ah, the pouch you refused me the knowledge of its contents. The pouch full of herbs which heal and kill. Should I worry you might use the wrong ones?" He had witnessed what she was capable of and vowed never again to underestimate her resourcefulness.

She rocked back on her heels, and Acastus lifted one brow, the movement further pulling apart the split skin. He wiped away a trickle of blood, even this minor effort taxing his strength.

"Did the gods addle your brain while the Argives pummelled your body. Why would I poison you now when I need you more than ever?"

Her face might be shadowed, but he did not have to see her expression to hear the light panic in her voice. Was she tacitly admitting he affected her in the same way she affected him? "You need me? That is interesting to know."

"You know what I mean," she muttered. "Tell me how to start a fire? It'll get cold in here; you need to keep warm."

"And have the smoke give our position away," he scoffed. "No, the cloaks of the bandits plus our own are enough." He had maintained enough presence of mind after regaining consciousness to grab the cloaks. The bodies would be disposed of in the morning.

"If you become feverish you must sweat to break the fever," she insisted.

Acastus inhaled sharply. What would it be like having her lie pressed to him, his body absorbing her heat? His groin clenched, reminding him how much time had passed since he had last held a woman in his arms. She was a woman, a woman moreover, considered ready for marriage in Sparta.

He harboured no illusions about the weight of expectations he faced to marry once this mission was completed. His father would expect it, and he recalled Diokles's hint, and his evasive answer, before he left. A different fate awaited Xanthia – she needed time with her family and time to familiarise herself with her new life.

The next words out of his mouth confirmed he had taken leave of his senses like she had accused him of earlier. "The best way is to lie close together, naked. That shouldn't bother you given your past."

She hissed like an angry cat. "My past what?"

"Don't pretend to not understand." He waved ruefully towards his half-erect manhood, barely covered by the short, ripped tunic he still wore. "Despite what you'd feel lying next to me, I lack the strength to ravish you, no matter how much my body insists. No fire will be lit until the morning."

"What about your past?" she challenged hotly. "You dare to throw what you think is my…*depraved*…past in my face and expect me to believe you've not taken women in passion. Then you show surprise at my low opinion of men."

Acastus heard the fury in her voice. She had every right to be furious. He shifted to ease the strain of lying unbalanced on one hip, sending excruciating spasms down his leg. It did not sit well with him to direct verbal attacks toward her. He pushed aside the riddle of how she managed to scramble his thoughts so completely without any effort on her part.

"Is that why you chose Kallios as a lover? Because he was weak and easy to control."

"I chose him because—"

Maybe it was his own renewed pain that enabled him to detect the sudden hitch in her voice, the abrupt termination of whatever she planned to berate him with, and the barely audible sob…

"You weep for your dove." A warrior was not trained to feel remorse, but in this case he felt it for her. "I'm sorry."

Though she remained silent, he heard muffled sobs which cut him like her dove had been cut – he shot upright and clutched his ribs, unable to prevent a sharp groan. "Where are my weapons?"

"Beside you," she sniffed, "the Argive's weapons I wrapped in one of their cloaks and carried them deep into the cave."

"The next time I march to battle I'll take you along." He jested, although boundless admiration filled him for her presence of mind. "You will fit effortlessly into your new life. The qualities of a true Spartan woman are in you already."

"So you say," she countered in a sad voice. "I wasn't raised in your ways. I've known freedom much more than most. The odd customs you've mentioned," she hesitated, "I don't know whether I would ever accept them."

"Time makes anything possible. You'll learn to use weapons to defend yourself in the army's absence. I'm surprised you didn't kill me. You had the chance."

She hmphed audibly. "I haven't given up the idea, although now is not the time."

"You placed us in danger trying to attract the attention of the wrong people. Drakon's betrayal ensured the ambush. Why didn't you go with the pirates?"

Acastus glanced towards the cave mouth where enough moonlight now filtered inside for him to see her bite her bottom lip. He would have given anything to know what thoughts filled her head in that moment.

"When I saw they were prepared to drag out your death, it sickened me. The same way it sickened me thinking I would have to give myself to all of them. Whatever you think of me or my past, I never descended to those depraved depths."

He narrowed his eyes, trying to read her features in the dim light. "Do you enjoy ensnaring men for revenge?"

She turned her face away. Mind racing, Acastus sifted through everything she had said, trying to comprehend why Xanthia nursed a contemptuous loathing of men in general. He stretched to ease his cramped back, succeeding in sending more shards of pain to riddle his chest and legs.

Silence sat heavily between them. He lifted the hand nearest to her, pushing aside the dark mane of hair hiding her face. Her cautious drawing back surprised him, but he released her hair immediately.

"I have to get more water," she mumbled, rising to her feet. "I'll return soon."

"No, you won't. Wild animals are out hunting. None of us will die of thirst before the morning."

"Maybe you won't, but I need water, so do the donkeys."

"The donkeys will survive. In many ways you've lived a sheltered life. You can endure more than you think."

He knew instinctively she could. She had already proven her courage against the Argives while he had called on Ares to grant him strength to saw through his bonds. Fury had consumed him seeing the last pirate attempting to hurt her, a fury that had dulled the sting of the rope flaying his skin.

Yet, was his assumption that the Argive would have forced himself on her, then taken revenge by killing her, correct? Her heritage was Spartan. She would have fought to the end, and if the gods willed, she would have succeeded in finishing off her attacker.

"Very well. If fever overcomes you, blame yourself, not me, if you die. Leave me alone here to be eaten by wild animals. I'll curse your soul so that Hades sentences you to Tartarus."

Acastus laughed loud and long at her petulant tone, the action sending more pain burning like a wildfire to every nerve point. "I'll probably end up in Tartarus atoning for much more than you know. Your curse will barely make a difference."

Maybe one day he could reveal to her the reasons why he believed this.

He listened to the sounds of a cloak being spread over the ground indicating she was preparing to sleep. The image of Xanthia nestled by his side summoned a gut punch of desire. He clamped down on his unruly thoughts to assess their current position, noticing the moon glowing less brightly than earlier. Clouds had drifted in, the certainty coming from knowledge gained after years of campaigns. Good, if it rained the likelihood of discovery diminished. Tomorrow, he would have recovered enough strength to not fear attacks from humans or animals. His left hand groped in the darkness, closing firmly around the xiphos.

To his right, he heard her breathing slow and then become light. He felt compelled to reassure her she was safe while he remained her protector but was forced to admit that mere words would never convince her. Acastus closed his eyes. "Sleep well."

A huff of breath was his answer. He sighed and petitioned Hypnos for restful, healing sleep.

CHAPTER TWENTY

She fought the rhythms of her own body to stay in the land of dreams, but to no avail. Only half-awake, Xanthia groaned and rubbed eyes dry and tired from a broken sleep. Joyous birdsong penetrated the fog in her brain, mocking her with remembrances of Calliope. A renewed wave of grief brought awareness of her dry mouth, which convinced her it was indeed morning. She stretched to ease stiff back muscles, the cloak she had slept on having provided little barrier to the unyielding ground.

Noticing the ache in her shoulders had eased a little, she stretched out once more, undulating her back to reach into each individual pain point. She rolled onto her side and collided with a solid form. Her eyes snapped open.

Fully awake now, Xanthia attempted to launch herself upright, except her momentum was abruptly stopped by the heavy arm draping over her waist. Face pressed to Acastus's skin, absorbing the heat of his body as he lay beside her, it was too late to wish she had stayed still and kept her eyes shut, since all they could focus on was a broad chest smattered with dark hair camouflaging numerous scars of battle. The softening of her body, the subtle, instinctive movement closer to him, brought a heat to her cheeks she had no business feeling.

"What? Let go—" she spluttered, squirming when the arm around her waist tightened.

"Stop moving."

The words vibrated through her. No wonder. Every part of her was in contact with Acastus, her breasts crushed against his chest, her pelvis…

Involuntary and unwelcome desire ran a sensuous course through her veins. *No!* her mind screamed. No man commanded her desire, and only she possessed the power to command theirs.

"Let me go, Acastus, or I'll make you sorry you were ever born."

"Even if you killed me right now, I wouldn't be sorry. I'd cross into the realms of the dead taking the memory of holding you like this."

How long had she slept curled up in his arms?

As soon as he loosened his hold, Xanthia wriggled away. The morning sunlight streaming in through the cave mouth enabled her to clearly see his face. A paleness lingered beneath the bronze skin, but the pinched look around his eyes from last night was absent.

Observing him with a practiced eye, she noted the livid bruises standing out on his face and torso. Thanks to her herbs, the open wounds had lost their redness and the swelling along their torn edges had subsided. Watching the rhythmic rise and fall of his chest, she heard no rattle in the breaths he took and slumped in tired relief.

"Are you Spartans human? After the beating you endured, I can't believe you aren't in greater agony today." She sat up, pulling her tunic down where it had ridden up over her legs, discomfited by the gleam in his eyes as he followed her movements. He was starting to worry her. A lot. No man had ever made her tremble the way Acastus did.

"Very human. We bleed the same as other men."

Her skin prickled, followed by tiny bumps rising all over her arms. A portent, perhaps? But of what? She refused to countenance the idea it had anything to do with the enigmatic half-smile lending his ruggedly good-looking features more potency. Xanthia swallowed over the knot of nerves in her throat and rose to stand on shaky legs. "Stay here and rest. I'll bring you fresh water."

Not waiting to see whether he would order her to remain with him, she hurried to untie the two donkeys. Leading them down the slope to the stream below the hill, she gave fervent thanks to Aphrodite for their placid natures. Although they rarely brayed, the air resounded with their relieved calls. She half-ran to keep pace with them as they, scenting water, pulled her to the bank and lowered their heads for a long drink.

Which gave her time to think of Acastus.

She stared across the small valley, not really taking anything in and shifted her feet uneasily.

He frightened her.

Not his strength, but the unwanted emotions he evoked. A sudden, deep yearning under her heart confirmed it. She had made a pact during the bleakest point in her young life never to allow any man to breach the impenetrable wall guarding her heart. For a long time she had continually reminded herself that men had abandoned her to her death. Grown to maturity, the reminder happened less often, but the decision whether she left them, once their usefulness was over, still rested with her alone.

A tug on one of the ropes she held brought her back to the present. While she had been troubled by where her thoughts were leading her, both donkeys had begun to crop the long, lush grass that covered the banks. A good look around revealed a plentiful supply of large, fallen branches providing the means to tether them while she refreshed herself. She tied the ropes around one sturdy branch. This way she could keep an eye on them while leaving them free to graze to their hearts content.

The stickiness of her skin begged to be washed and quickly if she was intent on taking water up to Acastus. Her mouth twisted as she recalled events of the previous night. She had come close to being violated and dying, thanks to some misguided belief she could fight a pirate. Well, she could partially lay the blame on Acastus who had sown the seeds in her mind that she was a woman of Sparta. She had yet to learn what that entailed.

Even if you are one by birth, you're untrained.

Xanthia let out a breath. She would ask Acastus to teach her to use weapons once he recovered. Would he trust her though? A grim chuckle gave her the answer – he would be wise not to trust her.

But more practical and immediate matters needed taking care of. Kneeling on the bank, she dipped a hand into the rapidly flowing water. Gritting her teeth, she argued with herself that no matter how cold it was, she desperately needed to bathe. Her gaze darted nervously in all directions. The morning was quiet, an occasional bird call breaking the silence. She watched both donkeys for a long time, and their contented demeanour emboldened her. Animals were so much better at sensing threats. She had seen it often enough with Euphrasia's sheep.

Wading into the stream, she found the deepest part although the water only came up to her knees. She washed her face first, splashing water over her puffy eyes, which still burned from the tears she had shed for Calliope during the long night. Wiping them dry with the back of her hand, she checked again to reassure herself that nothing, human or animal, lurked nearby. Satisfied, she gingerly knelt in the water, uncaring of smooth pebbles digging into her knees, and pushed her chiton off her shoulders.

Taking a deep breath, she threw a couple of handfuls of water over the back of her neck. Taught this trick on Melos to cool her body temperature quickly, still, her teeth chattered while she washed herself from the waist up as best she could.

"Again, I find you looking like Aphrodite rising from the water."

Xanthia screamed, lost her balance, and sat down hard on her rump, not even registering the cold. Eyes popping at the apparition standing on the bank, she slammed both of her fists into the water. "What are you doing here? I told you to stay in the cave!"

"The bodies had to be moved to keep scavengers away, not to mention betraying our presence."

Her mouth opened but no sound came out. How, by all the gods, did he have the strength to stand, let alone walk? His legs still bore bruises, where the Argives had taken turns to kick him. No injuries could heal that fast, yet he had summoned the strength to drag the bodies of five men away.

She gave an imperceptible shake of her head. "Were you fathered by a god, Acastus? Only a demigod would have the power to complete such a feat."

"I have to keep us safe."

What sort of people was she being returned to? The brevity, yet total certainty, of his manner of speaking disconcerted and frustrated her in equal measure. She found it almost impossible to discern his thoughts. Perhaps she would learn to speak with the same brevity if she chose to stay in Sparta.

Their eyes met. Her shivering ceased, replaced by a warm river curling around and through every vein and artery. She possessed no power to stop the tide spreading, even though she sat in a cold mountain stream. How could she, given the gleam in his eyes devouring her bare skin? Had Zeus thrown a thunderbolt in their midst less tension would have crackled between them.

Hastily, she gulped in air, then stopped when his gaze moved over her curves, rising and falling in time with her frantic breathing. The memory of Acastus pulling her chiton up to cover her on Melos taunted her composure. She grabbed both fibulas, dragging them onto her shoulders, teeth clenched together to ignore the slide of damp material over the now sensitive peaks. The half-smile playing around his mouth had her glancing down and silently groaning when she realised the damp chiton clung to every part of her and was almost translucent. The plunging sensation in her belly served to fuel her anger; anger directed toward her traitorous body's arousal, and toward Acastus for his ability to ignite her desires.

Attack was her best defence. Petty though it be, she was past caring.

"How much has that effort further weakened you? We may have to stay here for days." She stood up, wringing out the bottom of the tunic. Holding it clear of the water, she stomped to the bank, almost losing her footing on the stream bed before emerging to stand toe-to-toe with him. "What will we do for food? You dragged me away to starve to death. You—"

Her words trailed away when he clasped her shoulders and began to rub warmth into them, the action more soothing than sensual.

"Stop. I can hunt. There are dried figs and some honey still in the packs."

Xanthia twisted out of his hold. His large, capable hands felt too warm on her skin, providing a powerful distraction from her purpose. "Why can't you take me home? I've come close to losing my life twice since I left Melos, Calliope has been killed." She choked over the emotion which rose from her chest to clog her throat. "Why must I further risk my life to go to Sparta?"

"I *am* taking you home." Acastus threw his arms out wide. "Every step is a step closer to Sparta and safety."

Ignoring the exasperation in his tone, she planted her hands on her hips. "One day I'll find out the reason you insisted on placing my life in danger."

"And one day you'll tell me why a dove was so important to you."

He would wait until his dying day for the reason, and even then she would not reveal her secret. She made to move past him, but he caught her arm. Heat blazed across that part of her skin where his hand rested. Her gaze flew to his face, meeting dark eyes smouldering with…desire, lust? She stilled as an idea sprung into her mind with the speed of an arrow loosened from Eros's bow. Whatever her expression revealed must have given her away because ardour receded from his eyes, replaced by an intense, narrow-eyed study of her face. "Go back to the cave," he said slowly, releasing her arm and stepping away. "I'll bring something to eat."

Xanthia tossed her head and walked away. Better to not argue lest he see the stab of pain that had gone through her heart at the mention of her dove. If they remained here for a few more days, it would give her time to look for any opportunity to carry out her plan.

Regardless of the consequences.

CHAPTER TWENTY-ONE

Acastus lifted his face to the cloudless morning sky, grateful for the light breeze which cooled his skin, even as it battled to disperse the increasing warmth in the air. Sitting in the same place he had come across Xanthia two days ago, he swung his legs into the quick-flowing water, stretching them out until they were immersed up to his knees. He kept a close eye on the valley, while at the same time finding relief in the water's therapeutic embrace working its magic over his tight calf muscles and tendons.

He raked his fingers through his hair and blew out a sigh. Xanthia had driven him to his limits over the last two days, arguing unceasingly that he rest, followed by complaints of her 'abduction'. Though Sisyphus had incurred the wrath of Zeus, Acastus felt a strange kinship with the disgraced king. The unending twists and turns of Xanthia's demands frustrated him with his very own boulder.

To make matters worse, the ever-present attraction simmering between them only complicated their arguments, to the point where he simply wanted to tumble her to the ground and silence her mouth with his.

She desired him. The fire in her eyes dampened the provocation of her words. In turn, she drew out emotions he refused to acknowledge, much less consider, or act on, because of the debt he owed her. A debt that might prove impossible to repay, not even by marrying her, despite his body insisting he was a fool.

He cast a rueful glance at his manhood, which inconveniently kept reminding him of its presence ever since he had met Xanthia. He rubbed his eyes to dispel the vivid images crowding his mind, the long braid hanging from his scalp brushing across his bare back. Time to leave. They had lingered here long enough. Maybe a lesser man might require more time to rest but not him.

There were good reasons why Spartan boys were broken during their training, their bodies toughened, remade into the warriors opposing forces at times refused to engage. They bled, endured pain, learned to ignore it, welcome it even. Such a harsh, often brutal approach, enabled them to continue a fight, despite their injuries, and recover quicker afterwards. The beating he had received at the hands of the Argives was nothing compared to what he had previously experienced, both in battles and within the agoge environment. He flexed his muscles, muscles strong enough to resume their trek, enabling him to protect Xanthia.

The thought of staying in the cave another night was intolerable, so their speedy return to Sparta governed his plans. Pulling his legs out of the water Acastus braced his hands on the grassy bank, ready to leap to his feet.

A soft footfall was the only warning. His hand shot out to grab his kopis…

Vision blinded by a shaft of sunlight flashing on burnished iron, he ducked but was too late to avoid the weapon pressed into his throat.

Heartbeat accelerating, Acastus did not risk turning his head to identify his assailant. He knew who it was by her unique, subliminal scent. Her knees were jammed into his lower back, her other hand pulling his braid down without mercy, each individual root in his scalp screaming in protest.

Teeth bared in a feral grin, anticipation burning in his veins, Acastus went on the attack. "Does your goddess make you invisible that you're able to surprise a warrior?"

The low, sultry laugh failed to fool him.

"No," Xanthia purred in his ear. "I waited, patiently, for just such a moment ever since you abducted me."

The next tug of his braid forced his face up till only the blue of the sky filled his vision, leaving his throat exposed further. He had faced worse situations fighting enemies, but she was armed with his weapon, and he had nothing but his cunning and superior strength. Trained or not, she could inflict damage he might not recover from.

"I know any number of ways to disarm you."

Her warm breath brushed a laugh over his ear. "I hold the power, Acastus."

"Perhaps you need convincing."

Always decisive, he hesitated for perhaps the first time in his life. It was a matter of urgency that he disarm her, however his ability to think did the unthinkable – it retreated. Her breasts pressed into his back, their hard tips hardening him to the point of agony. The sweetness of her breath, steady now, warmed his face. How long would it take to have her panting beneath him, either through battling him for possession of the weapon or, battling him in a much more intimate tussle.

"Give me the kopis, Xanthia, before either of us is hurt." Acastus leaned back, attempting to gain some leverage. All he received was a harder yank of his braid. He winced, and for a brief, irreverent moment wondered whether any hair would remain on his scalp.

"Oh, no," she whispered.

The sharp edge of his weapon moved from his throat, down his torso, then pressed menacingly against his vital parts. He froze in place, fingertips digging painfully into the grassy bank.

"What are you doing?" The roughness of his voice conveyed panic, the likes of which he had never experienced in his life. If she unmanned him, the shame would leave no option except to kill her, then kill himself. The breath whistled between his teeth as the pressure increased against his burgeoning lower body. Pitiful that fear drove him to find the situation arousing.

"Making certain you listen to me. I want to know the real reason it is suddenly so important I return to Sparta. Deny me this knowledge and you lose the ability to ever father a child." She pressed the kopis harder into his flesh.

"Don't threaten me," he growled. "If you mean to kill me do so, but injure me this way and I will kill us both."

"How like a Spartan," she scoffed. "You still can't understand there are far worse things in life than dying. I was as one dead. Whatever life I choose to live is my choice alone. Neither you nor anyone else will take that decision from me. If I refuse to live in Sparta, I want your oath, now, that you will take me back to Melos, since it was you who forced me to leave there."

Acastus opened his mouth, then shut it, his mind working furiously. The threat of castration had certainly cleared his ability to think. She had time enough to cut his throat or wound him severely, yet she hesitated. If he revealed the reasons behind his mission, there would be no hesitation on her part.

His pulse raced as he assessed their relative positions. Her right arm imprisoned his in a way that made any sudden move dangerous if he startled her. His left arm remained free. Recognising his awkward position, he still remained confident he possessed the skill to knock her hand away from his vitals and avoid injuring either of them.

Very slowly, he turned his head to the right. Xanthia's breath feathered across his mouth. A finger-width separated their faces. He could see every pore of her smooth skin, read the determination in the depths of her dark eyes. Her lips, those full, honeyed lips whose sweetness he had tasted already, parted. Something flickered across her expression. He allowed himself a small smile, laughing silently when her gaze narrowed. The subtle hesitation he felt in her body convinced him her intention had begun to waver.

Passion flared to weave its tendrils around them, embracing them in a moment of shared emotions. Acastus pushed back against this weakness even as he conceded that in any other circumstance, he would have leaned in, taking his fill of sweetness from her delectable mouth. Triumph swelled in his chest and not just because he could easily distract her now, but first, he needed to allay her suspicions.

"You know the reason. You are Spartan by birth and blood, belonging to our people and your family who are eager to embrace you." His voice was low and gravelly from the effort of holding himself in check, when her tongue darted out as though tasting his breath.

"Why should I believe you?"

"I speak truth." Desire flared, hot as Hephaestus's forge, as her eyes darkened to the colour of the blackest night. Yes, there, the softening of her body. So subtle, but to his warrior-honed senses, an easily discernible change. His blood surged to a battle tempo, his muscles bunched…

Now.

His left hand shot out to seize the wrist of the hand holding his weapon. Surprised by the strength of her resistance, he still managed to push her right arm away from his vulnerable parts. In the same movement, he twisted to the right, giving himself more leverage, eyes watering from the pain in his scalp when she refused to let go of his braid.

Even though his ears bore the assault of her voluble curses, he was still loathe to use force but her tenacious resistance left him little choice if he was going to save them both. Acastus dug his right elbow hard into her midriff, his conscience smiting him when she gasped in his ear. He had to do this quickly to avoid injuring her.

Bracing his feet, he pushed, his greater weight sending her tumbling backwards. His own momentum flung him in the same direction until, with a quick, well-practiced pivot, he pinned her beneath him. "Let go of the kopis."

"No." The denial rushed out breathy and desperate.

"My weight will crush you. Let go. Now."

"Crush me then. I'll die here and your mission will fail."

It was a direct challenge and a strike at his honour, one he would not ignore. "It won't fail. Let go."

The pull on his braid lacked the power from before given her prone position. The time for games was over. Grasping a hank of Xanthia's hair he pulled without mercy. Her insult to his honour dissipated when he saw her eyes widen in shock, the sight of her bared teeth summoning an approving smile.

"You uncivilised brute!"

He had learned over their time together that she never looked more beautiful than when she spat venom at him in the form of words. "You possess spirit enough for twenty women. It won't help you. Let go of the kopis, or you'll regret the methods I'll use to make you."

He stilled when her eyelids drooped, tensing when she gifted him a smile that carried blatant provocation. She stretched invitingly beneath him, her softness grazing his aching length, stealing his breath away.

"How will you make me, Acastus?" she murmured in a low, husky voice. "By ravishing me? The thought holds no terrors. I am no sweet virgin fearful of a man."

"You taunted me on Melos that Spartan men had no idea how to pleasure a woman. Your lesson in how wrong you are begins now."

Ducking his head he fastened his mouth around one peaking tip and bit gently through the soft fabric. Rewarded with an almost inaudible moan, he suckled, relishing every gasp, every arch and twist of her body. From the corner of his eye, he saw her release her death grip on his weapon. Not giving her time to change her mind, he tossed the kopis out of reach.

Acastus took a moment to savour the woman beneath him. Her eyes were slitted, her lips full and parted, her chest heaving in time with his. Desire burned, coming to rest in the pit of his belly. He pushed away all reminders of whose sister she was and what he had done. All he wanted was to bury his guilt in the softness between the thighs she parted languidly for him.

"From the first day I saw you," he grimaced at the sound of his voice, roughened by passion held in check, "I watched and desired, craved to do this."

Bracing himself on his elbows, he hooked a finger under the shoulder brooch of her chiton. He drew the fabric down leisurely, letting the knuckle caress her skin, gratified by every soft whimper that escaped her lips. With a grunt of pleasure his fingertips traced the soft skin of her breast, a thumb rubbing over the rosy crown that budded beneath his ministrations. Almost desperately, he pushed the other side of her chiton out of the way, burning to feel those twin buds against his bare chest, rocking himself against her pelvis while she bucked like an unbroken filly. Pleasure shuddered through him at the way her throat muscles contracted as he bent his head to fasten his mouth to the wildly beating pulse below her jaw.

"Acastus!"

Her plea goaded him to kiss his way down the golden skin of her neck, relishing the rake of her nails across his broken skin, a discomfort he welcomed because it was Xanthia. Her breathy demands, urging him on, showed him clearly that she could no more deny this wild desire gripping them than he could. Wrapped in her scent, in how she felt pressed to him, he dropped his head until their lips almost touched.

"Now you will find out we Spartans aren't the brutes you think we are," he stated thickly, smiling when she finally released his braid to jam her hands into his hair.

"Show me."

A shuddering growl was wrenched from him at the promise of plunging into the warm moistness already dampening his thigh. Reaching deep for control, determined to make the experience pleasurable for both of them, he positioned himself…

Snap.

With a speed to make Hermes proud, Acastus rolled off Xanthia, grabbed the discarded kopis, and leapt to his feet, weapon held at the ready.

They were alone. No enemy in sight.

Snap.

He spun in the direction of the noise, raising his hand in readiness to hack whatever threat lurked. Then he saw the threat – one of the donkeys meandered towards them, searching out lusher grass. It stamped a hind foot, snapping one of the numerous twigs littering the ground.

Taking a deep breath, he scanned the area but saw nothing. After a few moments he relaxed his tense shoulders, eventually turning his gaze back to Xanthia. He had relinquished focus, allowed himself to be lost in a haze of lust. A grimace warped his mouth, and he swore to himself there would be no recurrence.

A difficult oath to keep given the stupefaction covering her face as she sat up and began to dress herself. The image of the day on the beach on Melos flooded his mind. He had clothed her there to prove his power over her. Yet, it seemed she possessed the power to grind his self-control to dust.

There was no enemy to fight and release the adrenaline flooding his body. Furious at himself, disgusted by his weakness, he demanded, "Would you have given yourself to the Argives in the same way?" and immediately regretted the accusation, when she impaled him with a livid stare.

"You dare, after everything that happened, you dare!"

Her low voice was filled with menace. He had never lost control, either with a woman or on the battlefield. Yet one look from Xanthia ignited a conflagration that reduced his prized discipline into ashes. Integrity was the one thing he had left, and it was demanding he apologise for his intemperate words.

"Perhaps I was wrong to accuse you."

"Perhaps! You implied I give myself to anyone for the asking."

"Deny you were prepared at the time to use whatever means to escape."

"I don't need to deny anything. Whatever you may think of me, I'd never debase myself like that."

Acastus straightened, amused despite his dressing down at her hands, when she averted her eyes from his nakedness and gaped at the delicate blush blooming in her cheeks. "I'd never have believed you capable of such discomfort."

She turned her head away, and he pulled his chiton off the branch where he had hung it to dry, slipping it over his head. He kept a close eye on her as she stood almost hesitantly while he fought a battle with himself as to whether she would welcome his comfort. How was he going to endure more time with her? Then he noticed her biting her lip, a far-off look in her eyes. "What is it?"

"Will my family judge me the same as you just did?" She turned to look at him. "Perhaps they might only see a worshipper of Aphrodite and not what blood runs through my veins."

"Your fears are unnecessary." Discomfited, he took a step back. He had insisted on this mission so both she and her father could return to their rightful home. If he told Xanthia her father's return depended on hers, she would only notch up another black mark against them all.

"That is no answer, Acastus."

"It is answer enough," he muttered and turned away, the angry hiss of her breath beating at him. He watched her stomp to the cave, disapproval emanating off her rigidly held body. He followed more slowly, mind working furiously. One wrong word would ensure she kept up a tirade all the way to Sparta.

Striding inside the cave, he studied Xanthia's bent head. Acastus shrugged, giving her credit for the ability to ignore him while he gathered the remains of their supplies. Strapping both kopis and xiphos around his waist, he arranged his cloak so they remained out of sight of anyone who might come across them. "I'll fill the water skins, then we'll go."

Once his mission was completed she would have her answers. And, once she did, there were many, himself especially, who would need shielding from her wrath.

CHAPTER TWENTY-TWO

Xanthia scooped her heavy mane of hair off her hot neck, allowing the mild breeze a chance to dry the sweat pooling on the nape. A quick glance at the sun's position, and she guessed it was around the middle of the day and the loud complaint from her stomach confirmed the hunch.

A strong desire to growl at the man walking in front of her was reluctantly quelled. He never seemed to tire and had only gotten stronger as their trek progressed. And, if she were honest, her own strength had provided a constant source of wonderment. The walk around the lower slopes of Parnassus had taken a toll on her the first week. Now, the spring in her step told her she had built up the stamina to climb even mountains, if the need arose.

She might just have to, given the looming range to her left, although she was not sure if the river forming a barrier between them and the range needed to be crossed. It was the largest water course they had come across. Xanthia licked dry lips as her stomach protested once again. "Where are we? Can we stop to eat?"

She halted in her tracks when Acastus did the same, waiting expectantly for his answer as he turned to face her. Taken aback by the smile on his face, and the way he appeared to have gained height and stature, a sudden premonition that they had actually arrived in Spartan territory sent a small chill through her.

"In the Eurotas Valley. That is the river." He stabbed a forefinger toward the flowing water, then swept his hand upward. "And that's the mountain range of Taygetos."

Seized by a sense of impending doom, she clenched her hands and stared at her nemesis. "So that's where I was abandoned to die?" Focussed on the mountain range, she missed seeing Acastus's lips and face turn pale.

"No. The main peak is located above Sparta itself. There is a place…"

"Where babies like me are taken to die," she lashed out when he hesitated, "at the command of some man who—"

"Your parents wanted you. What happened wasn't their fault."

His harsh interjection startled Xanthia into taking a step away from him. "How do you know this?"

His face closed against her. "Just know that your father will tell you everything when you finally meet."

She ran a hand over her face, grimacing at the moisture and grit coming off it onto her hand. "What if we never meet? I want to know, and you didn't answer me."

"You want to eat. We'll stop here. There is a place further upstream where we can ford across later."

If only she held something heavy to aim at his head. Throwing her hands up in the air, Xanthia stomped over to the tree where Acastus had taken the donkeys. It afforded relief from the noon-day sun and the grass underneath was cool as it brushed her sandalled feet.

"I'm going to wash my face and refill the waterskins."

She grabbed one of the skins before he could utter an objection and made her way to the riverbank. Staring into the water, one thought repeated in her head – *I'm in Sparta.*

Keeping her eyes averted from the mountain range, Xanthia filled the skin and splashed cool water over her hot face. Sitting back on her heels, she sighed and wondered what the gods had ordained for her. In the beginning she had prayed to Aphrodite to intervene and spirit her home to Melos. When nothing had happened to change her plight, she had grudgingly come to the realisation that the goddess meant for her to be here, although it did not mean she had to cheer about her present situation.

She ran damp fingers through her hair, trying to cool her scalp. Jumping to her feet, she trailed her way back to where she could see Acastus securing the saddle bags, having already arranged some of their remaining dried figs and olives on a cloak. How long had it been since she had eaten any fresh bread? Her mouth watered simply thinking of the taste.

"Be glad you have anything left to eat. In a few days we reach Amyklai."

She stopped in her tracks. "How did you know what I was thinking?"

"Your mouth twisted."

Xanthia planted her arms akimbo. "Is that it? '*My mouth twisted*'. Is this the way I can expect my husband to talk to me?"

Where had those words come from? She blinked but not before she noticed the slight jerk of Acastus's body. So, she had struck a nerve. Closing the gap, she sank to the grass, tucked her legs to one side and pressed home her advantage.

"Since you're not answering me, I'll believe the answer is yes. I'm glad you decided to teach me how to wield a xiphos over the last few days." She leaned over for a fig and popped it in her mouth.

She almost choked on swallowing it when Acastus sat opposite her, the bulge of lean muscle momentarily wiping her mind clean. Were all Spartan men built like this? She poured a measure of water into a kylix and drank a large mouthful to cool the heat consuming her.

"I have skill in reading people, and your feelings show clearly on your face. What else do you want me to say?"

Xanthia cocked her head. "Even on Melos I heard claims that Athenians are great orators. Obviously, Spartans have not learned that skill if you are any example."

"We speak what is necessary and no more. Why speak when actions are enough? I taught you the use of a xiphos to be able to defend yourself. A xiphos speaks more clearly to any attacker than words do."

"Aren't you afraid I'll kill you?"

The memory of holding the kopis to his throat, and what had happened afterward, hung like a golden orb of fire between them. The burnished glint in his dark eyes ignited the embers of an arousal which had proven unquenchable, ever since he had turned her world on its head.

"No."

She dropped her gaze to the food. The uncompromising reply carried absolute belief she would not be foolish enough to try. "Of course you don't. I still need you alive to ensure I don't starve until we reach wherever we're going." She selected an olive and chewed thoughtfully. "Are there other fighting skills I need to learn, and what other surprises can I expect?"

More than mere curiosity drove her to ask these questions. She wanted to be prepared to face whatever she had to in this land. She also wanted to know what, if any, of those skills would help her leave, if she chose to, on her own terms this time, and be able to survive.

"In our laws handed down from Lycurgus—"

"Who is he?"

"Our lawgiver who laid the foundation for Spartan society. These laws require the sons and daughters of citizens to be trained in singing, dancing and music, reading, and writing. And more."

Her mouth dropped open and shut quickly as a fly hovered closer, drawn by the scent of food. Never had she believed to be granted such a thorough education. She had learned from observing others, could read a little, but this was beyond her experience. Even less expected was the fascination she found in watching a man chewing his food. Mesmerised by the movement of his lips, she remained oblivious to her tongue darting out to moisten her own. "All this! I thought…"

"…that we were heathens and brutes." Acastus reclined back on both elbows. "You'll soon see for yourself the value we place on our women."

Xanthia failed to tear her gaze away from the play of shadowed light over his strong features. His words struck deep – she had to remain vigilant and guard against any softening toward the land of her birth.

"Well, you didn't give me any reason to think otherwise back on Melos. Did my half-sister go through all this?" She met his hard look with a toss of her head.

"She did, although it was easier for her," he conceded. "Callisto was raised being taught basic skills in defence, how to ride, swim, and wrestle. She will guide you for as long as you need her."

She sat up straighter, sudden hope making her chest light. Ride? Loathe to betray too much interest, she wondered how a woman rode in a chiton. "Wrestle. The same as I watched you wrestle back at the port on Melos. Women do this in Sparta?"

Acastus shook his head. "What you saw was a pankration match. Wrestling is a different discipline and one our young girls learn early."

An idea burst into her head like a shaft of sunlight bursting through morning fog. Her pulse skittered, then continued to beat thick and heavy as she envisaged the idea. Xanthia hesitated, worrying her bottom lip while she questioned her motivations.

Getting her hands on Acastus would assuage the fire in her belly, which had built up over their time together. She let herself remember how sensitised her skin had been after his large, capable hands had caressed her curves. Shifting to ease a passion-charged ache in her pelvis, she deliberated how making love with Acastus could be used to benefit her later. One look at the play of muscles in his arms and legs, as he moved into a different position on the ground, and her body shouted she was being a fool for even hesitating.

"Will you teach me how to wrestle? Right now."

"No."

CHAPTER TWENTY-THREE

The denial burst from between his lips before he even had time to form a coherent thought. Jaw tense, the warrior in Acastus punched down the part of himself insisting he take the opportunity being offered.

"Why not? You just said that I'm to learn all these skills, so why can't I start now?"

He closed his eyes and petitioned the gods to grant him patience. "Time enough after you reach Diokles's house."

"But what if someone attacks us and I can't use your weapon?"

The thought briefly crossed his mind whether banging his head against a tree would help but he settled for grinding his teeth. "You will learn to fight with other women. You don't have the strength to wrestle me or any other Spartan male."

He held his hand up when she went to complain further. She was watching him like a hawk surveying potential prey. What thoughts flitted behind those dark eyes? She was an intriguing mix of vulnerability and confident strength. Right now, the latter quality was in full flight and twisting his stomach in knots.

"I told you we only have a few more days to walk before we reach Amyklai, our first village," he said, answering her puzzled look, "and be able to get fresh food. Rest for a while, then we walk until nightfall…what are you doing?"

He scratched his head as he attempted to reason why she had ignored him and risen to her feet. His bafflement grew as she started rummaging in one of the large bags until, with a triumphant flourish, she pulled out one of his short chitons.

"Mine. Your chitons are in your bag." Every sense went on alert, when she favoured him with a slow, beguiling smile.

"I know it's yours, but mine are too long. I've at least watched the men on Melos wrestle, and they always wear short ones." Her smile deepened. "Or nothing."

Acastus jammed his tongue into the side of his cheek to stop the harsh words and stem the tide of envy consuming him. "You won't like the consequences if you keep goading me this way."

The seductive look she tossed over her shoulder before she stepped behind a wide tree trunk to change, he returned with a disapproving glare while cursing his vivid imagination which tormented him with images of wrestling a near-naked Xanthia. A swift check of their immediate vicinity revealed they were alone, when he had been hoping some shepherds at least were nearby. Now, his mind worked furiously to find a way to deny her stubbornness. Action was always his best recourse – he sprang to his feet, ready to stride to the tree and snatch his chiton away but froze before he took a step.

Never had his garment looked better than it did on Xanthia as she walked toward him, determination written over every plane of her face. The belt she had tied around her waist had been used to drape the extra length, luring his gaze to linger over legs only a sculptor could have created. Toned arms proved that she had done physical work in her life and her thick mane of hair had been tied in one heavy mass behind her. A fist of desire punched low and hard into his gut.

"I'm not wrestling with you." He clenched his hands to prevent himself from reaching out and tumbling her to the ground while she looked him up and down.

"How will it look if I arrive in Sparta not knowing anything, and you had all this time to teach me? Come, Acastus, are you afraid I might overpower you?"

His laugh was long and loud and genuine. "There is no chance of that happening."

"Then why don't you prove it. Otherwise, I'll think you're afraid."

He sobered instantly. Whatever Xanthia saw in his face, he heard her swift, indrawn breath. "Never accuse a Spartan, male or female, of cowardice. It's unwise."

"I'm willing to take that risk if it means I get a wrestling lesson."

He willed his anger to subside. She may have hurled the worst possible insult his way, but he could not fault her bravery, and teaching her a few basic moves would give her more insight into how well she could adapt to her new life. At least, that was what he told himself as blood roared through his veins in the expectation of grappling with a woman who could inflame his desires with a mere look.

"If you are so determined, then come closer." Watching her almost leap towards him in her excitement to begin, he fought back a smile, at the same time thinking of a few moves suitable for her height and frame. "You learn to fight standing upright. No biting, kicking, attacking eyes, or punching vital areas. Anytime your opponent falls to the ground is a point for you. Three points you win your match." He smiled as she clapped a hand to her forehead.

"I'll never remember all that!"

"Of course you will. It takes time. Upper body holds only."

He proceeded to show her how to engage a headlock, joint lock, and a shoulder hold, tempering the severity of each move to what she would experience when fighting another woman. His grin became wider in response to her showing quick aptitude in mastering the simplest holds for the first time. Acastus easily freed himself from the joint lock she'd applied to his elbow and stepped back. "Impressive. I see true warrior spirit in you."

The look Xanthia sent him wiped his mind clean. Her dark eyes challenged him, her cheeks flushed from her exertions, her chest heaved, the skin on her limbs gleaming golden in the sunlight. With predictable speed his body responded to the sight. The man who eventually won her heart would be blessed beyond all mortals.

Her voice startled him out of his unruly thoughts.

"All that walking has hardened me, Acastus. Losing my dove..." her voice broke only for a moment, "...losing Calliope the way I did has hardened me. Being torn away from another home has hardened me. If I'm to survive in such a brutal world, then I have to learn fast to take care of myself. No-one else will."

"Family will protect you," he asserted roughly. She possessed an uncanny ability to draw deeply from the well of his remorse. "Sparta will protect you and give you the means to protect yourself. Never doubt that."

"That remains to be proven. So how do I take you down since you are bigger and stronger than me? I can hardly lift and throw you to the ground."

"Against a man's strength there is little you can do. Where strength is evenly matched, a sudden twist can surprise your attacker. I'll show you how to trip an opponent."

He should have realised she would use the knowledge to her advantage.

The twists posed no problem to her. She had already demonstrated her ability to learn quickly. But, after showing her two ways of tripping he had found particularly useful in contests, her foot lashed out with unexpected force, and in the blink of an eye, he found himself off-balance and falling to the ground.

A weight crashed onto him, a weight that turned out to be Xanthia straddling his waist.

"My match." Her tone was gleeful as she poked his back.

"I said three throws to the ground. Get off me. Now!"

Lying face-first on the ground suddenly became a trial that had nothing to do with the dirt in his nostrils. He stilled and battled to draw breath when Xanthia lay lengthwise over him, pressing her chest to his back and leaning in close, her sweet breath whispering into his ear.

"My match, Acastus. You said biting is against the rules, but what about this?"

His braid was pushed aside, her teeth sinking into the back of his neck. "Whatever you think you're doing, stop right now," he growled. When she ignored him in favour of a playful nip, he resolved on immediate action.

Rolling over and taking her with him, he lifted himself on his forearms, and with a practiced move, pinned her beneath him. Staring into half-closed eyes clouded with desire, he heeded an inner caution and braced to lift himself off her. In a flash, she had wrapped her arms and legs around him, the heat of their lower bodies melding and forging a passion that burned hotter than the sun.

Memories of their last encounter consumed his mind. Taking fistfuls of her dark hair, enjoying the contrast against his skin, he bent his head and gave her a hard nip between neck and shoulder. Her startled yelp and the way she thrashed beneath him, almost sent him over the edge. "Why are you doing this?"

"Even when I hated you for tearing me away from everything I knew, I still wanted you."

Her voice was soft, her lips parted, her breathing hitched, yet never had he experienced distrust and desire so strongly and in equal measure. The rake of her nails down his back, until they sank hard into his buttocks, tightened him further. Battle raged between the part of his mind still capable of rationality and insisting her intentions were questionable, and his body, which cried out for him to stop acting like a fool and take what he had wanted from the very first. It was like two pankration fighters coming together inside of him, clawing and gouging for victory. Only one could emerge the victor.

Acastus let his hungry gaze roam over her, her eyelids drooping in response to his intense scrutiny. Desire shook him. "Look at me." He waited until she languidly opened her eyes. "You accused Spartans of being brutes. You were wrong."

Her lips parted further, and it was all the invitation he needed. He closed his mouth over hers, tasting and teasing, her impassioned gasps filling every corner of his soul. He lifted his head to suck in air for his starving lungs, tremors gripping him when she slid her soft hands around his neck to draw him back to her mouth. Vision obscured by her flushed face, he barely heard her breathy demand.

"Take me now."

He had had many women, except no words from any of them had ever sounded sweeter or aroused him so much. A part of him insisted he wait, think, but it had been a long time since he had been with a woman, and the strain of keeping Xanthia at arm's length had taken its toll.

Working one hand between their overheated bodies, Acastus pushed clothing out of the way. Fighting for finesse, he touched her warm centre, sweat breaking out on his forehead when he felt the moistness ready to welcome him. The light contact slammed her hips into him, testing his formidable control even further.

"Don't move," he grunted, muscles seizing from holding himself back. Sweat pooling over his scalp, he slipped inside her and began a rhythmic rock of his hips, which she mirrored immediately. Cocooned in her warmth, her hips rising and falling in perfect cadence with his, Acastus lost sense of time and place, his world narrowed to the woman beneath him whose hands raced over every part of him she could reach.

Driven by instinct, he increased the tempo, heart speeding up to match the pace. He could not wait any longer – the ache was building too fast, and his thrusts grew more urgent. Perfectly joined, he felt the first flutters of her climax, then without warning she wailed, her contractions driving him to his own peak. Head thrust back, Acastus rode the tidal wave until it receded.

Still joined with Xanthia, he rolled onto his side and wrapped his arms around her back and waist. Everything was now changed by that one act. His chest lifted on a deep breath. Given the revelations looming like storm clouds on the horizon, the dark thought filled his mind that this might be the only time he ever made love to her.

Like Pandora's jar, once the lid was lifted, there would be no second chances when those secrets were released.

CHAPTER TWENTY-FOUR

"Welcome to Amyklai, the furthest of our five villages."

Startled out of planning what she could possibly say when she came face-to-face with her kin, Xanthia stopped and stared at the cluster of buildings ahead of them. "What do you mean by furthest? How is this place defended if there are no walls around it?"

To her island-bred eyes, the vast vistas that had encompassed them during the entire trek through the fertile Eurotas Valley presented an alien landscape. Only the sheep, like white clouds framed by a backdrop of green and golden fields, roused any semblance of familiarity to her former home.

And always on their left, looming ever closer, the mountain range drew her gaze. The forbidding peak atop the crown frowned down on her as though castigating her for some unfathomable wrong. It was her nemesis.

Conquer the mountain or it will conquer you. Forever.

The warning reverberated through her head. She rubbed her upper arms to ward off a sudden chill.

"Xanthia?"

Acastus's deep voice broke the mountain's spell. Shaking her head to clear her thoughts, she challenged in a hoarse voice. "Is this it? Sparta? Everywhere I look, I see only vast fields until I don't even recognise myself anymore."

"You belong here. You'll adapt quickly."

"Tell me, is this what I was forced to leave my home for? A village?"

"Five villages. We have temples, an agora, and public buildings that make up the main city further away, but better to rest the donkeys and ourselves here for the night and march in the morning."

She hurried to keep abreast of Acastus as he moved off, every step that drew her nearer to the village adding to the tension she felt in her stomach and chest. A handful of inhabitants cast curious glances their way. She met and held their looks even though her body quaked from nerves. She would allow no-one to see her disquiet, especially the man beside her, whose demeanour kept her from seeking…what? Comfort? Support? She had noticed the subtle change in his step, the cloak of disguise falling away the closer they came to their destination – the 'merchant' gradually vanishing to reveal the warrior hidden beneath.

A magnificent temple caught her eye. "Who is the temple dedicated to?"

"Apollo. The Hyacinthia, a three day festival is held here each year."

"Is there a temple to Aphrodite in Sparta or is the goddess not warrior enough for you?"

"Your beloved goddess has a temple a little way off from the temple of Athena on the acropolis. Callisto will certainly take you there whenever you ask."

Flustered by the sound of her half-sister's name, Xanthia became painfully aware of how close she was to meeting a part of her family. She drew a shaky breath and half-glanced at him. "You said that Callisto had prayed to find me. Where was that?"

"Here, in this very temple. Apollo granted her a vision of Kythera, which helped my mission."

She rubbed her arms – yes, there was the warrior again. 'Marching' and 'mission'. Did her half-sister think and speak like this? To keep the nerves that threatened to collapse her legs at bay, she tried to imagine what Callisto might look like, but her musings were cut short by the tableau that suddenly appeared before them. "Oh! What are they doing?"

Four warriors in full armour emerged from behind the dwellings to their right. Spying the young boy in their midst, indignation swelled her heart – why, the child appeared no older than seven or eight! Two held his hands while the other two walked to the rear, constantly turning to check behind them. Puzzled by their behaviour, Xanthia looked in the same direction but neither heard nor saw anything that might constitute a threat.

They were almost upon them, the odd group heading out of the village in a way that ensured their paths crossed. Close up, Xanthia spotted the boy's watery eyes and trembling lips. The old ache tugged deep in her womb, the flash of memory of Calliope being torn open, merged into a wave of anger which overrode all caution.

"Let him go! How brave of you to imprison a child. Is this how you treat children in your much-vaunted Sparta?" Chest heaving, she whirled to face Acastus. Her eyes bulged when he smiled indulgently, his amusement echoed by the other hoplites.

"He's not being imprisoned. It's time for him to start his training to become a warrior of Sparta."

Open-mouthed, she watched Acastus approach the boy and run an affectionate hand over the youngster's wavy, brown hair. Studying both their faces, a cold dread brewed in the pit of her stomach.

Their features were so similar.

"Are you excited to finally begin your training, Nikandros?"

The boy gave a hesitant nod. She rolled her eyes, leashing the angry words rioting through her mind. Why would a child feel excitement in being taken away from his home? Suddenly, all the old angry hurts resurfaced out of the deep, dark well where she had banished them, to lodge a ball of emotion in her throat.

How did Nikandros's mother feel?

How had her real mother felt when she, Xanthia, had been snatched out of her arms?

Teeth clenched hard to dam the hot tears threatening to flood her eyes, she stalked past the group, nose in the air. Two steps past them she heard one of the hoplites speak.

"He'll do his family, and you, proud, Acastus."

A strange buzzing filled her head until she could barely think. Her legs grew heavier with every step till she halted, staring straight ahead. She saw nothing, every sense turned inward.

Acastus had a son? He was married? She never stole another woman's man. Even the acolytes on Melos strongly discouraged such behaviour.

Rage boiled in her stomach until she felt physically sick. Pressing a hand to her midriff she forced herself to take deep, slow, breaths in the hope of countering the bile burning up into the back of her throat. Yes, she had initiated their lovemaking, then by some unspoken agreement they had not mentioned it after, nor had either attempted to reignite the flames.

She gagged – he had not bothered to mention he was married at the time. Well, why would he, she asked herself cynically. He was a man after all. In her foolish belief she could control such a man as him by binding him to her, she had instead merely provided a warm convenient body for him to slake his hunger until he returned home. Gritting her teeth, she silently called herself all kinds of fool for agreeing to return to this place that had forsaken her, and of which she was absolutely convinced the gods had forsaken as well.

Not pausing to think, pain gripping her heart, she tightened her hold on the donkey she led, not caring in that moment whether the packs contained sufficient supplies, and blindly hurried back in the direction they had arrived, a seething sense of betrayal speeding her steps. *This could be her revenge.* To risk leaving alone, proving herself capable of surviving without any man, gloating at the thought of Acastus dealing with the loss of his honour.

She snorted indelicately. Did he truly possess any honour in his soul?

The shouted warning which followed her served to quicken her pace. Xanthia inhaled deeply and prepared to run, stumbling when a large hand clamped onto her shoulder.

"Where are you going?"

Pitifully, her skin tingled under the weight of his hand. "Leaving. Let me go or you'll be sorry." She prayed her gaze hurled daggers, then she dropped it to the deadly weapons sheathed either side of his waist. Her fingers itched and flexed.

"Don't try."

She pierced him with another sharp look, his rugged handsomeness blinding her for a moment, then bared her teeth. "You forgot to tell me you're married."

"I'm not married. I fathered the boy for his parents."

Eyes shut tight, she prayed for the strength to not fall into hysterics. "Explain how you, what did you say, 'father a child' for someone else?"

"If a man is unable to do so for whatever reason, he can ask another man to be genitor. Nikandros is his family's heir. He'll inherit part of my kleroi should I die without a wife and children of my own."

"Part of your…" Xanthia repeated in disbelief. Then her voice rose. "What kind of barbarity have you brought me to? This isn't done even among the acolytes. How many other children have you fathered?"

"There are two others."

Clutching her middle, she ran to the side of the road. Her stomach begged to empty itself. She bent over, heaved, but to no avail. Once she was certain her stomach really had nothing to throw up, Xanthia straightened to stare sightlessly across the fields. Acastus had fathered three children. Three healthy, living children. At least one of them a son.

Don't go back.

It was too late to restrain the memories. She pressed a hand over her belly, although such scant comfort could hardly undo the pain that had lodged itself permanently in her heart two summers ago.

She found herself unexpectedly wrapped in Acastus's strong embrace. Too distraught to object, she leaned into him, accepting whatever solace to her soul his arms contained.

"We aren't barbarians. That is another great insult you can hurl at us."

"How can any woman be forced to take part in something so soulless? Especially one already married."

"Not forced. A wife must agree, and if she doesn't, it's the end of the matter."

She exhaled a quiet sigh of relief, then stilled as another thought brought a cold dread to engulf her. "What if a woman doesn't want children?"

His sudden, questioning frown, had her struggling to keep her expression bland, while the most important question she burned to know the answer to trembled unasked on her lips.

"The duty of every Spartan, man and woman, is to bear children." He shrugged. "Once that duty is fulfilled, wives may decide they want no more."

Xanthia chewed her lip. Did she dare? Locking her knees to keep her legs from collapsing, she told herself there was nothing else to be done but ask. Every decision she made from now on, rested on this one answer. "What about women who may be barren but only discover this after they wed? Do their husbands cast them off?"

"How would I know? An agreement may be reached for another woman to carry a child for them. Why all these questions?"

She glanced up to find Acastus studying her keenly and she shrank back under the intense scrutiny. Had he seen through her feeble attempts to disguise why she asked such things? She knew he desired her, and there was no question she wanted him again after the first taste of what they could bring each other. Passion simmered, she could almost touch it, yet something held him back. Perhaps it was better this way. "So, can I decide not to marry?"

Her heart dropped to her toes when he stepped away, his face now the inscrutable face of a warrior.

"Given your heritage, the expectation is you will marry and birth children." He pointed to his right. "There is a place over there we can lodge for the night." He looked back at her and warned. "Don't try to escape unless you want me to tie you up."

Mouth open, Xanthia watched him commandeer the leads of both donkeys and start walking through the village. She remained where she stood, mind working furiously to find anything she could do to extricate herself from her present dilemma. With a heavy sigh, the practical side of her reluctantly chose restraint. She would go to her family, learn what she could, then wait for the right opportunity to silently slip away into the night.

She could not stay and endure, knowing he would father a child on another woman for her to raise. Given her past, she had no future here.

~*~

Out of the corner of his eye, Acastus studied the woman walking to his right but keeping one step behind him. Nothing about her demeanour suggested she would abscond, although he questioned whether her position was deliberate. Her frozen features hid whatever turmoil festered in her mind.

Your fault. Your fault. Your fault. The words echoed inside his head, keeping time with his footsteps.

A colourful oath escaped as his toes stubbed against a partially exposed rock in the middle of the sandy path between the houses. A warrior did not question his decisions, but watching Xanthia, doubts consumed him. Her ancestral ways were alien to her and he had forced her return, just as he had forced her expulsion from the privilege that ought to have been hers from birth.

He understood her shock at learning he had sired three children. What he failed to understand, though his determination to unlock the reason grew stronger, were her questions on the bearing of children. Alerted by their strangeness, his keen mind connected them to his own speculations that first night, before the Argive pirates ambushed them, about whether she had lost a child. A bleakness that overtook her whenever the discussion centred on children convinced him the answers held greater importance to her than she was willing to admit.

His chest tightened as an unpleasant thought struck him. Was she unable to bear children? Unthinkable he ask such a question. Unthinkable to consider proposing she…

No, he would never ask her to marry him. It was only a matter of time before his guilty secret came to light, and he truly believed Diokles would never forgive him, no matter how strong their friendship. Lives had been lost in one way or another. Too many people had suffered heartache. Scourging himself for the rest of his life might allow him to seek forgiveness.

Acastus ran a hand over his beard. More likely he would not live long enough to take Xanthia as a wife.

CHAPTER TWENTY-FIVE

Just place one foot in front of the other, Xanthia, you'll be out of this madness soon. The goddess will help.

She badly wanted to give her head a good shake, and make the persistent light-headedness go away, but was afraid to make it worse. She had once experienced the same feeling after unwittingly drinking too much wine during her first festival. The breaths she managed to inhale somehow did not reach her lungs – surely this was the reason for the dizziness. Clutching her midriff, she eventually succeeded in relaxing her tense muscles to deeply inhale a handful of breaths.

The sensation of her head spinning thankfully grew less, but the tremors shaking her legs persisted. They felt weighted, the same as the times she dragged them through the waters off Melos, when wading out to cool off on a blisteringly hot day. She stifled a sob at the recollection and pressed a hand to her mouth, unable to fathom the reason for her distress. Did she still really yearn that much for her former home or was it because of the visual and audible assault of her senses by the great agora of Sparta? Never in her life had she seen so many people.

Drawing her shoulders back, she stared straight ahead. She would not allow this place to cower her. "Do we have to walk through the agora?" she protested.

"Via the city is quickest to Diokles's house, and you can see the principal buildings."

What hope did she have of noticing buildings? Her whole focus was on keeping herself from running as fast as she could to somewhere less oppressive. She looked up and found herself trapped in Acastus's dark gaze. It took all her willpower to not roll her eyes with the speed at which her insides tumbled like a gymnast. Interlacing her fingers to find a measure of calm, she silently railed against the injustice of Eros's misdirected arrows. Of all the men in the known world, it had to be a Spartan who made her knees knock and feel truly alive.

She might be able to escape to Melos one day if she chose, but escaping the unexpected feelings for Acastus would not be so easy. Angry at what she considered her weakness, incomprehensibly angry at him for drawing out emotions better left buried, she sought relief for her jerky pulse by her customary habit of baiting him. "Are Spartans so over-confident that you leave the city wide open to attack?" She waved one hand in a disparaging semicircle. "I used to hear visitors, who came to our group from all over Hellas, tell of high walls being a city's first line of defence. I can't believe Sparta has none!"

While it was only a small victory when he stopped and looked at her askance, she nevertheless congratulated herself for her success.

"You just walked the distance between here and Amyklai. We can't shut them out."

Xanthia stared at his face, now glowing in pride as he explained, suddenly curious despite her misgivings. "How are the women and children defended from invaders?"

His sideways grin brought a scowl to her face.

"Spartan women are taught to fight as I've told you before. You will learn what they, and you, are capable of doing. As for walls…wiser heads than I say Sparta's walls are its men and the tips of our spears are its borders."

The words shivered through her heart. No false bravado, no exaggeration. Belief in himself, in his peers, resonated in his confident voice. She bit the inside of her lip and mused once more amidst what kind of people she had arrived. Oblivious to everything except her turbulent thoughts, Xanthia jumped when his warm hand settled on her shoulder.

"There's no time today to linger. There'll be time to visit the agora and other places after you're home."

Home. Conscious of his hand guiding her, Xanthia took a few hesitant steps when a drawling voice stopped them.

"So, Acastus, do you bring a wife, a slave…or a sacrifice?"

Despite the warm sunshine, the sinister query chilled her to the bone. She felt Acastus's fingers tighten on her shoulder, then he spun around, the momentum taking her with him, to confront the man accosting them.

"No business of yours, Theron."

"Perhaps not, but I am naturally curious that you return with a woman after leaving alone."

"Your curiosity might prove lethal."

Xanthia glanced between the two men, her breathing quickening at the hostile undertone to their words that neither bothered to hide. She scrutinised the newcomer, subtly moving closer to Acastus for protection. Theron's gaze bored into her, a thin white line circling his mouth. The narrow pinched look around his eyes gave her pause, and in that moment, caused her to question if she had suddenly sprouted horns from her head like the god, Pan. A jarring sense of something very wrong swirled in the air around her. She crossed her arms under her breasts and worked to convince herself to ignore the intuitive whispers insisting that Theron was her enemy.

How could he be, though? What possible reason did he have to hate her? She had never met the man until now.

"You threaten a peer?"

"Not a threat, a warning. I'll leave you here."

The hand at her waist seared away the chill of Theron's words. She held her head high, looking neither right nor left, while Acastus guided her through the agora. Conscious of the stares following their progress, she remained close by his side, the brush of their arms against each other setting off flutters in her chest. His remarks as he parried questions, the masculine laughter accompanying them, floated over her head without really being heard.

In what seemed like no time they were out of the city. Every so often, Xanthia glanced back until the buildings of this strange world she had arrived in were almost out of sight. Shaken by the realisation she was as a stranger in the land of her birth, she stopped suddenly and refused to move even when Acastus turned an impatient look towards her. "Who is Theron?" she blurted out.

Her urgency to understand Theron's identity rose to engulf her as Acastus's whole demeanour changed. He held himself so still, it was like looking at a statue, and his face was suddenly like a blank mask. "I sensed his hostility, and I want to know why he appears to hate me."

"He's no-one to be concerned about," he snapped.

Mouth open in shock, she tilted her head to one side and threw him a fulminating look. "Why not? If he's a danger to me I want to know, whatever the reason."

"Just know that your brother will protect you."

She threw her arms out wide, clutched the hair on her scalp, and stepped forward to stand toe-to-toe with him. "I don't need his protection," she enunciated slowly and in a way that almost spat out every word.

In the next moment she found herself pressed to him. Air rushed out of her lungs at the feel of his arms holding her tight, hindering any idea of escape.

"All that spirit and fire, Xanthia. You'll make someone a fine Spartan wife."

Anger erupted through the pores of her skin to flame her face. "I will not!" she yelled, slapping her hands to his chest, ready to push him away.

It was a mistake.

Her gaze darted upward to meet desire-filled eyes burning with the odd light she saw in them when he thought she was not looking. Her worldview narrowed to encompass only the two of them – her panting breath, the strong thud of Acastus's heart beneath her palm, the way her softness yielded to the flex of his body where their pelvises pressed together, sent her spirit soaring into the ether.

Her lips parted over a soft '*oh*' as he bent his head, his mouth coming ever closer to hers. Their lovemaking on the banks of the Eurotas had given birth to a smouldering passion, which lay dormant in both, never alluded to, but ready to ensnare both in its sensual net when they least expected it. She closed her eyes, vexed to have discovered that even knowing he had fathered children she still was drawn to him like a butterfly to the first spring blooms.

At the touch of his firm lips covering her mouth, Xanthia sank into him, opening herself to his kiss, needing to understand the power he possessed to summon this wild need. To make her desire to kiss him like no other man before or, she shuddered as the premonition intruded, no other man after.

She inhaled the clean scent of his skin, tinged with a light sprinkling of sweat, which enhanced, rather than detracted, her appreciation. Sliding her hands up his broad chest, Xanthia hooked them around his neck, pressing him to deepen the kiss. Never in her life had she wanted to savour the feeling of truly wanting a man rather than bending him to her will.

A simple confession that filled her with the first flutters of panic. Her eyes flew open. Tearing her mouth from his, struggling to breathe normally, Xanthia found herself drowning in eyes darkened by shock.

"Never kiss me like that again."

~*~

While his mind rationally agreed to her demand, his body throbbed in protest at her words. He refused to even consider the message his heart shouted.

Acastus released her and walked away to stare sightlessly at barley fields rippling out in a golden wave towards the mountains. Rubbing both hands over his face, he focussed on the tall stalks waving in a gentle breeze, the sight helping him to order his thoughts.

Clenching a fist, he ground it into the palm of his other hand. He had surrendered to weakness. He could be honest and admit he wanted Xanthia, but the chaos such an admission had the power to cause remained untenable. The thought of her becoming another man's wife made his head ache with an intensity that blind-sided him, yet his principles would not allow him to offer marriage until he confessed his role in her exile.

There existed no consolation in knowing he had been a young boy at the time, eager to prove himself, determined to do his father proud, to ensure his sister would not be shunned once she reached the age to wed. The past still hovered over him like a menacing Harpy waiting to pounce, the Harpy which held the knowledge of who had betrayed his innocent remarks to Diokles's father.

He ran an unsteady hand over his scalp. Standing here and waiting for Dice, the goddess of moral judgment, to condemn him would achieve nothing. Tasks remained unfinished, not least to deliver Xanthia to Diokles's house, report at the barracks first, then deal with Drakon, if the traitorous servant still lived and had foolishly chosen to return to his certain death.

He looked over his shoulder to find her watching him with wary eyes and biting her lip. A wry smile lifted one corner of his mouth. "I don't recall any objections. Are you certain you don't want me to kiss you again?" Acastus grinned when she bared her teeth.

"I pretended to enjoy it. Just because other women found you worthy to sire their children, doesn't mean I do!"

"One kiss doesn't lead to marriage. Or children." He folded his arms across his chest and looked down his nose when she tossed her head to stare insolently.

"Do you think I don't know that?" She stabbed a finger in his direction. "Why aren't you married if your whole purpose is providing children for this…this..?"

Acastus flexed his fingers to combat the heat flushing his face. "I have more than just one purpose and don't denigrate the land of your birth."

Her face blanched. Understandably, since he had spoken in a rougher tone than intended. He was not ready to explain to anyone why, at the age of thirty, he remained unmarried. Raking stiff fingers through his hair, he conceded the necessity of choosing a wife soon or face relentless mockery. He could take pride in completing the mission he had been insistent on taking, but Aeschylus still remained an outcast. To enable Xanthia's father to be restored to his rightful position, he still needed to present himself to the Gerousia and advise them of his success.

Silently, he gathered up the donkey's leads and motioned for her to follow. For the first time since he had met Xanthia, his attention was not on her at all, but on how he could find an opportune moment to warn Callisto to not reveal what the high priestess of

Olympia had foretold – that for Aeschylus to be welcomed back, the long-lost daughter trailing behind him in equal silence, had to be brought home first.

Given her reluctance to come to Sparta, her bafflement – even derision – of Spartan customs she had already learned about, he doubted she would listen to reason and accept that no-one, apart from her exiled father, had known she existed. Acastus sighed heavily. She had already tried to kill him twice. If she discovered that she had been brought back, against her will, in part to aid her father's return, he did not doubt she would be furious at what she perceived to be his deception and attempt to kill him a third time.

CHAPTER TWENTY-SIX

Cursing under his breath, Theron strode into his home's courtyard, lips twisting on witnessing servants shrinking back from him. The fury consuming him must be reflected on his face, and he did not care. Too much was at stake for him to care whether his servants feared him.

With no break in his stride, he flung open the doors of one room after another, without finding his sister. Thinking she might be overseeing the winemakers, who he needed to speak to anyway, he began to retrace his steps but saw the servant who had bribed Drakon approach him. The hunched shoulders of the helot, the tremble of his lip, did not bode well.

"What news?" Theron growled in an undertone.

"Master, I learned of Drakon's death. A kryptos sprang a trap on him before he could reach the helot villages outside of Limnai."

Theron clenched both hands and ground his teeth for good measure. Of course his servant's voice shook. Not only had Drakon, chosen on this servant's advice, failed to return with tidings of Xanthia's death, any mention of the krypteia struck terror into the slave class. "I've wasted money which could've been put to better use!"

He let out a bitter half-laugh as his servant jumped away from him. By the gods, he had every right to shout. The money was on its way to Hades along with Drakon, and the lethal blow to his plans might never be overcome. As things stood, he could barely afford to pay his share to the syssition, his mess group, in his current straits.

"Brother?"

Theron whirled to see Akantha descending the steps from the upper level. An angry jerk of his head sent the servant scurrying to another part of the house.

Motioning her to come closer, he whispered savagely, "Drakon is dead." He punched one fist against the white-washed wall, laughing sourly at the shock on her face. "Even worse, I saw your nemesis in the agora. Acastus has succeeded in his mission."

Akantha sucked in a breath. "I have been thinking the situation over. You mustn't lose any more time or money or place our own position under threat to deny Aeschylus's return." She spared her brother a hard stare. "Whenever he arrives, I'll throw myself on my knees before him if necessary to ensure our future."

Theron paced, anger driving his relentless steps. Stopping mid-stride, he turned to glare at his sister. "You've brought this upon us. Certain your husband won't take you back given you refused to leave with him. I told you at the time to stay on in his house."

"You'd rather I left our mother to a lingering death, alone? Yes, I refused to leave with him because I resented his preference for Ianthe. Whatever I brought upon us, according to you, was done at your urging. You used every opportunity to throw me in front of Aeschylus. For your advantage alone!"

Outrage stiffened his limbs. "Keep your voice down," he hissed, checking each of the open doorways to ensure no servant overheard their conversation. "Don't place all the blame on me. You couldn't wait to live the life Aeschylus's wealth provided. Not a very Spartan notion, my dear sister. Nor is it my fault that the one kleros I inherited is on poorer land, therefore less abundant than our elder brother's. I won't allow the shame of being unable to provide a share to my syssition and be cast out like a common helot. Is that what you want to see happen? If you'd stayed, Aeschylus's kleroi would have prospered with me overseeing the place."

He started to pace again, every agitated step matching the agitation of his mind. He had to remain calm and consider his next move rationally, since his future as a full citizen was at stake.

He met Akantha's worried look. "Are you losing your nerve?"

Her laugh, comprising derision and disbelief, grated over his hearing.

"I'm a woman of Sparta, I don't lose my nerve," she spat. "I'm worried for you and what you're planning. I abhor a constant reminder of Ianthe's child, still it remains unthinkable you're plotting to kill a fellow Spartan."

"She wasn't brought up a—"

He bristled when his sister cut him off with a chopping motion of her hand.

"She is a Spartan by blood of both parents. That's all anyone will care about."

"So you won't care of I tell you that Ianthe's daughter exactly resembles her mother. I thought I saw a ghost." Studying his sister, who wrapped her arms around herself as though warding off an evil spirit, Theron wondered how he could use the situation to his advantage. "Have you seen Callisto yet?"

"Of course not," she scoffed. "Nor would she welcome me. The gods cursed me with a daughter instead of a son. I couldn't even present a son to my husband to sway his heart away from Ianthe."

Theron rolled his eyes at her. "Must I remind you your son would have been taken away once he turned seven. There is no failure on your part giving birth to a daughter, a future mother of Sparta. She is married to an influential man. Consider the advantages to making your peace with her. Remember, she will inherit all of Diokles's wealth on his death, leaving Aeschylus's wealth to you."

Akantha tossed her head. "Ah, yes, Diokles," she sniffed. "The son of my husband's supposed love, Ianthe. The woman he would have cast me aside to claim given half a chance. I hated her, why should I nurture any children my daughter has by Diokles?"

"They will be your grandchildren, sister," Theron flung a hand out, impatient with her unreasonable long-held grudge, a grudge holding the power to ruin his plans. "You are not unintelligent. Think with your brain instead of your wounded pride."

"What do I say to her after all these years?" she exclaimed. "I'm sorry daughter for wishing I'd birthed a son instead of you. For not caring enough to find out what happened to you. For abandoning you because my own mother was at the door of Hades and my husband chose to take you away regardless of what I thought."

"And, dear child, while I cared for my mother, I had time to brew bitterness in my soul over your father's preference for another woman."

"You dare!"

Theron blinked. The vitriol in his sister's voice, the fire flaming from her eyes, gave him pause. The sudden cold filling his chest reminded him to never underestimate the women of his city-state, including his own sister even though they shared the same blood.

Rubbing his chin bought him a fraction of time to choose his words carefully. "You seem to forget it's expected of you to release your menfolk to war and the agoge. To allow them to be genitors if requested."

"You, brother, choose to overlook the expectation that the woman's consent is gained first. I never gave mine. I'm certain Ianthe never revealed the identity of her lover to her husband."

"No, she didn't."

"How do you know?"

He met Akantha's quizzical look with a blank stare and shrugged to indicate the conversation was over. From now on, he had to be vigilant and exercise control over his tongue, to not reveal secrets he had kept to himself for the last ten years, waiting patiently until he could use them to his advantage once more.

Especially the knowledge of the person who had betrayed to Ianthe's husband, Lysander, who the father of her child was.

CHAPTER TWENTY-SEVEN

Xanthia's steps slowed by degrees until she came to a complete halt. Open-mouthed, she circled on the spot, struggling to comprehend the sight before her. The imposing house on two levels, flanked by a number of smaller domed buildings scattered in orderly fashion to its rear, and the fields encircling it in all directions.

"My half-brother lives here?"

Disconcerted by the indulgent gleam in Acastus's eyes at her amazement of the home she had been brought to, she moved a few hesitant steps forward.

"Yes. Diokles inherited a wealthy kleroi. On his father's side they are related to our Agiad royal house."

The revelation shocked her into a misstep. Stumbling on an uneven patch of ground, she caught his arm to regain her balance. The familiar burning in her fingers at the contact jolted her into letting go the instant she found her feet. "Who are they?" It was his turn to stop and stare at her for so long, that she felt compelled to call him out on his disbelief. "Do you expect me to know or care?"

"You heard nothing of Thermopylae even from visitors to your festival? Of the sacrifice of Leonidas, the courage of our people?" He ran an agitated hand over his face. "You have much to learn."

"I'm not stupid, Acastus."

"I didn't say you were, nor imply it. You'll learn of this and much more now that you are here."

She rolled her eyes and retorted in a sharp voice. "Learn what? How to cook and clean for a husband?"

"Servants cook and clean," he informed her in a dry voice, making no effort to hide the amusement tugging at his mouth.

Her eyes narrowed – was he mocking her? She sniffed and kept walking towards an archway beyond which she spied a courtyard. There was no time to make sense of the snippets of information he had provided before she walked under the arch and into a much larger courtyard than she had expected to see. An unexpected bout of nerves set her hands trembling. *What is wrong with you?*

She had faced death twice, slashed a burly attacker to save her life and Acastus's, and here she was, shaking at the prospect of meeting kin who might only be in her life for a short time. In her confusion, she clutched his arm again to stop her falling into the power of her misgivings, and blurted out, "Am I expected to live here? Perhaps there is no room for me."

"Diokles's house is large enough to fit ten more people," he reassured her and covered her hand with his own. "He told me Callisto was already making plans which room to prepare for you when I left."

Turning away from his intent gaze, Xanthia took a deep breath. She could no more contain the resentment churning in her gut than restrain Kerberos with her bare hands. Her family were complete strangers to her. What had prevented them seeking her out before this? The answer, once she received it, would alongside the issue of marriage govern every choice she made about her life, whether in Sparta or anywhere else.

Conscious of Acastus still covering her hand, she tugged, her startled gaze flying to meet his as he resisted and pressed down to keep her by his side. For a brief, blissful moment they stood, absorbed in each other, her skin growing warm as though she stood unprotected in the glare of the noonday sun.

The sound of approaching footsteps broke whatever spell had been cast between them. She made a small noise of protest in her throat when he released her hand but stepped away, keeping her eyes averted as servants carried pitchers of water for their refreshment. She gratefully accepted a kylix filled to the brim with crystal clear water, gulping greedily to ease her dry throat. Handing the empty vessel to the servant, she looked nervously around the large courtyard, the many doors on both levels, seeming to proclaim wealth and position that rattled any attempt to compose herself.

"Xanthia!"

She tensed, her shoulders rising almost to her ears. Plastering a stiff smile onto her face she turned diffidently in the direction of the melodious voice calling her name. A woman, short blond hair glistening in the sun, glided down the stairs leading from the floor above them. Frozen in place, she clasped her hands in front of her, the rising tension forming a lump in her throat as she waited for – it could only be her half-sister – to come closer.

Xanthia held her breath until Callisto, carefully placing her feet, reached the last step and half-ran to her, a welcoming smile lending her features an ethereal light.

Their eyes met.

Witnessing Callisto clutch one hand to her chest, her smile waver and disappear to be replaced by a look of stupefaction, shattered her belief that she had done right by coming here. She lifted her chin, fighting the urge to run to the furthest reaches of the Peloponnese.

"Callisto?" There was a questioning lilt in her stiff voice. Given the pinched look on her half-sister's face, she longed to ask what part of her appearance offended. If this stranger she shared a father with could not stand the sight of her, she must begin to make plans to leave as soon as an opportunity presented itself. Xanthia drew herself up, pursing her lips the longer the awkward silence lingered, aware the silent man standing behind her was reading every nuance of emotion crossing their faces.

"Forgive me," Callisto whispered, "you so resemble your mother, Ianthe, I can't…"

Xanthia pressed her churning stomach and moistened her dry mouth. "That is something I will never see for myself."

A part of her, the part craving true acceptance, winced when Callisto's face paled. She battled the intemperate words rushing through her mind, fuelled by the betrayed, unhealed part of her soul and struggled to find something to say to soothe…and failed. Instead, she gripped her hands together in defence at the brightness of Callisto's eyes before her half-sister blinked rapidly and collected herself.

"If I could walk into the Underworld and beg Hades to return your mother from the dead, I would," Callisto replied in a remote voice. "If I had known of your existence earlier, I would have begged Apollo to show me where to find you sooner. I cannot undo the past, only welcome you as my sister, half-blood notwithstanding."

Xanthia felt her face heat at the rebuff. In her heart she knew Callisto was right. Although she questioned how long it would take to accept, if ever, the reality of her life. Lost in her chaotic thoughts, she had almost forgotten Acastus, whose interruption released her from the awkward moment.

"Where is Diokles?"

Yes, where was her brother? Watching closely, it appeared to her that Callisto drooped in relief for this turn their exchange took.

"Skirmishes on the northern border," she informed him. "He left some days ago to restore order. I received word he came home this morning."

"I should've been here to assist."

"You can't be in two places at once," Callisto reminded him. "What you accomplished is just as great."

"I'll go to the barracks and give him the news that Xanthia is here." He looked down at her. "Tonight, Diokles and I dine with our mess group as is customary. He will see you tomorrow."

Face stiff from holding her emotions in check, Xanthia raised her chin to lock gazes with Acastus. So, her half-brother could not be bothered to come and meet her on the day she arrived at his home. Regardless of Callisto's sentiments, the news deepened the sense of rejection that still lived inside her wounded heart.

"Is this what I can expect of a Spartan husband?" she said, not bothering to hide the outrage in her voice. "To see him only when he deems it expedient?"

She ignored Callisto's gasp but found it harder to ignore the flaring of displeasure in Acastus's eyes. Cursing the dance of butterflies in her belly, she took a step away from his overpowering presence, determined to stay unaffected despite the frown darkening his face.

"All of us are bound and live by these laws." He raised a hand in farewell. "I must leave."

"So, you too abandon me?" She stared, mesmerised, oblivious to her watching sister as the frown melted away and a wry glint entered his eyes.

"Remember you tried to *abandon* me in a different fashion when you attempted to push me over a cliff."

"What!?"

Xanthia opened her mouth, but Acastus spoke first. "Your sister shares the same fire and spirit you possess, Callisto. Diokles told me you tried to kill him not long after you left Apollysis."

Her jaw slackening, Xanthia tore her gaze away from Acastus and studied Callisto. The possibility of her half-sister being a kindred spirit had never occurred to her. Conscious of their stares, she shut her mouth. So what if she discovered she might have more in common with her kin than she expected.

"Yes, I tried to push him off a cliff. He deserved it for tossing me over his shoulder and taking me away from Aphrodite's festival."

Stunned by Callisto collapsing in peals of laughter, Xanthia felt the tightness of her skin relax and the knot of churning emotion in her stomach begin to dissolve. The air, thick with tension moments ago, became lighter, allowing her to think more clearly and decide how she might use the situation to her advantage.

"You will find our men are of few words," Callisto said, wiping tears of mirth off her cheeks, "they prefer to act rather than talk."

She sent a sideways glance at Acastus. "Indeed. I witnessed this remarkable talent many times during the journey here."

He gifted her a rare grin. Lifting her chin, she made the mistake of looking deep into his eyes. She drew a sharp breath and saw his grin fade as he read something in her expression and half-lifted a hand towards her. Slowly, reluctantly, she moved out of reach lest she did something foolish and kissed him, here, in front of her half-brother's entire household. He dropped his hand, a mask of inscrutability settling over his face.

"I must go. I may see you in a few days."

She released the breath jammed halfway up her chest. Lips trembling, she continued to watch him until he left the courtyard and then squirmed when she turned to see the measured look Callisto was giving her. "Is something the matter?" she challenged hotly.

"You desire Acastus."

"I don't!" She almost shouted the denial. "He kidnapped me, I was forced to nurse injuries he sustained…why are you looking at me like that?"

"Diokles kidnapped me and see how that finished. There is no shame in feeling desire for a warrior like Acastus. Spartan men are very hard to resist. Both Acastus and your half-brother wear an aura of power more so than most of their peers." Callisto tilted her head knowingly. "Both are very appealing to the eye."

Xanthia felt the blush start in her cheeks, carrying its heat all the way to the roots of her hair. No matter what Callisto thought, she would not let herself desire Acastus, much less love him. All she saw down that road contained hurt for herself. She jumped when Callisto placed a light hand on her arm.

"You must be exhausted and hungry. Come with me."

Surrendering herself to her sister's guiding hand, she entered a doorway that Callisto indicated to her left and gasped at the spacious bathing chamber, the likes of which she had never seen before. She stared longingly at the deep alabaster tub full of steaming water, barely listening to her sister directing the servants. Memories of swimming in the sea to refresh herself, of warming her own water and using a cloth to bathe, brought on a powerful wave of homesickness.

"If you wish to be left alone, there are garments and scented oils on the table. Call one of the servants when you are ready. I hope you'll join me for a meal, I so much want to learn of your life."

Xanthia took a deep breath and pushed the memories away. "Thank you. I will bathe alone." She had never bathed with anyone present, apart from the single time Acastus came across her in the stream. Clenching her thighs in a vain effort to lessen the throbbing in her intimate place, she pushed the memory away.

Callisto startled her with a swift, if hesitant, hug, banishing both her arousal and unexpected homesickness with this one simple act. Her throat tightened. Despite all of Euphrasia's efforts, the older woman had never felt comfortable hugging Xanthia. She had missed out on a mother's love and guiding hand. She reached out, hesitated, and then dropped her arms by her side, uncertain how to reciprocate the offered affection.

"Take all the time you need," Callisto said, her tone tempered with a sad understanding as she turned to usher the servants out, leaving Xanthia to her solitude.

She was used to being alone. Used to fending for herself even when surrounded by others. She had never let anyone get too close since the day her world fell apart. Wiping away a solitary tear, she remembered the exact moment she had even closed off from her foster parents.

Letting the old chiton she had worn for days fall to the floor, Xanthia stood naked in the steamy room. Closing her eyes, she cupped her breasts and relived the wild desire that had flooded her when Acastus had worshipped them; the sensual danger in the moment when she had caught him, naked and unawares, and held his own weapon to his throat.

Lost in the magic her mind conjured, she threw her head back, luxuriating in the feel of her long hair caressing her bare skin, impulsively circling a finger around the peaked crowns. Her lips parted, a low moan escaping, pressure built in the secret spot between her legs. One hand drifted downward…

"No!"

The emphatic denial echoed in the silence, breaking the dreamscape of her own making. Anger at needlessly causing herself frustration, she climbed into the deep tub, clenching her jaw against the sensation of warm water caressing her over-stimulated pleasure points. She could desire Acastus all she wanted but never marry him or any other man.

Would she become a pariah in her native land? Did it make her a coward in Spartan eyes if she pushed the potential consequences of her decision to the back of her mind right now and take simple enjoyment in cleansing her body? The day would arrive soon enough when she would be forced to reveal the secret heartache that had closed the door to marriage for her, perhaps forever.

~*~

Halfway across the training ground, Acastus spotted the man walking towards him, the familiar combative rivalry surging in his blood as it surged in all Spartans. His opponent mirrored his quick grin. Both unsheathed their weapons and dropped into the same fighting stance. Acastus half-heard the good-natured taunts their peers directed at them both, all accustomed to the way he and Diokles greeted each other whenever they met following separate campaigns.

"Callisto mentioned you'd returned." Acastus aimed his kopis toward Diokles, who blocked the blow in exactly the way he expected. Disengaging, he leapt backwards, thrusting again in one smooth move, going on the defensive as Diokles attacked swiftly. "No doubt the border has been secured with your usual efficiency."

"It's nothing to jest about," Diokles said. "Argives were raiding Arcadian territory. That band won't be raiding any longer."

"Neither will the ones I met after making port in Zarax."

Only his superb reflexes stopped him wounding Diokles, who had stopped in his tracks as though stunned by a body blow.

"You succeeded in your mission?"

A seed of doubt took root in his gut when the muscle spasmed in Diokles's right cheek. He had known his friend too long to not recognise the stress reaction. He had seen it often enough on the battlefield. His hand clenched around his weapon but not to deliver a blow.

"Yes. I came to report to the general, then I'll present myself to the Gerousia. What troubles you?"

"Instinct warns me bringing her home will cause chaos."

"Why doubt now? The gods willed it. Your own wife divined the help I needed. Are you saying you prefer Xanthia leaves?"

He met Diokles's hard look with one of his own. He had just risked his life to bring Xanthia to her native land. She had come near to death twice through Drakon's betrayal. An all too familiar fury flooded him. No hiding place existed for the treacherous servant that he would not fail to discover.

"No, I'm not saying that," Diokles rebuffed stiffly.

"Then what?" Acastus stood back, at a loss to make sense of the situation.

"I'll explain after I've seen her." Diokles nodded towards the barracks. "Report to the general, then I'll accompany you to the senate."

Acastus sheathed his kopis, not pressing Diokles further for an explanation. He knew with certainty something was wrong. Whatever the challenge was, it weighed heavily on his friend's mind.

"Wait here. I'll be back shortly."

Seeking out his general, Acastus gave him a brief report of his journey, focussing on the pirate activity they had encountered and other observations he had made. The information might one day assist in securing Sparta's safety in the event of an enemy attack.

Right now, there was no threat, leaving him free to continue his usual daily life of training.

Rejoining his friend, Acastus silently led the way out to the agora. As they crossed the large, central square, he grew more aware of the troubled air that hung around Diokles like a cloak and speculated why, all of a sudden, he was wary of his sister's return. What would his friend do if he knew what had transpired between himself and Xanthia? Until he discovered who had betrayed his innocent remarks all those years ago, his situation remained precarious. If that peer was still alive, there was nothing to stop him from whispering a quiet accusation in Diokles's ear.

And, in all probability, he and Diokles would end up in a fight, leaving one of them maimed. Or dead.

The senate building loomed ahead. Beating back his morbid imaginings, Acastus set his face in neutral lines. "Are the senators still here?"

"Yes. I've already spoken to some of them. There were many other matters to discuss."

Noting the distant tone, Acastus allowed the tingle in his gut full rein. The sooner this meeting finished, the sooner he would confront Diokles to openly state any reservations he nursed in relation to his half-sister. He endured a short wait, finally summoned to his audience before the senators.

"Welcome, Acastus. Your mission was successful?"

Acastus inclined his head in deference to the elder statesman. "Yes, Heliodoros. Thanks to Apollo, Xanthia has rejoined her family. Now it's time for her father, Aeschylus, to be restored as ordained by Olympian Zeus."

"Unnecessary to remind us," Heliodoros admonished. "We have already considered who can carry word to Apollysis."

"I leave that decision to your wisdom."

Then Diokles spoke. Acastus stood unmoving, staring straight ahead, and finally understood, in part, why his friend had been close-mouthed and aloof with him. Now all he needed was to discover why.

CHAPTER TWENTY-EIGHT

Arms stretched high above her head, Xanthia smiled as each muscle and tendon expanded and released the inertia of sleep. She stepped across the room to open the window shutters, where she spied a faint gleam of light peeping through, and drew in a long breath of fresh morning air. Eyes narrowed, she gazed out across the green and gold vista, past groves of olive trees abutting the mountain at their edge. The sight of the forbidding range tightened the back of her neck, forcing her to tilt her head from side to side to ease the dull ache.

The unfamiliar bed she had slept on was not the reason for the stiffness gripping every part of her body.

During the darkest point of the night, she had awoken to the sound of someone retching. Wanting to help, knowing she could blend the right herbs quickly, she had listened for some time and was convinced that the noise came from Callisto's room. Despite the cautious welcome she had received, Xanthia had made her way to her sister's door. The instant she had touched the handle, a powerful chill had frozen her in place. Stunned by the intensity, she heeded the inexplicable urgency that had pushed her to go back to her own room.

By the time she had fallen into a fitful sleep, the sounds had ceased.

Lost in the night's recollections, she jumped at the sound of someone knocking on the door of her room. One last wary glance at the mountain, she turned her back on it and went to open the door, finding Callisto standing on the threshold.

"Come in." Opening the door fully, she stepped aside to let her half-sister enter, surprised by the concern she felt over the lines of tiredness circling Callisto's eyes, although she also noticed a glow illuminating her face.

"Are you ready to break your fast?" Callisto enquired with a tentative smile. "The servants tell me the food is served. Our bread is best eaten while still warm."

"I'm a little hungry," Xanthia agreed in a neutral voice. The tension she had recently released returned as bands constricting her chest and back. She could hardly expect herself to feel comfortable with her family so soon, and the flutter of nerves in her stomach protested the very thought of food. She would rather eat alone, free from having to find something to talk about with a sister she barely knew.

Callisto drew back. "We eat in the same room where we ate our evening meal yesterday," she said in a constrained voice. "Do you want me to wait for you?"

Relieved to have a few more moments to prepare herself, Xanthia spurned the offer. "Please don't wait, I'll come down soon."

The moment Callisto left, she shut the door and returned to the window. Why did the mountain call to her so strongly? She shivered as dread engulfed her, the same way it had during the night. Wide-eyed, she stared at the distant peak of Taygetos, knowing she had been left to die there on the whim of some unknown man.

Was her father responsible? Or someone else? Her fingers flexed as the longing for a weapon consumed her.

Your bravery proved your heritage as truly a woman of Sparta.

Acastus's words returned to burn in her mind. She had not seen him since he had left her here like some unwanted burden. She rubbed the sleep out of her face and reminded herself yet again that there was no future with him. It did not matter what he made her feel, or she him, when they had made love by the river, men had always interfered in her life.

The leap of her heart at the loud voices floating up to her room made a mockery of her assertions. Furtively, she eased her face past the window and saw two men walking towards the house, their long, confident strides eating up the ground. A light sweat broke out along her skin at the sight of Acastus looking both serious and infuriated. She could not hear what he was saying but the harsh tones of his voice carried clearly on the still, morning air. Then her gaze fell on his companion and her mouth dried. It could only be her half-brother, who argued back in the same angry manner.

She retreated from the window before they had a chance to notice her. Xanthia paced the room, willing her heartbeat to calm and ease the small ache that had made its presence felt after seeing Diokles.

She pressed her fingertips to her temples, feeling the pulse throbbing beneath them. Why were they arguing so intensely? Everything she had been told pointed to a bond of friendship and brotherhood through their shared experiences as sons of Sparta. A relentless urge filled her to discover whether her presence caused the conflict between them

One last worried stare out the window, and she shook a fist in the mountain's direction, vowing Taygetos would never conquer her. Let her mind conjure Acastus in all his warrior glory as much as it liked, but she would keep her promise to never allow a man to conquer her heart.

~*~

Holding her breath, Xanthia ran lightly down the stairs, thankful there were no servants in the courtyard just then to see her. She edged along the wall to the archway, placing herself behind a large pot in which a tall, green-leafed plant flourished. She almost gave her position away, when she started, heart thumping wildly, on hearing Acastus shout her name, but both men were still arguing outside.

"She has just arrived, and I'm ordered to take her away!"

She bit her lip until she tasted blood. Rage, the intensity of which she had never felt before, grew until she began to fear she would burst from the pressure. Redeemed from one exile, she now faced the prospect of another? Bewildered by a sharp pain, she glanced down and unclenched her fisted hands, the deep bruise-like marks left by her nails drawing nothing but indifference to the state of her palms.

"You know why, Acastus. Better she meets her father in Apollysis and you can teach her survival skills along the way."

"Like how to use a xiphos. She's well on the way to mastering that skill."

Maybe I am. If I had one now I'd run it through both of you.

A lava tide of fury rose up into her throat, leaving her speechless when all she wanted to do was jump out and scream at them both, but desperate to hear more, she remained plastered to the wall, the only support to hand for her shaking body.

"I understand why I'm tasked to carry the news to Aeschylus, but why must Xanthia go with me?"

Why indeed? A long pause followed, where her thundering pulse resounded in her ears while her mind struggled to come up with a possible reason.

"I witnessed Aeschylus's anguish when told of my mother's death. If, as you say, Xanthia resembles her so closely, he will need time to accustom himself to this likeness, and I won't have Callisto upset."

"How does this affect Callisto?"

Senses heightened, Xanthia heard Diokles issue a short, derisive snort.

"Callisto has just reunited with her father. If he favours Xanthia, it will cause her more heartache given what she endured. Especially since she carries our first child."

She bit down on her knuckles to stop herself crying out her deep anguish. The reason for the glow on her sister's face was clear to her now. Collapsing in a wailing heap onto the stone floor would provide brief, but fruitless, respite. Xanthia squeezed her eyes shut to the point of pain, trying to give solace to her aching heart. Lost in misery, it took her a while to become aware of a deep silence that now hung in the air around her.

Eyelids snapping open, she gave profound thanks for the wall behind her because her legs had lost the power to hold herself up straight. A sensation akin to every muscle becoming as insubstantial as a cloud in the heavens, gripped her as two men approached, a mixture of unease and incredulity wreathing their features. Up close, Xanthia saw the taller man's face whiten beneath his bronze skin.

Staring into the eyes of her half-brother almost broke her. "Diokles?" she whispered.

Why did he stand there as though he had seen Medusa's face and been turned to stone? As her insensibility lessened, Xanthia spied turmoil in his dark eyes before he passed a hand over them, leaving them oddly blank as his arm dropped back to his side. Her sister had looked shocked yesterday, but it paled in comparison as she took in the pinched line of his mouth and the lack of any gesture from him.

She swallowed against the tears begging for release. Somehow this was worse than meeting Callisto. This man had lain in the same womb as her; been birthed by the same woman. *So what, she admonished herself? There was absolutely no reason to cry.*

"Is…" Xanthia took a breath and tried again, "is something wrong?" she managed past the constriction in her throat. Glancing at Acastus for support, she understood why Callisto had said Spartan men were hard to resist. Why, in the name of Aphrodite, did she think of that now?

"You are the image of Ianthe."

Xanthia stared and fought back a wave of hysteria. The lack of welcoming words angered and centred her at the same time. If these were the best words he could offer, she had no reason to be upset.

"Yes, I've already been told this," she retorted, uncaring if she sounded fretful. She was here under duress, and her presence undoubtedly unnerved her kin. Observing the way Diokles held himself rigidly aloof only hardened her desire to have this awkward meeting over with.

"Prepare to hear this often," he said. "Many remember my mother. Their surprise will be great."

My mother? Did he mean he did not consider her his sister? Why had he not said, 'our mother'? With effort, she stiffened her knees and pressed away from the wall, chin raised as she drew herself to her full height. "Does my presence upset you, brother?" If anything, she noticed his lips thin even more, so that a white line appeared around them.

"No."

There was that Spartan brevity again! She yearned to hit him. "Are you certain?"

Her mouth dropped open when Diokles turned away to enter the dining room that Callisto had shown her yesterday. Not knowing where to look, fist pressed against her trembling lips to hold back a strangled cry of grief and vexation, she clutched the front of her tunic and ran out of the courtyard.

The winding path leading to the city drew her far away from a place where she had no reason to stay. Desperation lent her a speed that surprised her even though she had no idea where she could run to for sanctuary, so long as she did not have to stay here and have her heart ripped to shreds.

A hand clamped around her upper arm, the abrupt pull backwards carrying her legs out from under her. The stony path loomed in her face before another hand wrapped around her waist just in time to pull her up before she crashed to the ground.

With every fibre of her being she resented the way her skin burned under Acastus's touch. Xanthia bared her teeth, furious with herself and with him. "Let me go before I make you regret coming after me."

An outrush of air left her lungs when he imprisoned her in his arms and slammed her against him. Xanthia fought to douse the fire melting pleasure points she never knew existed, asking herself how could this man rip desire from her in such a moment when she faced rejection by her family once again?

"I won't let go. Understand your brother. In you, he saw the ghost of the mother who never told him of your existence."

"I don't care. I won't go back to his house."

"Where else will you go?" Acastus challenged. "Your father's house is not fit to live in yet. Even if it were, you can't live there alone."

As her anger began to lessen, an awareness of his burgeoning manhood teased an answering response in her pelvis. Xanthia beat down a sudden rush of triumph. She summoned her most seductive smile and subtly angled her hips closer to his. "Would you allow me to live in your house if I have nowhere else to go?" she murmured, gloating when his face flushed a dark colour.

"One day you will push me too far." His hands slid down to cup her bottom and squeezed. "You may not enjoy the consequences."

She had no time to open her mouth in a rebuke before her hand was taken in an uncompromising grip and she found herself pulled along behind him. Mouth twisting, she dug her heels in and dropped into a crouch, forcing him to stop. "You don't need to lead me, I won't get lost!"

"You'll run as soon as I release you," he retorted, pulling her to her feet. "Heed my advice, there is nowhere to run unless you're willing to risk your life."

In the brief moment their eyes met, fear flitted through her, then disappeared on the wings of the knowledge that she must contain her resentment of her situation and prepare a viable plan for leaving in her own time.

"Give me my hand," she ordered in a cold voice while tugging at the same time. Amazed that he listened, she did not press her luck but lifted her chin and set her own quick pace back to the house.

On their return, she faced a new trial of nerves. Through half-closed eyes, she endured the astonished stares of the servants, some of whom gaped open-mouthed when they saw her features up close for the first time. Had circumstances been different, she might have grown up here, known her real mother, and seen with her own eyes why everyone remarked on their resemblance. The world spun around her. Perhaps the long walk had taken an unexpected or unknown toll on her physically. Perhaps she needed to see a physician, especially if another long journey beckoned.

Think!

Except she could not think, or worry, or settle the nerves twisting her stomach in knots because Acastus's hand at her elbow was ushering her into the light-filled, pleasant room where she had dined last night. Her stomach rumbled as the aroma of warm bread tickled her nostrils.

"Come, sit next to me."

The buzzing in her ears muted Callisto's voice. Xanthia willed her legs to move closer to the table, praying they would not collapse from under her. In this land of hard men and women, falling in an ignominious heap at their feet would surely invite their scorn.

Stiffly, she sat on the stool Callisto indicated. Clasping her hands in her lap, Xanthia half-glanced at Diokles, found him studying her intently, and hurriedly looked down. Her stomach, which scant moments ago had signalled hunger, now clenched, removing any desire for food. How could she possibly swallow anything past her tight throat. She forced a smile, hoping her discomfort was not apparent to the others. "Thank you, but I'm not hungry."

"You must eat," Callisto pressed, offering a platter of cheese, "to rebuild your strength after such a long trek."

Xanthia made a show of studying the white cheese, overcome by surprise when her mouth watered. "Of course you're right. I'm a little weary, but I survived." Indeed, she needed to regain her strength after days of walking, which at least had hardened her mentally and physically. Reaching for a piece of barley bread, she bit into it and chewed, relishing the taste.

"Acastus says you showed talent in wielding a weapon."

She choked over the mouthful she was about to swallow, blinked, and stared at her brother. Of all the things he could have chosen to speak of, he chose this?

"Yes," she replied slowly, locking gazes with Diokles. "I found it entertaining to hold Acastus's kopis to his throat." One corner of her mouth lifted when he gaped at her, the kylix he was about to take a drink from frozen in place near his mouth. The sideways glance he directed at Acastus satisfied her that she had found a chink in the armour guarding his emotions.

"You found it entertaining until I wrestled it back from you," Acastus cut in with a smirk.

She fought to keep her composure, not helped by the fact that Diokles and Callisto were listening to their exchange with rapt attention. A sinking feeling in her stomach almost undid the remains of her self-control. Surely, he was not about to tell them what had occurred afterwards?

"Only because you are stronger and I had no choice," she accused with a not so subtle warning in her voice to steer clear of further discussing the incident. Thankfully, he obliged.

"I leave soon to carry news of your return to your father."

Xanthia sat up. "So I heard," she announced, undaunted by the raised eyebrows of her companions. An idea burst into her mind, forcing her to suppress a shiver of excitement. "I'll gladly accompany you so I'm not a burden here." Let them take her subtle dig in whatever fashion they chose.

The various reactions around the table relieved her tension. Callisto dropped the fig she held to stare in distress. Diokles sat still as a stone, his lips compressed in a disapproving line. Only Acastus gave her a hard, distrustful look at the easy capitulation. Damn him! But her exasperation could not prevent her pulse skittering at the thought of sharing another long journey with him.

"You are eager to accompany me?"

Xanthia shrugged nonchalantly. "The sooner I meet the man who fathered me, the better." *Once my curiosity is satisfied, I can vanish among the denizens of the city where he lives if I choose to.*

She watched the play of Acastus's firm biceps as he rested his forearms on the table and became caught in the thrall of those knowing eyes, which appeared to bore holes into her brain and see the thoughts within. His ability to read her disturbed her more than she cared to admit.

"Your *father*," he emphasised the word, "will be grateful. I'll send word when I'm ready to leave."

"I go to the agora later and welcome your company," Callisto interrupted. "It's a good opportunity to see the city that is your home and heritage."

"I'm eager to learn more while I'm here," she agreed, taking the offer as a way to smooth over any rough edges which might linger. This place might be her heritage, but it was not yet her home and might never be. Her home had been on a distant island she had grown to love, and where she had discovered acceptance, happiness, and purpose.

Except one dark blight cast a pall over her life. A secret heartache she had revealed to no-one. A secret for which she could face banishment, or worse, if the reason came to light, why, in every sense, she could never take her place in the society she had been born into.

CHAPTER TWENTY-NINE

The bustle and noise made little impression on Xanthia as she skirted the agora with Callisto, secretly marvelling how the latter managed to look more beautiful with a veil covering her hair. To her surprise, this walk she had agreed to summoned an overwhelming desire to understand this land. She rubbed her arms – the need was beginning to concern her.

"Do you have a himation to take to Apollysis?"

"Acastus bought me one in Zarax," she replied. "Why didn't you insist I wear a veil, too? Everyone who's seen me has done nothing but stare."

"Some may have known your mother, Ianthe, well and stare for that reason. Don't fret, only married women are expected to wear a head covering." Callisto gave a rueful half-smile. "My hair should be much shorter. Diokles insisted I let it grow for a while since we lost so much time together."

The uncomfortable yearning to know more about her family took hold of Xanthia. She attempted to shrug it off but could not prevent herself from asking, "What happened?"

The haunted look in Callisto's eyes gave her a moment's pause, and she wished she had not voiced the question.

"It's complicated and the agora isn't the place to tell you, but I will soon."

Xanthia's nerves tightened. True, the agora was no place to talk about family history, or scandals, but she also sensed that Callisto wanted to delay telling her. Her need to know only deepened because of this mystery and gave her still greater reasons to seek out her father.

She turned their conversation to a more pleasant subject. "How did you and Diokles find each other before then?"

"One year during the *Gymnopaedia*," Callisto winked, "the festival where young people have the chance to discover a spouse and often will attend naked to enhance their chances."

"When you say young…"

"Usually, girls and boys who have not yet reached their twentieth year. Girls are not encouraged to marry before then, so our bodies have time to strengthen and carry healthy children and survive their birth."

The revelation caused more pain than if she had been cut open with a knife, like her beloved Calliope had been. She had lost this opportunity, and she would never have the satisfaction of seeing a child of her own participate either. Xanthia used the companionable silence that had settled over them to pour balm over her wounded heart before she spoke again to turn her attention away from the lingering pain.

"Is it normal women are out on their own?" The number of women walking alone or in small, animated groups, was one of the first things she had observed. "On Melos and Kythera, women don't travel much unless with their menfolk." She watched, surprised, as Callisto drew herself up, eyes gleaming.

"Sparta stands above all the other city-states in the freedoms accorded to us women. We can own land in our own right, we are educated, taught to defend ourselves, are free to move around the city on our own. And," she finished on an exultant note, "we rule our men!"

This confirmed what Acastus had already hinted at. Yet, a niggling thought, like an ill-wind, swept through Xanthia's mind. "You say we rule our men. Then why did my mother allow me to be taken away to die?"

Her sister's response was immediate. Callisto stood rooted to the spot, the hitherto healthy glow of her skin replaced by a dull flush. *I've hit a nerve and I need to know more.*

"That is for our father, Aeschylus, to tell you. Even I didn't know of the circumstances until he was able to tell me many years later."

Yes, now she was absolutely certain, Callisto was stalling for a yet-to-be disclosed reason. Her conviction to uncover the truth of this family scandal pushed her to press further, but Callisto, her eyes devoid of their customary sparkle, turned her face away. *Let the subject drop. Use your wiles to find out on the road to Apollysis.*

"I will ask him but let us go on." Xanthia lightly touched her sister's arm, wanting to ease the awkwardness between them. Casting her mind round for another topic, she hit upon something Acastus had said already, but she wanted confirmation from a woman. "Why don't Spartan men say much? All my life I've been around people who like to talk."

"In Lakonia, our Doric dialect has limited words compared to other dialects spoken elsewhere," Callisto explained. "They are men of action, not given to flowery words. Don't make the mistake of thinking they are unintelligent because of this. If anything, it gives them a formidable air."

Her attention was caught by the relief in her sister's voice, but she refrained from asking why a simple change of subject elicited such a response.

"I witnessed all this when Acastus threw me over his shoulder and carried me away from Aphrodite's festival on Melos. Our men pursued him. He swatted them away as easily as one beats away flies."

She stopped when Callisto did, both looking at each other as though seeing one another for the first time. A merchant selling bolts of cloth hurried around to extol the fine material's virtue. Xanthia smiled as he hastily unrolled a particularly beautiful weave, fumbling the length in his haste and just managing not to drop it. She ran a hand over the fabric, marvelling how anything could be so soft. With an apologetic shrug, she left him crestfallen in her wake, aware of Callisto hurrying after her.

"You mentioned Melos. Will you share something of your life there?"

Head held high, Xanthia turned to face her sister. Her past had to come out sooner or later. Now seemed the right moment. The great agora of Sparta would indeed provide a cathartic place to numb some of her hurt.

Leading Callisto to a quieter part of the marketplace, she began in a low voice, "I found out in the worst possible way of my exposure and exile. I came to hate all things Spartan. My foster parents left Kythera when questions were raised about my parentage, and we settled on Melos. Bitterness became my constant companion until I came across a group of Aphrodite's acolytes on the island. My homeland threw me out, they welcomed me. I became one of them and joined in the fertility festivals to the goddess of love."

Her chest lightened as though some great burden had been lifted off it. She looked at Callisto, expecting judgement, but saw only sympathetic acceptance in her gaze. To her great surprise, her sister laid a warm hand on her arm.

"I'm so sorry, Xanthia. One day I'll explain how I came to know of your existence. It wasn't easy for me to hear and far less easy for Diokles. As for your having taken lovers, don't be surprised at my lack of astonishment. It would take a man carved from rock to resist your beauty."

Her knees trembled and she quickly locked them in place. It was the last thing she had expected to hear. "I…thank you. Neither am I surprised my brother married you. You are beautiful too, sister." She returned Callisto's warm smile with a rueful one, "One day I'll become accustomed to referring to you both as my brother and sister without having to remind myself you are in no way related to each other."

"Understandable," Callisto agreed. "Although, sometimes distant, and not-so-distant, relations marry. Our great Agiad king, Leonidas, married his half-brother's daughter, Gorgo. Their son ruled till his death a few years ago. I think you've been told that Diokles is related to the Agiad dynasty through his father's lineage."

"Coming back to Sparta has proved…interesting." *What an understatement.* "I discover my brother is related to some kings, that women command an uncommon amount of freedom, that Spartan men—"

She bit her lip. One Spartan male in particular wielded the power to make her forget her vow to not let any man breach the walls of her heart. Xanthia swallowed and clenched both hands, catching Callisto's speculative look as she did so.

"How did you find Acastus's company?"

She waited until she felt confident her voice would not betray the state of her nerves. "Brash. Boorish. Obstinate. Do I sound like a Spartan now?" Watching her sister struggle not to laugh, she found herself hard-pressed to contain her own smile.

"Yes. But…I couldn't help notice the manner of glances you and Acastus exchanged. You are of an age to marry. He is Diokles's closest friend. Perhaps—"

"No!" She had objected so loudly heads turned their way. "I can never marry. I can never be a Spartan wife. What happened in the past…"

Averting her eyes from the slight bump of her sister's belly, she reminded herself she could never have a child. Not after her son had rejected her. After her body betrayed her.

Xanthia choked over a sob.

"I didn't mean to hurt you," Callisto said, wrapping a comforting arm around her sister's shoulders. "Come and have a drink of water, it will revive you a little."

Calling herself all kinds of fool for exposing her grief, Xanthia allowed herself to be led to where a man provided water for thirsty merchants and buyers alike. She took the proffered kylix and drank deeply. A few more sips and her hands stopped trembling and her legs grew stronger. Covertly studying Callisto, who sipped her own water pensively, she decided her sister had a way of drawing a person in. It was the only explanation why she had freely confessed her innermost thoughts.

The mention of marriage had lit a brief spark of joy before she ruthlessly extinguished it. Some other fortunate woman would marry Acastus. She choked on the final mouthful of water as her throat constricted at the thought of Acastus marrying and siring legitimate heirs. While she would probably have to return to Melos because no man in Sparta would marry a woman incapable of carrying a child.

She ran an agitated hand through her hair, promising to keep Acastus at arm's length from now on. She handed her kylix back and saw Callisto studying her with warm, affectionate eyes. "Thank you, I feel better now."

"Would you like to see the temple of Aphrodite?" Callisto pointed to an imposing temple sitting high and proud on the acropolis. "That is the temple of Athena Chalkioikos, the city's patron goddess. Aphrodite Areia's temple sits on the other side of the hill."

Her mouth fell open. "Areia? Since when does the goddess bear arms?"

"You will find it a unique temple. There are two levels. The first is dedicated to Aphrodite as Areia, the upper level is to Aphrodite Morpho."

Xanthia shook her head at this revelation. "At least 'Morpho' is appropriate since the goddess is acknowledged to be the most beautiful in shape as well as face."

It proved a long walk, although time passed quickly because Callisto pointed out various landmarks to her as they walked past them. Her heart raced as she entered the temple to pay homage, her mind returning to the halcyon days of her childhood, the festivals on Melos, and always her dove, and the tears she had shed on losing the one consolation to her grief.

Now a few welled and slowly trickled down her face, while she spent some time praying that Aphrodite smile upon Philodemos and Euphrasia, that they might reunite with her one day, either here or on Melos, finally praying for guidance on whether to stay in Sparta. Eventually, she rejoined Callisto, who had waited outside in the warm sun.

"What has upset you?"

Unused to such concern, she lied. "Nothing, I was just lost in memories of my life." Clearly, her shaky voice did not convince Callisto who's eyes held a sceptical look but she was grateful her sister did not press her further. Instead, they retraced their steps to the agora.

They were approaching the senate building, which caught her interest. So, this was where Acastus had hurried to on the day of their arrival. An imposing building, she was admiring the columns when she walked straight into Callisto's back.

"*Mother?*"

Xanthia stepped to her sister's side and placed a hand on her shoulder. Beneath it, she could feel Callisto trembling violently, one hand pressed to her mouth. In contrast, her mother's face flushed red, her lips thinned in a tight line. The silence between them brewed with all the turbulence of a raging storm. Glancing from one face to the other, she wondered whether she might not have missed anything in not knowing her own mother.

More closely, she scrutinised the older, though still attractive, woman whose stance appeared to give off waves of hostile uncertainty before Callisto's mother locked gazes with her. Her abdomen clenched in protest as though she had just received a superhuman punch to her middle. She heard the woman's loud hiss, but the disapproving sound paled in comparison to the loathing filling her eyes. Xanthia met the woman's inspection of her with a challenging stare. Angling her chin, she waited for the uncomfortable silence to break. *Why does Callisto's mother hate me?*

"Callisto."

Xanthia inhaled a sharp breath at the frigid tone, interlacing her fingers to stop herself giving both women a hard shake. She, who had never known a mother, could not understand their need to distance themselves from each other.

"I didn't know you had returned, mother. I wasn't even sure if you were alive. This is Xanthia, who is half-sister to Diokles and me." Callisto turned to her. "My mother, Akantha."

She had experienced jealousy from other women when men favoured her, but though she wracked her memories, Xanthia failed to recall a time she had been regarded with such an intense dislike, bordering on hatred. The fiery glare in Akantha's eyes was so heated she was surprised her skin remained unsinged.

"I greet you. May the—"

"Ah, yes, Ianthe's daughter," Akantha jeered. "I thought you were a ghost. Has your father seen you yet? Take care, Callisto, Aeschylus may favour his spawn from another woman over you, regardless that you are the offspring of his wife."

Xanthia clutched her throat, the wildly beating pulse in her neck throbbing against her fingers. This revelation of family history explained much of Akantha's vitriol and perhaps some of her sibling's wariness around herself. Her sister's face was splotched with colour, a hand stealing to her waist. The latter movement was akin to having icy water poured through her. It cleared her mind, allowing her to leap to Callisto's defence.

"It's true I have much to learn of my family," Xanthia asserted in haughty tones, "but I don't believe our father would do such a thing to my sister."

Akantha's face twisted as though she had bitten into the bitterest lemon. The satisfaction in putting a jealous woman in her place acted like a balm to her soul. She had had enough experience to make her a master of the art.

"You think not, girl? Perhaps you may discover differently once he meets you."

Xanthia opened her mouth to retort, then quickly shut it when Callisto laid a restraining hand on her arm. Relief flooded her when she saw that colour was stealing back into Callisto's pale cheeks, and her hands no longer shook. It took an effort not to retaliate given the hurt infecting mind and body, the hurt which she had shared with no-one; the agony of her body being ripped apart, the despair of losing a baby, the joy of motherhood snatched from her by some avenging Fury.

"I agree with Xanthia. Please dine with us this evening? I welcome the chance to hear about your life since we last saw each other."

If Callisto sought to heal open wounds, Xanthia could see by Akantha's face that her sister had failed miserably. What mother disliked her child so much to remain aloof in the face of a proffered olive branch? The little she had gleaned so far, she understood her own mother had wanted her and been given no say in the matter.

"Dine in that house? No." Akantha took a step back and averted her face. "I must find your uncle. Goodbye."

Slack-jawed, Xanthia watched Akantha's retreating form until she was swallowed up by the crowd of people going about their business. Later, she would question her mental lapse in taking Callisto's hand to comfort her. She well understood the rigid jawline obviously holding her sister's deep hurt at bay. She had overcome the anguish of losing a longed-for child, having had years to practice exerting control over her emotions.

"Don't concern yourself, Callisto, your mother's words didn't affect me." The lie slipped easily off her tongue. The words affected her more than she was prepared to admit, and she now had proof that the passing years had not altered the attitudes of some involved in this wider tragedy. She was still the interloper. The one to be cast aside and forgotten. "Shall we go home."

"Pardon?" Callisto shook her head. "Sorry…yes…yes, we'll go home. I'll help you pack some essentials for your journey to Apollysis. Diokles told me this morning that Acastus will be ready to leave in a day or two to escort our father home."

It was clear her sister was prattling and disturbed by meeting her mother. The skin between Xanthia's shoulder blades prickled. Casting an uneasy look behind her, she mused whether someone else carried a grudge over her very existence. Trying to make sense out of the awkward encounter, she trailed Callisto as the latter absentmindedly bustled out of the agora without a further word.

The walk back to Diokles's house passed in an uneasy silence and she grew concerned over her sister's behaviour. Callisto avoided eye contact, repeatedly dragged her fingers through her blond hair, having pushed her veil off her head. Not having to say anything gave her time to make an important decision – she would go to Apollysis, meet her father, then slip away before anyone realised she had gone.

She did not want to slip away, but to protect herself and others she must. Akantha's hostility had shown her how strong was her own deeply buried need for her family's acceptance and love. She shuddered, not wanting to consider the consequences if she failed to secure it.

CHAPTER THIRTY

No sooner did they reach the house than Callisto summoned a male servant. "Go to the barracks and ask for your master," she said, when the man arrived, "tell him I will follow you there shortly."

"Yes, mistress." The servant bowed and immediately left at a jog to carry out her instructions.

"Can I help in any way?"

Callisto started, flustered by both the question and that she had overlooked Xanthia's presence. Although she radiated her usual calm demeanour, a demeanour she had perfected during her time as Apollo's high priestess in Apollysis, her stomach was twisting itself into knots. She summoned a wan smile. "No, it's something important I forgot to speak to Diokles about." Then, seeing Xanthia's face fall into confusion, she sought to soothe her. "Let me change my chiton for riding, then come to see the horses. I won't be long."

A short while later, she had left Xanthia at the stables and was cantering her favourite mare, Astara, who she had ridden the first time Diokles had brought her here, towards the barracks. The mare's smooth, sure-footed gait enabled her to think over what had happened earlier.

Seeing her mother abruptly after so many years had left her shaken. Akantha's coldness towards her remain unchanged from when she was a child. Callisto had hoped that by extending an olive branch to her mother it would change their relationship but she had been wrong. The rejection had hurt, and hurt even more, knowing she was pregnant and would have welcomed her mother's happiness at the news. Instead, Akantha had spoken words that had carried the power to carve wounds into the joy she had felt at her sister's return.

She rode on, looking straight ahead, not hearing her name called out by friends, whom she left open-mouthed in her wake. Reaching the barracks, where women rarely, or never, went, Callisto let out a *whoosh* of air, only now realising how tight her chest was from having held her breath. A few hoplites stood outside, leaning against posts or the building. Dismissing their astonished looks as she dismounted, she recognised one as a member of Diokles's syssition, but asking him to summon her husband became unnecessary when he walked out to meet her.

"Diokles, if only you obeyed the general like you obey your wife!" one of them baited him good-naturedly.

"I remember you hiding from yours when you didn't obey her summons to come home for the night," he mocked his peer with a wide grin.

At any other time, she would have joined in the teasing and laughter, but she saw that the grin Diokles wore was forced. Without a word, she let him lead her a short distance away so no-one would overhear. His grin vanished immediately as he clasped her shoulders.

"What happened?" He swept a concerned glance over her hair, "you've even forgotten your veil."

"Ah, so that's why I received all those looks." She closed her eyes, then opened them to stare at her husband. "I met my mother in the agora." She felt his hands tighten on her shoulders. "I asked her to dine with us, but I think she still can't stand the sight of me."

"Interesting that your uncle has said nothing about her returning." His gaze swept up over the acropolis. "Both our mothers have failed us."

"Don't say that," she gasped. "Ianthe loved me like my own mother never did. She would never have said—"

Callisto bit her tongue, but it was not enough to put her overly observant husband off the scent.

"Said what?"

She sighed heavily, wanting to ignore the warning in his voice, but Akantha's words preyed upon her. "Xanthia was with me. By my mother's manner it's obvious she loathes her and hasn't forgotten or forgiven your mother. She said…she said that I should take care that our father doesn't favour Xanthia over me…" Her voice broke, and she winced at the brutal curse that flew from Diokles's mouth.

"It was a mistake to bring her back."

"Don't say that!" she cried. "How else will my father return if Zeus has willed this course. Not only that, Xanthia is one of us, she must take up her role as a Spartan, her courage demands it. She stood up to my mother in defence of me." She studied Diokles, the tension growing as she watched his face harden and grow cold.

"I salute her at least for that. Whenever I look at her all I see is my mother's failure to tell me and that Xanthia was the reason you were forced to flee."

"You can't blame her for that, she was a baby," Callisto stormed at him, watching the muscle in his jaw clench. "I thought you had made peace with the past, perhaps I was wrong—"

"Half the barracks will hear you." He threw his hands up to stall her. "Let me deal with this in my own way."

Callisto rubbed her eyes, knowing exactly what 'his way' meant. He would bury the problem like the warrior he was unless it ate away at him, and then…

"If my father does favour Xanthia, what will you do?" she probed. "Challenge him to a fight until one of you is killed?"

"Of course not," he raged in a furious whisper. "I wouldn't hurt you, nor do I fight my peers to the death."

Hearing Diokles's name shouted from the barracks, she pressed her lips together to forestall further discussion. Returning his light kiss of farewell, her heart danced as she watched him stride back into the quadrangle. Marriage, and carrying his child, had simply served to strengthen her desire. Callisto briefly wished she had inherited some of her mother's hard-heartedness. Because, if she were honest with herself, she would confess that the thought of her father favouring her sister hurt deeper than she believed possible.

CHAPTER THIRTY-ONE

Acastus's tireless strides swiftly covered the distance to his family's lands, which lay in an easterly direction from the agora and nestled close to the village of Limnai. He ran an assessing eye over the abundant vista. Crops swayed in a light breeze while sheep and goats grazed on still-green grass. This land would be his one day. To be passed on to his son – if he ever fathered one who was truly his heir.

He came to an uncertain halt as a sense of urgency he had never experienced plucked at his nerves. He had already fathered two boys, as well as a daughter, at the behest of their separate families. This feat, while worthy, would in no way save him from being ridiculed by his peers for remaining unmarried.

The dilemma played on his mind with the relentless regularity of waves breaking on the shore. Securing a wife presented him with his next mission. Prior to the campaign to take Apollysis, he had considered marrying a woman from a Spartiate family in Mesoa, a village to the south of Limnai. Young and healthy and attractive, she would have given him the children to carry on his family name and inherit his property after him.

Then the gods had intervened and brought him to Xanthia. His ordered world had been plunged into turmoil.

A shouted greeting pushed the niggling predicament to the back of his mind. He grinned at the sight of his father, still vigorous and healthy after surviving numerous battles and more than fifty summers of life. Acastus hugged him, both clapping each other on the back. He stepped back to study Pancratius. "You look well. Any tidings I should know of?"

Pancratius winked. "I was elected the first new ephor. I and my supporters shouted the loudest."

Pride filled Acastus despite laughing at his father's words. "Loudest or not, you deserve the position. No doubt you will keep our kings in line. Who else is joining you?"

His father named them.

"Worthy choices," Acastus agreed with a conspiratorial grin. "No doubt they shouted loudly, too. I remember their voices being easily heard even over the din of battle."

"You, too, are worthy of commendation, my son. I heard you succeeded in your mission to bring Aeschylus's estranged daughter back to her family."

An expectant look wreathed his father's battle-scarred face. Acastus released a resigned breath, readying himself for the inevitable questions. But first he needed answers of his own. "Safely returned, although with some challenges. Drakon disappeared not long after we left Zarax. Did he come back?"

His father's face tightened in anger. "He is dead. I have no doubt one of the kryptoi killed him, but his body was found close to Theron's kleros."

A fist of suspicion punched Acastus low in the gut. "What? Why wouldn't he return here first?"

"That, too, was my question."

He stared at his father, not really seeing him, his mind busily putting all the circumstances together. "I suspected something amiss with Drakon on the return journey," he said uneasily, as a seed of discomfort took root. "Although Xanthia insists he didn't attempt to push her overboard, I still have my doubts."

"He tried to kill her? Why?"

Acastus rubbed his forehead. "Everything that occurred suggested Drakon might have been bribed."

"To accuse a fellow Spartiate of such an act is dangerous without proof," Pancratius warned.

"I know, but it's the only explanation possible. Soon after he disappeared, I was attacked by Argive pirates."

"I hope you did what you needed to do."

He met his father's gimlet stare with a shrug. "Do you doubt otherwise? I was injured while dispatching some of them to Hades, but Xanthia healed me."

"Hmm. You became a full citizen in the spring. It's time you took a wife."

The sigh he heaved travelled all the way to his feet. "A fruitless distraction since my sister has already given you grandchildren." He pressed on with the important details, "Do you think Theron somehow managed to bribe Drakon?"

While his father stared over the land for a long time before answering, he used the pause to consider the best way to discover if bribery had been involved. It explained much except Theron's motive.

"The right questions in the right places will give us an answer," Pancratius finally replied. He rubbed his trim beard thoughtfully. "I hear rumblings of Theron paying less of his share toward his evening meal. Aeschylus was, or still is, his brother-in-law; perhaps he thinks to claim his kleroi since no-one has lived there since his sister left."

Acastus slapped a hand against his hip. "By Zeus, that makes sense. Aeschylus's land is even richer than yours. Diokles and I saw one of the new appointees to the Gerousia talking with Theron after I presented my mission. What do we do about him?"

"We do nothing without proof. Theron is cunning, so you must be equally so to outmanoeuvre him." Pancratius crossed his arms over his chest and studied his son with a calculating smile only a father could give. "Speaking of your friend, why don't you marry his sister?"

"She's tried to kill me," Acastus blurted out. To his chagrin, his father guffawed heartily and did not stop until tears of mirth ran from his eyes.

"A true Spartan woman, then," Pancratius chuckled, wiping his eyes. "She'd make you a fine wife."

The thought of Xanthia nursing his child summoned a desire that raced with blistering heat through every organ, nerve, and cell inside him. He was not ready to tell anyone of his part in her banishment, and certainly not until the opportunity presented itself to tell her first.

He managed a circumspect reply. "Xanthia has just arrived home. She has yet to meet her father. I'm ordered to Apollysis to apprise him that the conditions have been fulfilled for his return."

"Well, you can make him an offer of marriage for his daughter once you get there."

His father's talent for unflagging focus had ensured his rise to a general and now an ephor. Too bad that talent was now being directed at ensuring his son chose a wife and soon. "I'll collect my shield, provisions, and servants." He paused. Better his father hear it from him. "Xanthia travels with me to meet her father in Apollysis, and *my* father's smile is too smug."

"You know your duty, my son."

Yes, he knew his duty – marry, sire children. Acastus led the way into the courtyard, already planning ahead. The journey to Apollysis would provide valuable time to teach Xanthia more survival skills and about the society that was her birthright. All knowledge she had missed out on for twenty years of her life.

And to assess whether he could risk marrying her in a way guaranteed to leave him alive to cherish her as she deserved to be cherished as his wife and a future mother of Sparta.

CHAPTER THIRTY-TWO

Xanthia swung her right leg over the grey mare's back and landed lightly beside her. She had found herself remarkably pleased that Kyra, whom she had ridden from the time their unwieldy group had left Sparta, had accepted and then bonded with her. Patting the mare's neck, she whispered words of thanks to her mount for securely carrying her this day.

Stretching tired legs, she rejoiced that her muscles did not complain as much as they had the morning after her first full day of riding. She expelled an indignant breath recalling the stiff, protesting muscles on the second day, refusing to ride, then volubly cursing Acastus when he had swept her up to dump her unceremoniously on Kyra's back.

"Your riding ability improves."

She took her time turning to face Acastus who stood an arm's length away, studying her with a glint in his eye that spoke of both surprise and gratification. If only her traitorous heart would stop thumping madly every time she looked at him. "I have a good teacher." She tossed the jibe his way, thanks to her new-found understanding of Sparta's structured society. "I suppose I should thank my brother for insisting he accompany us."

One of the perioikoi – a free non-citizen – had been teaching her along the way. To her annoyance she had failed to rattle Acastus by praising a man of a lower class.

"He is renowned for his horsemanship skills, and a long journey provides time to hone your ability."

Xanthia sighed. She had been doing nothing but learning since beginning this trek to Apollysis. Her first lesson, apart from riding, had been to understand the nature of their companions. As well as her riding tutor, another perioikoi accompanied them to provide extra fighters should they be ambushed. The two helot servants – essentially a slave class – tended to the meals and horses. Her mind had melted, much like Icarus's wings, from all the information she had to absorb.

Wary of the helots after her encounter with Drakon, she found these two to be deferential and compliant. So much so that she had secretly dressed a wound for one of them. Thinking back to when she last tended to the man, she determined the dressing needed changing and had contained her impatience to do so until they stopped for the night. Given that the entire party had dismounted and were tethering horses, this was the place.

Digging through the saddlebag, her fingers closed around her bag of herbs, pulling it out and preparing her arguments against the objections she expected from Acastus.

"Where are you going?"

"Don't worry, I won't run away. I need to re-dress your servant's wound."

"They can see to themselves," Acastus ordered in a disapproving tone. "In Sparta, our women are not required to stoop to menial tasks, especially for a helot."

Xanthia tried hard but failed to stop the wave of temper flaring. Forgetting the watching eyes, she stomped over and poked Acastus in the chest. "Don't tell me what I can and can't do! I dressed the wound yesterday while you were busy hunting. I need to clean it again."

Her loud, startled yelp rang out as his hand shot out to grab her arm, and she found herself hauled out of earshot. She gulped and nervously questioned whether she had pushed him beyond his control or crossed some invisible cultural line. Brought to an abrupt halt, she tugged her arm, growling in her throat when he refused to let go.

"Don't challenge my authority in front of the others."

"I thought Spartan women did that all the time to their men. Or has Callisto told me a lie."

"No lie. Wives do challenge their husbands, but you're not my wife. Yet."

Yet?

Xanthia blinked, then studied Acastus, whose ruggedly handsome features were flushed a dull red, his head thrown back as though he had taken a direct hit in a fight. She looked down as he released her arm, the slide of his fingers along her skin an involuntary caress. Slack-jawed, she once again wondered what it would be like to tame him, rule his desires, bear his children.

Impossible.

She found herself fighting a longing for closeness that had crept up on her unawares. Suspecting he was just as shaken as herself, she stepped away to give the time and distance needed to collect her chaotic thoughts. "I will tend to your servant's wound. Please don't stop me. My own suffering has led me to detest seeing any other living being endure the same."

Why had she laid out her hurt for him to use as a possible weapon over her? Feeling like she had left part of her heart behind, Xanthia pivoted and hurried back to prepare the poultice she would need.

~*~

Acastus pinched the bridge of his nose and questioned at what point his sanity had abandoned him. After remonstrating with himself time and again that Xanthia remained out of his reach, for the moment at least, he had essentially announced to her face his desire to marry her. He blamed his father for pushing the idea that she would make his son a perfect wife.

Rubbing the back of his neck, he swore under his breath – it was not his father's fault at all. Xanthia had been gradually insinuating herself past his defences from the moment he had seen her. Her face and form – while taking his breath away – drew him in no less than her capacity for loyalty and love of those she held dear; the need inside of her to help those it was not her place to help, the spirit and energy which had carried her through life.

And always between them hovered the memory of the day they had made love by the banks of the Eurotas. He blew out a breath and relaxed his tight shoulders. By unspoken agreement, neither had ever mentioned their sudden 'lapse', although it remained a constant source of tension between them. Trained to notice everything, he had seen the covert looks under her lashes when she thought he was not looking; the slight hitch in her breathing whenever they brushed against each other; the constant teasing – as though she had been raised among Spartans – to get a rise out of him, in more ways than one.

He found himself waging an unceasing war between desire and duty. Watching her tend the helot's wound, the beauty of her face in profile, it required all his self-control to not march over and pull her away from a task she would in all likelihood never do again once this journey was over.

Dragging his gaze away from her, he noticed the other helot clearing a space to light a fire and two large branches struck into the ground, ready to suspend any wild game he caught. Time had been wasted while he stood here staring at a woman! A grunt of self-disgust was his cue to march off into the forest to hunt for their dinner.

It took longer than he liked, but the gods were with him when he came across a wild goat, his scent carried away from the animal by a moderate breeze. Acastus stalked it until he was satisfied the goat was in the best position for him to spring a trap. Dispatching it with one swift stroke, he carried it to the camp to find the fire had been lit and the larger pieces of wood sufficiently burned down to cook a meal. The two servants hurried to collect the carcass from him and set about preparing the goat for roasting.

"Are all Spartan men such great hunters?"

Acastus stilled as Xanthia came to stand beside him, the scent of her hair enveloping him.

"You should know better than to stray too far from the camp," he admonished, more concerned for her welfare than was healthy for his peace of mind. Her exaggerated sigh would have done any actor in the great theatre of Sparta proud.

"I only went as far as the stream you decided was the place to spend the night."

Recalling how he had found her in another stream, he frowned, the disapproval growing deeper when she laughed at him.

"I only washed my face and rinsed my hair with some herbs." She looked him up and down with a knowing smile. "Don't worry, I'm not so foolish as to try and bathe on my own."

This was not a path he wanted to go down, especially with others present. To relieve his discomfort, he searched around the perimeter of the camp until he found a decent sized log, which he then dragged near the fire and motioned for her to sit, answering her question when she obliged. "All Spartan boys learn to hunt. Some of us are better than others."

He watched her worry her lip as though she was wondering whether to voice another question which he sensed was coming. Captivated by the way her dark, glossy hair framed her face, he lost himself in the flicker of firelight reflected in her eyes. As she lifted her gaze to his, he fought against a powerful desire until it fled with the speed of Hermes's winged sandals at her next words.

"Tell me about my father. Will he be happy to see me? Others appear not to have welcomed my return."

"You'll see for yourself when you meet him." He could only give scant details, and of those, he needed to be circumspect about what he divulged. "Which others? You can't think Callisto and Diokles have regrets." He sat up, alert to the way her mouth thinned, suddenly speculating on what had passed between Xanthia and her half-siblings while he had been busy with other duties.

"Have they truly? I was with Callisto when we unexpectedly met her mother. I could survive Medusa's stare after the way that woman looked at me."

Acastus leaned back as understanding dawned. "You'll grow weary of hearing you're the image of your mother. I'm not privy to the past, only your father knows everything that occurred."

"Only if he chooses to be honest with me, and in my experience most men are not."

The pain in her voice struck deep because he was responsible for most of it. "Aeschylus is a good man, a man esteemed by his peers, who sacrificed his future to save Callisto." Against the light of the gloaming, he saw a wounded, disbelieving look in her eyes and wanted nothing more than to embrace her. He needed to give her something to make her understand her exile had been forced upon her parents. "Also to save you. Did Philodemos tell you how you came to be rescued?"

"I didn't want to know. When I overheard them speaking of how they smuggled me out, I was too furious to listen to reason and never wanted to talk about it afterwards."

Take care, Acastus, and be mindful of what you reveal.

"Philodemos told me your mother managed to get word to Aeschylus that you'd been exposed on Taygetos." Her flinch drove a dagger deep into his heart. "Your father entrusted him and Euphrasia with a perioikoi, who escorted them out of Sparta after you'd been recovered."

"How did they know where to find me?"

"You were exposed on a known place on the mountain. They looked there first and heard your cries."

The sparkle of tears illuminating her eyes, the clenched hands, checked him. The truth was painful, and it would become even more brutal for the both of them. "Aeschylus provided well for his servants. The perioikoi returned after he delivered you all to Gytheion. Without him, none of you would have survived."

"And, of course, my father's role in breaking some sort of honour code would be known."

Acastus stiffened. "Any kryptos would never believe whatever they told him, even if Aeschylus was mentioned. The hidden ones are out proving their survival skills and defending our sovereignty."

The scent of meat roasting turned his attention away from Xanthia, who stared unseeing into the embers of the fire. He welcomed the fact the meat was almost done so that this conversation, which had taken a turn he had not foreseen, could end. Enough had been revealed, for now, and she would need the remaining time to Apollysis to reflect on what he had told her.

"The food is ready. Eat well, we'll be in Apollysis in a day or two." The fine tremor in her hands hinted to him that she was not as ready to face her father as she claimed.

CHAPTER THIRTY-THREE

The tension behind, and around her eyes, blurred Xanthia's vision. She blinked repeatedly to focus – she needed to see clearly as she walked through the city gates of Apollysis. The beat of her heart was a dull thud in her chest that threatened to choke her. Desperate for a sip of water to moisten the dryness in her mouth, which had overcome her as soon as the city walls were in sight, she chose to endure the discomfort, reluctant to betray to Acastus how much this impending meeting was already affecting her.

After so much lost time, so much bitterness and hurt, she was close to seeing the man who she might one day truly regard as her father. With a toss of her head, she poured the cold water of reality over the thought. No matter how momentous this looming meeting, it was foolish to believe it carried the power to absolve all the pain of the past. If there was one thing she had learned from life, it was to guard her feelings and not voluntarily expose her heart to more grief.

She stole a glance at the man walking beside her in a subtle show of support. Chest pushed out, he forged ahead as though he owned his surroundings. Xanthia sighed and admitted he did that anyway, but there was an extra confidence in his step as they wound their way closer to the acropolis of the city. Her gaze darted everywhere, trying to absorb more sights and sounds than was manageable, comparing this place to the buildings of Sparta she had, however briefly, come to know. The further they walked, the more obvious it became to her that almost every denizen spared them a quick, nervous glance before giving Acastus and the two armed perioikoi a wide berth.

"The last time I was here, was with your brother," Acastus informed her, "to uncover a plot to invade Sparta."

Xanthia started. He had been silent since they had crested the hills which ringed the city that morning, so this spontaneous offering of information caught her unawares. "Ah, now I understand why the people are looking at you as if the Minotaur has been unleashed upon them. How many did you kill?"

"Only those who barred our way."

The level, confident tone the words were delivered in turned her blood cold. "I have spent time with you and time in Sparta, yet I can't embrace the way you think. I don't know whether I'll be able to ever understand, or come to accept, such a ruthless way of thinking." She met his hard gaze, astonished when his face softened into an encouraging smile.

"A Spartan, man or woman, is not forged in a day. Your heritage will prevail over any distaste you still harbour."

A breath shuddered through her parted lips. Would she live up to his confidence in her? The high expectations of the society she had returned to? There was only one way to find out and that was to meet her father. After that she would decide her own future and the means available to her to direct its course. Her admiring gaze fell on the magnificent temple to their left, which gleamed in the morning light. "Which god is the temple dedicated to?"

"Apollo. Your father and Callisto sought sanctuary there when they first arrived. She became its high priestess."

Xanthia came to an abrupt halt. "She never told me she was a priestess," she whispered in a tremulous voice. If she needed further proof that there was more, possibly unpalatable, family secrets to discover, the blankness spreading over Acastus's features convinced her. "Tell me more."

"I know little to nothing of their life here."

"But you know something?" She studied the flattened, uncompromising line of his mouth. He knew more than he was admitting to, she could feel remorse coming off him in waves. However, his inadvertent admission gave her the seed of an idea. If her father and Callisto had sought sanctuary here, then she could do the same if such a decision became necessary.

Certain she would get no more information at the moment, and after one last, lingering look at the temple, she followed when he motioned her to keep up with him. They were now walking past well-tended homes that were larger and more solid-looking than those she had first seen upon their arrival. This was very different to Sparta, where the homes of the wealthy were located on their private land, and as removed from her life on Melos as if she had walked into the halls of Olympus itself.

"These are homes of private citizens. We are almost at your father's house."

Xanthia shivered. "How did you know what I was thinking?"

"I didn't," Acastus returned in a neutral tone. "The order of life here must be very different from what you have known."

She wanted to snipe back that this way of life was not of her choosing but held her tongue. Soon. Soon, she would meet her father, the very thought speeding up her heart to such a tempo that her fingers went numb, and a sensation akin to the pitching of a boat in rough seas swamped her head. She tripped over her feet and righted herself before Acastus noticed.

Breathe, Xanthia. It will be alright.

For a fleeting moment, she considered clutching his arm for support. The impulse vanished as quickly as mist before the rising sun. She had heard over and over about the bravery and strength of Spartan women. Well, she was one of them by birth at least. She did not need his support in order to meet the man who had sired her and never seen her after that time.

Far too quickly, with no time to compose the storm of feelings assailing her, she trailed Acastus into a shaded courtyard. She came to a halt, knees trembling, and strove to compose herself by taking an interest in the pleasant space around her. A large well sat in the centre, the ground paved with stone, a luxury she had never seen. It brought to mind how the mud, after heavy rains fell, would envelop the compact dwellings she had lived in. No mud would dare encroach here, she mused.

Looking up, she spotted a riot of flowers growing out of nooks and crannies in the walls, her gaze drawn to a spike of purple flowers she could not recall having seen anywhere else. Fascinated by the innumerable blooms, she was drawn to the plant and pressed her nose to the flowers, enveloped by their sweet scent. Absorbed in the shape of the delicate petals, she failed to hear the low murmur of people approaching.

"Acastus! What brings you here?"

Xanthia's head shot up. She pressed a hand to the wall for support as alternate waves of cold and heat battered her. Anger, fear, longing, delight, swirled and foamed on the shores of her heart. Unable to tear her eyes away, she stared at the older man who had come out to greet Acastus. Was this tall, well-looking stranger with the neat beard, the same long hair as all the Spartan men wore, her father?

Her pulse beat heavily as though every beat required an effort to move through thick honey. She gulped air into her lungs as a loud sob escaped before she could clap a hand over her mouth to stop it.

Two pairs of eyes, like twin arrows loosed from the bow of Artemis, pierced her. Her gaze locked with her father's, and a ringing started in her ears as she fully beheld his face for the first time, a face so white it looked like all blood had been drained from him.

She tried to move, but her legs felt like dead-weights. Xanthia twisted her hands together, unsure of what to do, of what to say as both men came to her. She saw her father's chest heaving with the struggle to breathe, then, lifting one trembling hand, he gently cupped her cheek, grief and wonderment clearly written across his features. It took all the strength and courage she possessed to stop herself collapsing on the ground.

The silence was unbearable. She wanted to reach out somehow; she wanted to throw up to relieve the nausea in her gut. For the first time since she had met him, she truly felt gratitude for Acastus's presence, at the same time troubled to see his hands clenched and a nerve working below his eyelid.

"Xanthia, your father, Aeschylus. Once I've seen to the others, I'll return."

"But—"

It was too late; he was already disappearing out into the street. How could he leave her like this?

"Xanthia?"

Sweat broke out over her body, the material of the chiton clinging uncomfortably close to her skin. She did not want to be moved by a word that had been uttered in a way that conveyed pain, hope, and joy, all rolled into her name.

"Yes," she confirmed in a whisper, clasping her hands in front of her and falling silent. The adult Xanthia raged that she wanted to curse her father; the abandoned child within her longed to embrace him, touch his brown eyes, and feel for herself whether the light film of moisture covering them was real. "You are my father?" She winced at the inanity of the statement.

"I am, and my heart is gladdened to see you. Come inside." Aeschylus called out to the servants to bring food and drink. "This way," he indicated with his hand.

She walked through a door into a light-filled room, aware of her father following and watching her every move. A fierce desire to hit Acastus swamped her for having left her alone, not because she lacked courage, but because of the overload on her senses – seeing her father for the first time, unsure of what to talk about that would not bring them more hurt.

To give herself time, she took in the room, the space, the large table with a number of stools around it, a far cry from the small table and three stools her foster parents possessed. The room was sparsely furnished otherwise, similar to Diokles's home. With a wan smile at Aeschylus, she sank onto one of the stools while he chose to sit almost opposite her.

Servants silently appeared with kylikes filled with water and wine, plates filled with the customary cheese, figs, honey, and oil for dipping the freshly baked bread into. Her stomach rumbled in appreciation. Face warm, she explained, "Forgive me, I didn't eat much this morning." The truth was she had been too nervous to break her fast. The knowledge that she would meet this man today had sat like a stone in her stomach.

"There is nothing to apologise for," Aeschylus assured her. "Eat. Then we can talk."

To her immense surprise, his understanding and encouragement opened her appetite. She found herself relishing the food while her father barely ate, more occupied with looking upon her with a warm, benign smile. She finished the last morsel of her bread, exhaled in satisfaction, and sat back. At that moment, she noticed the tremor in her father's hands.

"Are you displeased with me?" she challenged, hiding her discomfort behind a show of boldness. "You have stared at me since I arrived."

"Never think that my child. I hoped for yet despaired of ever seeing you. I am only amazed at how much you are the image of your mother."

Xanthia gaped at him, unable to credit that his voice broke when he mentioned the woman who had borne her. All her old insecurities rose like hackles. Certainly, her father appeared overjoyed to see her but would he grow to love her for herself alone or because she reminded him of her mother, the woman he had loved and lost?

"I see." She shifted on her seat, then raised her chin. "Will you tell me about her?"

She watched Aeschylus reach for her hand, draw back, then take it between both of his. She pushed away the sudden onrush of joy and love that had risen from some buried place in her soul. Maintaining a distance was crucial to hearing anything he told her with a calm, clear head.

"Your mother and I loved each other, but I was sent on a campaign before we could marry. On my return, I found she had been forcibly married to Diokles's father, Lysander. After siring your brother, he sustained an injury in battle that left him unable to sire more children. He refused to accept me as a genitor when he wanted another son. Your mother, Ianthe, secretly came to me." His grip on her hand tightened. "You are the child of our love."

Two opposing forces battled with the might of a phalanx in her heart. One pushed her to throw her arms around her real father and sob on his shoulder; the other pushed her away, insisting she hang on to the anger and betrayal to protect herself. She looked away, unable to meet Aeschylus's steady gaze. The look in his eyes spoke of sincerity, but how could she trust him?

"I…" she drew a deep breath and tried again. "I don't know what I want or what I feel. It would be so easy to accept that everything is healed and forgiven, but you know nothing of what happened to me or my foster parents."

"We can begin to know one another on the way home," Aeschylus assured her. "Now that you are here, I, too, can return to Sparta."

Xanthia opened her mouth, then shut it like a trap, mind working furiously. "What do you mean you can return to Sparta now that I'm here?" Her heart felt as though it had dropped to her toes and back again as Aeschylus drew back with a troubled expression.

"Didn't Callisto tell you why I was unable to return with her and Diokles?"

It was warm inside the house, but it felt like ice was freezing her chest. "All I was told was that you still lived here and would want to see me," she said slowly, watching his face like an eagle watched its prey before swooping. She had been right to trust her instincts and hold back from opening her heart, directing much of her fury towards Acastus. He had lied to her by omission and been complicit in not revealing vital details she obviously needed to know. "What else has been kept secret from me?"

Aeschylus cleared his throat. "To protect you, Philodemos, and Euphrasia, I never tried to discover where they had gone. When Lysander threatened Callisto's life, I followed Athena's counsel and fled Sparta. After Diokles invaded Apollysis, he and Callisto were reunited after many difficulties faced by all of us. To atone for what I had allowed to happen to Callisto, the high priestess of Olympia ordained that I could return to Sparta only if you were found and returned, too."

Another violent wave of nausea hit her. She wrenched her hand away from him, stood up, swayed, and walked away to stare out of a window overlooking the courtyard. Her hands clenched so hard the nails dug deep into her palms.

Screaming her frustration out might help, but there were other ways of gaining revenge. Damn the Spartans and their ridiculous notions. Consumed by red-hot anger, she could have sent her father, and Acastus, and every Spartan male to the realms of Hades, smiling while she did so.

Fighting for control, she turned back to Aeschylus, sniffing contemptuously at the plea in his eyes. "It appears I have something other than a father in common with my half-sister. Our lives were ruined by men. What happened to her?"

Her father rose from his seat, the plea replaced by a look of power she met with a bravado she was far from feeling. Once again she had underestimated a Spartan male.

"Your lives were blighted, but it was preferrable than seeing you both dead. Your sister found it in her heart to forgive me. I pray to Zeus, that one day, when you know and understand me and our ways better, you may find it in your heart to do the same."

The sting of tears forced her to shut her eyes. When she opened them, she discovered herself alone in the room. Xanthia pressed a hand to her chest and leaned back against the cool wall. How many more blows could she endure? Would she ever learn the entire truth of the tragedies that had struck her family?

All her problems came back to Acastus. If he had never forced her from Melos, she would still be there, living peacefully and not exposed to more heartache. Yes, he possessed the power to rouse her passions to a pitch that rendered her unable to think, but that did not mean she could not bend him to her will and extract Callisto's past from him.

Her belly tightened, the sudden burst of arousal clearing the fog of distress in her mind. Acastus desired her, and for some inexplicable reason, her goddess had decreed she desire him. The ghost of a smile flickered across her face as a plan began to unfold in her mind.

CHAPTER THIRTY-FOUR

The piece of cheese, that was halfway to her mouth, dropped in Xanthia's lap as she stared at Acastus and her father. "What do you mean men and women don't eat together? Why am I eating with you now?"

She met the gleam of humour and indulgence in Aeschylus's eye. "Because we aren't in Sparta at the moment," he answered. "Didn't Acastus speak of the custom where our men eat their evening meal with their syssitia? It's important our warriors bond and understand each other and communal eating provides this opportunity."

"And what about bonding with, and understanding, their wives?" Xanthia challenged. To her chagrin both men threw back their heads and laughed heartily.

"No Spartan is foolish enough to not bond with his wife," Aeschylus remarked, "everything our society demands of its men is for their betterment and increased chance of survival on the battlefield."

Flushing, she looked down and retrieved the cheese, placing it on the table. She understood the merit in what she had just learned, although…"I've grown up differently. Men and women dine together. All these customs are so odd."

"I say again – acceptance will come in time."

She turned to Acastus who had said very little during the meal, suspecting that in part he had deliberately left her and Aeschylus the greater share of the conversation. Their gazes clashed and the all too familiar warmth burned through her. She turned her head away in case something in her look betrayed to Aeschylus her feelings for Acastus, and it was a source of constant annoyance that the latter's feelings were always ably controlled.

When her father cleared his throat, Xanthia became aware of how far the silence had stretched. She gave a nonchalant shrug to mask her confusion. "Perhaps it will," she hedged and breathed a sigh of relief when, after a last, lingering look, Acastus swung his attention to her father.

"Arrangements need to start tomorrow for your departure."

"I began those when Callisto and Diokles left for Sparta in anticipation of this day. I always believed Zeus would smile kindly on me and he has."

Xanthia met her father's look and shivered from the warmth she read in his eyes. It was obvious he expected she had been restored to him permanently while for her ambivalence still ruled. Her heart had been broken, and she hoped she would not have to do the same to Aeschylus, whose sincerity and delight became more apparent the longer she spent in his company.

She listened to the talk turning to how long it would take to load pack animals, what needed to be carried back to her father's home in Sparta, and what could be left behind. The mention of Callisto reminded her of her plan, and she warded off a thrill of anticipation. Hunger sated, she rose from the table and retreated to the room set aside for her to sleep in and to wait until Acastus would do the same.

The murmur of voices outside her door jolted Xanthia out of a light doze. *For the love of Aphrodite, I pray that means they are finally retiring for the night!* Struggling to keep her eyes open, she muttered under her breath, waited, and waited some more as the voices moved away. How did they maintain their stamina with so little sleep?

Getting up from the bed to walk around the small room helped to dispel the drowsiness threatening to scupper her plan. After a few circuits she paused by the door. Nothing. Not a sound disturbed the quiet that had fallen while she had paced. Carefully turning the handle, she clenched her teeth together as if this would help her not make a noise and stepped silently onto the landing.

Only to realise she had no idea in which of the remaining rooms Acastus had been quartered.

Fingertips pressed to her lips, she remained rooted to the spot and tried to come up with possible excuses she could use if she walked into her father's room by mistake. Nothing came to her. Feeling like her brain was swimming through thick mud, she squared her shoulders and kept going. She would just have to cover her tracks somehow.

The only noise was her heartbeat thumping in her ear. Moving like a silent wraith, she reached the first door after hers and wrapped trembling fingers around the handle. Holding her breath, Xanthia turned it and eased her head around the open door.

Eyes growing accustomed to the darkness, she could just make out that no-one was lying on the bed to her right. Diokles's servants did not sleep on the upper level, so she assumed the same rules applied here. She dismissed the empty room and began to carefully back out.

In the blink of an eye, she found herself thrown forward with the opening door's momentum. A strong arm grabbed her around the waist and pulled her into the room. It all happened so quickly that by the time she opened her mouth to scream, a hand had been clapped over it, and she found herself pinned against a wall.

"Are you pining for my company?"

Her eyes widened as she recognised Acastus's voice, low and guttural to avoid waking the household. Xanthia mumbled furiously behind his hand, choking in outrage at his quiet chuckle.

"I'll remove my hand. Don't scream."

As her galloping heartbeat started to settle into its usual sedate rhythm, she noticed several things at once – Acastus's shield and weapons behind the door, his chiton and cloak neatly folded over a table. Which meant—

She glanced down and licked her lips. Then she remembered why she had sought him out. Her gaze wandered back up, but she drew the journey out, stopping to linger on every chiselled muscle along the way. There was enough moonlight to allow her to see the shadowed planes of his face. The heat coming off his body easily permeated the light chiton she wore, and a stab of desire pierced deep inside her.

It would be so easy to simply lose herself in the passion they had once brought to each other, but she had her own mission to accomplish. She had to discover what had happened to Callisto after she had been taken from Sparta and in what way their father was responsible.

Callisto had been banished, too. Xanthia touched her throat and wondered how she had not made the connection before.

"Well?"

She tilted her head back and allowed a half-smile to curve her lips. "I've had your company constantly since we left Melos. You knew I was outside." The lilt of her voice carried a question, and her breathing hitched when he leaned even closer to whisper in her ear.

"A warrior develops an awareness of his surroundings. Even asleep I would have sensed someone outside the door."

His short, neat beard tickled the sensitive skin where jawbone met ear, forcing her to fight the urge to whimper. It rankled that an innocuous act such as this possessed the power to arouse her. "I see," the words rattled out unsteadily. "Tell me about the time you spent in Apollysis."

He drew away to stare at her. "You want to speak of this now? Impossible, and there's no reason for you to know."

Damn him! Xanthia squirmed restlessly as she tried to find the right words to persuade him. Best not to mention that Aeschylus had already told her about Zeus's decree. The feeling of betrayal she harboured over this knowledge, she kept well-hidden.

She slid her palms over the dark hairs covering his chest, revelling in the strength she found there, a sultry smile widening her mouth as she linked her hands around his neck and felt the tension in the corded muscles. "Why not? I want to learn about my sister, to try and form a bond with her. Is that wrong?"

"Not wrong, but this you need to do with Callisto, not me."

Xanthia stood on tiptoe and pressed against him, lips almost touching his. "Please tell me what happened to Callisto while she was here."

"I don't know."

~*~

Which was the truth. No matter how much this beautiful, maddening woman tried to seduce him, no answer would be forthcoming. It was taking all his strength of will to stop himself from tumbling her to the bed, but he would not in conscience abuse a fellow peer's hospitality, especially as that peer was her father.

Not to mention the life-altering secrets still hanging over them all.

"You mean you won't tell me."

"I mean exactly what I say. Neither Callisto nor Diokles has spoken of it to me. It would be strange if they did."

When she pressed herself closer, so that their bodies were almost forged together, Acastus unhooked her arms from around his neck and gently pushed her away, although it required every particle of his formidable self-control to do so. Having once been taken to the halls of the gods in her arms, the temptation to relive the moment almost broke him. Almost, but not quite.

To take his mind away from what his body was demanding, he strove to find amusement in her pouting mouth. "Understand that no amount of seduction will get you what you want. Why didn't you ask Aeschylus?"

"I did. He gave me no answer."

He released her hands and cupped her face. "Neither can I. Leave now while you have the chance."

"Acastus, please."

Her soft plea came close to breaching his defences. "No. Not here." He stepped back to open the door. "Get some sleep."

She threw him a disparaging look. "If I can sleep."

Shutting the door after she flounced out, he stared at it for a long time. His entire system still throbbed with the desire she had ignited, so in all likelihood he would not sleep much himself. He was used to it. The forced marches, an entire night or nights without sleep. All that he had lived through and then some.

He rubbed a hand over his face and walked over to open the shuttered window. The streets of Apollysis were quiet. Memories poured in of the campaign he and Diokles had waged here. Having stayed behind to hold the city, he knew nothing of what had transpired to bring Callisto's memory back or how she had lost all memory of her life in Sparta in the first place.

A cold gust of air coming off the surrounding hills wafted over his skin, leaving a chill behind in his soul. He still had no idea who had carried his innocent remarks to the ears of Diokles's father. Perhaps the time had come to confess with the courage of a true Spartiate. A caustic laugh escaped his lips as he speculated whether Aeschylus, Diokles or Xanthia would be the first to drive a spear into him once he did.

CHAPTER THIRTY-FIVE

The late afternoon sun still warmed the air when Acastus called a halt for the day. Xanthia marvelled at the rising tide of anticipation she had been experiencing ever since that morning when he announced that in another day and night they would be in Sparta.

Blessed with mostly clement weather and Acastus's knowledge from the previous campaign, they had made good time, even with Aeschylus's servants, carts, and animals in tow. The distance had been covered too quickly for her liking, only because she wanted to spend more days coming to understand her father before they reached home and the secrets waiting to be unveiled. She looked over to where he stood still and solid as only a warrior could be, facing southward, an air of impatience and longing hanging over him like the travelling cloak he wore.

A sudden desire to be near him directed her footsteps to his side.

"Father?" She met his light-filled gaze and was seized by a trembling that had nothing to do with fear, when he draped an arm over her shoulder.

"The first time you address me as father, and…" He straightened, chest expanding over a deep, long inhale, "…once again I breathe the air of Lakonia."

Xanthia shifted her feet and looked down, unable to fathom the reason that had prompted her to openly acknowledge their kinship. Aeschylus still refused to disclose, no matter how many ingenious ways she had contrived to ask, what had happened to Callisto while her sister had been priestess in Apollysis. She had come to a resigned determination to be patient and extract the truth from Callisto herself. She needed to know before she could fully open herself to trust, yet the journey had given her a glimpse into the remarkable man who was her father.

From the time they left Apollysis, astonishment had been her constant companion, observing him demonstrate the stamina and strength of a much younger man. He had hunted for food alongside Acastus and, to her fascination, had even prepared breakfast one morning, explaining he needed to resurrect some of the skills he had lost living as merely as a citizen and not a warrior.

Moving out from under his arm, she took his hand in both of hers and confessed honestly, "I'm happy for you. The changes happening inside of me frighten me. While I still need answers, these days of travelling have helped me see you differently."

They both spun round as a shout behind them filled the camp. A cart, one wheel caught in a rut, listed badly. Xanthia held her breath as servants rushed to help Acastus, who held it up, preventing the cart from toppling over. Watching this demonstration of strength, her lips parted and released a sigh of longing without being aware of doing so.

"Answers will come. Perhaps a husband also."

Her neck cricked from the speed she turned it. Wincing, she rubbed at the sore spot and glared at her father, who peered back at her in good-natured amusement. Her mind suddenly caught up with his meaning. "No. I cannot marry. Please don't make me."

Aeschylus's forehead creased. "Why is the idea abhorrent to you? Every Spartan, man and woman, is expected to marry and produce children."

"I've already discussed this with Acastus." And could have bitten her tongue off for the revealing words when her father drew back to study her with a speculative half-smile.

"You have? I would welcome him as a son-in-law."

"Diokles is already your son-in-law."

Acastus had come upon them without either noticing. Xanthia grimaced, confounded anew by the level of training that enabled Spartan men to move with the speed of Boreas but as light as Zephyrus and leave no mark. She winced as her father clapped

Acastus on the back in a way certain to topple anyone, other than a warrior, face-first into the ground.

"Ah, you show me how much my senses have dulled that I didn't notice your approach. I meant *you* would make a fine son-in-law."

Xanthia gasped and looked away, but not before she saw Acastus's jaw grow rigid and the colour drain from his face. Was the idea of marrying her so repugnant to him? Even more unsettling, it was now clear to her how the idea of marrying him had crept up on her unawares, and she angrily reminded herself that marriage was closed to her.

However, convincing herself she did not care proved much more difficult, and the hurt deepened when she noticed Acastus's mouth stretch into the parody of a smile.

"There are worthier men than I, Aeschylus. I have to hunt."

Eyes wide at his abrupt departure, she stared after him as he disappeared into the forest which provided shelter for their camp, at a loss to understand why he had thrown Aeschylus's compliment back at him. If he truly considered himself unworthy, she would have to change his mind. Her heart skipped a beat – or did he consider her unworthy to marry him?

"The river is nearby, perhaps you want to refresh yourself."

Not trusting her voice, she nodded mutely and followed Aeschylus, observing that his face mirrored the same perplexion she felt. Acastus's manner presented yet another mystery she needed to unravel. How many more would she find? Would all the answers she needed ever be revealed?

~*~

The sun was dipping below the horizon when Xanthia finished eating and sat watching her father spar with Acastus. Every so often she caught her breath when their xiphoi clanged against each other. Heart in her mouth, she marvelled at the lack of fear shown by the two men who had upended her world and brought her to a new understanding of herself.

Though proud and full of admiration for her father's skill, it was his younger opponent who made her heart skip and dance. The fact she could not tear her gaze away from the ripple of bicep muscles, whenever Acastus moved to strike a blow, the contraction of thigh muscles whenever he propped and readied for the next move, worried her as much as either man injuring the other.

In defence, she closed her eyes to the fight playing out before her, then glanced up into the cloudless sky, where blinking stars were gradually becoming visible. The gods had indeed blessed them with mild, sunny days, only having to take shelter from light rain a handful of times. The sudden absence of clanging iron brought her gaze back to the two combatants, who stood talking to each other with barely a heave of their chests to indicate they had expended any energy.

"You surprise me, father," she called out, "I've been watching your fights these last few days and can only wonder at your skill and strength."

Aeschylus threw his chest out and smiled. "I am always a Spartan. Toughened from birth and by the agoge. Only death can weaken me."

A cold shiver passed through her at his words. Xanthia studied her father anew, seeing the warrior who had emerged over their days on the road. He seemed to have grown in stature from the moment he had insisted on training – as he had called it – with Acastus. "Then I pray Aphrodite give you the protection of many years yet. Acastus began teaching me the use of a xiphos on our way to Apollysis."

"As he ought to." Aeschylus walked over to rifle through a bag and emerged brandishing a spare xiphos. "Come, daughter, show me what you have learned."

Her jaw dropped when he offered her the handle of the weapon. Dimly, she heard Acastus say something and laugh while her father took a few steps back, handed Acastus the weapon she had refused to take and dropped into a fighting stance. He was serious! "I can't…"

"You can and you will."

The skin of her hand burned when Acastus took it, placed the grip of the xiphos in her palm, and closed her fingers over it. Her mind whirled in a confused eddy. "Have you both lost your reason? How can either of us live with the knowledge of hurting the other?"

"You relished the fights with me," Acastus reminded her. "I have no doubt you did so because you wanted to kill me."

"I might still want to," she flung back, but accepted there was only one way to show them she was no coward. She brought the xiphos into position as Acastus had shown her for one-on-one duelling and said, "attack me, father."

Momentarily disconcerted when Aeschylus lunged without hesitation, Xanthia found herself equal to parrying the blow…just in time, she admitted ruefully. Like Acastus, he tempered his blows without showing her any favours.

"Don't chop wildly. Straight arm thrust with all your force behind it," Aeschylus directed, "imagine carrying a shield and fighting around it as it covers your body."

Irked that she could hear her breath labouring, while Aeschylus sounded as though he was taking a stroll around the agora, her determination to try and best her father grew in proportion to the number of people in the camp who had stopped to watch. The lock she had placed on the Spartan part of her loosened and fell away, allowing the warrior in her soul to emerge. The longer they fought, the wider her grin grew despite the tiredness she sensed creeping into her untested muscles.

Then her over-confidence defeated her. Closing in for what she planned to be the winning blow, Xanthia let slip the focus that Acastus had taught her to develop, and in the blink of an eye felt one foot swept out from beneath her, landing painfully on her bottom.

She glowered at her father. "That was unfair!"

"There is no fairness in war. Focus and use *all* your senses. Acastus has taught you well, and I'm proud of you."

Still sat in the dirt, she peered at her father and saw that his eyes did indeed gleam with unmistakeable satisfaction. Xanthia straightened her back, believing she had crossed a bridge to understanding him and more importantly, the sense of belonging had grown and strengthened.

Her chin trembled when Acastus approached and held out his hand. The xiphos slipped from her suddenly clumsy fingers, nervous energy prompting her to use pettiness like a shield. "Don't you think I can stand by myself?" She was rewarded for her baiting by Acastus blowing out a voluble, world-weary sigh.

"I never underestimate you. If you had been trained in Sparta from childhood you would be leading our armies into battle. Either give me your hand or give me the weapon…without stabbing it into my heart."

Xanthia tilted her head to one side to study him and, too late, realised her mistake when her legs seemed unable to move. She wanted him, but she could never have him. While parts of her were healing, there still remained a tiny corner of her heart, which yearned to return to Melos and to everything she knew and had loved and lost.

Shoulders slumping, she picked up the weapon, wrapped her fingers around his, and allowed him to pull her up. Honesty prodded she admit that a large part of her heart had been yielded to Acastus – it was the part beating wildly as they stood close together. The camp and her father, melted away, leaving only awareness of the warrior beside her. Mouth parting over an outrush of breath, she swayed toward him, delighting in the way his dark eyes turned obsidian.

His fingers clenched around hers.

Xanthia blinked. What had come over her? Mutely, she held out the xiphos for him to take, then on unsteady legs lurched over to where her father stood conversing with the perioikoi. She reached them in time to hear Aeschylus organising the watch for the night.

"Can I help with the watch?" The words had left her mouth before her befuddled brain could regroup itself.

"No. Your life is worth more than mine." He pressed a fatherly kiss on top of her head. "Night brings out hidden predators."

She hugged him in affectionate gratitude for his concern, then stepped back, reeling at how natural it felt to hug her father. Aeschylus turned his head and she read warm surprise in his look when out of nowhere chaos enveloped them.

In the flicker of an eye an arrow cut a shallow groove across her father's cheek.

CHAPTER THIRTY-SIX

Her scream tore through the camp and behind her, she heard Acastus roar a battle cry. The breath left her lungs as she found herself tackled to the ground and dragged to safety behind one of the carts. She heard servants yelling, saw them scrambling to seek shelter behind whatever solid they reached first. Pulse racing erratically, she wanted to crawl to be with Acastus, who along with her father and the two perioikoi, had taken position behind their heavy shields in front of her.

"Only cowards fight with arrows! Show yourselves and fight us like men."

Ears ringing from Acastus's furious shout, Xanthia frantically scanned the line of trees and low shrubs that hid the threat. Memories of the Argive ambush summoned a wave of intense nausea. How could four men defeat an unknown number of assailants?

Four men and a Spartan woman.

Everything inside her went into stasis – did she just entertain such an insane idea? Movement at the edge of the clearing to the south drew her gaze there. A sob hitched halfway up her chest at the sight of a band of men breaking cover and closing in with menacing intent. If it was only those nine, she quickly counted, they might stand a chance. Then she took a closer look at the three men in the centre of the group. "No!"

"Release Xanthia. She's coming with us."

"Prepare to die!" Aeschylus roared in a strained voice. "No-one will ever again take my daughter."

Xanthia pressed a fist to her mouth to stop the howl of misery rising from the depths of her being. On one side stood Kallios and two worshippers from Melos, flanked by a group of ragged men she did not recognise. Opposing them were the father she barely had time to get to know and the man she…

Never would she forgive herself if she caused the death of two men who had come to mean more to her than she had ever dreamed possible.

"Kallios, why are you here?" She made to rise but stopped when Acastus yelled at her to stay down.

"Has madness gripped you since leaving Melos!? You sent a message, and we left everything to come to your rescue."

"What message?" she spluttered, then with a sinking feeling saw her father and Acastus staring at her, the latter's face hardening into lines of distrust.

"The one that begged us to follow you to Sparta," Kallios yelled back.

"You were deceived," she cried, "who told you I wanted you to follow?" Even as she voiced the question, suspicion widened her eyes as her mind grappled with how he could have told them.

"His servant," Kallios spat, stabbing a finger in Acastus's direction, "gave me the message before you left port."

Mouth open, she looked at Acastus and in his expression she saw the same comprehension that had dawned in her. Drakon! He had started his plot to ensure she never reached Sparta before they even sailed. The reason remained shrouded, and she swore it would not remain so for long.

"He lied," she insisted, "leave while you have the chance."

"No," he snarled, "I'll take you home once we finish these Spartans off."

Before she could berate Kallios that one of the Spartans he mocked was her father, Acastus's growling laugh rent the air.

"Twice I've beaten you to claim Xanthia. With the gods on my side, I will again. All of you combined are no match for us."

"Four against nine," Kallios mocked, "the gods have addled your wits."

The barbed words they hurled at each other made no impression on her. She lay unmoving, thinking of all she had lost to come this far – Philodemos and Euphrasia, her beautiful Calliope, the friends she had made, the life she had known – and had twice come close to losing her life. Still not fully certain of where her path would take her, now, at this moment, the decision she arrived at settled harmoniously in her heart and mind.

Ignoring the loud protests, she stood, unafraid, and calmly walked to retrieve the abandoned xiphos she had fought with earlier. Heart thudding against her ribcage, she positioned herself between the rivals.

"Five against nine."

She risked a swift backward glance to find Acastus looking at her with fierce pride, her father torn between pride and alarm. The guffaws which greeted her from Kallios and his cohort only served to send a surge of blood through her veins, the spirits of her ancestors entwining with hers, strengthening and imbuing her with their courage.

Her hand tightened around the grip. "Who is brave enough to fight me?" The laughter only grew louder. Xanthia brought her weapon to bear and called out in a louder voice. "Which of you cowards is brave enough to fight a Spartan woman? No shields. Once it is over, the remaining eight leave us in peace."

One by one the guffaws trailed off into silence. If the situation were not so dire, she would have patted herself down to discover what strange creature inhabited her body. The expressions of utter consternation on the men's faces were worth whatever injuries she might sustain in a fight. Lives hung in the balance because she had stamped her foot like a child and that petulance had been used as a weapon against her.

It was up to her to right the wrong. To stand firm and do honour to her heritage. Laughter came from behind her, stiffening her posture. Who dared to laugh in this moment?

"I'll not let you be killed. I will fight this Kallios." Aeschylus sauntered up to stand beside his daughter, holding his shield across both and glaring at their attackers. "I want answers how you knew to find us on this road."

Yesterday, she would have pushed her father aside to protect him. This night she truly understood for the first time what it meant to be Spartan. Blood stained her father's tunic and continued to seep from the gash across his face. At first chance she would tend to his wound.

She heard someone else approach and found herself flanked by Acastus and the two perioikoi, all overlapping their shields, their weapons thrust between the gaps, the glint of firelight giving the xiphoi a dangerous glow. She edged closer to his solid strength, pressing her arm against his as though to absorb some of his courage and skill.

Every beat of her heart pounded the warning that it was up to her to end the standoff. Kallios and his band had retreated a short distance, their hand gestures and furious whispers appeared to indicate that some were wavering. Having witnessed Acastus dispatch the Argives, she made one last attempt to prevent total bloodshed.

"Kallios, please, go back to Melos. It will be solely my decision whether I return. You may be nine in number, yet with my own eyes I saw Acastus kill three Argives. You are no match for two trained warriors and these free men. And I will not forgive the attempt on my father's life."

Above her head, she heard Acastus mutter to Aeschylus. "There are three I recognise from Melos. The others are helots by their clothes."

"Agreed, but whose helots are they?" Aeschylus muttered in return.

Whose indeed Xanthia questioned. "Listen to me, Kallios, before patience is lost on this side." She could almost feel Acastus vibrating on the spot, eager for the fight. The light of battle in her father's eye was no different. The look Kallios sent her would have pulverised a stone.

"Whether truth or lie, we risked our lives to come for you. Now you refuse to return with us."

"I need to understand my birthright. My mistake was to defy Acastus, though I didn't foresee how this would be used to trick you."

"My daughter speaks with wisdom granted by Athena," Aeschylus interrupted. "Any further attempts to harm us will see you all take your last breath."

The tension in the air was so thick it could have been sliced with the weapon she held. Quietly mouthing a prayer to Aphrodite, she exhorted the goddess to make Kallios see sense, while keeping an eye on two helots, whispering to each other, who stood a little apart from the main group. No doubt her father and Acastus were doing the same. She tensed when Kallios stepped forward, angling her body to block any sudden moves from the men flanking her.

"We'll go," he bitterly agreed, "but know that you won't be welcomed back. From this moment you are an outcast from our group."

Xanthia released the breath she had not even realised she had been holding. "Banishment is nothing new to me. May the goddess grant her protection for your journey home."

She might have made her decision, but it was still with a heavy heart that she watched Kallios and his band turn and walk away from them. A part of her life was walking away too, including the memory of the worst moment of it. She sagged against Acastus and clutched his arm, the toll on her emotions manifesting in her trembling legs. The arm encircling her waist gave all the comfort she needed, although clearly his thoughts were elsewhere.

"Aeschylus, I will take first watch with one of the perioikoi, you and the other, will take second. We cannot risk them changing their minds and planning an ambush."

"Agreed. Shields and armour since they have arrows."

The mention of arrows enervated her. "Let me tend to your wound," Xanthia protested. "You men of Sparta believe you are indestructible, but I've seen infection settle in less."

"So, my daughter is a healer," Aeschylus said approvingly. "I will try to be a good patient for—"

She spun round, when they all did, and sucked in a breath. The man shuffling towards them, hands splayed out to show he was unarmed, set her nerves on edge. The helot stopped just out reach of the weapon her father trained on him and bowed. "Master, if I tell you who sent us, will you spare my family from punishment."

"No Spartiate makes deals with helots," Aeschylus returned sternly. "Tell us, and I may forget who you are."

The helot bowed again and gave a name. The chill in Xanthia's core grew and spread until every hair on her arms stood on end. She looked at Acastus, whose rugged features betrayed nothing, although instinct told her he was unsurprised by the news. She looked at her father, the stupefaction covering his face increasing her uneasiness, along with a sense of foreboding so strong that she wished she knew what it portended.

CHAPTER THIRTY-SEVEN

Xanthia lifted a hand to shade her eyes from the late morning sun, letting her sweeping gaze encompass the scene which greeted her. The fields appeared to stretch out forever, a number of outbuildings dotted over the land needed some repair but still managed to convey wealth and position. Her brother's kleroi was large, her father's larger still.

You are home now.

Aeschylus's words echoed in her mind as goosebumps rose along her arms. Home. All around her there was a muted bustle of activity as Aeschylus's servants unloaded carts and carried his belongings inside the house she knew he had been forced to flee ten years earlier. If anyone had told her, when she left the home she had shared with her foster parents, that she would feel this intense yearning to grow closer to her blood relatives, to learn more of this land which had bred her, she would have laughed in their faces and then offered prayers to Aphrodite for them.

Prayed harder for a restoration of their sanity if they had said she would come to feel – she could not bring herself to say the word – what she felt for a man she had wanted to see dead before he could remove her from the only life she had known.

"Xanthia."

She caught her breath as the desire, which grew stronger every day she spent in his company, leapt and danced in her pelvic region. With something akin to despair, she wondered whether this excitement would calm over time; whether the sound of his voice, as deep as the halls of Poseidon beneath the seas, would never fail to move her heart.

She looked up at Acastus, who had materialised by her side. "It's much larger than Diokles's," she observed in an awed voice, "even crops are growing."

"Some of your father's helots stayed on to tend the land."

"I see," she sighed, "does he speak to these helots like he did to the one who gave him information after Kallios left?"

"Your father is an honourable man." The disapproval was evident in Acastus's voice. "He treats his servants well but doesn't do deals, no Spartiate does."

Placing a hand on her waist, she tilted her hip in a way meant to convey her disbelief. "Mmm, so he didn't make a deal with my foster parents?" She then leaned away from the dark frown Acastus turned on her. What had she said wrong?

"Philodemos confessed to me he went to Aeschylus and offered to rescue you. He said it pained him and Euphrasia to witness your father's despair when Ianthe's message was brought to him."

Xanthia chewed her lip. Letting go of a lifetime of beliefs was proving a challenge. "Well, of course he agreed, what are two helots less?" She instantly could have bitten off her tongue at the look of astounded disgust on his face.

"Do you hear yourself? Aeschylus set himself against our laws to free his servants so they could save and then escape with you. Let two helots raise his child rather than leave you to die!"

By the goddess, what had she done? *Hated your father because you refused to listen to Philodemos and Euphrasia when they tried to explain.* She turned her back to Acastus and pressed a fist to her mouth to stifle the urge to throw up. A rock sat in her stomach, a rock formed by regret and all the darkest emotions that had swamped her from the time she left Kythera. She found herself facing in the direction of Taygetos. At least it was further away here, although she could still see its formidable peak frowning down on her, foretelling danger, deceit, death. Or maybe that she was losing her mind.

Strong hands clasped her shoulders, and she allowed herself the luxury of resting against Acastus's comforting bulk.

"You did well stopping Kallios and the men with him."

Though not yet completely understanding a Spartan male's way of thinking, she understood enough to know he had just paid her the highest of compliments. "Why did Drakon try to kill me if he left that message?" She hung her head. "I placed us all in danger. I saw Drakon steal away the night before we sailed but didn't tell you because I was still angry."

"He wanted to make certain he succeeded in what he had been paid to do. If he failed, there were others ready to complete the task."

Leaning so close against him allowed the rage in his voice to vibrate through her. "Are you angry I didn't tell you? Or that I tried to push you off that cliff?" She tilted her head to look up at him, and the smile on his face left her reeling.

"You did what you thought best. One of our tests as young boys is being sent out to fend for ourselves. I had to hunt or steal food. One night I was caught stealing and whipped." He rubbed the back of his neck, then shrugged. "For being caught."

"That's…that's…" she spluttered, unable to wrap her mind around the idea that stealing was encouraged.

"No-one is punished for being resourceful. Out on campaign the army often has to live off the land to provide enough food."

"I still think it's wrong but accept your reasoning." She blew out a troubled sigh. "It will be hard to change the beliefs I've held. I…"

She stopped talking because breathing had become impossible. Acastus had taken her hand and pressed it briefly to his lips, enough to ignite a blazing trail of warmth from the spot he had kissed that now scorched into every intimate point she possessed.

"Some, yes. It will be easier now that you are back with your people."

Lips puckering, Xanthia stared as his features settled into thoughtful lines. The air around them grew thick and heavy, weaving a blanket of desire that enveloped their two selves. She swayed toward him, shivering when his strong fingers tightened over her own. His eyes turned opaque, a signal for her to take a step closer.

"Acastus, I'm ready to accompany you to the barracks."

Her whole body jerked at the sound of her father's voice. She swayed when Acastus dropped her hand as though it had singed him, feeling like being cut loose from a safe anchorage. The approving way her father observed them, the small smile playing around his mouth, rattled Xanthia's nerves. They were rattled further when he grasped Acastus by the shoulder.

"A Spartiate should be married by now," Aeschylus declared in an innocent tone. "You are much too worthy to be ridiculed."

If her body grew any hotter she would erupt in flames. She stared at her feet and desperately searched for something to say, anything to steer the talk away from an expectation she could never fulfil.

"Did the gods spirit you away to speak to my father?" Acastus returned drily.

"Ah! How is my friend, Pancratius?"

She wanted to hear about Acastus's father, but the opportunity was denied her when a feminine voice exclaimed over their conversation.

"Father!"

Her heart jumped against her ribs. Turning, she saw Callisto running towards them, which gave her the opportunity to distance herself and gather her scattered wits. A sensation she avoided naming froze her mutely in place as she watched her half-sister throw herself into Aeschylus's arms, laughing and crying in turns.

"Thanks to Zeus, you have come home," Callisto exulted.

Envy. There, she had acknowledged it even if it was just to herself. Callisto had years of their father's love, years she could never make up. She, Xanthia, had no memories of a mother or father's love. Her mother was dead, her father still essentially a stranger, no matter how much he welcomed her. She bit the inside of her cheek as the injustice of the day she had learned of her past rose up to swamp her with the old, familiar bitterness. Her hands clenched when Aeschylus cupped Callisto's face.

"I have much to do before I rejoin my peers," said Aeschylus, running a keen eye over his fields. "This land needs to come alive as it was before we left. The house needs to be made liveable." He peered at Callisto, "Your face glows, daughter."

"Because I carry your first grandchild."

A knife through her heart would have caused less pain than what engulfed her seeing Aeschylus sweep Callisto into an enveloping hug. A surreptitious glance showed Acastus perusing her face as though he was working out some complex battle manoeuvre. An imperceptible shake of her head did not stop his scrutiny, which only ended when she heard the mention of her name.

"Xanthia, go with your sister for now. After I present myself to the Gerousia and this place is made habitable, you will move here."

"She can continue living with me," Callisto argued.

Xanthia squared her shoulders, aware of undercurrents the others may not have noticed. With a swift intake of breath, she remembered the meeting with Callisto's mother. Ah, so the truth was surfacing. For all her fulsome welcome, it appeared that deep down Callisto was concerned her mother might be right.

Well, she was here now and not going anywhere. "By Spartan custom, where does a daughter live before she is married?" she challenged.

"With her mother," Callisto interposed swiftly.

"But my mother is dead." It was a brutal reminder for everyone there, but then Spartans could be brutal and she was one of them. "Would a wife not live in her husband's home? Then I should stay with my father. Is that not so?"

Her brow rose when Acastus and her father retreated but stayed within earshot. Was this an example of Spartan men fearing their women? She wanted to laugh at the thought but hard determination prodded her to stand her ground.

"I'm certain you know Ianthe was the wife of Diokles's father. By rights you stay in your half-brother's house."

"That may be so, sister, but Diokles's father is also dead. My only parent is Aeschylus. Do you begrudge me the chance to finally come to know all my family?"

There! She had drawn her battle line. A mixture of fear, annoyance, and sadness flashed through her sister's eyes, leaving Xanthia to wonder how her welcome had descended into conflict so easily.

"No. However, our father speaks truth. You can't stay here for the moment."

She planted her hands on hips and glared at her father and Acastus. "Then so be it. I leave with Callisto and await your summons."

Without giving anyone a chance to answer her, she stalked away in search of her bag. Her practical side admitted that all her belongings were still at her brother's house. The gulf that had opened between herself and Callisto hurt. The greater hurt was that she had been used as a pawn to enable Aeschylus's return.

Her father's words to Acastus haunted her mind. She would have to have lost all her senses to not see he would welcome Acastus as her husband. Her insides quivered with anticipation, but Xanthia reminded herself that marriage was impossible unless the gods saw fit to heal her. One day soon, she would slip away to the temple of Aphrodite to pray. For healing, for guidance, for the ability to trust a man for whom love had grown before she could stop it.

Head held high and with barely a farewell, Xanthia brushed past them all and strode in the general direction that would take her to her brother's house. Out of the corner of her eye she saw Callisto come up beside her, appearing as lost in thought as she was. The silence, as they made their way to Diokles's home, remained deafening.

CHAPTER THIRTY-EIGHT

The scent of bread baking woke Xanthia from an uneasy night's sleep. *Was it morning already?* Groaning, she opened her eyes to mere slits and saw light streaming in through the half-open window shutters. She propped herself up on her forearms, fighting the sleep clouding her brain, eventually realising as the sleep-induced fog cleared, that she was in her brother's house. Her eyes snapped open as she recalled the events of the previous day, and with another groan, sank back onto the bed.

Callisto's cold insistence she remain in this house had both hurt and placed Xanthia on guard. Rubbing her eyes, she confronted the stark possibility that her life path would once again be left to the mercy of others. Thumping a fist on the bed, she vowed to not meekly accept such a fate.

Right now, though, she had little to no choice but to rise and endure another painful meal with her half-sister, grimacing at the recollection of the awkward dinner they had shared the previous night. Without the men present all talk had centred around the food, an uncomfortable silence punctuating their desultory attempts to find something else to talk about. Neither of them were willing to be the first to broach their disagreement.

Her stomach growled, reminding her of how little she had eaten. Xanthia rolled to her feet, reaching for a chiton draped over the table. The shallow dish beside it was filled with water which she splashed over her face, then ran a comb through her thick tangle of hair. She had to go down. Hiding in her room would achieve nothing except to increase her hunger. It was up to her to insist on returning to her father's house once it became habitable and push back on any objections. Not giving herself time to change her mind, she marched to the door and pulled it open.

She stepped onto the landing and started to make her way to the steps leading to the ground level, when a door at the end of the house opened and Callisto emerged. She froze, then angled her chin to meet Callisto's gaze. "Good morning."

For a fleeting moment she thought she spied guilt, or was it regret, cross her sister's face, but it was quickly covered by an uncertain half-smile which lent a conciliatory air to Callisto's demeanour.

"Please come into my room, Xanthia. I'm sure you're hungry, so I won't keep you too long."

Hmph… Callisto had obviously noticed her lack of appetite last night. Hounded by misgivings, Xanthia dragged her feet to Callisto's room. As soon as she reached the threshold, her skin turned clammy, and she fought back a violent nausea. Through eyes watering from the effort of labouring for every breath, she saw Callisto's eyes widen, then in two swift steps, her sister was at her side to wrap a supporting hand around her waist.

"I'm so sorry! I had no idea the room would affect you like this."

She cast an incredulous gaze at her sister whose voice was thick with tears. "What do you mean? Tell me why I feel like my heart has been pulled from my body."

"I have the gift of sight, and now it's clear to me that you have a similar gift to sense the unseen," Callisto said softly, paused, then went on, "This was your mother, Ianthe's, room, the room you were born in and from where you were taken from her."

Xanthia wrapped her arms around herself and collapsed to her knees. Her past was catching up to her with a vengeance. Haunting images of her escape from Kythera, the fear she had sensed from Philodemos and Euphrasia until they had reached sanctuary on Melos, her child. Hot tears spilled down her face, and she silently rocked back and forth, body trembling because she stifled the keening wails she longed to release.

In an instant, Callisto was kneeling beside her, cheek pressed against her temple, holding her shoulders, absorbing the wracking sobs. The warmth flowing into her from her sister's presence helped to calm her and stifle the sobs until they subsided to an occasional hiccup. Feeling drained, but also filled with purpose, Xanthia pushed her damp hair off her face and sat back on her heels.

It was time. In her mother's room, the mother who had endured the same pain before her, it was time to speak of the hidden heartache she had carried for years. The breath she took was deep and long and filled with the power of life.

"I lost a child." She began without preamble and felt the small jerk of Callisto's body. "A son. He came too early, rejected me as I believed my father had rejected me, as my foster father did, too, by siding with Acastus and sending me away. The pain was unbearable, blood everywhere." Her voice trembled, but Xanthia forced herself to speak on. "I prayed to Aphrodite, the midwife prayed to Eileithyia. To no avail. My son ripped himself from my womb. The midwife said it was impossible I would ever be able to carry another child after what happened." She turned burning eyes to her sister. "I can never be a true Spartan wife."

The protective hand Callisto placed over her belly felt like a slap in the face. Sadness engulfed her, then came the first stirring of anger. "Is that what you think of me, sister? Not just a rival for our father's love, but that I would be vengeful enough to harm the child I will be aunt to?" Only when Callisto placed a soothing hand on her arm, did Xanthia notice her sister's watery eyes and wet face.

"No!" Callisto insisted. "I wanted to talk about yesterday, but it seems you haven't been told what happened to me."

"Acastus mentioned you'd been priestess in Apollo's temple in Apollysis. He wouldn't say anything else and neither would our father, no matter how many times I asked them."

Her sister began to speak, words flowing out from her that Xanthia listened to with rapt attention. Callisto related the events that had led up to her being taken from Sparta by Aeschylus, then seeking sanctuary in Apollysis. Even though he had not sired her, Xanthia experienced a twinge of shame at hearing the part that Diokles's father had played in her sister's banishment. Her life by comparison had been idyllic before the truth had hit like a charging Minotaur.

The same feeling of having the wind knocked out of her came with the revelation of how Callisto had lived without her memories for ten long years. Grief and bitterness forgotten, Xanthia leapt to her feet. "You drank water from the Lethe, and you are still here, alive!! How could our father agree to that?" She paced the room, wringing her hands, the old belief of men being nothing but her enemy, merely playthings to be used and discarded at her whim, returning to grip her in its clutches.

Engrossed in trying to comprehend how Callisto had survived the loss of her memories, Xanthia started when her sister's hands gently clasped her shoulders from behind.

"Don't blame him. He did what he believed best for both of us, including taking counsel from Athena. Whatever has happened, you and I are both here, alive, and restored to each other."

Xanthia inhaled sharply and turned to face her sister. Callisto's face glowed with health and contentment. "I don't understand how you can be so calm after all you endured."

"I prayed to Apollo. By wearing his coronet, my memories were restored to me, and I came to an acceptance of our father's reasons. Was there a better way? I don't know, but the gods ordained my path. Yes, I have had more time with our father than you, and yes, I felt fearful that, after all the trials we endured together, he would prefer you for many reasons." Smiling, she gripped Xanthia's hands. "A sleepless night praying and discerning brought me back to my senses. Stay with Aeschylus. You will come to see and appreciate his qualities and strength."

Xanthia struggled to form words past the tightness of her throat. Callisto was so strong – could she be just as brave? Two fears remained cradled in her heart, unvoiced except to herself. Had she been restored to her homeland simply to enable Aeschylus's return or had her family really not known she had survived until the revelation in Olympia? And her biggest fear – would Acastus still want her if she was unable to bear him children? She managed a tremulous smile. "I'll do as you have done. Pray for guidance. I remember the way to Aphrodite's temple and will go there after breakfast."

Thunder suddenly rumbled, its displeasure echoing in the room. After standing for a moment to try and absorb any echoes that might remain of her mother's presence, Xanthia hurriedly followed Callisto downstairs. Overhead, clouds had massed and the scent of rain was in the air. Bowing to her sister's knowledge of the weather, she blinked the first raindrop out of her eye and enquired, "Will the storm pass soon?"

She followed Callisto out of the courtyard and waited while her sister studied the sky. The peak of Taygetos brooded beneath a cover of clouds.

"No," Callisto predicted. "See how closed the heavens are. The rain will set in for some time."

Xanthia sighed in resignation. "Then I will wait and hope for better weather tomorrow and hope nothing else stops me from going."

"We can go together tomorrow. I can accompany you some of the way. Even though my mother was cold towards both of us, I still want to take her the news that I'm with child."

Yet again her sister's strength and perseverance amazed her and eased some of the heartbreak that she had never known her own mother. Xanthia nodded and followed as Callisto led the way back inside to the dining room. Remembering Akantha's hostility, she prayed Callisto would have success in that quarter. Her sister deserved it.

CHAPTER THIRTY-NINE

Silvery light poured through the open window of her room. Xanthia leaned her elbows on the sill and gazed up at a glorious full moon, its brightness bathing her brother's land as far as her eye could see. A deep sigh escaped her lips.

The rain, which had eventually stopped late in the afternoon, had kept her indoors with very little to do but meditate on everything she had learnt, her conversation with Callisto, and especially on a certain warrior. Although she had accompanied her sister as the latter carried out her duties, the day had dragged on, and she had only absorbed a fraction of what Callisto had explained would be expected of her once she was mistress of her own home.

She pushed her thick hair over her shoulder and wondered whether all the soul-searching was the reason she remained too restless to sleep; pacing around her room then kneeling by the window. Doubt tormented her. Long ago she had accepted her feelings for Acastus went beyond the physical. This was as much as she could bring herself to admit. Xanthia buried her face in her hands. Admitting love for a man, something she had guarded her heart against with the same fiery resolution the dragon guarded the Golden Fleece, would leave her heart exposed to more hurt.

A cool breeze brushed over her skin, causing small bumps to rise from its smooth surface. Chilled, not just physically but somewhere in her deepest self, she raised her eyes to Taygetos, its dark bulk thrown into relief against the backdrop of the moonlit sky. Since she had arrived in Sparta, the mountain had always called to her in a subliminal way she had yet to understand. It commanded her gaze, her presence, her giving over of herself to this unfamiliar land. Hands clenching into fists, she whispered, *"No,"* without having any idea of what she was refusing to do.

I need to break the mountain's spell.

Preparing to push herself up, Xanthia froze as the sound of voices broke the silence enveloping the house. As they drew closer, the deep sound of male laughter reached her ears. She frowned and drew back from the window. One of them had to be Diokles, since neither bothered to stay quiet, and the other—

Her heart slammed against her ribs, when she saw it was Acastus. Even though his face was shrouded by the night, she would have known him in the deepest, darkest corner of Hades' realm. Their nightly meal with their peers had obviously finished and her brother had decided to come home to his wife. Of all the odd customs in the land, this was the one she least understood and could not fathom: how or why their womenfolk accepted it.

"I will see you tomorrow."

Acastus's farewell drifted up to her – surely, he would stay awhile. He had not come near her since the day she had left Aeschylus's house. Disappointment forced her to admit she had, in all likelihood, misread his intentions.

"Stay here tonight. We can return to the barracks together in the morning."

"Very well."

She sat back on her heels, body slumping in relief. Earlier, she had decided a course of action and tonight presented her the chance to fulfil it. Rising, she hurried over to open the door, just enough so that it enabled her to see her brother and Acastus ascend the steps as, with her tummy dropping to her toes and back, she saw which door the latter was entering. If the midwife was right and she could not bear a child, then she would give the proud warrior, who had risked everything to bring her here, a gift by which he would always remember her.

Even though that very same gift would haunt her for the rest of her life.

~*~

A whisper of movement floated along the landing of the upper floor. A woman's form momentarily outlined by a sliver of moonlight.

Keeping her step light was easy. Keeping herself from panting, and giving away her presence, proved much more difficult, given the excitement churning in her belly and chest. Heart in her mouth, Xanthia crept past doors until she reached the room where Acastus slept. Not daring to breathe, she cautiously turned the handle and slipped inside, shutting the door and the world behind her.

Acastus lay in naked glory before her avid gaze. His broad chest lifted and fell with his breathing, every muscle deeply defined from the life-long training regimen Spartan men were subjected to. The breeze fluttering in through the open shutters whispered over the light tunic she wore, the delicate material caressing the budding peaks of her breasts.

"I asked you once before if you were desperate for my company. It seems I have my answer."

Xanthia choked over a nervous giggle. "I shouldn't have expected less from you," she whispered. "Lie there and pretend a strange nymph has come into your dreams."

"I'm a Spartan hoplite, I don't pretend."

The deep timbre of his voice, kept intentionally low, curled around her senses. "Keep your eyes closed, Acastus." She said his name as though tasting the essence of it for the first time. Seeing his eyelids were indeed closed, she divested herself of her chiton, sensual heat permeating every pore of her body despite the night's freshness.

Her bare feet made no sound as she walked to the bed. Kneeling to straddle him, she lowered herself to rest against his hard form, purring deep in her throat when his arms clamped her to him as though he wanted to absorb her deep into himself.

"What are you doing—"

A slumberous smile curled her mouth as she placed a finger to his lips, asking for silence. She would make love to him, let him make love to her in total silence. It would be an expression of life like no other.

The glitter in his half-open eyes betrayed the control it cost him to relinquish power to her. Relishing his compliance, she rolled off him to nestle by his side. With her head cushioned on his chest, Xanthia swept her hands over his torso, revelling in the feel of his skin against her fingertips. Threading those same fingers through the coarse dark hair that smattered his chest, she luxuriated in the texture then moved her hand to linger on his flat stomach, a soft sigh of satisfaction escaped when his abdomen clenched.

Rubbing her cheek over his pectorals, she closed her eyes, all the better to appreciate the discoveries she made – the rough edges of a scar from some battle, the ridge of muscle that sculpted his torso, the line of hair narrowing to the burgeoning evidence of his arousal. Purposely avoiding it, she explored his thigh, then drew her fingers all the way back to caress his neck. The fine sheen of sweat over his face and body told her everything she wanted to know.

Tonight, she would be his and he would be hers alone.

She moved onto him, flattening her breasts against his broad chest. Never had she experienced this depth of passion simply from watching a man. She traced a light finger over Acastus's firm, well-defined lips, which were parted over the sharp breaths he drew into his lungs. Xanthia ran her tongue over her dry lips, heart leaping when his body spasmed beneath her. A silver beam of moonlight glimmered over his face for her to see his absolute absorption as he stared fixedly up at her. The corners of her mouth lifted in a soft smile that failed to express the emotion filling her heart.

As swift as a lightning bolt, passion erupted when his large, capable hands, slid down her back to shape the rounded globes of her bottom, lingering at the indentation of her waist. Xanthia rocked to an elemental rhythm, bending to take his lips in a soul-shattering kiss that drove her to the edge of a divine madness. The caress of his fingers over the sides of her breasts unleashed a wildness she never knew she possessed.

Sitting up, she grabbed his long hair and tugged until his head lifted to her breast. She saw his fierce smile before he fastened his mouth over the tender peak, knowing he was recalling the moment by the stream the same as she was. He suckled hard, forcing her to thrust the knuckles of one hand into her mouth as a wild moan threatened to escape. Robbed of all rational thought, she thrust mindlessly against him.

Cold air flowed over her moist peak as Acastus drew back to prop himself on one arm while his free hand rubbed the hidden bead begging for release. She pressed wildly against his clever fingers, knuckles protesting the pain as she bit down on them in her struggle to not make a sound. The hot flame of her desire rose higher, then white light flashed behind her eyes, all sense of self swept away on a violent tide of release.

Guttural moans were trapped in her throat for fear she would be heard. It was as if Zeus had thrown a thunderbolt through her, the sizzling, blinding light consumed her mind, body, and spirit. No matter how much she wanted it to, it could not last. No human could survive an outpouring of ecstasy of this magnitude for long. She gradually became aware of the ragged beat of her heart, the light breeze cooling her skin, and the deep rise and fall of Acastus's chest. Xanthia lifted a trembling hand to cup his jaw, closing her eyes to better savour his warm skin beneath her fingertips.

As if in a dream, or a trance, she watched him sit up, then turn her under him, taking care to support his weight and not crush her leg. She lay in the middle of the bed, still warm from his body heat, waiting in breathless anticipation as he settled himself over her. Wrapping her arms around his waist, her hands explored the bunched muscles of his back, which betrayed the control he was exerting over his own desires. His hot breath over her mouth melted into a kiss that conveyed a meaning she dared not hope for. With every successive kiss planted on her eyelids, her cheeks, her jaw, her legs liquefied in time with them and parted to grant him access to the moist heart of her.

She whimpered in protest when he stopped short of her mouth. In the moonlight his features were taut, but his eyes blazed with an emotion she had not seen before. Lifting herself, she fluttered a kiss over his lips, the sensation in turn fluttering through to her belly and the secret place, aroused and eager to envelop the manhood pressed over it.

Reward came when his mouth covered hers, their tongues meeting in a timeless lover's dance, where nothing existed except their two selves. Knowing it could well be the last time she would be with him like this, Xanthia poured every last shred of desire and love into the kiss, implanting herself onto his memory so that he would never forget her, no matter where fate led their two selves.

In a silent command as old as time, she signalled her need with a seductive curl of her hips. A long, sensuous murmur of approval vibrated deep in her throat as he granted her wish and slid into her warmth. Languidly closing her eyes, she rejoiced in the erotic, yet tinged with a sweetness, dance of their bodies moving in unison. Seeking fingers greedily traced his back, his shoulders, and the corded muscles in his arms. Arms she would always remember and forever mourn the loss of. She began to lift her hips higher, inviting him to thrust deeper, suppressing a rapturous cry when he immediately answered her wordless plea.

A wild need to once more experience the release only Acastus could give her gained in strength, so that her hips rocked faster and her whispers of encouragement became huskier. Nails digging into his buttocks, Xanthia urged him to quicken his thrusts so that both were panting and gasping for air. Impossible as it might be, she felt his manhood swell further, stretching her, while she thrust her head from side to side, excitement driven to intolerable levels.

She forced her eyes open, needing to see him reach his peak so she could forever carry the memory of his face in that moment of ecstasy. Clenching her inner passage around him, she kept up the action until sweat rolled off his forehead, his teeth bared in agony, and then his proud head thrust back as the apex of human pleasure crashed through him. Then, her spirit once more soared into the halls of the gods as another release swept her away into timeless pleasure.

~*~

His breath mingled with hers, their heartbeats settled into a matching rhythm. For a short time, Acastus allowed himself to revel in the feeling of Xanthia's warmth burrowed beneath him. Groaning under his breath, he rolled onto his side, taking her with him. The feather-light brush of her lips above his heart prompted him to tighten his arm around her waist.

"You know I can't be found here in the morning," she warned in a low, unhappy voice.

"Stay with me tonight," he murmured. "I will wake you before the household stirs."

He doubted he would get much sleep, if any at all. His emotions and expectations had been ripped apart and handed back to him by an experience that would stay with him to his dying day. All done by the woman now seeking a comfortable spot within his arms. Despite her unconsciously provocative wriggling, he was too drained to attempt to make love to her again.

"I thought you and Diokles would sleep at the barracks. I'm glad you didn't."

He breathed in the scent of her hair laced with the fragrance of roses. "Diokles wanted to spend time with his wife. They have been parted a while."

"Oh."

"What?" There was a stillness and sudden chill radiating from her. "All husbands and wives accept this is the way."

Acastus sighed, when she fell quiet. He began to rub her back rhythmically, releasing the tension he found there and in her shoulders. It bothered, and concerned, him, that she had not at least begun to foster an acceptance of the way of life in Sparta. And he knew exactly why he felt this way.

His father, Diokles, and Aeschylus were right. It was time he took a wife and the feisty woman lying warm and peaceful beside him was the one he wanted to see bear his children. Which meant it was time to unburden the secret he had carried since that day in Apollysis when Diokles had told him of Xanthia's existence. He could not, in honour, ask Aeschylus for his daughter without explaining first how he had been the unwitting pawn in an exile that should never have happened.

He glanced down at Xanthia and judged by her breathing that she had fallen into a peaceful sleep, free of the impediments weighing him down. An ironic laugh shook him. He felt like Paris, but instead of holding a golden apple to bestow to one of three beautiful goddesses, Acastus saw himself holding an immense kopis ready to be handed to one of three figures arrayed in front of his vision.

Open to debate was whether Aeschylus, Diokles, or Xanthia herself, would be the one to hack his soul out of his body and send it to Hades after he confessed his guilt.

CHAPTER FORTY

Having fulfilled her promise to accompany Xanthia part of the way to Aphrodite's temple, Callisto parted with her sister before they reached the agora and proceeded to make her way to her uncle's house. She lifted her face to the morning sun, enjoying the warmth and the air, fresh and clean, after the rain. She offered up a prayer to Apollo that a fresh start with her mother would prove attainable even after the years of estrangement.

Callisto blew out a breath and reminded herself of the two powerful motivators that drove her to extend the olive branch to her mother. She ran a comforting hand over her belly, where her and Diokles's child grew. As the wife of a Spartiate, and an influential one at that, she would have the best servants and midwives available to her, but an instinct she could not casually brush aside, prompted her to seek her own mother's wisdom at this time.

The other reason was more complex. She could attribute Akantha's abrupt dismissal of herself to Xanthia – who bore an extraordinary likeness to Ianthe – being present when she encountered her mother in the agora. But, her mother's accusations that Aeschylus would favour Xanthia over her, she could not so easily dismiss.

An uneven patch of ground turned her ankle, and Callisto berated herself for not taking more care and lifted her head. A small '*oh*' escaped her lips on seeing her uncle's house up ahead. Absorbed in reflecting on what she and her mother would find to speak about afterwards, that would not be disagreeable to either, she could barely credit that the distance had been covered already.

"In the name of Zeus, what brings you here!?"

Callisto gasped and spun to find that Theron, his eyes bulging, had appeared from behind the winemakers building. "I greet you, Uncle. I hope to visit with my mother. Is she inside?" His unwavering stare set her teeth on edge, and she remembered that she had never warmed to him as a child.

"Who told you she was here?"

The demand behind his question put her on guard, deeming it wise not to reveal that a long-time friend of Akantha's had mentioned her mother was now living with her brother. "Does it matter?" she challenged, wary of the malicious look appearing in his close-set eyes.

"You should've sent a message. Your mother is inside, but don't expect any welcome from her."

Her uncle's warning sounded gleeful. Maybe her pregnancy was playing with her connection to the unseen, but Callisto found herself unable to shake off a suspicion that he hid some heinous plan or secret. The morning suddenly felt colder. "Thank you," she replied, overlooking his animosity.

Chin lifted at an aggressive angle, she resumed her path to the house, her rigid back daring him to say or do anything. She might be pregnant, but it was early days and her hand-to-hand fighting skills had been sharpened since returning home. After all she had endured and done, he would need to watch his back if he tried to hurt her or anyone of her family.

As she passed beneath the arch into the courtyard beyond, Callisto glanced over her shoulder. Theron had disappeared, but the uneasiness his attitude had caused stayed with her. A servant approached, and after she asked for Akantha, she was led to an airy room where she found her mother seated, facing a large window and seemingly oblivious to what was happening behind her. She drew a deep breath, "Mother?"

It hurt to see Akantha leap to her feet, one hand clutching her throat and taking a step backwards. The corners of Callisto's mouth turned down and her hopes for an amicable reunion vanished, but she remained unwavering and had no intention of wasting the time she had taken to come here.

"May I enter? I've wanted to see and talk to you since we crossed paths in the agora."

"I'm surprised you didn't bring that half-sister with you," Akantha finally found her voice. "You look well." She paused, and a small pleat appeared between her eyebrows. "Are you—"

"I'm with child." Callisto smiled and walked in to take her mother's hands in her own. "I would appreciate my mother's wisdom during this time."

She held her breath, wanting, unable to ask for love. Akantha's face was a study in fleeting emotions – anger, guilt, fear, and to her surprise she spied a glimmer of hope, too. "If you will tell me, I want to hear from you why you never sought me out after father took me away." She might reopen old wounds, but to heal them, she had to ask, "and why you hated Ianthe so much."

Her mother's fingers tightened over hers in a death grip that turned her fingertips white, so she was relieved when Akantha grimaced and released her hands.

"Sit down, daughter. You may not like what you hear, you may despise me at the end, but if you want the truth you shall have it."

A tiny, hidden corner of Callisto's heart cried. Akantha had never referred to her as '*daughter*' before now. She struggled to summon the patience to sit still while her mother ordered bread, honey and figs to be brought to them. Their conversation while the servants served the food centred on the weather and other obscure topics out of necessity.

The last platter having been set on the table, the servants left them. Callisto clasped her hands, watching Akantha finish drinking the water she had poured.

"Your uncle recently accused me of marrying Aeschylus for his wealth," Akantha began, "and in a way he's correct. I did so at Theron's behest. The kleros he inherited was not as valuable as what was given to our older brother. Theron urged me into Aeschylus's notice without telling me your father planned to marry Ianthe, nor did he mention the political manoeuvrings behind the scenes that instead saw her married to Lysander.

"By the time of our wedding, I had developed strong feelings for Aeschylus. Whether it was love I never found out. What I did find out was his passion for Ianthe. I began to be resentful of her, even though her own marriage continued in unhappiness. In time, I bore you and *still* I failed to secure my husband's interest in me. I'd borne him a daughter instead of a son."

"How can you say that," Callisto interjected, "a daughter is just as valuable in her own right. You know this is our way."

"Of course she is but think for a moment. My husband favoured another woman. I could not even give him a son to be proud of. Then he went and secretly became a genitor for Ianthe, without my or Lysander's knowledge, the ultimate betrayal. You know how that turned out."

For Callisto, the missing links in her family history were revealing themselves and now many incidents in her childhood made sense. "Is that why you never allowed me to visit Ianthe? Except when I sneaked away. I don't want to cause you hurt, but she was a wonderful woman in many ways, and now it's clearer why she loved me. Withdrawing your love pushed me her way. She taught me little things I thought my own mother would, but you couldn't see past your hurt and anger to see my hurt at what I saw as your rejection of me."

Her mother looked away for a moment, then back again, and Callisto saw nothing but sorrow in her face.

"I did reject you. I bore my lot with bitterness colouring every word and action. When Aeschylus whisked you away, I refused to leave, and perhaps it was best because not long after you left I received word that my mother was unwell. I stayed with her for the next few years until she died. Your uncle's wife died during that time, and he offered me a home after I returned."

Callisto stared at her mother, at the smooth face showing little change other than a few lines near her mouth. It would take time for both of them to heal their bond, if it ever completely did; nevertheless, her sympathy was aroused for her mother being used as a means to securing her uncle's status and wealth.

"I'll be equally honest with you and confess that I was almost shocked out of my wits when I first beheld Xanthia. For a moment, I thought Hades had released Ianthe's spirit from the dead and allowed her to take human form again. The warning you gave me in the agora about father favouring Xanthia." Callisto pushed her hands through her hair. "I confess it played on my mind. I've made my peace with Xanthia and with Father. I pray the gods grant you the same blessing."

Callisto held her mother's searching gaze before the latter stood up to pace the length of the room. *And this is how I may look if I reach my mother's age. Sleek of body, still beautiful in face with barely a grey hair to dull the blond sheen.*

"Where is Xanthia now?"

"Seeking guidance in Aphrodite's temple. Acastus found her on Melos, where she had joined worshippers of the goddess after discovering the truth of her past. She hated Sparta and everything it stood for. He didn't have an easy time bringing her back."

"And your husband?"

Callisto bit her lip. Should she voice her reservations over Diokles distancing himself? No. He would come to acceptance in his own way. "He also needs time. Seeing Xanthia brings back memories of his mother and her failure to tell him she'd borne his half-sister."

Receiving no response, she looked at her mother, a tingle starting at the base of her neck when she noticed Akantha's fixated attention to something outside the window. "What's happened?"

"I'm wondering where your uncle is going in such a hurry," Akantha replied slowly. "He has already been out this morning and said he would stay to oversee the fields until he returned to the barracks in the evening."

"Perhaps someone brought him word that he is wanted in the city."

"I didn't see or hear anyone arrive before you came."

Suddenly, her mother whirled and stalked to the door, flinging it open and calling a servant. The hum of conversation was muted, so she leaned closer to try and overhear what was being said. Even then she only caught the word 'listening'. The first flicker of trepidation travelled through Callisto after Akantha shut the door, a troubled look on her face. "Did Uncle receive bad news?" But she somehow just knew that was not the case.

Her mother rubbed a shaky hand over her jawline.

"I don't think so. His leaving now is very odd. The servant I spoke with reluctantly admitted your uncle stood outside this door for some time. I don't know how much he overheard."

Callisto leaned her forearms on the table. "Why would he do that and not join us?" The fact Akantha continued to stare past her renewed her earlier fears that scheming was underfoot. She had had enough experience of that in the temple halls of Apollysis to detect subterfuge.

Akantha gave a derisive laugh. "Has Diokles never wondered how Lysander uncovered who fathered Ianthe's baby?"

The blood in her veins seemed to screech to a halt. Mutely, Callisto shook her head which made the light-headed feeling worse.

"Theron told him." Akantha wrung her hands, as though uncomfortable to be betraying her brother this way. "I don't know how Theron found out anything about the circumstances, but he used it to his advantage. If anyone loathes your half-sister more than myself, it is my brother, who sees her as an obstacle to my reconciliation with Aeschylus and assistance with building up his land."

Mouth agape, Callisto struggled to find her voice. "But, then, Xanthia is in danger depending on what Uncle overheard! Aphrodite's temple sits away from the main part of the city. I have to go to her." She rose, then the realisation hit. "Thank you for telling me this."

Akantha shook her head. "I don't understand why I betrayed this to you except that after I returned from the agora that day, I began to think of you more and more. There may be hope for us yet."

Grasping her mother's outstretched hands, Callisto moved in closer to hug the older woman who appeared unable to return the embrace, although she felt a brief, affectionate pat on her back. But there was no time for longer embraces if Theron had indeed gone to look for her sister. "I must hurry to the temple and find Xanthia if she has already left."

"And I'll send a message to your father," Akantha decided on the spot. "If you need help, he'll provide it."

Taking the biggest gamble of her life, Callisto leaned in to kiss her mother's cheek, smiling at the bemused look the small gesture left on Akantha's face. Once outside, an urgency pushed her into a shuffling jog, and she prayed for the stamina to maintain the pace. Her one goal was to get to Xanthia. Forehead creasing, she speculated on who had told her uncle all those years ago?

CHAPTER FORTY-ONE

Decision made, the night he lay sleepless with Xanthia wrapped around him, Acastus sought out her father, prepared to be either thrust through with a spear or, unlike the forever cursed titan, Atlas, have the weight of the heavens shifted off at least one of his shoulders. He was crossing the agora when he ran into Aeschylus coming out of the senate building and hailed him.

"Acastus! On your way to the barracks?"

He motioned to his shield and kopis. "To a sparring match, but first," Acastus steered him away to a quieter spot, "I have something to tell you."

"You have my blessing to marry Xanthia," Aeschylus said, grasping the younger man by the forearm as though an agreement had been settled. "Why the surprise? From the time we left Apollysis, it was obvious to me, that I wondered what took you so long to ask."

This then, was the moment. "You may withdraw your blessing, when you hear what I have to say."

The words poured out like the Hyades' tears poured out as rain. He held nothing back – from espying the small group furtively making their way south, while he was stealing food, the laughing wager with his mentor as to how far they would get before a kryptos finished them off. "I was ten," he paused to draw breath, "the first I knew the gods had protected them, or that it was Xanthia, was at the end of the siege of Apollysis."

"One day I will tell you how I am to blame more than you, and my orders are to marry Xanthia."

Acastus gaped at his future father-in-law, who proceeded to lecture him to give up his misplaced guilt, how it could ruin him and endanger his life, in addition to the lives of his peers, during a battle. The pressure he had not noticed in his head eased. "I don't deserve—"

"You do," Aeschylus corrected him sternly, "go on your way, I'll join you shortly."

He jogged to make up time, and along the way gave thanks to Athena he was still alive to reflect on whether he would remain breathing after he confessed to Xanthia. The quick pace warmed and loosened his muscles by the time he arrived for his match.

"Homoios!"

The furious challenge roared over the training ground. Not being called by name was enough to tell Acastus that this fight, agreed with his opponent the previous day, had morphed beyond a simple exercise. He took a moment to focus and relax muscles that had tensed in anticipation. Back straight, he strode forward without hesitation, ready to face whatever the gods had ordained for him.

A brief glance was sufficient to show his opponent ready and waiting, hand clenched so hard around the handle of his weapon that the knuckles were white. A small knot of onlookers had gathered. Acastus heard their murmurs, unsurprised by their perplexed expressions. But it was the hard, blazing look in his opponent's eyes that sent both anger and regret washing through him.

He could not afford to feel either emotion, especially since he prepared to spar with his oldest and closest friend. The friend whose half-sister he intended to marry. The friend who, by some means, obviously knew that a few simple words from him had ruined the lives of those closest to them. His own included.

Shifting to a tighter grip on his kopis, Acastus came to a halt and gave Diokles a hard look. "Aeschylus couldn't have told you, so how did you discover my supposed disloyalty?"

"You expect me to forget your betrayal? Whoever you told, they must have carried the news to my father. No. We have this out like Spartans."

Acastus laughed, a hollow, bitter sound. "Be careful you don't make the same mistake as you did with Aeschylus, my friend." It gratified him to witness Diokles jerk back and hesitate, but this small display of uncertainty was swiftly recovered when Diokles signalled his readiness to begin.

Acastus took a step back and started to circle Diokles, who mirrored his movements. Strategy raced through his mind like a river in full flood. They were equally matched as fighters, both having survived the harder krypteia training. His best chance to win was to finish the fight quickly.

He cleared his mind in time to see Diokles leap toward him, kopis bearing down like the vengeance of Hera on Alcmene. In less time than it took to blink, Acastus swept his shield up to meet the downward hack of a weapon that could have cleaved his arm off at the shoulder. He pushed the shield into his friend, hard enough to knock him off-balance.

Nonplussed when Diokles regained his footing and leapt back to regroup, Acastus speedily followed up with a strike of his own. The clang of his kopis striking the heavy, bronze covered shield sent the familiar reverberations up his arm. The tingle in his fingers was a nuisance he easily ignored, managing to get another strike in, and then compelled to go the defensive as Diokles retaliated.

The fight dragged out. Thrust, parry, slash, parry. The intensity of their blows turned a practice bout into a vicious honour fight, leaving Acastus striving hard to dampen his frustration. In the back of his mind, he knew neither would gain the advantage. They knew each other's strengths and weaknesses too well after all the years of fighting and training together.

Time to try something else, even if he hated himself for it afterwards.

Keeping a keen eye on Diokles's every move, he called out, "Perhaps the gods don't want you to win, Diokles, because they know you are in the wrong."

"You dare," Diokles growled. "After what you did, you are fortunate they didn't smite you down."

The injustice of the remark lessened the stab of any remaining guilt. "What did I do? Escorted Xanthia and Aeschylus safely back. I was ten and made an innocent remark as we were taught to observe everything. I never knew those words were overheard and carried to your father."

It was the fire burning in Diokles's eyes that showed him he would not get through the rekindled urge to lash out, which still haunted his friend. He comprehended the wound was too raw, even if Diokles thought he had come to terms with his family's past.

Acastus stepped back and placed his shield on the ground. "If you are determined to kill me, then do so."

There was no room for regret or any other emotion in a fight. He waited while Diokles divested himself of his own shield. They had not sparred like this for years. Always it had been half-serious, half-fun to see who could outdo each other.

Now his heart told him it might prove a fight to the death.

He pushed all thoughts of Xanthia out of his mind. Pushed aside all reminders of past battles, where he and Diokles had stood shoulder-to-shoulder in a phalanx, sometimes grinning at each other as they pushed through an enemy force with ease. He parried Diokles's strike and came in with strikes of his own. The sun glinted off the two, wickedly curved swords the Spartans were renowned for wielding.

Acastus leapt in and hacked the kopis down towards Diokles's left arm, where the white scar stood out as a reminder of the echoes of the past, when he had injured Diokles, who had been weakened by a whipping administered by his father, Lysander. The words he had spoken as a boy had borne bitter fruit for his friend, and Aeschylus, ten years later.

The loss of concentration cost him. Losing his balance when Diokles disengaged, he swiftly regained his footing, and in the corner of his vision saw the glint of a blade slashing down as he leapt, too late, to his right.

His enraged shout of disgust at himself echoed around the ground. A quick glance showed him a deep cut on his left arm, blood flowing out to splatter the ground. *No retreat, no surrender.* The words every Spartan warrior lived by echoed in his head and blinded his vision. Acastus did not see the momentary disconcerted look flicking across Diokles face. He let out another roar and attacked.

All his focus was on the flashing of blades, the defensive blocks, the attacking strikes. The gathered onlookers were mere dots in his side vision as he fought with the man who was like a brother to him. Acastus had no awareness of how he breathed, pain from his injury blocked by the greater instinct for survival…and winning.

Round and round, until he felt dizzy. He felt a subliminal connection to his opponent so that they both moved in unison, neither able to gain the advantage. In the next clash of weapons, Acastus disengaged immediately, leapt back and came in, weapon raised, ready to strike with his whole weight behind the blow. His kopis hacked down toward Diokles, whose own came down toward him, only for both weapons to hit a shaft of wood thrust between them.

Taken aback, he stood unmoving, keeping a wary eye on Diokles, whose features wore an astonished glare. Chest heaving, Acastus stared blankly at the shaft of a spear in the dirt beneath their feet, neatly sliced in three pieces by the force of two kopides severing it.

"Enough of this madness!"

The voice of Aeschylus blasted his eardrums. The primary rule of never turning away from your opponent was lost to Acastus as he stared at the older man, whose eyes blazed with a fury he did not bother to dampen. He had never seen Aeschylus this angry before. He and Diokles were breathing heavily from their combat, allowing the verbal assault to continue.

"You should both be punished for this. You could have killed each other over a wrong that has been righted."

Acastus opened his mouth, but the man who might be his father-in-law waved him silent. Shutting his mouth, he spied a look a complete stupefaction on Diokles's face and, regardless of what had just transpired, wanted to laugh.

"I mentored you, Diokles, and expected better. I don't care you are now a celebrated commander. This was unworthy. Of both of you!" Aeschylus folded his arms and spared neither man his glare. "Acastus, come with me, that wound needs tending. Diokles, consider your actions carefully."

Acastus spared his friend a tight nod, the gesture reciprocated in a silent agreement the fight was concluded. He turned and half-jogged to catch up with Aeschylus, who had already summoned a healer.

Seating himself on a log, he surrendered his arm to the physician's care. Teeth gritted, he endured the stinging pain of having it cleaned and bandaged without complaint. He had suffered worse injuries, but to succumb to an infection after such a fight was the most ignoble way he could think of to die. The physician left, after completing his ministrations, and Acastus braced himself for further chastisement.

"You were both fighting to kill."

Adrenaline still pumping through his body, he lifted a shaky hand to wearily rub his face. "Diokles has discovered my blunder. I don't know who told him. Despite what he asserts, I believe he hasn't fully made peace with the past."

"Perhaps you know me better than I know myself." Acastus swivelled to find Diokles almost upon them. "A message was delivered to me this morning implicating you. The details were such that there could be no doubt."

"Who sent it?"

Aeschylus's sharp demand moved Acastus to raise his hand to stop Diokles from answering. "I'd returned from a physical test at dusk. As expected, I told my mentor of seeing two helots carrying a baby escorted by a perioikoi. He laughed and wagered with me how long it would be before a kryptos found them."

"Did anyone else hear?" Diokles demanded, "or did your mentor betray this?"

"He had no motive," Acastus insisted. "As he said, any kryptos would do their duty. Neither of us knew or cared who those helots were."

Aeschylus grunted. "If I have to knock both your heads together to finally put this long-gone tragedy to rest, I will do so."

Acastus studied Xanthia's father, not being fool enough to underestimate the man's strength or tenacity. "It's fitting Diokles injured my left arm since I injured his." He sighed when Aeschylus grunted in disgust, understanding that his attempt at levity had not been appreciated.

"Fitting? And how would you fight if the army was on a war footing?"

Acastus laughed loud and long. "We are Spartans. If my left arm was missing, I'd still continue fighting. Pain is nothing. You know that as well as I."

"Of course. But why court death before you even start out? And that with your brother-in-arms."

Because he had lost focus and allowed emotion to rule. Because of what had been said. Acastus flexed the fingers of his left hand. The wound smarted, but he barely winced. Bones had been broken and reset during his passage through the fire that was the agoge. He had come out the other end, re-made, a fearless warrior.

"Aeschylus, will you leave us."

"Remember what I said." Aeschylus speared both with a warning look as he left them to settle their argument.

He sensed that Diokles waited until the older man was out of earshot.

"I don't hate you."

Acastus leaned forward to rest his elbows on his thighs. "Right now, I think you do. I told Aeschylus this morning because I intend to marry Xanthia." He half-smiled when Diokles's eyes widened and almost popped out of his head. "I would've needed to defy three years of training to keep what I saw to myself. Would you have done differently?"

As Diokles crouched to sit beside him, Acastus again worried over how Xanthia would take the news of his… mistake. And the news that he wanted to marry her. Would what they had shared override her natural disdain and anger for losing her family and homeland because of a few simple, but careless, words. Could he convince her that he loved her and not because he felt he needed to make amends for the past.

"How much does it hurt?"

"As much as the Nemean lion's claw hurt Herakles."

Their full-throated laughter was met with approving glances by those standing nearby. It was a verbal sparring that had grown up with them over the years. Belief in their nation's descent from the demi-god, Herakles, imbued pride into every Spartiate. And a bravery beyond any other.

He watched Diokles run a hand over his neck, a sure sign his friend was hesitating over what to do. "You need time and I need courage to confront Xanthia. She is no less a formidable opponent than you are."

"I'm proud to know that," Diokles said, holding out his left hand.

Acastus gripped it with his injured one. "We are brothers-in-arms in every way now," he said, looking at his wound and Diokles's scar on the same arm. "And, if Xanthia doesn't kill me first, brothers through marriage."

"She's shown herself true to her Spartan heritage," Diokles replied in an approving voice. "Watch yourself."

"After what you endured with her sister, I will!" They grinned at each other, yet beneath the light-hearted jesting a niggling portent of disaster ran up his spine. It had been a constant burr for some days, and he debated whether to voice his unease. The decision was made for him by an ashen-faced Aeschylus's hurried return.

Acastus jumped to his feet. "What happened?"

"We may have our answer," Aeschylus spoke rapidly, "a message just came to me from my wife—"

"Is Callisto—"

"She's well, though she mentioned that Xanthia intended to pray at Aphrodite's temple. Almost immediately after, Akantha saw Theron hurrying away from his house. Why she's chosen to tell me this after everything that has happened and the ill-will between us is a mystery to me."

"Theron told your father." Acastus clenched a fist, a cold lump of dread settling in his stomach. Both his peers wore identical sceptical expressions. "Explanations later, this is the final confirmation, and Xanthia must be found and brought to safety."

There was no time to lose. He snatched up his kopis, retrieved his shield and sprinted towards the city's acropolis, disregarding their calls to wait. The sooner Xanthia was under his protection, the better.

CHAPTER FORTY-TWO

Xanthia entered the temple of Aphrodite with a bemused shake of her head. Even as she bowed low, her credulity was yet again strained to behold the goddess of love and fertility adorned in full armour. The sigh she released carried a kind of amused tolerance. "Will I ever accustom myself to this warrior ethos?"

There was no-one else in the temple, and her light chuckle mocked her foolishness in talking to herself. Rather than pray to the goddess in this form, she chose to climb to the upper level, where the manifestation of Aphrodite Morpho, or the Shapely one, sat veiled and with tethered feet. Making a mental note to ask Callisto why the statue had been carved in this manner, Xanthia knelt and stretched out her arms to petition the goddess she had served for four long years.

"Aphrodite, hear my prayer. Send me a sign whether I should remain in this strange land of my birth or return to Melos and my foster parents. Help me to truly understand whether my family want me and not just because of my father. To know," Xanthia swallowed over the sudden lump in her throat and resumed in a whisper, "to know whether Acastus will want me, barren as I am. I love him."

There. She had verbalised her greatest hopes and fears. For what seemed like an eternity, she waited, arms growing heavy, but no sudden vision, no instinctive voice in her head, no outward sign, answered the plea that had been wrung from the depths of her heart.

A sob of disappointment was wrung from her, and she sat back on her heels, letting her arms fall to her sides.

Staring at the shackled feet of the statue, inspiration struck. Xanthia chewed on her bottom lip as she considered her own fetters. They tied her to the mountain where she had been abandoned. If she confronted the mountain that embodied her fears, she could throw them off and lift the invisible veil covering her mind, in order to clearly see her way forward.

She inclined her head to thank the goddess for this guidance and jumped to her feet, for the first time eager to make her way to Taygetos. She retraced the route she had taken with Callisto, past the theatre, skirting the agora, marvelling that her presence was barely acknowledged by the men and women she passed. This freedom of movement was the first thing she had learned to appreciate in her new home.

Her only companions were her thoughts and memories. The desire that had smouldered since her first meeting with Acastus ignited with a fiery roar at the memory of the secret night they had shared in her brother's house. Try though she did to convince herself her hunger for him had been satisfied, the loving had only stoked the flames higher.

She wanted to stay. But at what cost? If she could not give Acastus a child, she might be forced to watch him marry someone else, driving a stake through her heart. She would be forced to live with a constant reminder of her lost child. Would she end up dying alone when Death came for her? Her chest grew tight recalling that her mother had died, perhaps because of her. She had been reluctant to ask Callisto about Ianthe. What strength could she draw from her mother's memory?

Brooding, she made her way through the fields, reaching the lower foothills of Taygetos and then looked up, her neck cricking. A chill gripped her spirit so much so that the world whirled around her. If only she knew where she had been exposed as an infant, she would go there, sit and try to feel the echoes of that child, alone, abandoned, belly cramping with hunger pains. A wave of grief engulfed her. She pressed a hand against her belly, which was indeed twisting itself into knots, and wondered what she had eaten to make it cramp in such a fashion. She stopped walking, frowned, and stared unseeingly at the forested sides of the mountain. Even when she had lost her child in such—

Xanthia gasped. Unable to form a coherent thought, it was if her mind had gone numb, her legs trembling as alternate waves of hot and cold pushed sweat out of her pores.

She had missed her moon dark bleed.

Twice.

At the very least.

Her wildly beating pulse made a mockery of her attempts to calm her mind and enable her to count the days since she last recalled it had occurred. Delving into her memory, she retraced the journey to Sparta, Apollysis, and the intervening time until today. Her breathing grew faster as she struggled to remember when she and Acastus had lain together in shared passion. The sound of a stream gurgling over stones brought her up short, and in a blinding flash, she remembered the day by the Eurotas.

Had Aphrodite, through the great river of Sparta, blessed their union that day? Had Acastus given her the child she believed she could never have? If it was true, it changed everything.

"Aphrodite, give me a sign. Show me there is hope." The desperate, heartfelt prayer flew out, borne on the wind to the heavens. She glanced at the mountain once more. If she was pregnant, the fetters binding her to it would be broken.

A flash of white sped past her and landed on the grass to her left. Xanthia sucked in a breath and stared, her mind wiped clean of thought. A dove. A female by the song it cooed softly to her. She sank to her knees and let joyful tears fall freely. Memories of Calliope returned; the dove who had been the solace to her grief; the dove she had nursed back to health and nurtured; the dove she had poured all her love onto in place of the child taken from her. Now another had come to bring warmth and hope to her soul. It was either a sign from Aphrodite or the goddess herself had taken this form to show that her prayer had indeed been answered.

For a few precious moments she rejoiced in the emotional cleansing that washed away the lingering bitterness of spirit, releasing the resentment that had kept her heart shackled in its own fetters. Laughter mingled with the tears. Xanthia hiccupped and comforted herself she was *not* becoming hysterical.

Heart light, she stretched a hand out to the dove. Its bright red eye watched her for a moment, and, with a last coo, it flew up towards the mountain peak where grey clouds were scurrying quickly over the range. No clouds, however forbidding, could darken the light in her spirit, and Xanthia swore she could feel the shackles that had bound her melting away. She would recall this blessed moment for all her days, but more urgently, she needed to return to the city and seek out Acastus.

A smile as wide as the Eurotas stretched her mouth as she half-jogged, half-skipped back the way she had come, almost floating over the ground. In the distance, a man was walking to meet her. She stopped, squinted, and dismissed whoever it was, since his stature in no way resembled the height and build of her lover.

Her pace slowed as he came nearer, a sinking feeling leaving her queasy. She had only met the man once, but his words to Acastus at the time had left an indelible imprint on her mind. His smile alone was enough to freeze the blood in her veins and her feet dragged to a reluctant stop. Her heart came into her throat as he planted himself in a wide-legged stance across her path.

Theron?

"I'm glad I found you all alone, Xanthia. How fortuitous that we should meet here at the foot of Taygetos. It must hold much meaning for you."

The first fingers of fear began to pluck at her nerves, leaving her weak and shaky. *Remember who you are*! The admonition reminded her of her ability to fight, her bravery facing down the Argives to save Acastus and herself, and defying Kallios to save her father. Hands on hips, she thrust her chin forward, strength returning to her legs. She would not cower before any threats Theron could make. "You dare to mock me. I could ask how you know Taygetos has meaning for me, even how you knew I'd be here?"

The avid smile on Theron's face could be trusted as much as trusting Kerberos laying down and meekly waiting for her to pat all three of its heads. She looked everywhere but found no sign of human life, no sign of anyone who might witness this meeting, and prayed for Acastus to miraculously arrive.

"No-one knows I'm here," he gloated. "When one listens, one often hears important details. I kept watch on Aphrodite's temple. I would've accosted you there but saw you walk in this direction which aided my plan. I doubted you would ever return once my niece discovered you were still alive. Now that you foolishly have, I can send you to Hades as you were meant to at your birth."

"You will not," she snarled, ready to scratch his beady eyes out to save the precious life growing within her. "Be warned, I'll fight you at every turn and take you into Hades with me!" The meaning of his words pierced the red mist of anger. "You lie! You know nothing about my birth."

Theron's expression turned ugly. Xanthia tensed, feeling her heart pumping blood to her legs, readying herself to run faster than the legendary Atalanta herself.

"My sister was never afforded her due by her husband because of his obsession with your mother. It was I who told Lysander, Diokles's father, who had sired you. I, who told him you had been saved after he had ordered you to be exposed on the mountain. Did you know it was your precious Acastus, who betrayed he'd seen three people escaping with a baby."

Fury coiled up her spine, ready to strike. Menace hovered in the air, but Theron's words haunted her mind until she could not think about anything else. "You lie, Theron. Why would Acastus care? He was only a child himself."

"Three years into his training is enough to harden a boy. It was his duty to report anything out of the ordinary. I overheard him tell his mentor. They wagered how far the group would get before they were stopped. Not for a moment did I believe you would get out of Sparta until the perioikoi returned with the information that your father's helots had safely boarded a boat."

A huge raindrop splattered on the crown of her head, followed by a low rumble of thunder. "Even if this is true, you are at fault," she shouted. "You, supposedly a Spartiate, reduced to listening to others, lurking in the shadows like the meanest of beasts."

"You dare insult me, girl. Come, let me show you where the unwanted and deformed are left to die."

Gathering up the length of her chiton, she shot past him, side-stepping when he leapt after her, but was not quick enough to evade the hand that clamped around her arm in a vice-like grip. Xanthia screamed, rage and desperation adding power to the blood-curdling sound emerging from her throat. She dug her heels in, letting her body sag like a deadweight.

Nothing deterred the man, who fuelled by a long-held grievance, laughed while he dragged her closer to her doom. Real fear began to sink its talons into her. Hoping someone would hear, Xanthia tried to scream again, but her mouth and throat were now so dry only a strangled croak emerged.

As Theron pulled her up the face of the mountain, she caught sight of a dove, perhaps the same one, fly above them. A well-spring of elation bubbled up to fight the fear as she whispered a prayer, imbuing it with the belief it would be carried to the halls of Olympus.

Aphrodite Areia, gird me in your armour that I may defeat this madman and save the child you have blessed me with.

CHAPTER FORTY-THREE

Weaving around people making their way to the agora, brushing off both the greetings and curious looks directed his way, Acastus began the sprint uphill. Sucking air into his lungs to keep his heartbeat steady and strong, his vision tunnelled to encompass only the temple of Athena commanding the peak of the hill, and his goal beyond that, Aphrodite's temple where Xanthia had gone to.

"Acastus! Wait!"

Recognising the panicked voice, he stopped with such force he almost tripped over his own feet before checking himself and jogging to meet the woman running towards him. "Where is she?"

"I think I may know," Callisto half-sobbed, gasping for air and holding her side. "The temple is empty, and a member of my uncle's syssition saw him passing the Hall of the Ephors in a great hurry towards Pitane." She clutched his arm, "I didn't divine this, but it can only mean one thing – she has gone to the mountain and my uncle followed."

His gut contracted. "You were right before, I believe you are right now. I'll bring her back." He briefly pressed Callisto's hand to reassure her, then turned to sprint in the direction of Pitane, the village closest to the mountain range. The grip on his kopis tightened painfully. If Theron succeeded in his murderous plan, he would have no qualms in killing him, even if it meant his own death or banishment from Sparta.

~*~

Heart threatening to burst through his chest, Acastus started the ascent up the face of Taygetos. He had reached the base of the range in time to see Xanthia, her black hair swinging out behind her, being dragged by the arm around a rock face and out of sight by a man who his keen eyesight confirmed to be Theron.

There was no time to lose. He knew exactly where she was being taken.

He spared a glance upward and started to climb – fast. Dark, grey clouds were racing across the peak. If rain fell, the slippery rocks would aid Theron while slowing his own ascent. His heartbeat accelerated to keep his strong warrior's legs climbing, eating up the distance to the place where sickly and deformed infants were sometimes left to the mercy of the gods.

Knowing Xanthia, she would fight her captor all the way, risk losing her footing, and fall. He climbed faster, fighting to erase images of the woman he loved impaled on a rock, or worse, battered if she fell too far, leaving her out of sight to die a slow, painful death, alone. A furious shout from above echoed between the rocks. He re-doubled his efforts as a light drizzle touched his skin. Fighting for each foothold, he cursed whenever a foot slipped out from under him. He was risking safety for time in this climb.

"Stop! Stop, or I'll take you with me."

The sound of Xanthia's voice nearby – half desperate, half the snarl of a lioness – stopped Acastus in his tracks. Having reached a level spot of ground, he unsheathed the kopis and pressed himself against the side of the rock face. Inching forward, he risked a glance, his blood boiling at seeing how close Xanthia teetered near the edge. Unable to get to them without revealing himself, Acastus settled on the path of least resistance, the element of surprise and blind luck. A battle cry roared from his mouth, and he leapt out from behind the rock he was using as cover.

The tableau he beheld froze and then fell apart as a clap of thunder sounded overhead and rain began to fall in earnest. Acastus threw himself forward as Theron pushed Xanthia towards the edge of the rock ledge they stood on. Her yells mingled with Theron's but nothing could penetrate the battle focus that had taken hold of him, all senses attuned to one goal – saving Xanthia from death.

No time to do anything except throw his weapon aside and grapple Theron by the waist and pull him away from Xanthia. Not caring whether he broke ribs or not, Acastus tightened his hold as Theron kicked out at her in a last vengeful attempt on her life. Acastus saw her jump out of the way, her foot slip on the wet rock, and with a scream that seared itself into his memory, the inexorable slide of her legs over the ledge.

Rage and loathing lent him power beyond his already formidable capability. In a swift, calculated move he released Theron, catching the other man by his braid and flinging him away, immune to the howls of pain which filled his ears. The arrival of someone else went unnoticed as he dived to where Xanthia's fingers had found purchase in a fissure, holding on in a dogged will to live, her head just clearing the edge.

Acastus slid forward on his knees and grabbed both her arms. The clamp-like grip of his fingers to counter the dampness of her skin would leave bruises but better bruised than dead. There was one way to alleviate her fear…somewhat. "We've done this before?" He grinned at her bulging eyes, which held no terror, only implicit belief he would save her.

"Pull me up!" she shrieked.

From behind them rang the shouts of two men and the clang of metal as weapons clashed. The noise was a distraction, to be pushed aside, until Xanthia was safely on firm ground. He began to pull, feeling her body sway a little as she searched for a toehold to brace herself. She said nothing, eyes fixated on him, his chest swelling with pride at her lack of tears and screams, not attempting to climb in a panic, which would have endangered her and his ability to help.

He pulled, the movement of her body telling him she walked her feet up the rockface as best she could. His knees scraped over hard rock as he moved backwards to gain better leverage. As more of her torso appeared, he painstakingly repeated the slow, precise movements, listening to her harsh breathing, the grunts of effort, feeling the rain dissipate to a gentle drizzle again, which provided blessed relief to cool his skin.

The tense silence which had fallen was broken by a triumphant exclamation of joy as Xanthia propped a knee up on the ledge, and one final effort saw her safely over to collapse beside him as he broke her fall. His harsh breathing mingled with hers as she lay with her chest heaving against his. The touch of her fingers on his face reminded him of the first soft flakes of snow signalling the start of winter. Acastus closed his hand over them. "I've rescued you twice from falling. There won't be a third."

He blinked as her face suffused with an angry red colour. "*'We've done this before'*," she mimicked his words threateningly, "and I recall saying all Spartans were mad! You just proved me right! How could you say such a thing in that moment!?"

Acastus wrapped her close in his arms. If she ever needed final confirmation, this was it. "You just proved yourself a woman born and bred of warriors, Spartan warriors," he declared, his voice strong despite the adrenaline still shaking his body. He sat up, helping her to do the same, frowning over the discolouration on her arms, where the imprint of his fingers still showed. He closed his eyes, sending a prayer of thanks to Athena that he was not searching for Xanthia's broken body at the bottom of a crag.

"Xanthia, give me your belt."

Acastus swung round to see Theron lying face-first on the ground, yelling muffled threats and curses, Aeschylus's knees jammed in his back, the point of his xiphos held tucked against Theron's neck.

"You followed?"

"I couldn't trust that Theron was alone."

He stood and helped Xanthia to her feet. Watching her calmly hand her father the belt that had cinched her chiton, he marvelled at her strength but knew that reaction would set in later. He searched out and retrieved his own weapon, which Theron had obviously used to fight his own brother-in-law with, and dug the point into his peer's – he could barely acknowledge him as such – back while Aeschylus securely tied his wrists behind him. Together, they hauled the vanquished betrayer to his feet.

"Stare at me murderously all you want, Theron, it will not help," Acastus glared back at him, "you will be punished for this attempt to kill one of our own." He looked at Aeschylus, "I'll escort you back."

"No need," Aeschylus demurred. "The bonds are secure. Attempts to overpower me will be met with a xiphos through his heart."

Acastus took a half-step forward as Theron turned his murderous gaze on Xanthia and then Aeschylus.

"My sister was a fool to not heed my advice, but I was a bigger fool for not killing your spawn outright."

Cold, merciless anger, the kind that sustained his clear-headedness in battle, swept through Acastus. He lifted his weapon.

"No! Killing Theron like this makes you no better than him. The Gerousia will decide what punishment to mete out."

Aeschylus's harsh tone penetrated the anger. Slowly, he lowered his weapon and nodded. "I bow to your wisdom. I'll take Xanthia home and meet you there." Now that the danger was over, he saw Aeschylus's face soften.

"My house is almost ready to welcome you. We'll speak later."

The delight on Xanthia's face warmed Acastus's soul. He waited until Aeschylus led Theron out of earshot, then lifted her hand to plant a kiss on the knuckles. "I salute your courage. Do you need me to carry you down the mountain?" Her quiet chuckle lifted his spirits.

"I can walk." She stepped closer to him. "But before we leave I have something to tell you."

"As I do." Consumed by uncertainty how she would take the news, he pressed on, "It's my fault—"

Acastus shuddered when she pressed her hand across his mouth and restrained himself with the utmost difficulty from tumbling her to the ground. Adrenaline still surged through his body, fuelling his desire for this woman who had claimed his heart.

"I know," she said quietly. "Theron took great pleasure in telling me. You were a boy, and you didn't even know it was me being rescued. Release any guilt you may still carry. I want to believe you want me and our child out of love, not guilt."

He opened his mouth, then shut it like a trap. Her face shone with the light of a thousand suns. Drawing his head back, he eyed her warily. "Our child?"

"Yes," she affirmed, her smile warm enough to melt the clouds away. "I was told I could never carry another child after the trauma my body suffered when I lost my first. This, in part, made me determined to never return to Sparta. I couldn't be a Spartan woman in every sense."

"You are a Spartan woman in every sense," he rebutted fiercely. "I resented the hold you had over me until I realised it was too late to escape. I've already spoken to your father, and he agreed to my request to marry you." The outrage shimmering on her face drew a loud laugh that echoed around the mountain.

"Without talking to me first?" She huffed and stamped her foot. "Were you planning to ask me at all?"

Acastus lunged and drew her into his arms, to the approval of his body and hers, if the way she softened against him was any indication. He lowered his head to murmur over her lips, "I would've spoken today. What made you come here?"

"I needed to break whatever part of my psyche was still chained to Taygetos. To come to terms with the past and free myself for the future." She wrapped her arms around his neck with a pert smile: "and to plan how to chain you to me."

"You've already won that battle."

He wasted no more time in talking, instead claiming her lips in a kiss celebrating life and victory, the thump of her heart beating a message older than time against his chest. Acastus buried one hand in the tangle of hair at her nape, massaging the base, revelling in the soft sounds of approval emanating from her throat. He broke the kiss to rest his forehead on hers. "We need to go while there is good light. I want to assist your father, too."

Taking her hand, he guided her down the now slippery rocks back to where he had begun his climb. Apart from wanting to ensure Theron was still subdued, it became a matter of honour to support Aeschylus when he fronted the Gerousia and to see that justice was served to Theron for his attempt at taking Xanthia's life.

Then he would have time to prepare his home to welcome his bride.

CHAPTER FORTY-FOUR

"Fellow elders, we have two matters to judge today. One, to decide whether to accept back a peer and the other, what punishment is to be meted out to another."

Aeschylus stood to attention before the Gerousia. Heliodoros's words, and more importantly the tone they were spoken in, gave him hope that he would not be permanently exiled for fleeing his duty ten years ago. If he had any say in the matter, his own brother-in-law would be justly exiled. Otherwise, nothing would stop him dragging Theron up the face of Taygetos and throwing him off the side of the mountain for what the man had intended to do. He held his breath when Heliodoros rose to face him.

"All present here know from Acastus's testimony why you fled. While a Spartiate fleeing is to be frowned on, we must take into account it was the will of our patron goddess that you should do so. A show of hands to welcome Aeschylus back as a peer."

Heart racing, Aeschylus scanned the hands in the air, including those of the relatives representing the kings who indicated their favour. Even better, the cousin of the Agiad king had given him a barely perceptible nod of reassurance, and he wondered if Diokles had spoken to the man beforehand. Whatever, he relaxed his tensed shoulders and released a relieved breath. He waited, but Heliodoros did not call for a show of hands for those in opposition. The outcome was obvious.

"Aeschylus, it is good to have you with us once more! May the gods grant you many more battles and a peaceful life after them."

"I pray that is so," he agreed in all sincerity. "I plan to restore my kleroi to its former prosperity for my grandchildren to inherit."

"Ah, so Callisto is to give Diokles a child."

Aeschylus smiled. Very little remained secret within the ruling class. How he and Ianthe had managed to keep their love and Xanthia hidden for so long could only be attributed to the benevolence of the gods. "Yes, but Xanthia, too, is to bear Acastus a child. Had Theron succeeded in killing her, he would have killed her unborn child as well."

A storm of disapproval broke out among the elders. The birth of a Spartan child, no matter whether male or female, was considered a gift of utmost importance, the continuance of Sparta and its legacy. For a peer to raise his hand in cold blood against another was unconscionable.

"Have Theron brought in," Heliodoros ordered as he sat back in his chair. "Aeschylus, you may stay if you wish but make no attempt to intervene in any way."

Aeschylus nodded and moved to stand partially behind a column. He pursed his lips as Theron – face set in resentful lines, the hint of a sneer around his mouth – was marched in, restrained by two hoplites. He knew his brother-in-law well; knew the humiliation which would be seething within his spirit. Two major rifts had plagued his marriage to Akantha, one of which would be exposed today of how Theron had sought to profit off himself in any way he could. Including blackmail.

"Theron, you lifted a hand against a fellow peer," Heliodoros began sternly, "there is little to be said—"

"I know exile awaits me," Theron interrupted with a cynical laugh, "but, before I go, do you know Aeschylus defied a peer's orders to expose the daughter he fathered without agreement from that peer or his own wife."

Aeschylus drew in a swift breath. His brother-in-law faced the worst punishment a Spartiate could be given, yet his malice was such that he would take others with him. No wonder Theron had no conscience in trying to kill Xanthia. Many of the Gerousia had fallen silent, and he speculated whether any of them had done similar in the past. Then he heard Heliodoros calling him forward and stepped out from behind the pillar with his head held high.

"Theron speaks true," he stated without fear, "what he does not know is that I offered to be genitor. Lysander refused, knowing that his wife and I had planned to marry before political intrigues bound her to him. When he ordered Xanthia exposed, two trusted servants offered to escape with her. I paid a perioikoi to escort them to safety."

Heliodoros gaped at him in disbelief and was forced to raise his voice over the volume of condemnatory shouts. "You released two helots!?"

"Yes, to save my daughter, a future mother of Sparta with no blemish or deformity on her other than jealousy. You might ask Theron how he came to know of their escape. How he blackmailed me with that knowledge."

The previous words of censure changed abruptly to shouts of outrage from amongst the senators. Aeschylus silently praised himself for keeping a hard, triumphant smile off his face, despite Theron glaring at him with murder in his eyes.

"What do you have to say, Theron?"

"I overheard Acastus and his mentor laughing about how long it would take for them to be stopped," he sneered. "I knew what Lysander had done, he was raging about it during the mess dinner that night. I intercepted the group, recognised the servants, and demanded the identity of the baby."

"Then what?" Heliodoros thundered.

"I let them go and accosted my brother-in-law," he admitted in a cold, spiteful voice, "told him what I knew, told him I would take it to the Gerousia if he didn't agree to help pay my share of the evening meal, which I struggled to do. I was not going to be cast out like a common helot."

"Even the release of two helots is nothing compared to this," Heliodoros announced in a hard voice and leaned forward in his seat. "You will leave Sparta and never set foot within our borders again. Are we agreed?" He looked around, counting the hands held high. "It is unanimous. You will be allowed time to provision yourself, and your kleros will be given to your sister."

Aeschylus briefly met Theron's gaze as the latter was led out of the chamber. The utter loathing, the promise of revenge, burned in his eyes. A coldness gripped Aeschylus as though the winds of destiny had blown past him. Out of nowhere came the recollection of Demaratus's exile, who had fled to the Archimedean empire to live amongst the Persians, eventually to fight against his fellow Greeks. Was this a portent of the future?

The senators were beginning to disperse, some stopping to congratulate him, and he was swept outside with a group of them eager to hear of his life since he had left. He stepped out into the sunshine in time to see Theron being marched across the agora, no doubt towards his home to collect whatever he would take with him. Again, foreboding swept through him like the rush of an icy river as he remembered the look on Theron's face. He had to remind himself that, although Theron was capable of anything, he would be dead before he took a handful of steps into Spartan territory. The krypteia would see to that.

He turned his footsteps towards his home, then stopped short, eyes bulging. "Akantha!"

Regret, anger, and an odd kind of hope simmered in the cauldron of his stomach, rendering him incapable of thinking. He had not set eyes on his wife for ten years. She had barely changed, her hair still the crisp colour of golden wheat, the bearing as proud as ever.

"Husband," she inclined her head. "I came to learn what has happened to my brother."

Suspicion clamped a cold hand over his heart. "Did you spur your brother to kill Xanthia?" He noted the bitter look at the mention of his younger child. "You still harbour resentment for a dead woman."

Her eyes flashed at him. Arguing outside the senate building was ludicrous. He went to steer her away, but she evaded his hold.

"You still don't understand why," she laughed harshly. "Nor did you ever care to understand. Any love I bore for you died when I learned you had fathered Ianthe's second child without agreement from me or Lysander."

A whip lashing would not have been as effective in expressing her displeasure as her verbal barrage. He could have retreated. Any Spartan would not condone retreat in battle but in the face of a wife's tongue-lashing was another matter, although this airing of grievances was cathartic in some odd way.

"I always assumed you'd married me for the wealth and prestige I could afford you. A plot fomented while I was away with the army to ensure Lysander marry Ianthe." He shrugged and looked away. "Perhaps I see plots where there are none, although this has proved useful in the past." Explaining the events in Apollysis, their daughter's pain, was not a discussion to be had in public.

"Is that meant to make me feel better?"

"Perhaps, in time." He looked back at her. "Have you seen Callisto?"

"She came to see me, and we've made our peace."

"Ah, thank you for the warning, but what made you do it?" He stared at the way she clasped and unclasped her hands. She had always carried herself with an air of assurance, especially before the fallout of all that had occurred.

"I don't understand it myself," she admitted, biting her lip. "I knew little of what had transpired after your…indiscretion…was uncovered, but I couldn't bring myself to condone killing anyone. My brother, though…"

Aeschylus restrained himself from reaching out to still the nervous twitching of her hands. It was too soon, and whether past bitterness could be truly healed remained to be seen. "He is banished from Sparta, and his kleros will pass to your ownership."

She closed her eyes. "I thought that might be the verdict. Well, at least I have somewhere to live."

He searched his soul with a calm that surprised him. There were still many things he did not understand, including why she had never felt the need to be with her child, but in the course of time he felt certain he would hear the reasons and gradually bring himself to accept once again Akantha's presence in his life. "There may be another home waiting for you one day. Xanthia leaves to marry Acastus, and it is a large house."

Her eyes shot open. "What?" She then collected herself. "I don't know. We're married still, but…I…there's much to come to terms with."

He knew she referred to Xanthia. Her presence would be a constant reminder of Ianthe, and trust would not be easy to rebuild.

"Send word when you are ready to talk further." His mouth quirked in a smile. "I'll need someone to hand me my shield when I go to battle."

She tilted her head to one side, a habit he remembered from early in their marriage. It boded well since, in the time before Eris had sown discord between them, the gesture had always indicated a softer, playful side to his wife. "So that is why you hint of a new home," she chided him in jest. "If you can escape the clutches of the barracks and your syssition, I will see you soon, Aeschylus."

His name sounded strange from her lips after all this time. He watched her walk across the agora until she was out of sight. Rubbing his jaw, he wondered whether Xanthia would always remain an obstacle to any truce he could come to with his wife. Yet, there was something in Akantha's manner that hinted at a possible softening towards the daughter who had so recently come into his life.

Aeschylus whistled through his teeth as he made his way to the barracks. A good sparring match with one of his peers would energise him. Let the winds of destiny threaten all they liked, his future was not bleak at all.

CHAPTER FORTY-FIVE

Xanthia eyed the shears hovering near her neck and heaved an exaggerated sigh. "If you aren't brave enough to cut my hair, then let me do it." She made to grab the shears, but Callisto moved them out of reach. She moved restively on her seat and glanced out the window. The sun dipped low on the horizon. Acastus would arrive as soon as darkness fell to abduct her. She looked up to see her sister wearing a wistful, somewhat sad, smile.

"You have such beautiful hair, the same as your mother's. After you were taken away, Ianthe grew hers long enough to braid. Her spirit was broken, and she didn't care about society's conventions anymore."

An arrow pierced Xanthia's heart at the mention of the mother she had never known. The faraway look in Callisto's eyes only made it worse, even though it was not her sister's intention. She swallowed, refusing to break down, refusing to allow herself to be broken by memories that were not her own.

"I can never know her, but at least I can learn a little of her through you and our father." She turned to clasp Callisto's free hand and squeezed it hard with heartfelt joy. "I'm so glad we healed the rift between us. I couldn't have borne being the wedge that drove everyone apart once more."

Callisto placed the shears on a small table, then rested her hand over their joined ones. "I was hurt and wounded and scared after you came back. I saw how our father looked at you and treated you.

I'd just begun to know him again and suddenly you were there, his child born of the woman he loved. I was frightened of losing him and being pregnant did not help. I felt so fragile."

"I'm happy my family grows around me. Soon I will be an aunt." Xanthia examined her sister. "You are even more beautiful now than when I first saw you. Your face glows, your whole demeanour is serene." Her eyes bulged when Callisto laughed hard enough to rock back on her heels.

"Serene," she chuckled, "when you get a chance, ask Diokles his opinion of how serene he considers me."

Xanthia grinned. "He loves you, anyone can see that. I've never said anything, but when I first came here I was amazed at how you command him and how he accepts your orders."

"Our men are our rocks. They are Sparta's walls; we need no other. But every man has a weakness and for our men it's their women." She leaned forward to whisper conspiratorially, "Always remember that last part."

Heart dancing at the thought of ruling her soon-to-be husband, she urged her sister to action. "Then hurry up and cut my hair, although I don't really understand why it has to be done this way."

"An unmarried woman wears her uncovered hair any length she likes," Callisto explained. "It's shaved on her wedding day as a symbol of entering a new life, and in a way, symbolises your inclusion in the citizen body. A married woman usually wears a head covering after that. Diokles insisted I grow my hair just so he can see it once again as it was. When he took me hostage in Apollysis, it was hennaed. I'll cut it back after the birth of our child."

"I envied you, you know. From your birth, you grew up with our customs." Xanthia chewed her lip pensively. "Maybe it would've been easier for everyone, including me, if I had stayed on Melos."

"Never say that again," Callisto admonished in a sharp tone. "And not just for the sake of our father returning. You complete our family and deserve to be with your people."

Callisto's words filled her heart to bursting. Now she could finally believe she belonged. Sending her a warm smile, Xanthia presented her back and waited. This time, she heard the shears snap together and watched the dark, shining strands fall to the ground with a light heart.

~*~

A smile played around Xanthia's lips as she lay on the bed in her room in Aeschylus's house. A half-moon shone through the window with enough brightness to outline the sparse furnishings contained within. As it would outline the man she waited for with increasing impatience. Where was he?

The throb of anticipation playing havoc with her pelvis was so strong she placed a hand there, certain she could touch it. She shifted to ease its intensity, the intensity of need only one man could assuage.

The door creaked open. Her heartbeat accelerated, the rapidity almost choking her.

Framed in the doorway stood the outline of power. Her man. Xanthia curled her hands into the bed to stop herself bolting upright and dragging him down beside her.

"Have you come to abduct me or just stare?" she purred in a sultry voice, hips wriggling invitingly as he came into the room, standing over her like a Titan. The predatory half-smile he wore, and the rampant arousal beneath the thin chiton, pulled a moan of longing from her throat.

"Will you ever stop baiting me," he countered with light mockery. "I'd planned to marry a respectful woman, but the gods addled my mind and I chose one who—"

To her delight, he fell silent when she caressed his leg, the calf muscle like warm rock beneath her fingers. "Who what, my brave Acastus?" she mocked in turn. "A woman who loves you, who will challenge you, but who will always pray to Aphrodite to bring you safely home from battle to me." She held her breath as he crouched beside her.

He ran a finger lightly down the side of her face. "Remember what happened at the festival on Melos."

"Are you going to abduct me in the same way?"

He moved so swiftly she had no time to pretend to struggle. The breath left her lungs as he picked her up and swung her over his shoulder, exactly in the same way when he had forcibly taken her from everything her world had encompassed. Then she had beaten his back with her fists, furious at his high-handedness. Now, she ran her hands over him revelling in every taut muscle she was able to touch.

"Does this answer your question?" he rumbled in a deep voice before giving her a playful slap on the bottom.

Xanthia giggled, catching her breath when the slap turned into a caress. "Yes," she replied, unsurprised by the jerkiness of her voice. No man had ever aroused her to the fever-pitch that Acastus could do.

She found herself bouncing against him as he raced from the room and down the steps, obviously filled with the same urgency that left her teetering on the verge of breaking point. They were both silent as his long strides covered the distance to his father's house, where they would live until their own was built on his land. "How will this look if anyone sees us?"

"They will cheer me for successfully abducting my bride."

She heard the smile in his voice. With her face pressed to his back, she was unable to see how far they had travelled until he strode through another courtyard and climbed yet more steps. Set back on her feet, she studied the large room with interest. Her eyelids drooped when she saw the bed, large enough to fit both of them comfortably. Soon, she told herself, soon he would be hers alone. Desire kindled when he pulled her against his muscular body.

"Do you think I look like a boy," she whispered when he ran a hand over the short spikes of her hair.

"Nothing about you declares anything but that you're a woman," he replied in a smouldering voice. "From your face," cupping her cheeks, "to your form," shaping her breasts, waist, and hips with his large hands.

Xanthia stood on tiptoes. "Then make love to me as my husband," she murmured over his lips.

The short, plain chiton she wore was ripped from her and discarded to the floor. She clawed at his with the same desperation until he stood before her in naked magnificence. Love swelled her heart for this proud warrior, the bravest man she could have ever met and whose eyes glinted in the moonlight. Filled with love and desire. For her.

Taking his hand, she brought it to her lips, then fell back against the bed, pulling him down over her. Their loving was more intense tonight, she branding him as hers, the same way he branded her as his. When he finally claimed her, their two bodies moving as one form, the release surpassed anything she had experienced before, even with him.

For long, sublime moments, her ears were filled with their harsh breathing, gradually gentling to soft intakes of breath as a caress or a touch made its impact felt. She slid her palms over his sweat-slicked back, her contentment growing and deepening within their shared silence. It was if she had been whisked away to feast on ambrosia and nectar with the Olympian gods and then returned to earth.

She smiled against his broad chest. "Are we going to stay like this forever?" Inertia kept her eyelids down, so she only felt him roll to one side and lie beside her, warm tides of contentment flowing out from where their skin touched.

"No-one will disturb us." He ran a lazy hand down her side, then rested it over her belly. "Do you think the gods will bless us with a future warrior or a mother of Sparta?"

Xanthia clapped a hand over her forehead and shook with silent laughter. "It's too early to know. I've barely had time to rejoice that I'm carrying your child."

Draping herself half across him, she pressed a light kiss over his heart. The heart of a warrior that beat for her alone. "You know I wasn't raised in Sparta, that my beliefs were shaped differently. I don't know whether I can hand your shield to you and say come back carrying it or carried on it. I'll always worry whenever you leave with the army."

"You've proven your courage over and over. In time, our way of life will become second nature to you." Acastus caressed her face. "We're not always at war. There has been peace since the surrender at Ithome. Sometimes armies won't engage us because of our reputation."

"Ah, yes, the fearsome Spartan warriors." Despite the tiny cloud of worry in her heart, she grinned to convince herself and him. "I've just returned to my homeland and family, become yours. I want our child to know both father and mother. Is that too much to ask?"

Acastus shrugged. "No, but sometimes the gods will ordain otherwise." He pulled her on top of him with a growl. "My wife isn't using her time wisely. Leave the talking for another day."

Xanthia wriggled higher, pulse leaping as she heard the harsh hitch in his breathing. Ducking her head, she nipped his neck, revelling in the sudden spasm of his body beneath her. "You may command me tonight, husband. Afterwards, we shall see."

Any further words were subdued by a long, searching kiss. This man would always have the power to soften her limbs, her very being. The room around them melted into nothingness, the call of night birds in nearby trees remaining unheard. Passion grew, stoked higher by their mutual need, until her world narrowed down to entwined hearts, bodies, and minds.

She had come home.

Thank you for reading. If you enjoyed this book, please consider leaving a review and/or rating at your point of purchase.

Please turn the page for more.

ACKNOWLEDGEMENTS

Special thanks to my fabulous editor, Stephen Black, at **Black Thoughts Editorial Services**, whose insights always take my stories to another level.

Sheridan, you've outdone yourself on the covers for this trilogy. Thank you from the heart.

As always, grateful thanks to my fellow authors, A L Maze and Vanda Vadas, who take time out to proofread and lift my game where it's needed.

GLOSSARY

AGIAD: Sparta maintained dual kingship – one from the Agiad dynasty and one from the Eurypontid line.

AGOGE: the training program pre-requisite for Spartiate status. Spartiate-class boys entered at the age of seven and completed the program by thirty.

APHRODITE: goddess of love and beauty. The temple in Sparta was likely unique in that was built on two levels each depicting the goddess in a very different form.

APOLLO: worshipped as the god of light, healing, music, poetry, amongst others. Both he and the titan Helios were worshipped as sun gods.

ATHENA: goddess of wisdom and war. Though Sparta and Athens warred each other many times, both worshipped Athena as their patron goddess.

EILEITHYIA: goddess of childbirth and midwifery. Her name means – she who comes to aid.

GERONTES: senators/elders aged over sixty who were elected to the Gerousia for life.

GEROUSIA: council consisting of twenty-eight Gerontes plus the two kings of Sparta. The council wielded significant influence over Spartan politics and governance.

HADES: ruler of the Underworld and brother of Zeus.

HEPHAESTUS: god of blacksmiths and fire.

HERMES: messenger of the Olympian gods. A divine trickster and the god of roads, flocks, commerce, and thieves.

HOMOIOS: meaning 'alike', similar to peers, how Spartiates addressed each other.

HOPLITE: citizen-soldiers of Ancient Greek city states.

HYADES: Nymphs that caused rain to fall. They had one brother, Hyas, who was killed while hunting. The tears they shed fell as rain upon the earth.

HYDRA: The Lernean Hydra was a serpentine water monster with nine heads and blood that was poisonous.

KLEROS: an allotment of land given to each newborn Spartan boy (pl. – kleroi).

KOPIS: single edged cutting or "cut and thrust" sword with forward curving blade (pl. – kopides).

KRYPTOS: a member of the KRYPTEIA, young men singled out for further elite training and high office later in life (pl. – kryptoi).

KYLIX: drinking cup with a stem, two handles, and a broad, shallow body (pl. – kylikes).

LYCURGUS: a legendary figure credited with creating the Spartan constitution and society.

NEMEAN LION: a legendary creature known for its invulnerable hide and immense strength.

PANDORA: the first human woman created by Hephaestus on the orders of Zeus.

PERIOKOI: members of an autonomous group of free but non-citizen inhabitants of Sparta.

PHALANX: rectangular mass military formation, usually composed entirely of heavy infantry armed with spears, swords and overlapping shields.

POLIS: a city-state in ancient Greece, with its own walls, constitution, and loyalty.

POSEIDON: god of the sea and earthquakes, brother of Zeus.

SPARTIATE: elite full-citizen male Spartans coming from families who could trace their ancestry to Sparta's first settlers, the Dorians, in the 9th century BC.

SYSSITIA: group dining clubs (mess groups) to which all citizens (males in good standing over the age of twenty) were required to belong, contribute food to, and attend most nights for dinner.

TARTARUS: a deep abyss in the Underworld used as a dungeon of torment and suffering for the wicked and as the prison for the Titans.

XIPHOS: a double-edged straight short sword. The classic blade was about 45–60 cm long, although the Spartans preferred to use blades as short as 30 cm (plural – xiphoi).

ZEUS: king of the Olympian gods.

ABOUT THE AUTHOR

Anthea fell in love with Greek mythology at the age of thirteen. Her love of the Spartans, especially, came after reading Roger Lancelyn Green's THE TALE OF TROY where she cheered on Menelaus to take his Queen back! She left a career in IT to write stories of adventure, family intrigue, and of course, love, set in Ancient Sparta, and pander to an extremely spoilt German Shepherd called Zali.

A former horse-rider, Anthea enjoys keeping fit through power walking and interval training. She loves travelling and has a bucket list of destinations yet to be fulfilled.

You can find Anthea at:

Website: www.anthealaurelton.com

Goodreads:
https://www.goodreads.com/author/show/18937882.Anthea_Laurelt
on

Instagram: www.instagram.com/anthealaureltonauthor

Facebook: www.facebook.com/AntheaLaureltonAuthor